Jean-Paul Sartre – possibly the best-known and most discussed modern French writer and thinker – was born in Paris in 1905. He was educated in Paris and later taught in schools at Le Havre and Laon. In 1934 he spent a year in the French Institute in Berlin where he became acquainted with modern German philosophy. He then taught at the Lycée Condorcet in Paris. He played an active role in the Resistance during the war, and afterwards left the teaching profession. Since 1946 he has spent his time writing, and editing the magazine *Les Temps modernes*.

Sartre is a Marxist and the founder of French existentialism. His philosophical works, such as *L'Étre et le néant* (1943), have had a profound effect on modern thought. His books available in Penguins are the plays *Altona*, *Men Without Shadows*, *The Flies*, *Lucifer and the Lord*, *The Respectable Prostitute*, *In Camera*, *Kean*, *Nekrassov* and *The Trojan Women*; the novels belonging to the 'Roads to Freedom' trilogy: *The Age of Reason*, *The Reprieve*, and *Iron in the Soul*; the novel *Nausea*; and *Words*, reminiscences of his childhood.

The Reprieve

JEAN-PAUL SARTRE

TRANSLATED BY
ERIC SUTTON

PENGUIN BOOKS
In association with Hamish Hamilton

Penguin Books Ltd, Harmondsworth, Middlesex, England
Penguin Books Australia Ltd, Ringwood, Victoria, Australia

—

Le Sursis first published 1945
Eric Sutton's translation first published in Great Britain by
Hamish Hamilton 1947
Revised translation published in Penguin Books 1963
Reprinted 1964, 1966, 1968, 1970 (twice)

—

—

Made and printed in Great Britain
by Cox & Wyman Ltd,
London, Reading and Fakenham
Set in Monotype Garamond

Friday, 23 September

FOUR-THIRTY in the afternoon in Berlin, three-thirty in London. The hotel stood bleakly on its hill, a desolate, solemn edifice with an old gentleman inside it. At Angoulême, Marseilles, Ghent, and Dover, people thought: 'What can he be doing? It's past three o'clock, why doesn't he come out?' He was sitting in the lounge behind half-closed shutters, his thick-browed eyes staring into space, and his lips slightly parted, as though he were recalling some ancient memory. He had ceased to read; his hand – the freckled hand of an old man – still grasping some typewritten sheets, hung loosely from his knees. He turned to Horace Wilson and said:

'What is the time?'

'About half past four,' Horace Wilson replied.

The old gentleman lifted his big eyes, laughed a short, genial laugh, and said: 'It's very hot.'

A crimson, crackling, glistening heat had descended upon Europe: there was heat on men's hands, behind their eyes, and in their bronchial tubes: and they waited, sickened by heat and dust and fear. In the vestibule of the hotel, journalists waited. In the courtyard, three chauffeurs waited, motionless at their driving wheels: on the far side of the Rhine, motionless in the vestibule of the Hotel Dreesen, tall black-clad Prussians waited. Milan Hlinka was no longer waiting. He had ceased to wait two days ago, on that awful day, lit by a flash of certainty: 'They've let us down!' Then time flowed on once more in its usual random fashion, individual days no longer seemed to exist – there was nothing but next days, henceforward all days would be next days.

At three-thirty Mathieu was still waiting, on the threshold of a dreadful future: at the same moment, at four-thirty, Milan no longer possessed a future. The old gentleman rose, walked with stiff, pompous steps across the room, and said, 'Gentlemen!' smiling affably: he laid the document on the table, and smoothed out the pages with his closed hand: Milan was standing by another table: the outspread newspaper covered the whole breadth of the waxed cloth. For the seventh time Milan read:

'The President of the Republic, in association with the Government, had no alternative but to accept the proposals of the two great Powers, concerning the basis of our future attitude. There was nothing left for us to do, being now alone.' Nevile Henderson and Sir Horace Wilson had gone up to the table, the old gentleman turned to them, looking very elderly and inoffensive, and said:

'Gentlemen, this is what we must now do.'

And Milan thought: 'What else could be done?' A confused murmur drifted through the window, and he thought: 'We are now alone.'

A small squeaky voice rose up from the street: 'Hitler for ever!'

Milan ran to the window.

'Wait a moment!' he shouted. 'Wait till I come down.'

There was a wild scurry down the street, and clattering of clogs. At the far end of it, the urchin turned, groped in his apron, and began to wave his arms. Two sharp thuds on the wall.

'It's little Liebknecht,' said Milan, 'he's going his round.'

He leaned out: the street was as deserted as on a Sunday. The Schoenhofs had hung out red and white swastika flags from their balconies. All the shutters on the green house were closed. And Milan thought: 'We haven't any shutters.'

'We must open all the windows,' he said.

'Why?' asked Anna.

'When the windows are shut, they aim at the window-panes.'

Anna shrugged her shoulders:

'In any case . . .'

Songs and shouts burst in gusts into his room.

'They're still on the Square,' said Milan.

He had laid his hands on the window-rail, and thought: 'It's all over.' A tall man appeared at the corner of the street carrying a rucksack and leaning on a stick. He looked exhausted, two women were following him, bowed beneath enormous bundles.

'The Jägerschmitts are coming back,' said Milan, without turning round.

They had fled on the Monday evening, they must have crossed the frontier during the night of Tuesday or Wednesday. And now they were returning exultantly. Jägerschmitt went up to the green house, and walked up the front steps. His face was grey with dust and he was smiling strangely. He felt in his jacket pockets and produced a key. The women had put their bundles on the ground and stood watching him.

'You come back when the danger's over,' shouted Milan.

'Milan!' said Anna briskly.

Jägerschmitt had raised his head. He saw Milan, and his light eyes flashed.

'You come back when the danger's over.'

'Yes, I come back,' shouted Jägerschmitt. 'And now – it's your turn to go.'

He slipped the key into the lock, and opened the door: the two women followed him in. Milan turned round:

'Dirty cowards!' he said.

'Don't provoke them,' said Anna.

'Cowards,' said Milan, 'dirty Germans. They were licking our boots two years ago.'

'Never mind. You shouldn't provoke them.'

The old gentleman stopped talking: his mouth remained half-open, as though silently expressing views on the situation. His large round eyes were full of tears, he had raised his eyebrows, and was looking questioningly at Nevile and Horace. They said nothing; Horace abruptly averted his head: Nevile walked to the table, picked up the document, considered it for a moment, then pushed it irritably aside. The old gentleman wore an expression of perplexity; he opened his arms, in token of his impotent goodwill. And he said for the fifth time:

'I found myself faced by a quite unexpected situation: I thought we should quietly discuss the proposals I brought with me. . . .' And Horace thought: 'The old fox! Where does he get that grandfatherly voice?' He said: 'Very good, sir: in ten minutes we shall be at the Hotel Dreesen.'

'Lerchen has come,' said Anna. 'Her husband is in Prague: she's worried.'

'Why doesn't she come here?'

'She won't feel much less worried,' said Anna, with a curt laugh, 'in the company of a lunatic like you, who stands in the window and insults the people in the street.'

He looked at her small head, delicate and serene, at her drawn features, narrow shoulders, and swollen belly.

'Sit down,' he said. 'I don't like to see you standing.'

She sat down, and clasped her hands in front of her: a man was brandishing newspapers, muttering: '*Paris-Soir*, latest edition. Only two left – here you are.' He had shouted himself hoarse. Maurice took the paper and read:

'Prime Minister Chamberlain has sent a letter to Chancellor Hitler, to which, it is intimated in British circles, the latter will reply. The meeting with M. Hitler, which was to have taken place this morning, is consequently postponed to a later hour.'

Zézette looked at the paper over Maurice's shoulder.

'Anything new?' she asked.

'No. Same old story.'

He turned over the page, and they noticed a blurred photograph showing a kind of castle, a medievalized erection on the summit of a hill, with towers, belfries, and hundreds of windows.

'It's Godesberg,' said Maurice.

'Is that where Chamberlain is?' asked Zézette.

'Apparently police reinforcements have arrived.'

'Yes,' said Milan. 'Two gendarmes. That makes six gendarmes altogether. They've barricaded themselves in the police-station.'

A cartload of shouts poured into the room. Anna shivered; but her face remained calm.

'Should we telephone?' said she.

'Telephone?'

'Yes. To Prisecnice.'

Milan showed her the newspaper without answering: 'According to a dispatch from the D.N.B. dated Thursday, the German population of the Sudeten regions have taken over the maintenance of public order as far as the linguistic frontier.'

'Perhaps it isn't true,' said Anna. 'I was told that that had only happened at Eger.'

Milan crashed a fist on to the table:

'God Almighty! Must we ask for help again?'

He stretched out his hands; they were large, gnarled hands, dotted with brown spots and scars: he had been a woodcutter before his accident. He looked at them, and splayed his fingers, saying:

'They may turn up. In twos or threes. There'll be some fun for five minutes or so.'

'There'll be six hundred of them,' said Anna.

Milan bent his head: he felt alone.

'Listen,' said Anna.

He listened: they could be heard more clearly now, they must be on the march. Anger shook him: he could no longer see clearly, and his skull ached. He went to the chest of drawers, breathing hard.

'What are you doing?' Anna asked.

He was bending over one of the drawers, still breathing hard. He bent down lower, and grunted, but did not reply.

'That's unnecessary,' she said.

'What?'

'You mustn't. Give it me.'

He turned: Anna had got up, and was leaning against the chair, looking quite composed. He thought of the child: and he handed her the revolver.

'Right,' said he. 'I'll telephone to Prisecnice.'

He went down to the ground floor, and into the school-room, opened the windows, and picked up the telephone.

'Give me the police-station at Prisecnice. Hullo!'

His right ear caught a dry zigzag crackle. His left ear heard *them*. Odette laughed vaguely: 'I have never really known where Czechoslovakia was,' she said, plunging her fingers into the sand. After a moment or two there came the click of an unhitched receiver.

'*Na?*' said a voice.

Milan thought for a moment. 'I am asking for help.' He gripped the receiver hard.

'This is Pravnitz,' he said. 'I'm the schoolmaster, twenty of us here are Czechs, and there are three German democrats hiding in a cellar, the rest are Henlein's men: they're officered by fifty fellows of the Free Corps who crossed the frontier last night, and have drawn them up in the square. The mayor has joined them.'

9

A silence followed, then the voice said insolently:

'*Bitte – Deutsch sprechen.*'

'*Schweinkopf!*' exclaimed Milan.

He replaced the receiver, and limped upstairs again. His leg was hurting him. He entered the room and sat down.

'They've got there,' he said.

Anna went to him and laid her hands on his shoulders:

'Darling,' she said.

'The bastards!' said Milan. 'They know what's happened, they just jeered at me.'

He pulled her between his knees. Her big belly touched his.

'Now we are quite alone,' said he.

'I can't believe it.'

He raised his head slowly and looked her up and down; she was steady and dependable when there was something to be done, but like all women she always needed to confide in someone.

'There they are,' said Anna.

The voices seemed nearer: they must be marching down the main street. From a distance the jubilant shouts of a crowd sound very like shrieks of terror.

'Is the door barricaded?'

'Yes,' said Milan. 'But they can always get through the windows, or go round by the garden.'

'If they come upstairs . . .' said Anna.

'You needn't be afraid. They can smash up everything, I won't lift a finger.'

He suddenly felt Anna's warm lips against his cheek: 'Darling, I know it's for my sake.'

'Indeed it isn't. You are myself. It's for the child's sake.'

They started: there was a ring at the bell.

'Don't go to the window!' exclaimed Anna.

He got up and went to the window. The Jägerschmitts had opened all their shutters: the Hitler flag was hanging above the door. As he leaned out he saw a tiny shadow.

'I'm coming down,' he cried,

He crossed the room.

'It's Marikka,' he said.

He went downstairs, and opened the front door. Bangs,

shouts, and music floated across the roofs: it was like a holiday. He eyed the empty street, and his heart turned over.

'Why have you come here?' he asked. 'There's no school today.'

'Mummy sent me,' said Marikka. She was carrying a little basket, filled with apples and slices of bread spread with margarine.

'Your mother must be crazy: go home at once.'

'She said you wouldn't send me back.'

She held out a sheet of paper folded into four. He unfolded it and read: 'Father and George are terrified. Please keep Marikka until the evening.'

'Where is your father?' asked Milan.

'He's behind the door, with George. They've got axes and rifles.' And she added with a touch of importance: 'Mummy sent me out by the yard, she said I should be safer here because you're sensible.'

'Yes,' said Milan. 'Yes, I'm sensible. All right, come up.'

Five-thirty in Berlin, four-thirty in Paris. Slight depression in the north of Scotland. M. von Dörnberg appeared on the staircase of the Grand Hotel, the journalists crowded round him, and Pierryl said: 'Is he coming down?' M. von Dörnberg had a paper in his right hand: he raised his left hand, and said: 'It is not yet settled whether Mr Chamberlain will see the Führer this evening.'

'It's here,' said Zézette. 'I used to sell flowers here, on a little green stall.'

'Very nice too,' said Maurice.

Obediently he inspected the pavement and the street, that being what they had come to see, since lately she had begun to talk about it. But it meant nothing to him. Zézette had let go his arm, she was laughing to herself in silence, as she watched the traffic gliding past.

'Did you have a chair?' Maurice asked.

'Sometimes: a folding chair,' said Zézette.

'It can't have been much fun.'

'It was all right in the spring,' said Zézette.

She was talking to him in an undertone, without looking at him, as one talks to a sick person: and she had suddenly begun to wriggle her shoulders and back in an affected sort of way. She had ceased to be natural, and Maurice was getting bored: twenty people were gathered in front of a shop-window, he went up to them and peered over their heads. Zézette remained in a trance on the edge of the pavement: after a moment she rejoined him and took his arm. On a bevelled glass plaque stood two scraps of red leather with red fluff around them, rather like a powder-puff. Maurice burst out laughing.

'What is it?' whispered Zézette.

'Those shoes,' laughed Maurice.

Two or three heads turned round. Zézette said: 'Sh!' and drew him away.

'Look here, we aren't in church,' said Maurice.

However, he spoke in an undertone. People were padding along the street, looking as if they were all acquainted, but not uttering a word.

'It must be five years and more since I was here,' he whispered.

Zézette pointed proudly to Maxim's.

'That's Maxim's,' she said, into the hollow of his ear.

Maurice looked at Maxim's, and abruptly turned his head away. He had heard about it, and a loathsome hole it was where the bourgeois swilled champagne in 1914 while the workers fell in battle. And he said between his teeth:

'Filthy bourgeoisie!'

But he felt ill at ease, without quite knowing why. He walked with a brisk, springy step: the passers-by looked so fragile to him that he was afraid of bumping into them.

'Maybe,' said Zézette. 'But it's a fine street, don't you think?'

'I don't go for it,' said Maurice. 'Not enough air.'

Zézette shrugged her shoulders, and Maurice found himself thinking of the avenue de Saint-Ouen: when he left his lodging in the morning, the men passed him whistling, with satchels on their backs, bent over the handlebars of their bicycles. He felt happy: some stopped at Saint-Denis, and others went on farther, everybody was going the same way, the workers were in motion. And he said to Zézette:

'This is a bourgeois neighbourhood.'

They walked on a little way enveloped in a smell of face-powder, then Maurice stopped and begged pardon.

'What did you say?' asked Zézette.

'Nothing,' said Maurice with embarrassment; 'nothing at all.'

He had bumped into somebody again: other people might walk with their eyes on the ground, yet they always managed to avoid each other at the last moment: it must be a matter of habit.

'Are you coming?'

But he no longer wanted to walk on, he was afraid of breaking something, and besides this street didn't lead anywhere, it had no direction, some people were making their way towards the boulevards, others down to the Seine, and others standing with their noses glued to shop-windows – eddies, but no coordinated movements, a man felt isolated. He reached out a hand, laid it on Zézette's shoulder, and gripped the yielding flesh beneath the fabric. Zézette smiled at him, she was enjoying herself, she eyed everything eagerly without losing her air of assurance, swaying her small hips neatly as she walked. He tickled her neck and she laughed.

'Stop it, Maurice!' she said.

He liked the strong colours she put on her face – the sugary white, and the crimson on her cheekbones. From near by she smelt of honey. He said to her in a low voice:

'Are you enjoying yourself?'

'I remember it all so well,' said Zézette with shining eyes.

He let go of her shoulder and they walked on in silence: she had known many bourgeois, they came to buy her flowers, she smiled at them, and indeed there were some who tried to be familiar. He looked at her white neck, and an odd feeling came over him, he wanted to laugh and cry at the same time.

'*Paris-Soir*,' cried a voice.

'Shall we buy one?'

'There won't be anything new in it.'

People thronged round the paper-boy, and silently snatched the papers. A woman emerged from the crowd, in high-heeled shoes and a ludicrous hat perched on the top of her head. She unfolded the paper, and read it as she pattered off. Her features suddenly sagged and she heaved a deep sigh.

'Look at that woman,' said Maurice.

Zézette looked at her. 'Perhaps her husband will be called up.'

Maurice shrugged his shoulders: it seemed odd that anyone could be really unhappy in that hat and those alligator shoes.

'Oh well,' he said, 'her husband will be a bloody officer.'

'Even if he is,' said Zézette, 'he can leave his skin behind like our chaps.'

Maurice threw her a sidelong glance. 'You make me sick with your bloody officers. Did they leave their skins behind in 1914?'

'They certainly did,' said Zézette. 'I thought lots of them were killed.'

'It's the peasants who were killed, and then our lot,' said Maurice.

Zézette snuggled up to him. 'Oh, Maurice,' she said. 'Do you really think there's going to be a war?'

'How can I tell?' said Maurice.

That morning he had been sure of it, and the chaps were as sure as he was. They were on the bank of the Seine, looking at cranes and the dredger, lads in shirt-sleeves, toughs from Gennevilliers who were digging a trench for an electric cable, and it was evident that war was on the way. After all, it wouldn't make much difference to the chaps from Gennevilliers: they would be somewhere in the north, digging trenches in the sunshine, in peril from bullets, shells, and bombs, just as they were now in peril from earth-slides, falls, and all the accidents of labour: they would wait for the end of the war just as they waited for an end to their poverty. And Sandre had said: 'The chaps will do the job. But when we come back, we shall keep our rifles.'

Just now he was no longer sure of anything: at Saint-Ouen it was war all the time, but not here. Here was peace: shop windows, displays of luxuries, coloured fabrics, mirrors, every implement of civilized life. The people looked depressed, but they were born that way. Why should they fight? They were waiting for nothing, they had all they wanted. It must be rather grim to hope for nothing except that life might continue indefinitely in its present course.

'The bourgeoisie don't want war,' observed Maurice suddenly. 'They are afraid of victory, because it would mean the victory of the proletariat.'

The old gentleman got up and escorted Nevile Henderson

and Horace Wilson to the door. He looked at them for a moment with an air of deep emotion, he was very like all those old gentlemen with rather worn-out faces who gather round the newsvendors in the rue Royale and Pall Mall, and ask no more than that their life should terminate as it had begun. He thought of these old gentlemen, and of their children, and he said:

'Furthermore you will ask M. von Ribbentrop if Chancellor Hitler considers it desirable that we should have a last conversation before my departure, drawing his attention to the point that an acceptance in principle would entail on M. Hitler the necessity of putting fresh proposals before us. You will lay particular stress on the fact that I am determined to do all that is humanly possible to settle the issue by means of negotiation, as it seems to me incredible that the nations of Europe, who do not want war, should be plunged into a bloody conflict over a question on which agreement has to a large extent been reached. Good luck.'

Horace and Nevile bowed and went downstairs, the ceremonious, nervous, tired, suave voice still ringing in their ears, and Maurice looked at the flabby, worn, civilized flesh of the old men and women all around him, and he thought with disgust that they would be better for a little bloodletting.

They must be bled: it would be a nastier process than squashing slugs, but there was no help for it. The machine-guns would rake the rue Royale, which would lie desolate for several days, windows broken, star-shaped smashes in the shop-fronts, the tables outside the cafés scattered in a litter of glass: aeroplanes circling overhead above the corpses. Then the dead would be removed, the tables picked up, the glass replaced, and life would resume its course, sturdy citizens with strong red necks and leather jackets would repopulate the street. That indeed was what had happened in Russia, Maurice had seen photographs of the Nevsky Prospect: the proletariat had taken possession of that resplendent avenue and were walking up and down it, no longer dazzled by the palaces and the great stone bridges.

'I beg your pardon,' said Maurice with confusion.

He had swung his elbow into the back of an old lady, who was eyeing him indignantly. He felt tired and depressed:

beneath the great advertisements on the hoardings, under the blackened gold letters on the balconies, among the confectioners' and bootmakers' shops, in front of the columns of the Madeleine, it was impossible to imagine any other crowd than this – old ladies trotting on their way, and children in sailor suits. The melancholy, golden light, the smell of perfume, the overpowering buildings, the honeyed voices, bemused and anxious faces, the bleak shuffling of footsteps on the asphalt, all this was self-consistent, all this was *real*: the Revolution was nothing but a dream. 'I oughtn't to have come,' thought Maurice, with a malicious glance at Zézette. 'This is no place for a proletarian.'

A hand touched his shoulder: he blushed with pleasure as he recognized Brunet.

'Good morning, young fellow,' said Brunet with a smile.

'Morning, comrade,' said Maurice.

Brunet's fist was as hard and horny as his own, and it had a powerful grip. Maurice looked at Brunet, and burst into a hearty laugh: he imagined all the chaps around him, at Saint-Ouen, Ivry, Montreuil, in Paris itself – at Belleville, Montrouge, and La Villette, squaring their shoulders and preparing for the fray.

'What are you up to here?' asked Brunet. 'Are you out of work?'

'It's my paid holiday,' explained Maurice with some embarrassment. 'Zézette wanted to come because she used to work here once.'

'Ah, here's Zézette,' said Brunet. 'Hello there, comrade Zézette.'

'It's Brunet,' said Maurice. 'You saw his article this morning in the *Huma*.'

Zézette looked boldly at Brunet, and gave him her hand. She was not nervous of men, whether they were bourgeois, or big noises in the Party.

'I've known him from a lad,' said Brunet, pointing to Maurice. 'He was with the Red Falcons, one of the singers, and I never heard such a voice. In the end it was agreed that he should only pretend to sing during the processions.'

They laughed.

'Well?' said Zézette. 'Is there going to be a war? You ought to know: you're in a position to hear what's going on.'

It was a silly question, a woman's question, but Maurice was glad she had asked it. Brunet looked serious.

'I don't know if there's going to be a war,' he said. 'But anyhow we mustn't be afraid of it: the working classes ought to realize that it can't be avoided by concessions.'

He talked well. Zézette gazed at him with trustful eyes, and smiled softly as she listened. Maurice was annoyed: Brunet talked like a newspaper, and said no more than appeared in newspapers.

'Do you think Hitler would cave in if we showed him our teeth?' asked Zézette.

Brunet had assumed an official expression, he did not appear to understand that he was being asked his personal opinion.

'Quite possible,' he said. 'Besides, whatever happens, the U.S.S.R. are with us.'

'It's only to be expected,' thought Maurice, 'that the Party nobs shouldn't feel inclined to give their views on demand to a paltry mechanic from Saint-Ouen.' None the less, he was disappointed. He looked at Brunet, and all his satisfaction vanished: Brunet had strong peasant's hands, a powerful jaw, and purposeful eyes: but he was wearing a collar and a tie, a flannel suit, and seemed at ease among these bourgeois.

A dark window mirrored their reflections: Maurice saw a woman without a hat, and a tall strapping fellow with a cap on the back of his head, bursting out of his jacket, talking to a gentleman. However, he remained standing, with his hands in his pockets, he couldn't make up his mind to leave Brunet.

'Are you still at Saint-Mandé?' asked Brunet.

'No,' said Maurice. 'Saint-Ouen. I'm working at Flaive's.'

'Ah? I thought you were at Saint-Mandé. Fitter?'

'Mechanic.'

'Good,' said Brunet. 'Excellent. Well ... 'bye then, comrade.'

''Bye, comrade,' said Maurice. He felt ill at ease and vaguely disappointed.

''Bye, comrade,' said Zézette, with a toothy smile.

Brunet watched them move off. The crowd had closed upon them, but Maurice's huge shoulders emerged above the hats.

No doubt he had an arm round Zézette's waist: his cap was close to her tousled hair, and with heads together, they sped through the throng. 'A good chap,' thought Brunet. 'But I don't like the floozie.' He walked on with a serious air, conscious of a twinge of remorse. 'What answer could I give him?' he thought. At Saint-Denis, Saint-Ouen, Sochaux, Creusot, hundreds of thousands of them were waiting, with the same anxious, confiding look in their eyes. Hundreds of thousands of heads like that one, good round solid heads, rough-hewn, cropped heads, the heads of true men, had turned towards the east, to Godesberg and Prague and Moscow. What answer could be given to them? There was nothing to be done now except to protect them, protect their slow tenacious minds against all the bastards who try to muck up their thinking. Today he had to see old Mother Boningue, tomorrow Dottin, secretary of the Teachers' Union, and on the following day the Pivertistes: such was his lot: well, he would go from one to the next, and try to soothe them all. Mother Boningue would look at him with velvety eyes and talk to him about 'the horror of shedding blood', waving idealist hands. She was a large woman of about fifty, with a florid complexion, white down on her cheeks, short hair, and a suave, priest-like expression behind her spectacles: she wore a man's jacket, with the ribbon of the Legion of Honour in the lapel. 'I shall say: Women always get it wrong: in 1914 they bundled their men off to the front, when they should have lain down on the rails to prevent the train from starting, and now when there might be some sense in fighting, you're founding peace leagues and doing all you can to break your men's morale.' Maurice's face reappeared before his vision, and Brunet shrugged his shoulders angrily. 'One word, just one word, does help them sometimes, and I couldn't think of one.' Bitterly he thought: 'It was that girl's fault, girls have a knack of asking silly questions.' Zézette's floury cheeks, her lewd little eyes, her vulgar scent: they would go about collecting signature after signature, gently persistent; corpulent Radical doves, Trotskyist Jewesses, Oppositionists of the S.F.I.O., so utterly barefaced that they would descend upon an old peasant woman in process of milking a cow, thrust a fountain-pen into her large damp hand and say: 'Sign there, if you are

18

against war.' *No more war. Negotiations, not war. Peace first.* And what would Zézette do, if she were suddenly offered a fountain-pen? Had she retained sufficient class reflexes to laugh at these large benevolent ladies? She had dragged her man into the fashionable districts, she was looking excitedly into the shop windows, and she had plastered her cheeks with make-up. ... Poor chap, it would be a bad job if she hung round his neck to stop him going. That would be too much. ... (*Intellectual. Bourgeois.*) I can't stand her because she plasters her face and bites her nails. (*Intellectual. Bourgeois.*) Still, all the comrades can't live without sex. He felt tired and sluggish; all of a sudden he thought: I criticize her for making herself up, because I don't like cheap makeup. Like them. He ought to like them, one and all, men and girls, without distinction. And he thought he shouldn't even *want* to like them, he should do so as naturally as he breathed. (*Intellectual. Bourgeois. Perpetual isolation.*) No use, we shall never share the same memories. Joseph Mercier, aged thirty-three, congenital syphilitic, Professor of Natural History at the Lycée Buffon and the Collège Sévigné, was walking up the rue Royale, sniffing, and from time to time sucking his lips with a faint damp smack; he had his usual pain in his left side, he felt wretched, and he was wondering whether the salaries of mobilized officials would be paid. He looked at his feet to avoid all those merciless faces, and bumped into a tall red-haired man in a grey flannel suit who jostled him against a shop window. Joseph Mercier looked up and thought: 'Hulking brute!' He was a proper human wall, one of those callous, cruel brutes, like that hulking boy Chamerlier in the elementary mathematics class who snapped fingers in his face at school, one of those types who never question anything, least of all themselves, who are never ill, never suffer from nerves, take women and life as they come, and march straight to their goal, shoving all who get in their way against shop windows. The rue Royale flowed quietly towards the Seine and Brunet flowed along with it, someone had bumped into him, he noticed an emaciated creature with a corroded nose, a bowler hat and a tall celluloid collar, making its escape, he thought of Zézette and of Maurice, and all the old familiar anguish came back into his mind, his shame at the memories for which he could never make amends, the white house on the banks of the Marne, his father's library, his mother's tapering, perfumed hands, which set him apart from them for ever.

It was a lovely, golden evening, of a true September vintage. Stephen Hartley, leaning over the balcony, murmured: 'The vast slow eddies of the vesperal crowd.' Hats – a sea of felt, with a few bare heads afloat among the billows – 'like gulls', he thought: two fair heads, and a grey head, a fine, conspicuously red cranium already slightly bald. 'A French crowd,' thought Stephen, with a touch of emotion. A little crowd of heroic little old men. He would write: 'The French crowd awaits events with calm and dignity.' A heading for the *New York Herald,* in heavy type: 'I have felt the pulse of the French people.' Little men, not too clean, interspersed with large feminine hats, a silent crowd, serene and rather shabby, gilded by that hour: the calm of a Paris evening between the Madeleine and the Concorde. He would write: 'The face of France' – 'The eternal face of France.' Shuffling feet, decorous whispers of astonishment – no, astonishment was rather too strong a word: a tall red-haired, slightly bald Frenchman, serene as a sunset, gleams of sunshine in the windows of the passing cars, bursts of voices: sparkles of voices, said Stephen to himself. And he thought: 'My article is written.'

'Stephen,' said Sylvia, addressing his back.

'I'm busy,' said Stephen curtly, without turning round.

'But you must answer me, dear,' said Sylvia; 'there are only first-class berths left on the *Lafayette.*'

'Take first-class, take a luxury cabin,' said Stephen. 'The *Lafayette* is very likely the last boat that will sail for America for a long while.'

Brunet walked quietly on, breathing in the smell of face-powder, he looked up and noticed some tarnished gilt letters affixed to a balcony: war had come: it was there, in the depths of that luminous haze, inscribed for all to see on the walls of that frail city: it was an arrested explosion that had split the rue Royale: people passed and did not see it: but Brunet saw it. It had always been there, but people were not yet aware of it. Brunet had thought: 'The sky will fall upon our heads.' The city was in the act of falling, he had seen the houses as they really were; petrified collapse. Above that elegant shop were tons of stone, and each stone, interlocking with the rest, had been falling steadily for fifty years past; a heavier thrust, and the columns would swell and reel and splinter into gashes: the plate-glass window would be smashed; cartloads of stone would hurtle into the cellar, and overwhelm the stores of merchandise. They have ten-thousand-pounder bombs. Brunet's heart contracted: just now, upon those symmetrical façades, there had been a human smile shining through the powdered gold of evening. It had vanished: a hundred tons of stone: men wandering about among poised avalanches. Soldiers among the ruins – he would be killed, perhaps. He saw the blackish furrows on Zézette's plastered cheeks. Dusty walls, blank walls with yawning gaps in them, strips of blue and yellow paper dangling here and there, and leprous patches everywhere: red tiles among the wreckage, upthrusting weeds between the flagstones. Then lines of timbered huts; encampments. In time vast monotonous barracks would come into being, like the buildings on the outer boulevards. Brunet shuddered: 'I love Paris,' he thought with anguish. The vision vanished, and the city encompassed him once more. Brunet stopped: he was overwhelmed by a vague feeling of defeatism, and he thought: 'If only there were no such thing as war! If only war need not exist!' And he gazed avidly at the great arched gateways, Driscoll's glittering shop window, the royal-blue hangings of the Brasserie Weber. Then he felt ashamed, walked on, and thought: 'I am too fond of Paris.' Like Pilniak, in Moscow, who had been too fond of ancient churches. The Party rightly distrusts intellectuals. Death is imprinted upon man, and ruin upon objects; other men will come and rebuild Paris, and rebuild the world. I shall say to him: 'So you want peace at any price?' I shall speak gently, looking straight into his eyes, and I shall say: 'Women must not be allowed to interfere with us. This is not the moment to pester men with their follies.'

'I wish I were a man,' said Odette.

Mathieu raised himself on one elbow. He was already deeply tanned. Smiling, he asked: 'So that you might play at soldiers?'

Odette blushed. 'Oh no,' she retorted. 'But I find it silly to be a woman at this moment.'

'It can't be very comfortable,' he agreed.

She looked, as she often did, like a parakeet: the words she used always came back against her. And yet she felt that Mathieu could not justly have found fault with her, if she had been able to convey her real meaning: the point was that men always upset her when they talked about war in her presence. They were not natural, they displayed too much assurance, as though they wanted to make her understand that this was a man's affair, and yet they always looked as though they expected something from her; a sort of judgement, because she was a woman and could not fight, and because she remained above the fray. What could she say to them? Stay? Go? It was not for her to decide, just because she could not go. Perhaps she ought to say: 'Do what you wish.' But what if they had no preference? She stood apart, she pretended not to understand them, she produced coffee and liqueurs for them, and listened to their heated talk. She sighed, picked up a handful of sand, and let it trickle, warm and white, on to her tanned leg. The beach was deserted, the sea sparkled and rustled. On the wooden balcony of the Provençal three young women in beach trousers were having tea. Odette closed her eyes. She lay on the sand, enveloped in a dateless, ageless heat: the heat of her childhood days, when she closed her eyes, lying on that same sand, and played at being a salamander in the depths of a huge red-blue flame. The same heat, the same damply caressing swim-suit – which always seemed to be steaming in the sunshine; the same scorching sand against the back of her neck: in other years she melted into the sea and sky and sand, she no longer distinguished the present from the past. She sat up, wide-eyed: today there was a real present: there was a pain in the pit of her stomach: there was Mathieu, tanned and naked, sitting cross-legged on his white wrap. Mathieu was silent. She would so have liked to be silent too. But if she did not force him to speak to her directly, she lost him: he would politely acquiesce, just so far as to make a little speech in his resonant, rather rasping voice, and then he was off, leaving his body in pledge, a very lithe, athletic body. If only he had been absorbed in pleasant thoughts: but he looked straight ahead with a heartrending expression on his face, while his large hands were busily constructing a sand pie. The pie dissolved, and the hands unweariedly remoulded it: Mathieu did not once look at his hands: at last she could bear it no longer.

'You can't make pies with dry sand,' said Odette. 'Even children know that.'

Mathieu burst out laughing.

'What are you thinking about?' asked Odette.

'I've got to write to Ivich,' he replied, 'and I don't know what to say.'

'I'm surprised at that,' she answered with a short laugh. 'You send her pages.'

'I know I do. But some fools have frightened her. She has taken to reading the newspapers and she doesn't understand what's going on: she wants me to explain. It's going to be an awkward business. She mixes up the Czechs and the Albanians, and she thinks that Prague is by the sea.'

'How very Russian,' said Odette drily.

Mathieu grimaced and did not answer, and Odette began to feel hostile. He added with a smile: 'What complicates everything is that she's furiously angry with me.'

'Why?' she asked.

'Because I'm French. She was living quietly among the French, and here they are suddenly proposing to go to war. She thinks it's abominable.'

'Well, really!' said Odette indignantly.

Mathieu assumed a bland expression. 'Put yourself in her place,' he said quietly. 'She disapproves of us because we are putting ourselves in a position where we risk being killed or wounded! She regards the wounded as tactless sort of people because they force us to think of their bodies. That's what she calls physiological, and she hates anything physiological, both in herself and others.'

'Little darling,' murmured Odette.

'She's quite sincere,' said Mathieu. 'She fasts for days together, because it disgusts her to eat. When she feels sleepy at night, she drinks coffee to wake herself up.'

Odette did not answer: she thought, 'A good spanking is what she wants.' Mathieu was shuffling sand about with a sentimental sort of air: 'Never eats, eh? But I'm sure she keeps pots of jam hidden in her room. Men are too silly.' Mathieu had gone back to making sand-pies: he was off again, God knew where, nor for how long: 'I eat red meat, and sleep when I feel sleepy,' she thought bitterly. On the balcony of the Provençal the band was playing the *Sérénade Portugaise*. There were three musicians. Italians. The violinist wasn't too bad: he closed his eyes when he was playing. Odette felt quite moved: music in the open air always sounded strange, so slight and drawn out. Especially at such a moment: a vast tonnage of heat and war weighed heavily upon sea and sand, and here were these mouselike noises mounting up into high heaven. She turned to Mathieu, and was on the point of saying to him: 'I like that tune.' But she did not: perhaps Ivich detested the *Sérénade Portugaise*.

Mathieu's hands stopped moving, and the sand pie collapsed.

'I like that tune,' he said. 'What is it?'

'It's the *Sérénade Portugaise*,' said Odette.

Six-ten at Godesberg. The old gentleman waited. At Angoulême, Marseilles, Ghent, and Dover, they were thinking to themselves: 'What is he doing? Has he come down? Is he talking to Hitler?' Perhaps even then the two of them were in process of arranging a settlement. So they waited. In the drawing-room with the half-closed shutters the old gentleman waited. He was alone; he belched, and walked towards the window. The hill sloped down to the river, green and white. The Rhine was black, like a tarred road after rain. The old gentleman belched again, there was a sour taste in his mouth. He began to drum on the window, and scared flies darted round him. It was a white and dusty heat, a pompous, sceptical, antiquated heat, a high-collared heat of the time of Frederick II: and in the midst of it an elderly Englishman was waiting wearily, an elderly Englishman of the time of Edward VII, while all the rest of the world belonged to 1938. At Juan-les-Pins, at five-ten on 23 September 1938, a large lady in a white linen frock sat down in a deck-chair, took off her blue spectacles and began to read the paper. It was the *Petit-Niçois*, Odette Delorme could read the large type headline; 'Keep calm', and, with an effort, she deciphered the sub-title: 'Mr Chamberlain sends a message to Hitler.' And she said to herself: 'Do I *really* hate war?' And she thought: 'No, not all the way.' For if she had done, she would have leapt out of her chair, rushed to the railway-station crying: 'Don't go! Stay at home!' She saw herself for an instant erect, arms outstretched, and crying out, 'Don't go!' and she felt dizzy. Then she reflected with relief that she was incapable of so gross an indiscretion. Not all the way. A decent woman, a Frenchwoman, sensible and discreet, with many duties, with one particular duty never to think anything out for herself. At Laon, in an ill-lit room, a frantic girl rejected war with her whole being, blindly, doggedly. Odette said: 'War is a dreadful thing!' and she added, 'I keep on thinking of the poor fellows who must go.' But she really had no thoughts as yet, she waited placidly: she knew she would soon be told all that she must think and say and do. When her father had been killed, in 1917, people had said to her: He was a fine fellow, you must be brave; she had very soon learnt to wear her mourning veils with a sort of jaunty melancholy, and look at people with the ingenuous eyes of a war-orphan. In 1924 her brother had been wounded in Morocco, he had come back lamed, and people used to say to Odette: 'He's a fine fellow, you must be careful not to pity him'; and Jacques had said to her, a few years afterwards: 'It's very odd, I thought Étienne had more strength of mind, he has never got used to his disability, he has grown embittered.' Jacques would go, Mathieu would go, and all would be well, she was sure of that. For the moment the newspapers still wavered: Jacques said: 'It would be a silly war', and *Candide* said: 'We are not going to war because the Sudeten Germans want to wear white stockings.' But very soon the country would come together into one vast chorus of approval: the Chambers would unanimously approve the Government's policy, the *Jour* would sing the praises of our heroic *poilus*. Jacques would say to her: 'The workers are splendid': the passers-by would smile in sanctimonious complicity: it would be war, Odette too would approve, and start knitting woollen helmets. He was there, he appeared to be listening to the music, he knew what he really ought to think, but he did not say it. He wrote letters twenty pages long to Ivich to explain the situation. To Odette he explained nothing at all.

'What are you thinking about?'

Odette started. 'Nothing . . . nothing at all.'

'You don't play fair,' said Mathieu. 'I answered your question.'

She bent her head and smiled: but she did not want to talk. He appeared to be quite alert at the moment; he was looking at her.

'What's the matter?' she asked in a tone of annoyance.

He did not answer. He laughed with an air of surprise.

'Have you just noticed I exist?' said Odette. 'I suppose it gave you quite a shock. Is that it?'

When Mathieu laughed, he screwed up his eyes, and looked like a Chinese child.

'Do you suppose you can escape notice?' he asked.

'I'm not very exciting,' said Odette.

'No. Nor very communicative either. Added to which you do what you can to help people to forget you. Well, you don't succeed; even when you're absolutely quiet and withdrawn, look at the sea, and keep as quiet as a mouse, it is obvious that you are there. It just happens like that. On the stage they call it "presence": some actors have it, and some haven't. You have.'

Odette flushed. 'You have been spoilt by your Russian friends,' she said quickly. 'Presence must be a very Slavic quality. But I don't think it's in my line.'

Mathieu eyed her gravely.

'What exactly is in your line?' he asked.

Odette felt her eyes getting a little out of control, and begin to flutter in their sockets. She steadied them, and fixed her gaze on her bare feet with their lacquered nails. She did not like discussing herself.

'I'm a bourgeois,' she said gaily. 'A French bourgeois, nothing very interesting.'

This was obviously not conclusive enough, so she added forcibly, to clinch the conversation: 'A nonentity.'

Mathieu did not answer. She looked at him out of the corner of her eye: his hands were scraping up the sand again. Odette wondered what kind of brick she had dropped. In any case, he might have protested a little, if only from politeness.

In a moment or two she heard his rich, husky voice: 'It must be rather trying to feel a nonentity, eh?'

'One gets used to it,' said Odette.

'I suppose so. I haven't yet.'

'But you aren't a nonentity,' she said briskly.

Mathieu stared at his sand-pie. This time it was an excellent and solid pie. With a blow of his hand he swept it into ruin.

'We are all nonentities,' he said, and laughed.

'How depressing you are,' said Odette.

'Not more so than other people. These threats of war have got on all our nerves a bit.'

She raised her eyes and was about to speak, but was met by a calm affectionate look. And she was silent. Nonentities: a man and a woman looking at each other on a beach. And war was there, all round them: it had entered into them, and transformed them into the semblance of everybody else. He feels he's a nonentity, he looks at me, and smiles, but it's not me he's smiling at, it's a nonentity. He demanded nothing of her, except to be silent and anonymous, as usual. Better say nothing: if she had said to him: 'You aren't a nonentity, you are handsome, strong, romantic, not at all like anybody else' – and if he had believed it, he would then have slipped between her fingers, and drifted away into his dreams, he would perhaps have fallen in love with another woman, that Russian girl, for instance, who drank coffee to keep herself awake. A stab of pride stirred her into speech. 'It will be dreadful this time,' she said rapidly.

'It will be flat folly,' said Mathieu. 'They'll destroy everything within reach. Paris, London, Rome. . . . Just imagine the result!'

Paris, Rome, London. And Jacques's white and homely villa by the seashore. Odette shuddered: she looked at the sea. The sea was now no more than a glittering expanse of vapour: a water-skier, tanned and naked, crouched forward, sped past, towed by a motor-boat. No human agency could destroy that luminous sheen.

'That at least will be left to us,' she said.

'What?'

'That – the sea.'

Mathieu shook his head. 'No,' he said. 'not even that.'

She looked at him with surprise: she did not always quite understand what he meant. She thought of asking him, but suddenly she felt that she *must* go. She leapt to her feet, put on her sandals, and flung her wrap round her.

'What are you doing?' asked Mathieu.

'I must go,' she said.

'Did it suddenly come over you?'

'I've just remembered that I promised Jacques some *ailloli* this evening. Madeleine won't be able to manage it by herself.'

'You never stay long in the same place, anyway,' said Mathieu. 'Well, I shall have another swim.'

She walked up the sandy steps, and when she reached the terrace she turned. Mathieu was running down to the sea. 'He's right,' she thought. 'I'm fidgety. Always on the move, always making a fresh start, always trying to get away from something.' As soon as she felt she liked a place a little, she became uneasy, she felt guilty and insecure. She looked at the sea, and thought: 'I'm always afraid.' Behind her, a hundred yards away, there was Jacques's villa, a buxom Madeleine, the *ailloli* to be made, reasons for living, meals: she walked on. She would say to Madeleine: 'How is your mother today?' And Madeleine would answer, with a faint sniff: 'Just about the same,' and Odette would say: 'You must make her a little soup, and take some of the white of the chicken – cut a wing off before you serve it, she'll like that,' and Madeleine would answer: 'Indeed she won't touch anything, madame.' But Odette would take the chicken, and she herself would cut off a wing, and that would be a reason for being alive. 'Not even that!' She threw a final glance at the sea. 'He said: "Not even that".' And yet it was so gentle, so like the sky upside down, what could they do to damage it? Oily, viscous, coffee-hued, flat, monotonous, the sea of every day, smelling of iodine and medicaments, *their* sea, *their* breeze, at a charge of a hundred francs a day: he raised himself on his elbows and looked at the children playing on the grey sand, little Simone Chassieux laughing and limping about, her left leg clamped into an orthopaedic boot. Near the stairway there was a small boy he did not know, a new arrival, no doubt, fearfully emaciated, and with enormous ears; he had put a finger in his nose and was gravely eyeing three little girls who were making sand-pies. He hunched his narrow, pointed shoulders and flexed his knees, but his bulbous torso remained as rigid as stone. Corsets, of course. Tuberculous scoliosis. 'He must be crazy into the bargain.'

'Lie down,' said Jeannine. 'Flat on your back. You're so restless today.'

He did as he was told and looked at the sky. Four little white clouds. He heard the wheels of a trolley-bed creaking along the road. 'He's coming back early, who can it be?'

'Hello, my boy,' said a hearty voice.

He flung up both arms, and swung the mirror round above his head. They had already passed, but he recognized the nurse's large behind: it was Darrieux.

'When are you going to get your beard cut?' he shouted.

'When you get yourself castrated,' replied Darrieux's distant voice.

He laughed, in high good humour: Jeannine didn't like such talk.

'When am I to go in?'

He watched Jeannine's hand feel in the pocket of her white blouse and produce a watch.

'In another quarter of an hour. Are you getting bored?'

'No.'

He was never bored. Pots of flowers are not bored. They are taken out when the sun shines, and brought in when dusk begins to fall. Their opinion is never asked, they have nothing to decide, nothing to expect. It is unimaginably absorbing to soak in air and light through all one's pores. The sky reverberated like a gong, and he saw five little grey specks in triangular formation gleaming between two clouds. He stretched himself, and twiddled his toes: sound came in great copper waves, pleasant and caressing, rather like the smell of chloroform on an operating table. Jeannine sighed, and he looked at her from the corner of his eye: she had lifted her head and seemed uneasy, there must surely be something on her mind. 'It's true: there's going to be a war.' He smiled.

'So,' he said, turning his neck slightly round; 'the stand-ups are going to have their war.'

'You know what I said,' she observed acidly. 'If you talk like that I shan't answer.'

He was silent, he had all the time there was, the aeroplane roared in his ears, he felt perfectly at ease – I don't mind being silent. She couldn't hold out, stand-ups are always agitated,

29

they have to talk or move around: at last she said: 'Yes, I'm afraid it's true: there's going to be war.'

She spoke with her operation-day expression, suggesting, somehow, a poor pathetic child, as well as a trained nurse. When she came into his room on the first day, and said to him: 'You must hoist yourself up, I'm going to take the bed-pan,' she had worn that same expression. He was sweating, inhaling his own smell, that awful stable smell, while she – erect, expert, unknown, held out manicured hands, with just that expression on her face.

He licked his lips slowly: well, he had had his way with her since then.

'You look quite upset.'

'Do I?'

'What difference can war make to you? It's no business of ours.'

She turned her head away, and drummed irritably on the ledge of his trolley. She oughtn't to be bothering about war. Her job was to look after her patients.

'I don't give a damn about the war,' said he.

'Why do you pretend to be so wicked?' she said quietly. 'You wouldn't like France to be beaten.'

'I shouldn't care.'

'Monsieur Charles! You frighten me when you talk like that.'

'It isn't my fault I'm a Nazi,' he jeered.

'Nazi!' she said despondently. 'What will you think of next! Nazi! They beat up the Jews and everybody who doesn't agree with them they put in prison – the priests too; they set fire to the Reichstag, they're a pack of gangsters. No one has a right to say such things. A young man like you mustn't say he's a Nazi, even as a joke.'

He smiled a knowing little smile, just to provoke her. He felt no hostility towards the Nazis. They were violent, dreary sort of people, who apparently wanted to devour everything they could lay hands on: well, how far they would go remained to be seen. A comical idea came into his mind.

'If there was a war, we should all be on a level.'

'Ah, you're looking pleased,' said Jeannine: 'What have you got into your head now?'

'The stand-ups,' he said, 'are sick of standing up, they'll lie

30

flat down in holes. I on my back, they on their faces: we shall all be like as like.'

Too long had they bent over him, cleaned and scrubbed and rubbed him down with those competent hands of theirs, while he lay motionless, looking at their faces from the chin upwards, scabby nose-holes above protruding lips, and black line of eyebrows on the horizon: it would be their turn to lie down. Jeannine did not respond: she was less vivacious than usual. Gently she laid a hand upon his shoulder:

'You naughty boy,' she said. 'You naughty, naughty boy.'

It was the moment of reconciliation.

'What's for dinner this evening?' he asked.

'Rice soup, mashed potatoes, and your favourite fish.'

'And what sort of sweet? Plums?'

'I don't know.'

'Sure to be plums,' he said. 'It was stewed apricots yesterday.'

More than five minutes: he lay full length, filled his lungs in order to enjoy the respite, and viewed his little bit of a world through his third eye. A dusty, fixed eye, dotted with brown spots: it tended to distort all movements slightly, making them look comically stiff and mechanical like early films. And, at that very moment, a woman in black on a trolley slid into it, across it, and vanished: a small boy was pushing the trolley.

'Who is it?' he asked Jeannine.

'I don't know,' said Jeannine. 'I think she's at the Villa Mon Repos – you know, the large red house by the sea.'

'Where André had his operation?'

'Yes.'

He drew a deep breath. The fresh, silky sunshine flooded into his mouth, his nostrils, and his eyes. That soldier – what was he doing there? Did he want to breathe the air of sickness? The soldier passed into the mirror, stiff as a figure in a magic lantern, he looked worried, Charles raised himself on an elbow, and watched him curiously: he walks, he is conscious of his legs and thighs, his feet carry his whole body. The soldier stopped, and began to talk to a nurse. 'Ah, it's some local man,' thought Charles with relief. He talked gravely, and nodded, looking rather grim: he washes and dresses himself without help, he goes where he likes, he has to think about his doings, he feels quite strange because he is standing up: I had that experience. Something is going to happen to him. To-morrow there will be war, and something is going to happen to all these people. But not to me. I am an object.

'Time's up,' said Jeannine. She looked at him sadly, her eyes were full of tears. Ugly creature.

'Do we love our little doll?' he said.

'Oh, yes.'

'Don't shake me like you did on the way out.'

'No.'

The tears welled up and trickled down her pale cheeks. He eyed her mistrustfully.

'What's the matter with you?'

She did not answer, she sniffed as she bent over him and smoothed his bedclothes: he could see into her nostrils.

'You're hiding something from me.'

Still she did not answer.

'What are you hiding from me? You had an argument with Madame Gouverné, didn't you? Look here – I won't be treated like a child.'

She stood up again, and eyed him with hopeless affection.

'You're going to be evacuated,' she said, bursting into tears.

He did not understand, and said: 'Me?'

'All the patients at Berck. It's too near the frontier.'

He began to tremble. He grabbed Jeannine's hand and squeezed it. 'But I want to stay.'

'They won't leave anyone here,' she said in a despondent tone.

He squeezed the hand with all his strength. 'I won't go!' he said. 'I won't go!'

She took her hand away without replying, went round to the back of the trolley, and began to push. Charles half-rose, and began to twist a corner of the coverlet.

'But where are they sending us? When are we to go? Will the nurses go too? Tell me.'

She still did not answer, and he heard her sigh above his head. He fell back, and said savagely:

'The brutes, they've done me down all right.'

I won't look into the street. Milan is standing by the window, looking out: he has little hope. They aren't here yet, but their footsteps are shuffling round the houses. I can hear them. I bend over Marikka, and I say:

'Stand over there.'

'Where?'

'Against the wall, between the windows.'

'Why was I sent here?' she says.

I don't answer, and she goes on: 'Who is that shouting?'

I don't answer. Shuffling feet. The stealthy sound of them – shoo-shoo-shoo – all round the house. I sit down on the floor beside her. I feel so heavy now. I take her in my arms. Milan is at the window, absently biting his nails. I say to him:

'Milan: come here: don't stay by the window.'

He grunts, he leans out over the window-rail, he leans out deliberately. Shuffling feet. In five minutes they'll be here. Marikka puckers her little brows.

'Who is that marching?'

'The Germans.'

'Ha?' says she, and her face clears. She listens submissively to the shuffling feet, just as she listens to my voice in class, or the rain, or the wind in the trees: just because it's there. I look at her, and she looks at me with untroubled eyes. Just that look – to be absorbed into that uncomprehending, unforeseeing look. I wish I were deaf, that I might plunge into those eyes, and read the sound in them. A sound devoid of sense, like the sound of moving leaves. It's the sound of shuffling feet. Soft, and softly they will come, and they'll beat him to a jelly. There he stands, a tall strong man, looking out of the window: they will hold him in their outstretched hands, a poor limp wretch with a gaping, battered face: they will thrash him, stamp on him, and tomorrow he will shrink from looking at me. Marikka quivers in my arms –

'Are you afraid?' I ask her.

She shakes her head. She's not afraid. She looks solemn, as she does when I write on the blackboard, she watches my moving arm with parted lips. She tries so hard: trees and water, walking animals, people, and the letters of the alphabet. For the moment what has to be understood is the silence of these grown-up people; and the feet shuffling down the street. We are a small country. So they will come; they'll drive their tanks across our fields, they'll shoot our men: just because we are a small country. Pray God the French will come to our aid, pray God they don't desert us.

'There they are,' says Milan.

I can't look at his face: only at Marikka's, because she doesn't understand. They're in our street, their feet are shuffling down it, they shout our name, I hear them, I am here, sitting on the floor, heavy and still, Milan's revolver is in my apron pocket. He looks at Marikka's face: she opens her mouth, her eyes are unclouded, she doesn't understand.

He was walking along the tram-lines, looking at the shops and laughing contentedly. He looked straight ahead of him at the white street, blinked, and thought: 'So this is Marseilles.' The shops were closed, the iron shutters lowered, the street deserted, but this was Marseilles. He stopped, put down his bag, took off his leather jacket and slung it over his arm, then wiped his forehead, and hoisted the bag on to his back again. He longed for a chat with someone. He said to himself: 'I've got twelve fag-ends, and a cigar-end in my handkerchief.' The tram-lines sparkled, the long white street dazzled him, and he added: 'And a litre of red wine in my bag.' He was thirsty, and would have liked to drink it, but he would have preferred to have a glass or two in a bar if only they hadn't all been shut. 'I wouldn't have believed it,' he said. He walked on between the tram-lines, the street glistened like a stream between the low dark houses. On the left there were a number of shops, but what they sold one couldn't tell, since the iron curtains were lowered: on his right were houses, open-fronted and deserted, looking like railway stations, and then from time to time, a brick wall. But this was Marseilles.

'Where can they be?' said Gros-Louis.

'Come in quick,' shouted a voice.

At the corner of an alley, there was a café still open. A hulking young fellow with a couple of tipsy bacchantes stood in the doorway and shouted: 'Come in quick'; and people Gros-Louis had not noticed suddenly appeared from nowhere and began to run towards the café. Gros-Louis ran too: the other men jostled their way in, he tried to get in behind them, but the man with the bacchantes clapped him on the chest and said: 'Get out.'

A boy in overalls had hold of a round table rather larger than himself, and was trying to get it back into the café.

'All right, old boy,' said Gros-Louis: 'I'm going. You haven't got a drop of spirits, have you?'

'I told you to beat it.'

'I'm going,' said Gros-Louis. 'Don't be afraid: I don't stay where I'm not wanted.'

The man turned his back on him, jerked the outside latch off the door, and went inside, closing it behind him. Gros-Louis eyed the door: in place of the handle there remained a small round hole with raised edges. He scratched the back of his neck, and repeated: 'I'm going, he needn't be afraid.' Even so he went up to the window and tried to peer into the café, but someone drew the inner curtains, and he could see nothing. 'I wouldn't have believed it,' he said to himself. He could see the street to the right and left of him as far as eye could reach, the shining tram-lines, and on them a deserted black truck. 'I wish I could get in somewhere,' said Gros-Louis. He wanted to buy a drop of spirits in a café, and have a chat with the landlord. And he added, by way of explanation, scratching the top of his head: 'It isn't that I'm not used to being out of doors.' But when he was out of doors, other people were out of doors too, there were the sheep and the other shepherds, which made for company anyway, and when there was nobody, well – there was nobody, and that was that. Whereas now he was outside, and everybody else was inside, behind their walls and their locked doors. He was quite alone outside, he and the little truck. He tapped on the café window and waited. No one answered: if he had not seen them go in with his own eyes, he would have sworn that the café was empty. He said: 'I'm off,' and he went: he began to feel strangely thirsty: he wouldn't have imagined Marseilles could be like this. He walked on. The street surely smelt very stuffy. 'Where am I going to sit down?' he said to himself, and he heard a noise behind him, like a flock of sheep on the move. He turned, and in the distance saw a group of people carrying flags. 'Ah well, I'll watch them pass,' he said. And he recovered his good humour. Just on the other side of the lines there was a sort of square, a fair-ground, with two little green huts backing on to a high wall: and he said to himself: 'I'll sit down there to watch them pass.' One of the huts was a shop, from which came the smell of sausage and fried potatoes. Gros-Louis saw an old fellow in a white apron raking out a stove inside the shop.

'Give me some fried potatoes, Dad.'

The old man turned. 'Go to hell,' he said.

'I've got some money,' said Gros-Louis.

'Get to hell, and your money too, I'm shutting up.'

He came out, and began to turn a crank. An iron curtain clattered downwards.

'It isn't seven o'clock yet,' said Gros-Louis, shouting to drown the clatter.

The old man did not answer.

'I thought you were shutting because it was seven o'clock,' shouted Gros-Louis.

The iron curtain was down. The old man removed the crank, stood up and spat.

'Say, dopey, you didn't see them coming, did you? I don't want to hand out my taters for nothing,' said he, going back into his hut. Gros-Louis looked at the green door for a moment, then he sat down in the middle of the fair-ground, propped his back against his bag, and warmed himself in the sun. He remembered that he had a hunk of bread, a litre of red, twelve fag-ends, and a cigar-end, and he said: 'Well, well, let's have a bite.' On the other side of the lines, the men began to file past, waving their flags, and shouting and singing: Gros-Louis had pulled a knife out of his pocket, and munched as he watched them pass. Some of them raised their fists, and others shouted: 'Come and join us!' he laughed and hailed them as they tramped past; he rather liked noise and movement, it cheered him up a bit.

He heard footsteps, and turned round. A tall Negro was coming towards him, bare-armed and wearing a faded pink shirt: at every stride his blue calico trousers flapped and flattened against his lanky thighs. He did not seem in a hurry. He stopped, and wrung out a swim-suit with his pinky-brown hands. The water dripped on to the dust in small round patches. The Negro rolled the swim-suit into a towel, and then stood nonchalantly watching the procession, and whistled.

'Hi!' exclaimed Gros-Louis.

The Negro looked at him and smiled.

'What are they up to?'

The Negro came towards him swaying his shoulders.

'It's the dockers,' he said.

'Are they on strike?'

'The strike's over,' said the Negro. 'But these chaps want to start it again.'

'Ah – so that's it,' said Gros-Louis.

The Negro eyed him for a moment in silence, he seemed to be mustering his thoughts. Finally he sat down on the ground and began to roll a cigarette. He continued to whistle.

'Where have you sprung from?' he asked.

'Prades,' said Gros-Louis.

'Where's that?' said the Negro.

'Aha! So you don't know where Prades is,' said Gros-Louis with a laugh. They both laughed, and then Gros-Louis explained: 'I'd got fed up.'

'You're looking for work?' said the Negro.

'I was a shepherd,' explained Gros-Louis. 'I kept sheep on the Canigou. But I got fed up.'

The Negro wagged his head.

'There are no jobs here,' he said severely.

'Oh, I'll find one,' said Gros-Louis. He displayed his hands. 'I can do anything.'

'There's no work here,' the Negro repeated.

They fell silent. Gros-Louis looked at the people filing past and laughing. They shouted: 'Hang him! Hang Sabiani!' There were women with them: they were flushed and dishevelled, their jaws were open wide, but whatever they were saying was drowned by the men's yells. Gros-Louis was quite content, he had company now. What a lark! he thought. A fat woman passed along with the rest, her titties swinging as she walked. Gros-Louis thought he could have had some fun with her, at least she'd have been a handful. The Negro burst out laughing. He laughed so violently that the smoke of his cigarette choked him. He laughed and coughed; Gros-Louis clapped him on the back.

'What are you laughing at?' he said, laughing too.

The Negro had recovered his gravity. 'Dunno,' he said.

'Have a drink,' said Gros-Louis.

The Negro took the bottle and tipped it into his throat. Gros-Louis drank too. The street was again deserted.

'Where did you sleep?' asked the Negro.

'I don't know,' said Gros-Louis. 'It was a sort of square, with trucks under a tarpaulin. It smelt of coal.'

'Got any money?'

'Maybe.'

The door of the café opened, and a knot of men came out. They stopped for a moment in the street: looked the way the strikers had gone, shading their eyes with their hands. Then some walked slowly away, lighting cigarettes, others stayed around in little groups. One, a red-haired, rather corpulent fellow, said angrily to a wizened lad beside him:

'We've got war at our backsides, and you come and talk about syndicalism!'

He was sweating, he wore no jacket, his shirt, with two large damp patches under his armpits, was open at the collar. Gros-Louis turned to the Negro:

'War?' he asked. 'What war?'

'A bench!' said Daniel. 'Just what we need.'

There was a green bench, set against the farm wall, under an open window. Daniel swung open the gate and entered the yard. A dog barked, and leapt at them, dragging at his chain: an old woman appeared in the doorway of the house with a saucepan in her hand.

'Now then!' she said, brandishing the saucepan at the dog. 'None of that!'

The dog growled once or twice and lay down.

'My wife is a little tired,' said Daniel, taking off his hat. 'Might she sit on that bench?'

The old woman blinked dubiously; perhaps she did not understand French. Daniel repeated in a louder tone:

'My wife is a little tired.'

The old woman turned to Marcelle, who was leaning against the gate, and her suspicions vanished.

'Of course the lady can sit down. That's what benches are for. And she won't wear ours out – it's been there long enough. Have you come from Peyrehorade?'

Marcelle came in too and sat down with a smile.

'Yes,' she said, 'we meant to get to the cliff: but it's rather far for me, at present.'

The old woman winked knowingly: 'Ah well,' she said, 'in your condition you've got to be careful.'

Marcelle sank back against the wall, her eyes half-closed, with a little gurgle of contentment. The old lady looked at her belly with a professional eye, then turned to Daniel, nodded and smiled at him with an expression of respect. Daniel clutched the knob of his stick and smiled too. Everybody smiled, their thoughts centred on the self-contained assurance of pregnancy. A small boy came tottering out of the farm-house, stopped dead, and looked dubiously at Marcelle. He wore no knickers: and his little buttocks were red and scabbed.

'I did so want to see the cliff,' said Marcelle, peevishly.

'But there's a taxi at Peyrehorade,' said the old woman. 'It belongs to the Lamblin lad, the last house on the Bidasse road.'

'I know,' said Marcelle.

The old woman turned to Daniel, and shook a finger at him: 'Ah, monsieur, you must be very kind to your lady: you must always let her have her way just now.'

Marcelle smiled: 'He is kind,' she said. 'I was the one who wanted to walk.'

She stretched out an arm and stroked the boy's head. For the last fortnight she had felt an interest in children: it had come to her suddenly. She smelt them and touched them when they came within her reach.

'Is he your grandson?'

'He's my niece's boy; nearly four years old.'

'A nice child,' said Marcelle.

'When he behaves himself.' The old woman added in an undertone: 'Is it to be a boy?'

'Ah,' said Marcelle. 'I hope so.'

The old woman laughed: 'You must pray to Sainte Marguerite every morning.'

A reverent hush fell upon them; in the silence one could hear the wings of angels. All eyes were turned on Daniel. He leaned on his stick, and looked down, with a modest, manly air.

'I'm going to trouble you still further, madame,' he said politely. 'Might I ask for a drink of milk for my wife?' He turned to Marcelle: 'You would like a drink of milk, wouldn't you?'

'I'll go and get it,' said the old woman. She disappeared into her kitchen.

'Come and sit down beside me,' said Marcelle.

He sat down.

'How thoughtful you are,' she said, taking his hand. He smiled. She looked at him with a bewildered air, and he continued to smile, stifling a vast yawn. And he thought to himself: 'Women shouldn't be allowed to look quite so pregnant.' In the moist, slightly feverish clotted air, smells, like strands of seaweed; Daniel stared at the green and red glitter of a bush on the far side of the gate: there was greenery in his nostrils, and in his mouth. Another fortnight. Fifteen green and glittering days, fifteen days of the country. He hated the country. A timid finger moved over his hand, as hesitant as a branch swaying in the wind. He looked down at the finger. It was white and rather plump, and it wore a wedding-ring. 'She adores me,' thought Daniel. Night and day that humble, insistent adoration percolated through his being like the living fragrance of the fields. He half-closed his eyes, and Marcelle's adoration melted into the rustling foliage, into the smell of manure and clover.

'What are you thinking about?' asked Marcelle.

'The war,' replied Daniel.

The old woman returned with a bowl of foaming milk. Marcelle took it and drank deep draughts. Her upper lip protruded over the liquid in the bowl, and drew it in with a faint noise. The milk gurgled down her throat.

'That does one good,' she said with a sigh. A white moustache had appeared above her mouth.

The old woman eyed her pleasantly. 'Milk fresh from the cow – that's the stuff for baby.' They laughed with female complicity, and Marcelle got up, leaning against the wall:

'I feel quite rested,' she said to Daniel. 'We'll go on when you like.'

'Good-bye, madame,' said Daniel slipping a note into the woman's hand. 'Thank you for your kind hospitality.'

'Thank you, madame,' said Marcelle with a special smile.

'I hope to see you again,' said the old woman. 'Go back slowly.'

40

Daniel opened the gate, and stood aside for Marcelle; she tripped over a large stone and nearly fell.

'Hi!' cried the old woman from behind them.

'Take my arm,' said Daniel.

'I'm so clumsy,' said Marcelle in confusion.

She took his arm: he felt her against him, a warm top-heavy figure: 'And Mathieu actually desired the creature,' he thought.

'Above all,' he said, 'take small steps.'

Dark hedges. Silence. Fields. A black row of pines on the horizon. With slow and heavy steps the men were returning to the farms: they would sit at the long table, and swallow their soup in silence. A herd of cows crossed the road. One of them took fright, and broke into a prancing trot. Marcelle drew close to Daniel.

'Just imagine – I'm afraid of cows!' she said, in a low tone.

Daniel squeezed her arm affectionately: 'Go to hell!' was what he thought. She drew a deep breath and was silent. He threw a sidelong glance at her, and noticed her vague eyes, her sleepy smile, and her beatific expression. 'That's done it,' he thought with satisfaction. 'She's off again.' She was taken like this from time to time, when the baby stirred within her, or an unfamiliar emotion shook her. She must think of herself as a sort of illimitable, teeming entity, a kind of milky way. However, here were ten good minutes gained. 'Here am I,' he thought, 'walking in the country, cows are passing by, and this fat woman is my wife.' He wanted to laugh: he had never seen so many cows in his life. It's your own fault. You wanted a quick, high-powered catastrophe; and you've got it. They were walking slowly, like two lovers, arm in arm, and the flies were buzzing round them. An old man, leaning motionless on a spade, at the edge of his field, watched them pass and smiled. Daniel felt himself blushing fiercely. At that moment, Marcelle came out of her trance.

'Do you really believe that there's going to be a war?' she asked abruptly.

Her gestures had lost their aggressive angularity, they were now rather clumsy and languid. But she had kept her abrupt, emphatic voice. Daniel looked at the fields. Fields of what?

He couldn't have distinguished a field of maize from a field of beetroot. He heard Marcelle repeat:

'Do you?'

And he thought: 'Oh for a war!' She would be a widow. A widow, with a child, and six hundred thousand francs in cash. Not to mention memories of an incomparable husband. What more could she ask? He stopped abruptly, the prospect caught him by the throat, he gripped his stick, and thought: 'Oh God, if only war would come!' A thunderbolt that would shatter this smooth-faced world, plough the countryside into a quagmire, dig shell-holes in the fields, and fashion these flat monotonous lands into the likeness of a storm-tossed sea – war, the hecatomb of righteous men, the massacre of the innocents. That translucent sky – they will smash it with their own hands. How they are going to hate each other! How frightened they're going to be! And I – how I shall wallow in that sea of hatred! Marcelle looked at him with surprise. He wanted to laugh.

'No, I don't believe there's going to be a war.'

Children on the road, their shrill innocent voices, and their laughter. Peace. The sun flickers in the hedges as it did yesterday, and as it will do tomorrow: the steeple of Peyrehorade appears at the turn of the road. Every object in the world has its smell, its long, pale evening shadow, and its individual future. And the sum of all these futures – is peace: it glows on the worm-eaten wood of this gate, on that small boy's rosy neck, it can be read in his eager eyes, it rises from those sun-warmed beds of nettles, it is heard in the clangour of those bells. Men are gathered around steaming soup-tureens, they break bread, they pour wine into glasses, they wipe their knives, and their daily gestures constitute peace. It is there, enmeshed in all those futures, as slow and obstinate as Nature herself; it is the everlasting return of the sun, the quivering immobility of the countryside, and the purpose of man's toil. Not a gesture that does not evoke and express it, even the sound of Marcelle's padding footsteps at my side, even the affectionate pressure of my fingers on Marcelle's arm. A hail of stones through the window: 'Get out! Get out!' Milan only just had time to fling himself backwards. A raucous voice shouted his name: 'Hlinka! Milan Hlinka! get out!' Someone began to chant: 'The Czechs are lice in the German fur.' The

42

'I loathe new places.'

They have made decisions, they took responsibilities, they had health and strength and leisure: they voted and chose their leaders, they had the use of their legs, they ran about the earth with their pompous busy airs, they arranged the destiny of the world, and in particular that of the unfortunate sick people whom they treat like grown-up children. And here is the result: war: bloody war. Why should I pay for their stupidities? I was sick, no one asked for my opinion. They have just remembered my existence, and now they want to involve me in their mess. They are going to pick me up by the arms and the legs, and say: 'Excuse us, we are at war,' and they dump me in a corner like rubbish, so that I shan't have a chance of interfering with their sport of massacre. The question he had suppressed for the last half-hour suddenly rose to his lips. She would be painfully gratified, but no matter: this time it had to come out:

'You . . . will the nurses come with us?'

'Yes,' said Jeannine. 'Some of them.'

'Will . . . you?'

'No,' said Jeannine. 'Not me.'

He began to tremble, and said hoarsely: 'You mean to desert us?'

'I am posted to Dunkirk hospital.'

'Ah well,' said Charles. 'One nurse is as good as another, eh?'

Jeannine did not answer. He sat up and looked about him. His head swung from left to right and right to left, it was all very tiring, and there was a dry tingling at the back of his eyes. A trolley was trundling towards them propelled by a tall, elegant old gentleman. On it lay a young woman with a haggard face and golden hair, and a magnificent fur cloak spread over her legs. She glanced at him, dropped her head and muttered a few words up into the old gentleman's face.

'Who is she?' asked Charles. 'It's a long time since I've seen her.'

'I don't know. I think she's a music-hall artist. She lost the use of a leg and then of an arm.'

'Does she know?'

'What?'

'The patients, I mean – do they know?'

'No one knows, the doctor forbade us to tell anyone.'

'That's a pity,' he grinned. 'She might be a little less haughty.'

'I think a drop of Fly-tox is needed,' said Pierre, before getting into the carriage. 'There is a strong smell of insects.'

The Arab promptly sprayed a little insecticide over the white covers and cushions.

'There,' he said.

Pierre frowned. 'Hm!'

Maud put a hand over his mouth. 'Hush,' she said with an imploring look. 'Hush! That'll be quite all right.'

'Very well. But if you catch any fleas, don't come and complain to me about it.'

He handed her up, and then sat down beside her. Maud's slim fingers left a dry and living warmth in the hollow of his palm: she was always slightly feverish.

'Drive round the ramparts,' he said curtly.

It was not to be denied that poverty breeds vulgarity. Maud was vulgar, he hated her freemasonry with coachmen, porters, guides, and waiters: she always took their part, and even if they were caught red-handed, she managed to find excuses for them.

The driver whipped up his horse, and the cab clattered forwards.

'What old rattletraps they are,' said Pierre with a laugh. 'I'm always afraid of a spring breaking.'

Maud leaned out and looked at everything with large, solemn, conscientious eyes.

'It's our last drive.'

'So it is,' he said. 'So it is.'

She is feeling poetical because it is the last day, and we are sailing tomorrow. It was annoying; still, he preferred her contemplative to her vivacious mood. She was not pretty, and when she tried to display charm or animation, the result was at once disastrous. All would be well, he thought. There would be next day, and the three days' crossing: and then, at Marseilles – good night; they would each go their own way. He congratulated himself on having booked a first-class berth: the four women would be travelling third-class; he would

46

invite her into his cabin when he wanted her, but being timid she would never venture to come on to the first-class deck unless he fetched her.

'Have you booked your seats on the coach?' he asked.

Maud looked a little embarrassed: 'As a matter of fact we aren't taking the coach. We are being driven by car to Casa.'

'Who is driving you?'

'A friend of Ruby's, a very nice old gentleman, he'll take us round by Fez.'

'Pity,' he said politely.

The carriage had left Marrakesh, and was passing through the European town. In front of them, an expanse of desiccated decay stretched away into the distance, littered with opened petrol-cans and empty food-tins. The cab rattled on between great white cubes with gleaming windows: Maud put on her dark spectacles, Pierre winced under the strong sunlight. The cubes, decorously located side by side, stood poised upon the desert: a sudden wind would blow them all away. A sign-board had been fixed to one of them, bearing the words: 'rue du Maréchal Lyautey'. But there was no street: merely a shaft of tarred desert between buildings. Three natives watched the carriage pass: the youngest had a wall eye. Pierre sat up straight, and fixed them with a steady look. Show your strength, that you may not have to use it – that was good policy, not only in a military sphere, it was a sound rule of conduct for colonists, and even for the mere tourist. No need to make a display of power: the point was never to lose grip – to stand, in fact, upright. His morning gloom had disappeared. Beneath the witless gaze of those Arabs, he felt he represented France.

'What shall we find when we get back?' said Maud suddenly.

He clenched his fists without replying. Fool: in a flash, she had revived his gloomy mood. She persisted:

'War, perhaps. You'll have to go: and I shall be out of a job.'

He hated to hear her talk about being out of a job, with that serious air, like a worker. After all, she was second violin in Baby's female orchestra, which toured the Mediterranean and the Near East, and could properly be described as an artist. He replied, with a gesture of irritation:

'Look here, Maud, don't let us talk about what's happening. Just for once, do you mind. It's our last evening at Marrakesh.'

She snuggled up to him: 'Yes – it's our last evening.'

He stroked her hair; but there was still a bitter taste in his mouth. Not fear, not anything like it: he was not to be shaken, he *knew* he would never be afraid. It was a feeling of . . . disillusion.

The carriage was driving under the ramparts now. Maud pointed to a red door, above which could be seen the green fronds of a palm tree.

'Pierre! Do you remember?'

'What?'

'It's a month, to the very day. That's where we met.'

'Ah, yes. . . .'

'Do you love me?'

She had a thin, rather bony little face, with large eyes and a sensitive mouth.

'Yes, I love you.'

'Say it better than that!'

He bent over her and kissed her.

The old gentleman looked very angry, he glared at them, knitting his heavy brows. 'A memorandum! Are these the only concessions!' Horace Wilson nodded, and thought: 'Why does he put on such an act?' Didn't Chamberlain know there would be a memorandum? Hadn't everything been decided the day before? Hadn't they agreed on the whole performance when the two of them were left alone, face to face with that shyster of an interpreter, Dr Schmitt?

'Put your arms round your little Maud. She's got the blues this evening.'

He clasped her in his arms, and she began to talk in a sort of girlish whimper:

'You're not afraid of war, are you?'

An unpleasant shiver trickled down his neck:

'My poor little girl – no, I'm not. A man is not afraid of war.'

'Well, I bet Lucien was!' said she. 'In fact that's what put me off him: he was too much of a funk.'

He leaned over her and kissed her hair: and he wondered why he suddenly wanted to box her ears.

'Anyway,' she continued. 'How could a man look after a woman if he's always got the jitters?'

'He wasn't a man at all,' he said quietly. 'I am.'

She took his face in her hands, sniffed at it, and went on: 'Yes, you were a man, monsieur. With your black hair and black beard, I took you for about twenty-eight.'

He drew back a little: he was feeling limp and stale, a sense of nausea rose from his stomach into his throat, and he did not know which disgusted him most – the shimmering desert, the red earth walls, or the woman in his arms. How sick I am of Morocco! He longed to be at Tours, in his parents' house, in the early morning, with his mother to come and bring him his breakfast in bed. Well, you will go down to the Press room, he said to Nevile Henderson, and you will kindly announce that in response to Chancellor Hitler's request, I shall arrive at the Hotel Dreesen about twelve-thirty.

'Driver!' he said. 'Driver! Go back to the town by that gate.'

'What's the matter?' asked Maud in astonishment.

'I'm sick of the ramparts,' he said to her violently. 'I'm sick of the desert, and I'm sick of Morocco.'

But he soon controlled himself, and taking her chin between two fingers he said: 'If you are a good girl, we'll buy you a pair of slippers.'

The war *was not* in the merry-go-round music, it *was not* in the swarming cafés of the rue Rochechouart. Not a breath of wind. Maurice was sweating, he felt Nenette's warm thigh against his own (and very nice too); it *was not* in the fields, in the shimmer of the heated air above the hedge, in the clear white twittering of the birds, in Marcelle's laugh, *it had come forth in the desert*, round the walls of Marrakesh. A red, hot wind whirled round the carriage, swept over the waves of the Mediterranean, and struck Mathieu in the face: Mathieu was drying himself on the deserted beach, and he thought, 'Not even that'; and he felt the blast of war.

Not even that! It had grown a little cold, but he was not inclined to go in at once. One after another, the people had left the beach: it was dinner-time. The sea itself was empty, it lay, like a solar desert, a vast expanse of fallen light, and the black water-ski plank shot through it like a shark's head.

'Not even that,' thought Mathieu. She would knit, by the

open window, while waiting for Jacques's letters. From time to time she would lift her head, with a feeling of vague hope; and she would look out at *her* sea. *Her* sea: a buoy, a diving-raft, a little water, splashing against warm sand. A quiet little garden within the compass of humanity, with a few broad avenues and countless little paths. And each time she would take up her knitting again with the same sense of disappointment: they would change her sea. The inland country, bristling with bayonets and packed with guns, would have absorbed the sea-coast: the water and the sand would have receded, each into its own melancholy existence. Barbed-wire entanglements streaking the white steps with starred shadows; guns on the promenade among the pines; sentries outside the villas: officers would grope like blind men through that desolate watering-place. The sea would return to its solitude. No bathing: the water, guarded by the military, would assume an official aspect by the seashore; the diving raft and the buoy would no longer seem any distance from the land; all the paths that Odette had traced upon the waves since her childhood would have been wiped out. But the open sea, in contrast, the swelling inhuman sea – with its navy battles fifty miles off Malta, its clusters of ships sunk near Palermo, with its depths furrowed by iron fish – the open sea would be omnipresent, on all the waves she would detect its glacial menace, and the open sea would rise up on the skyline, like a wall without hope. Mathieu sat up: he was now dry; he began to dust the sand off his bathing-dress. 'War must be a filthy business,' he thought. And when it was over? Yet another sea. The sea of the vanquished? Or of the victors? In five years' – ten years' – time he would perhaps be here on a September evening, at this same time, sitting on this same sand, confronting that vast expanse of gelatine, the same red rays skimming the surface of the water. But what would he see then?

He got up and slipped on his wrap. The pines on the promenade were black against the sky. He threw a last glance at the sea: war had not yet broken out: people were dining quietly in their villas: no guns, no soldiers, no barbed wire, the fleet at anchor off Bizerta or Toulon; it was still permissible to view the sea in splendour, the sea of the last evenings of peace. But it was inert and non-committal: an expanse of salt water, moving, but indicative of nothing. He shrugged his shoulders, and walked up the stone steps: for some days past his contacts with this world had dwindled. Smells had gone, the multifarious smells of the south; then tastes. And now the sea. 'Like rats leaving a sinking ship.' When the day of departure came, he would be quite desiccated, with nothing left to regret. He returned slowly to the villa, and Pierre jumped out of the carriage:

'Come along,' said he. 'You shall have your pair of slippers.'

They entered the *Suks*. It was late: the Arabs were in a hurry to get to the Place Djemaa-el-Fnâ before sunset. Pierre felt in better humour: the bustle of the crowd had a stimulating effect on him. He looked at the veiled women, and when they returned his look, he preened himself in their admiring eyes.

'Look,' he said. 'There are some slippers.'

There were all sorts of objects on the stall – a bric-à-brac of fabrics, necklaces and embroidered shoes.

'How pretty!' said Maud. 'Do let us stop.'

She plunged her hands into the jumble, and Pierre drew back a little: he did not want to provide the Arabs with the spectacle of a European inspecting feminine adornments.

'Choose anything you like,' he said nonchalantly.

On the neighbouring stall there were French books for sale: he amused himself by turning them over. Mostly detective stories, and film novels. On his right he could hear the click of rings and bracelets on Maud's fingers.

'Have you got what you want?' he asked her over his shoulder.

'I'm having a look,' she replied. 'I can't decide all at once.'

He returned to the books. Under a pile of Texas Jacks and Buffalo Bills, he discovered a book with photographs. It was a work by Colonel Picot, on facial wounds: the first pages were missing, the rest were tattered. His impulse was to put it down at once, but he was too late: the book had fallen open by itself: Pierre glimpsed an awful head, from nose to chin there was nothing but a void, no lips nor teeth: the right eye had gone, and the right cheek was seamed by a great scar. The tortured face retained a human intelligence, and wore a sort of ghastly

51

grin. Pierre felt an icy tingling all over his scalp, and wondered how on earth the book had found its way here.

'Now here's a book for you,' said the shopkeeper. 'You'll get a kick out of it.'

Pierre turned over the pages. Men without noses, eyes, or eyelids – their eyeballs bulging as in anatomical illustrations. He was fascinated, he looked at the photographs one by one, and he repeated to himself: How did it get here? The most frightful was a head without a lower jaw: the upper jaw had lost its lip, and displayed a gum and four teeth. He can see – he thought. That fellow is alive. He raised his eyes: a mottled mirror in a gilded frame returned his reflection: he gazed at it, horror-struck.

'Pierre,' said Maud. 'Come and look. I have found the very thing.'

He hesitated: the book scorched his hands, but he could not force himself to drop it, to get away from it, to *turn his back* on it.

'I'm coming,' he said.

He pointed to the volume, and said to the shopkeeper: 'How much?'

The boy was pacing up and down the office like a caged animal. Irène was typing an interesting article on the evil effects of militarism. She stopped, and raised her head.

'You're making me dizzy.'

'I shan't go away,' said Philippe. 'I shan't go away until he has seen me. . . .'

She burst into a laugh:

'What a to-do! So you want to see him? Well, he's there, on the other side of that door: you have only to go in, and you'll see him.'

'Quite,' said Philippe.

He took a step forward, and stopped:

'I . . . no, that would be stupid, it would set him against me. Oh, Irène! – won't you go back and ask him? For the last time – I swear it's for the last time.'

'You silly boy,' she said. 'Let the thing drop. Pitteaux is a nasty bit of work: can't you understand that it's lucky for you he won't see you again? It would bring trouble.'

'Trouble!' he said ironically. 'Is it possible to harm me?

It's quite clear you don't know my parents: they have all the virtues, so what can I do but take the side of Evil?'

Irène looked him in the eyes: 'Do you suppose I don't know what he wants from you?'

The lad blushed but did not reply.

'Really, really!' said she, with a shrug of her shoulders.

'Go and ask him again, Irène,' said Philippe, in an imploring tone. 'Do. Tell him I'm just about to take a major decision.'

'A lot he cares!'

'Go and tell him all the same.'

She opened the door and entered without knocking. Pitteaux looked up grimly. 'What is it?' he boomed.

She was not alarmed. 'That'll do,' she said. 'No need to shout. It's the boy: I'm sick of having him on my hands. Would you mind taking him on for a bit?'

'I have said – No,' said Pitteaux.

'He says he's going to take a major decision.'

'And what the hell do I care?'

'For God's sake do something about it,' she said impatiently. 'I'm your secretary. I'm not his nurse.'

'All right,' he said, with a glitter in his eyes. 'Let him come in. He's going to take a major decision, is he? Well, he'll find I shall undertake a major execution.'

She laughed derisively and returned to Philippe.

'Go in.'

The boy hurried across the room, but on the threshold of the office he stopped, somewhat in awe, and she had to push him in. She shut the door behind him, came back and sat down at her table. Almost at once, angry voices started up on the other side of the door. She began to type with an air of indifference. She knew the game was lost for Philippe. He pretended to be worldly, and he had been fascinated by Pitteaux: Pitteaux had taken advantage of him out of sheer perversity: he was not even a homosexual. But at the last moment the boy's nerve gave way. Like all boys, he wanted to get all he could for nothing. At the moment, he was begging Pitteaux to remain his friend, but Pitteaux had told him where to get off. She heard him shout: 'Get out of it. You're a little coward, a bourgeois, a wretched little rich kid, playing it tough.' She laughed, and typed a few lines of the article. 'Can one imagine

more sinister ruffians than the high-ranking officers who condemned Dreyfus?' 'Oh, what's going on?' she thought with
amusement.

The door opened and then slammed. Philippe stood in front
of her. He had been crying. He leaned over the desk and
pointed a finger at Irène: 'He's driven me to breaking-point,'
he said, with a wild look on his face. 'And no man can get
away with that.' He flung his head back and began to laugh:
'You'll hear from me again.'

'Don't get excited,' sighed Irène.

The nurse shut down the lid of the trunk: twenty-two pairs
of shoes – he'd certainly made work for the bootmakers, when
a pair showed signs of wear he had thrown it into the trunk
and bought another; more than a hundred pairs of socks, with
holes in the heels and the big toes: six suits much creased from
hanging in a wardrobe – the place was filthy, a proper
bachelor's den. She could quite well leave him for five
minutes, so she slipped into the corridor, entered the w.c. and
lifted her skirts, leaving the door wide open in case of emer-
gency. She relieved herself rapidly, on the alert, listening for
the slightest sound: but Armand Viguier remained alone in
his room, decorously extended, his yellow hands resting on the
sheet, his gaunt head with its bristly grey beard and hollow
eyes tipped backwards, and on his face a far-off smile. His
skinny legs were stretched out beneath the sheet, his feet lay at
an angle of eighty degrees to each other, with his toe-nails
upturned – those horrible great toe-nails, which he pared with
a penknife every three months, and which for the past twenty-
five years had worn out all his socks. There were sores on his
buttocks, despite the india-rubber cushion on which he lay,
but they bled no longer: he was dead. On the night-table lay
his spectacles, and his false teeth in a glass of water.

Dead. His life was there and everywhere, intangible, complete, as full and hard as an egg, so compact that all the forces
of the world could not have introduced an atom into it, so
porous that Paris and the world passed right through it; scattered at the four ends of France, and yet condensed at every
point of space, a vast, motionless, rowdy country fair: shouts,
laughter, the whistle of the locomotives, and the shrapnel-
bursts on 6 May 1917, the savage buzzing in his head when he

fell between two trenches – all those sounds were there, but frozen; and the listening nurse could hear nothing but a trickle underneath her skirts. She got up, not pulling the plug out of respect for the dead, went back and sat by Armand's bed, passing through that still, bright sunlight that shone for ever on a woman's face, by the Grande Jatte in the canoe on 20 July 1900. Armand Viguier was dead; his life was a thing adrift, enclosing agonies now still, the month of March 1922, streaked through and through with inward grief, imperishable little jewels – the rainbow over the Quai de Bercy on a rainy Saturday evening, slippery pavements, two cyclists laughing as they rode past, the patter of rain on a balcony one stifling March afternoon, a gipsy melody which brought tears to his eyes, drops of dew gleaming in the grass, and a flight of pigeons on the Piazza San Marco. She unfolded the newspaper, adjusted her spectacles, and began to read: 'Latest news: M. Chamberlain: no meeting with Chancellor Hitler this afternoon.' She thought of her nephew who was certain to be called up, put the paper down beside her, and sighed. Peace was there, like the rainbow, like the sunlight on the Grande Jatte, like the glimmer of light on a fair-skinned arm. The peace of 1939 and 1940 and of 1980, the great peace of mankind: the nurse tightened her lips and thought, 'It's war,' she looked straight ahead into the distance, and her gaze pierced through that peace. Chamberlain shook his head and said, 'I'll do what I can, of course, but I have no great hopes.'

Horace Wilson felt an uneasy shiver down his back, and said to himself: 'Can he be sincere?' and the nurse thought: 'My husband in '14, in '38 my nephew: I shall have lived between two wars.' But Armand Viguier knows that peace has just been born, Chantal asks him: 'Why did you, with your ideas, join the army?' and he answers, 'To ensure that this should be the last war'. 27 May 1919. The very last. He listens to Briand talking, a small figure on the platform, under a clear sky; he is lost in the crowd of pilgrims, peace has come to them, they touch and see it, and they shout: 'Peace!' Peace everlasting. He sits in the Luxembourg garden, on an iron chair, now he can look forever at the chestnut trees in bloom, the war has receded into the past, he stretches out his skinny legs, he watches the children at play; they, he thinks, will never know the horrors of war. The path of future years will be splendid, peaceful, time spreads out like a fan. He looks at his ageing hands now warmed by the sunshine, he smiles and thinks: 'It's thanks to us. No more war. Neither in my lifetime, nor in time to come.' 22 May 1938. Peace everlasting. Armand Viguier was dead, and no one could now declare him right, nor wrong. No one could change the indestructible future of his dead life. One day more, one single day, and all his hopes might well have collapsed; he would discover that his life had been crushed between two wars, between the hammer and the anvil. But he had died on 23 September 1938, at four o'clock in the morning, after seven days in a coma, and he had taken peace away with him. Peace, the whole peace, the peace of all the world, implacable, out of gear. There was a ring at the front-door bell: she started, that must be his sole relative, the cousin from Angers, who had been notified by telegram on the previous day. She opened the door to a little woman in black, with a rat-like profile, and dishevelled hair.

'I am Madame Verchoux.'

'Ah yes, we were expecting you, madame.'

'Can I see him?'

'Certainly. There he is.'

Madame Verchoux went up to the bed, looked at the hollow cheeks, and sunken eyes.

'He is greatly changed,' she said.

Half past eight at Juan-les-Pins, half past nine in Prague.

'Listeners, please stand by. An important announcement will follow immediately. Stand by. An important announcement . . .'

'All over,' said Milan.

He was standing in the window-recess. Anna did not reply. She bent down, and began picking up the broken glass, putting the largest pieces in her apron, and then threw it all out of the window. The lamp had been smashed, the room was plunged in bluish darkness.

'Now,' she said, 'I'll give the floor a thorough sweep.'

She repeated: 'A thorough sweep' – and began to tremble.

'They'll take everything we have,' she said, weeping: 'They'll break everything, and they'll throw us out.'

'Be quiet,' said Milan. 'For God's sake, don't cry.'

He went over to the wireless, turned the knobs, and the lights came on.

'It's all right,' he said in a tone of satisfaction.

The shrill, mechanical voice suddenly filled the room:

'Stand by, please. An important announcement will follow immediately. Stand by, please. A very important announcement . . .'

'Listen,' said Milan in an altered voice. 'Listen.'

Pierre was striding along, Maud ran beside him clutching her slippers under her arm. She was overjoyed.

'They're just lovely,' she said to him. 'Ruby will be mad with jealousy: she bought some in Fez which aren't half as nice. And they're so convenient. You slip them on as you jump out of bed, you don't even need to touch them, ordinary shoes are such a bother. You just have to get the knack of keeping them on, by arching the foot, I think: I'll ask the maid at the hotel. She's an Arab.'

Pierre still did not answer. She glanced at him uneasily and continued.

'You ought to have bought some too, you're always running about the room in bare feet; they're just as useful for men, you know.'

Pierre stopped right in the middle of the street.

'Shut up!' he bellowed.

Disconcerted, she also stopped.

'What's the matter?'

'They're just as useful for men,' said Pierre, mimicking her words. 'Look here, you know quite well what I was thinking about all the time. And you were thinking about it too,' he added grimly. He passed his tongue over his lips, and smiled ironically. Maud was about to speak, but she looked at him, frozen into silence.

'The trouble is that people won't look reality in the face,' he continued. 'Women especially; when they are thinking of one thing, they promptly talk about another. Isn't that so?'

'But, Pierre,' said Maud frantically. 'You're crazy. I don't understand. What do you suppose I'm thinking about? What are you thinking about?'

Pierre produced a book from his pocket, opened it, and held it to her nose:

'That,' he said.

It was a photograph of a shattered face, noseless, with a bandage over one eye.

'You . . . you bought that?' she asked in stupefaction.

'Well, yes,' said Pierre. 'What about it? I'm a man and I'm not afraid: I want to know what I shall look like next year.'

He shook the photograph in Maud's face.

'Will you love me when I look like that?'

She did not want to understand, she'd have given anything for him to keep quiet.

'Answer. Will you love me?'

'Don't!' she said. 'Please don't.'

'Those men,' said Pierre, 'live in an institution on the Val-de-Grace. They go out only at night, and always masked.'

She tried to take the book away from him, but he snatched it from her hands, and put it in his pocket. She looked at him with quivering lips, afraid of bursting into sobs.

'O Pierre,' she said gently. 'So you're afraid!'

Abruptly he fell silent, and eyed her dully. For a moment they stood motionless, then he said thickly:

'All men are afraid. All. A man who isn't afraid isn't normal: fear has nothing to do with courage. And you haven't the right to judge me, because you don't have to fight.'

They walked on in silence. And she thought to herself: 'He's a coward.' She looked at his high, tanned forehead, his Florentine nose and handsome mouth, and thought: 'He's a coward. Just as Lucien was. I have no luck.'

Odette's head and shoulders emerged into the light, the rest of her was still shadowed by the half-lit dining-room, she stood with her elbows on the balcony, looking at the sea; Gros-Louis thought: 'War be blowed!' He walked on and on, the red light of the setting sun flickering on his hands and beard. Odette felt, upon her back, the dusky, homely room, the white tablecloth glimmering in the darkness, but she stood in the light – light, knowledge, and war came in through her eyes, it would soon be time for him to go, the electric light congealed into egg-yellow patches against the fluid light of the fading day. Jeannine had turned the switch, Marcelle's hands were moving back and forward in the yellow lamp-light, she asked for the salt and her hands threw shadows on to the tablecloth, Daniel said: 'It's all bluff, if we hold on, he'll put his cards on the table.' The light that rasps one's eyes like sandpaper – it's like that in the south, up to the last minute. Twelve o'clock and then night falls, Pierre babbled on, he wanted to make her believe that he had recovered himself, but she walked beside him in silence, and the look in her eyes was as hard as the light. When they arrived in the square, she was afraid he might suggest she should spend the night with him, but he took off his hat and said coldly: 'As we must get up early tomorrow and you will have packing to do, you had better go back and sleep with your little friends.' She replied: 'Yes.' And he said: 'Till tomorrow, then.' 'Till tomorrow,' she said: 'tomorrow on the boat.'

Stand by, please, a very important announcement will follow; he was stretched out with his hands behind his neck, feeling miserable. 'We love our little doll,' he said. She shivered: 'Yes.' She was frightened, just as she was every evening. 'Yes, I do love you.' Sometimes she said yes, sometimes no, but tonight she didn't dare come out with a straight refusal. 'Well then, we'll give him his little petting, his little evening petting?' She sighed, visibly ashamed – it was funny. 'Not tonight,' she said. He breathed heavily: 'Poor little doll,' he said, 'he's so restless, it would be good for him. Don't you want to help him to sleep? No, you don't? You know it always calms me down.' She put on her matron's face, the look she wore when she put him on a bedpan, her head stiffened up on her shoulders. She didn't actually close her eyes but it seemed as though she wanted to see nothing, and underneath, her hands deftly unbuttoned him – skilful hands – and her face was so sad, it was very funny. Her hand slid in, soft as almond cream. Odette started and said: 'You frightened me. Is Jacques with you?' Charles sighed, Matthieu said 'no'. 'No,' said Maurice, 'it can't be helped.' He had taken the key from the rack, 'the place still stinks of dog, it's sickening.' 'It's Madame Salvador's puppy,' said Zézette, 'she throws him out when she's entertaining her men, and he amuses himself by piddling all over the place.'

They went upstairs: 'Stand by, please, an important announcement . . .' Milan and Anna leaned over the wireless, sounds of victory came through the windows, 'Turn it down a bit,' said Anna, 'you mustn't provoke them,' soft hand, soft as almond cream, Charles budded, flowered, opened up like a huge fruit, the pod about to burst, fruit shooting towards the heavens, juicy fruit – a springtime of stifling sweetness: silence, the clink of forks, on the wireless, a sound like material rent apart, the touch of the wind on downy fruit, hairy, Anna started and clutched Milan's arm.

Citizens!

The Czechoslovak Government has decided to proclaim a general mobilization: all men of less than forty years of age, and specialists of every kind, must come forward at once. All officers, non-commissioned officers of the Reserve, and the Second Reserve, of all ranks, and all men on leave, must report to their depots without delay. All must wear their oldest civilian clothes, and be provided with their military papers, and with food for two days. The final date for rejoining their respective units is four-thirty tomorrow morning.

All vehicles, automobiles, and aeroplanes are hereby mobilized. The sale of petrol is authorized only on permit issued by the military authorities.

Citizens! the decisive moment has arrived. Success depends on each and all of us. Let everyone put all his strength at the service of our country. Be brave and loyal. Our struggle is a struggle for justice and liberty.

Long live Czechoslovakia!

Milan stiffened, he was ablaze, he laid his hands on Anna's shoulders, and he said:

'At last! It's all right, Anna. It's all right.'

A woman's voice repeated the decree in Slovak, they understood nothing more except a few words now and again, but it sounded rather like a military band. Anna repeated: 'At last! At last!' Tears rolled down her cheeks. Then, they once more understood. '*Die Regierung hat enschlossen,*' it was in German, Milan turned the knob right round, and the radio began to roar, the voice crushed their loathsome songs and sounds of festival against the walls, the voice would issue from the windows, smash the Jägerschmitts' window-panes, the voice would penetrate into Munich drawing-rooms, into little family gatherings, and freeze their very bones. The smell of dog and of sour milk had been there awaiting him, he breathed it into his very being, and with the sweep of a broom it cleansed him of the upper-class perfumes of the rue Royale; this was the smell of penury, the smell that was his own. Maurice stood motionless outside his room, while Zézette slipped the key into the lock, and Odette said gaily: 'Come along to dinner, Jacques, there's a surprise for you'; he felt firm and strong, he had re-entered the world of anger and revolt; on the second floor the children were yelling because their father had come home drunk; in the next-door room could be heard the pattering footsteps of Maria Pranzini, whose husband, a tiler, had fallen from a roof last month, sounds and colours and smells, all had an air of *reality,* he had woken up, he had re-entered the world of war.

The old gentleman turned to Hitler, he looked at that evil, infantile face, the face of a human fly, and he was stricken to his very soul. Ribbentrop had appeared, he said a few words in German to Hitler, and made a sign to Dr Schmitt: 'We are informed,' said Dr Schmitt in English, 'that Monsieur Beneš' Government has just ordered a general mobilization.' Hitler flung out his arms without a word, like a man lamenting that the event has proved him right. The old gentleman smiled amiably, and a red gleam came into his eyes. A gleam of war. He had only to sulk like the Führer, he had only to fling out his arms with an air of – 'There you are!' and the pile of plates which he had been balancing for the last seventeen days would crash on to the floor. Dr Schmitt eyed him curiously; it must be tempting to drop a pile of plates after balancing them for seventeen days, and he thought: 'Here is the historic moment, the last appeal; the naked will of an elderly London businessman.' The Führer and the elderly gentleman looked at each other in silence, and an interpreter was no longer needed. Dr Schmitt stepped backwards.

He had sat down on a bench in the Place Gélu and put the banjo beside him. It was dark and blue beneath the plane trees, bands were playing, dusk had fallen, the straight, black masts of the fishing-boats seemed to rise out of this earth, and on the far side of the harbour countless windows flashed. A boy was spurting water from the fountain; on the next bench some other Negroes sat down and hailed him. He was not hungry, he was not thirsty, he had bathed behind the pier, he had met a large hairy fellow who seemed to have fallen from the moon, and who had stood him a drink; he had enjoyed all that. He took the banjo out of its case, he felt like singing. For one moment, one single moment, he coughs, he clears his throat, he is going to sing, Chamberlain, Hitler and Schmitt awaited war in silence, and in a moment war would enter, his foot had swollen but in a moment he would wrench it out of the shoe, Maurice, seated on the bed, was tugging at his foot, in a moment Jacques would have finished drinking his soup, Odette would no longer hear that irritating little crackle of fireworks, the sizzle of rockets before they went off, in a moment suns would swirl upwards to the ceiling, her little doll, in a moment, a warm, copious discharge, smelling of absinthe, would flood his paralysed thighs, and the voice would rise, richly sentimental, through the foliage of the plane trees: in that one moment, Mathieu ate, Marcelle ate, Daniel ate, Boris ate, Brunet ate, their instantaneous souls were brimming with clammy little joys, in that one moment – war – war that Pierre dreaded, Boris accepted, and Daniel welcomed, would enter clad in steel, the great stand-up war, the white men's crazy war. In that one moment: it had exploded in Milan's room, it was pouring out of all the windows, it surged into the Jäger-schmitts' abode, it prowled round the ramparts of Marrakesh, it breathed upon the sea, it crushed the buildings in the rue Royale, it filled Maurice's nostrils with the smell of dog and sour milk; in the fields and cow-sheds and farmyards it *did not exist*; but it played heads or tails between two pier-glasses in the wainscoted salons of the Hotel Dreesen. The old gentle-man passed his hand over his forehead and said in a toneless voice: 'Well then, if you agree, we will discuss the clauses of your memorandum.' And Dr Schmitt understood that inter-preters were once more needed.

Hitler approached the table, and the clear, resonant voice rose into the translucent air: on the fifth floor of the Massilia hotel a woman on her balcony heard it, and she said: 'Gomez, come and listen to the Negro singing, it's charming.' Milan thought of his leg, and his joy collapsed, he squeezed Anna's shoulder: 'They won't want me, I am no good for anything now.' The Negro sang on. Armand Viguier was dead, his two pale hands lay outstretched on the sheets, the two women sat beside his bed, discussing events, they had taken to each other at once. Jeannine wiped her hands on a turkish towel, then she began to dry his thighs. Chamberlain said: 'As regards the first clause, I have two objections,' and the Negro sang: *'Bei mir, bist du schön'*, which means: 'For me you are the loveliest of all'.

Two women stopped, he knew them, Anina and Dolorès, two tarts from the rue du Lacydon. Anina said: *'Té!* How nicely you sing!' but he did not answer, he sang on, and the women smiled at him, Sarah called out impatiently. 'Gomez, Pablo, come here, what are you up to? There's a Negro singing so beautifully.'

Saturday, 24 September

IN Crevilly, on the stroke of six o'clock, Daddy Croulard entered the gendarmerie and knocked on the office door. And he thought to himself: 'They've woken me up.' He would say to them: 'Why have I been woken up?' Hitler was asleep, Chamberlain was asleep, snoring shrilly through his nose, Daniel was sitting on his bed streaming with sweat, and he thought: 'It was just a nightmare!'

'Come in,' said the gendarmerie lieutenant. 'Ah, it's you, Daddy Croulard? Well, you'll have to be getting busy.'

Ivich moaned faintly and turned on her side.

'The lad woke me up,' said Daddy Croulard. He eyed the lieutenant venomously and said: 'It must be pretty important. . . .'

'Ah, Daddy Croulard,' said the lieutenant. 'You must grease your boots.'

Daddy Croulard didn't like the lieutenant: and he said: 'What's all this about boots? I haven't got any boots. I've only got clogs.'

'You'll have to grease your boots,' repeated the lieutenant. 'There's a job to be done.'

Without his moustache he would have looked like a girl. He wore pince-nez, and his cheeks were as pink as those of the schoolmistress. He was leaning forward with his arms apart, the tips of his fingers resting on the table. Daddy Croulard looked at him, and thought: 'This is the man that had me woken up.'

'Did he tell you to bring the paste pot?' said the lieutenant.

Daddy Croulard was holding the pot of paste behind his back: he silently displayed it.

'And the brushes?' said the lieutenant. 'You must hurry. You haven't got time to go home.'

'The brushes are in my jacket,' said Daddy Croulard gravely. 'I was woken up all of a sudden, but I shouldn't have forgotten the brushes.'

The lieutenant handed him a roll of paper. 'You will put one on the front of the *Mairie,* two on the main square, and one on the notary's house.'

'Maître Belhomme's? Sticking posters isn't allowed on his house.'

'I don't give a damn,' said the lieutenant. He looked alert, but rather nervous as he added. 'I'll take the responsibility for that, and for everything else.'

'I suppose it's mobilization at last.'

'I should say so,' said the lieutenant. 'There's going to be a scrap, Daddy Croulard, there's going to be a scrap.'

'Is there?' said Daddy Croulard. 'Well, I fancy you and I will stay at home.'

There was a knock at the door, and the lieutenant opened it smartly. It was the mayor. He was in clogs, with his scarf across his jacket. He said: 'What's this the lad told me?'

'Here are the notices,' said the lieutenant.

The mayor put on his spectacles, and unrolled the notices. He read in an undertone: 'General Mobilization,' and slammed the notices on to the table as though afraid of scorching his fingers. And he said: 'I was in the fields – I went home to get my scarf.'

Daddy Croulard reached out a hand, rolled up the notices, and put the roll under his jacket. He said to the mayor: 'I wondered why they woke me up so early.'

'I went home to get my scarf,' said the mayor. He looked at the lieutenant uneasily, and said: 'It says nothing about requisitions.'

'There's another notice about that,' said the lieutenant.

'God rot it,' said the mayor. 'So that's going to start again.'

'I've been through one war,' said Daddy Croulard. 'Fifty-two months and not a scratch.' He crinkled his eyes in glee at the recollection.

'That's all right,' said the mayor. 'You did the other one, you won't do this one. Besides, you don't need to worry about requisitions.'

The lieutenant tapped authoritatively on the table. 'Well, get on with it.'

The mayor looked bewildered. He had slipped his hands into his scarf and tried to look important: 'The drummer is ill,' he explained.

'I can play the drum,' said Daddy Croulard. He smiled. For ten years it had been his ambition to play the drum.

'Drum?' said the lieutenant. 'You'll have the tocsin rung – that's what you'll do.'

Chamberlain was asleep, Mathieu was asleep, the Kabyle put the ladder against the charabanc, hoisted the trunk on to his shoulder, and scrambled up it without holding on to the rungs. Ivich was asleep, Daniel swung his legs out of bed, a bell echoed in his head, Pierre looked at the pink and black soles of the Kabyle's feet, and thought: 'It's Maud's trunk.' But Maud wasn't there, she was to leave a little later with Doucette, France, and Ruby in the car of a rich elderly gentleman in love with Ruby: in Paris, Nantes and Mâcon men were pasting white notices on to walls, the tocsin was ringing in Crévilly, Hitler was asleep, Hitler was a little four-year-old child, wearing his best suit, a black dog passed, he tried to catch it in his butterfly-net: the tocsin rang, Madame Reboulier awoke with a start and said:

'There's something burning.'

Hitler was asleep, he was slitting his father's trousers into narrow strips with a pair of nail scissors. Leni von Riefenstahl came in, picked up the strips of flannel, and said: 'I'll make you eat them in a salad.'

The tocsin rang and rang and rang. Maublanc said to his wife: 'I bet the sawmill's caught fire.'

He went out into the street. Madame Reboulier, in a pink nightdress, peered through the shutters, saw him pass, and hail the postman who was running down the street. Maublanc shouted: 'Hi! Anselm!'

'It's mobilization,' shouted the postman.

'What? What did he say?' said Madame Reboulier to her husband, who had now rejoined her. 'It's not a fire, then?'

Maublanc looked at the two notices and read them in an undertone, then turned and went back home. His wife was on the doorstep, and he said to her: 'Tell Paul to harness the cart.' He heard a noise and turned round; it was Chapin, on his cart; he said to him: 'Hullo! Where are you off to?' Chapin looked at him without answering. Maublanc looked at the back of the cart: there were two oxen lumbering behind it, haltered to the back. 'Bloody fine beasts!' he said in an undertone. 'You can say that again,' said Chapin wrathfully: 'bloody fine beasts they are.' The tocsin rang, Hitler slept, old Fraigneau said to his son: 'If they take the two horses and you, how am I to carry on?' Nanette knocked at the door and Madame Reboulier said to her: 'Is that you, Nanette? Go to the Square and see why they're ringing the tocsin.' And Nanette answered: 'But doesn't Madame know? It's general mobilization.'

Just another morning. And Mathieu thought: 'Just another morning.' Pierre had elbowed his way to the window, and was looking out at the Arabs sitting on the ground or on multicoloured trunks, waiting for the Ouarzazat coach; Mathieu had opened his eyes, which felt limp and clammy in their sockets, the eyes of a newborn baby, still sightless, and he thought: 'What's the good of it all?' as he did every morning. A morning of terror, an arrow of fire aimed at Casablanca, at Marseilles, the coach vibrated, the engine began to tick over, the driver on the outside seat, a tall fellow wearing a beige cloth cap with a leather peak, calmly finished his cigarette. He was thinking: 'Maud despises me.' A morning like all other mornings, stagnant and blank, a pompous, daily ceremony with brass bands and bugles and a public sunrise. In other days there had been other mornings: something had begun: Mathieu got up with a start, his eyes steady and his mind alert, as though awakened by a trumpet-call. There was nothing to look forward to any more, nothing whatsoever to undertake. And yet he would have to get up, join in the ceremony, find his way through the enveloping heat, and perform all the gestures of the cult, like a priest who has lost his faith. He slid his legs out of bed, stood up, and took off his pyjamas. 'What's the good of it all?' Then he lay back on the bed, naked, his hands beneath his head, peering through the white haze at the ceiling. I'm a wash-out. An utter wash-out. Once I used to carry the days upon my back from one river-bank to the other: now they carry me. The coach throbbed and clattered under his feet, the floor grew hot, he felt as though the soles of his shoes were cracking. Pierre's great cowardly heart throbbed and hammered against the warm cushions, the window was scorching to the touch, and yet he felt frozen, and he thought: 'This is the beginning.' The end would be a hole near Sedan or Verdun, and this was the beginning. She had said to him: 'So you are a coward,' and eyed him with contempt. Once again he saw the grave, flushed face, the dark eyes, and thin lips, his heart turned over, and the coach shot forward. It was still very chilly: Louisa Corneille, the sister of the level-crossing guard, who had come from Lisieux to help her sick sister keep house, went out to lift the barriers, and said: 'It's pretty nippy.' She was feeling glad because she was engaged. She had been engaged for two years, but every time she thought of it, she felt glad. She began to turn the lever, then suddenly stopped. She was sure there was someone on the road behind her. She had not looked as she came out, but she was sure. She turned, and caught her breath: there were more than a hundred barrows, carts, ox-wagons, and ancient carriages, waiting, motionless, in single file. The farm-lads were sitting stiffly on their benches, whip in hand and grimly silent. Others were on horseback, others had come on foot, dragging a cow behind them at the end of a rope. It was so comical a sight that she took fright. She hurriedly turned the crank, and stepped briskly back to the side of the road. The drivers whipped up their horses, and the vehicles filed past her, the coach rolled through a land of long, red steppes, a swarm of Arabs huddled at their backs. Pierre said: 'Bloody wogs! I never feel comfortable when I feel them behind me, I keep on wondering what they're up to.' Pierre flung a glance into the back of the coach; there they lay in silence, their faces mottled green and grey, their eyes closed. A veiled woman had collapsed on to her back, between the bags and bundles, her closed eyelids were visible beneath her veil. 'How tiresome,' he thought. 'They'll start to be sick in five minutes, these fellows have got no stomachs.' Louisa recognized them as they passed, they were lads of Crévilly, all lads of Crévilly, she could have put a name to each of them, but they did not look as usual – that fat red-faced fellow was young Chapin, she had danced with him at the Saint-Martin, and she cried: 'Hi! Marcel, you're a very stuck-up lad today!' He turned, and eyed her savagely. And she added, 'Off to the wedding, eh?' He said, 'By God, you're right. Off to the wedding!' The cart jolted across the rails, followed by two sleek oxen. Other carts passed: she watched them, shading her eyes with her hand. She recognized Maublanc, Tournus, Cauchios, they ignored her and passed on, erect in their seats, carrying their whips like sceptres, looking like angry monarchs. Her heart contracted, and she shouted to them: 'Is it war?' But no one answered. They passed in their jolting, rocking rattle-traps, the oxen following with comic dignity; the vehicles disappeared one after the other round the bend in the road, she stood for a moment with her hand arched over her eyes, looking into the rising sun, the coach sped like the wind, roaring round the corners, she thought of Jean Matrat, her fiancé, who was doing his service at Angoulême in a Pioneer regiment, the carts reappeared like flies on the white road, sticking to the side of the hill, the coach plunged into a brown, rocky gully, turned, and turned again, and at every corner the Arabs tumbled over each other and squealed pathetically. The veiled woman suddenly sat up, and her mouth, invisible under the white muslin, emitted the most appalling curses: she brandished two thigh-like arms and two delicate plump hands with painted nails flickering at the tips of them: finally she tore off her veil, leaned over the door, and began to vomit, groaning as she did so. 'That's the last straw,' said Pierre to himself: 'They'll all be sick over us.' The carts seemed motionless, looking as if they were glued to the road. Louisa eyed them for a while: they were moving, they were moving all the same, one by one they reached the summit of the hill, and then disappeared from sight. Louisa dropped her hand, her dazzled eyes blinked, and she went in to the children. Pierre thought of Maud, Mathieu thought of Odette, he had dreamed of her, they were standing with their arms round each other singing the Barcarolle from *The Tales of Hoffmann* on the balcony of the Provençal. At the moment he was lying naked on his bed, sweating as he looked up at the ceiling, and Odette kept him company. 'If I am not dead of boredom, I owe it to her.' A white haze quivered in his eyes, a faint affection still quivered in his heart. A blank affection, the sad little affection that comes with the wakening hour, a pretext to remain lying on one's back for a few moments more. In five minutes cold water would flow on to his neck and into his eyes, frothing soap would crackle in his ears, tooth-paste would smear his gums, he would feel no more affection for anyone. Colours, lights, smells, sounds. And then words, polite words, serious words, sincere words, funny words – words all day until evening. Mathieu – pah! Mathieu was merely a future. There's no future now. There's no Mathieu now except in dreams, between midnight and five o'clock in the morning. Chapin thought: 'Two grand beasts.' Who cared about the bloody war, anyway? But those beasts, he had looked after them for five years, he had gelded them himself, it would break his heart to lose them. He lashed at his horse, and pulled him towards the left; his cart slowly overtook Simeon's. 'What are you up to?' asked Simeon. 'I'm sick of all this,' said Chapin: 'I want to get there.'

'You'll tire your oxen out,' said Simeon. 'Don't care if I do,' said Chapin. He wanted to get past them all: he stood up, clicked his tongue, and shouted: '*Hue! Hue!*' He slipped past Popaul's cart, past Poulaille's wagon. 'Are you racing us?' asked Poulaille. Chapin did not reply, and Poulaille shouted after him:

'Mind you don't founder your oxen!' Chapin thought: 'I wish they'd drop dead.' There came a sound of blows: Chapin was now ahead, pursued by the others, all whipping up their horses: a sound of blows, Mathieu had got up, he was rubbing his eyes: *the sound of blows*; the coach swerved to avoid an Arab on a bicycle carrying a large veiled Mussulman woman on the handlebars. THE SOUND OF BLOWS, knocks on a door, Chamberlain started up, and said: 'Hullo! Who is it? Who's knocking?' and a voice replied: 'It's seven o'clock, your Excellency.' At the entrance to the barracks there was a wooden barrier.

A sentry stood on guard in front of it. Chapin tugged at the reins and shouted: 'Hi! you there!' 'Well?' said the sentry: 'Well? And where do you come from, eh?' 'Just lift that up,' said Chapin, pointing to the barrier. 'I've no orders,' said the soldier. 'Where do you come from?' 'Lift that up, I tell you.' A sergeant emerged from the guard-post. All the carts had halted: he contemplated them for a moment, then he whistled: 'What the hell are you doing here?' he asked. 'We're mobilized, of course,' said Chapin. 'Are you going to tell us to go away?'

'Have you got your papers?' asked the sergeant. Chapin fumbled in his pockets, the sergeant eyed all those silent, grim young fellows, motionless on their seats, holding their whips as though they were presenting arms, and felt proud without quite knowing why. He took a step forward and shouted: 'What about the others – have they got their papers too? Let me see your army book?' Chapin had found his army book. The sergeant took it, and turned over the pages: 'Well,' he said. 'You've got Form 3, you bloody fool. You were in too much of a hurry, wait till next time.'

'I tell you I'm mobilized,' said Chapin.

'You know better than I do, I suppose,' said the sergeant.

'Yes,' said Chapin angrily. 'I read the notices.'

Behind them the others were getting restive, Poulaille shouted: 'Look here, have you finished? We want to go in.'

'The notices?' said the sergeant. 'Look, here's your notice. You've only got to look at it if you can read.' Chapin laid down his whip, jumped to the ground and walked up to the wall. There were three notices. Two in colours: 'Join or Rejoin the Colonial Army'; and a third which was entirely white: 'Immediate call-up of Certain Categories of Reservists.' He read slowly, in an undertone, and said, wagging his head: 'That isn't the one that was put up in our village.' Maublanc, Poulaille, Fraigneau had got off their carts, they looked at the notice, and they said: 'That isn't our notice.'

'Where do you come from?' asked the sergeant.

'From Crévilly,' said Poulaille.

'Well,' said the sergeant, 'I've got an idea that there's a prize fathead at the Crévilly gendarmerie. Anyhow, give me your army books, and come along to the officer.'

On the main square in Crévilly, in front of the church, a throng of women clustered round Madame Reboulier, who was such a friend to the place – Marie, and Stephanie the tobacconist's wife, and Jeanne Fraigneau. Marie was crying quietly, Madame Reboulier had donned her large black hat, and said as she brandished her umbrella: 'You mustn't cry, Marie, you must bear up bravely. Your husband will come back to you, you'll see, with all sorts of honours and medals. And I dare say he won't be one of the worst off either. Because this time everybody will be mobilized, women as well as men.'

She pointed her umbrella towards the east, and felt ten years younger. 'You'll see,' she said. 'You'll see. I dare say the civilians will win this war.' But Marie had assumed her stolid look, her sobs shook her shoulders, she peered through her tears at the monument to the fallen in the last war, and refused to answer.

'Very good, sir,' said the lieutenant. He pressed the receiver to his ear and said: 'Very good, sir.' And the quiet, angry voice flowed on without pause: 'You say they've started? Well, my poor friend, you've put your foot in it. I'll tell you straight out that this may mean dismissal.'

Daddy Croulard crossed the square with his pot of paste and his brushes, and a roll of white paper under his arm. Marie shouted: 'What's up?' and Madame Reboulier was annoyed to notice a gleam of hope in her foolish eyes. Daddy Croulard laughed good-humouredly, waved the roll of white paper, and said: 'It's nothing. The lieutenant gave out the wrong notices!' The lieutenant hung up the receiver and sat down, his legs felt very limp. The voice still rang in his ears: 'This may mean dismissal.' He got up and walked to the window: on the opposite wall, quite fresh, still damp, and white as snow, shone the placard: 'General Mobilization.' Anger took him by the throat: he thought to himself: 'I told him to take that one off first, he'll carefully leave it till the last.' He swung himself out of the window, ran to the notice, and began to tear it to shreds. Daddy Croulard dipped his brush into the paste-pot, Madame Reboulier watched him sorrowfully, the lieutenant scratched at the wall until his nails were edged with little blobs of paste: Blomart and Cormier had remained in the barracks: the others had returned to their horses and were eyeing each other dubiously: they wanted to laugh and lose their tempers, they felt as flat as on the morrow of a fair. Chapin went up to the oxen and stroked them. Their muzzles and chests were covered with foam, and he thought gloomily: 'If I had known, I wouldn't have gone so fast.'

'What are we going to do now?' asked Poulaille, behind his back.

'We can't go back at once,' said Chapin. 'We must rest the animals.'

Fraigneau looked at the barracks; and that brought back memories, he nudged Chapin and said slyly: 'What about dropping in you know where, eh?'

'Where do you mean, my lad?' asked Chapin.

'Why,' said Fraigneau, 'the knocking-shop, of course!'

The lads of Crévilly gathered round him, clapped him on the shoulders, and said: 'Good old Fraigneau! He always has the right idea.' Chapin brightened up, and said: 'I know where it is, boys: get back on to your carts, I'll lead the way.'

Eight-thirty in the morning. A skier was already circling round the diving-board, towed by a motor boat: now and again Mathieu caught the purr of the motor and then the boat shot off, the skier dwindled to a black spot, and nothing more was heard. The sea, flat and hard and white, looked like a deserted skating-rink. Very soon it would turn blue and sparkle, it would become liquid and deep, the every day sea, echoing with shouts and dotted with little black heads. Mathieu crossed the terrace, and strolled along the promenade. The cafés were still shut, two cars passed by. He had gone out with no definite purpose: to buy a paper, to breathe the thick smell of seaweed and eucalyptus that hung about the harbour, and also to kill time. Odette was still asleep, Jacques always worked until ten o'clock. He turned into a street of shops that led towards the station, two young English girls passed him laughing: four people were gathered round a placard. Mathieu joined them, just to get rid of a moment or two. A small man with a pointed beard eyed it and wagged his head. Mathieu read:

'By order of the Minister of National Defence and of War, and of the Minister for Air. All officers, non-commissioned officers, and men of the Reserve, in possession of a white

mobilization order or form, numbered " 2 ", will start immediately, without waiting for an individual notification.

'They will report at the depot designated on their mobilization order or form, under the conditions specified on that
document.

'Saturday, 24 September 1938, nine o'clock.

'The Minister of National Defence, of War, and of the Air.'

'Tut-tut,' said the little man, with an air of disapproval.
Mathieu smiled at him, and re-read the notice carefully: it was
one of those tiresome but instructive documents which had,
for some time past, filled the newspapers under the heading:
'Foreign Office Announcement', or 'Statement by the Quai
d'Orsay'. They always had to be read twice to be fully understood. 'They will report at the depot designated . . .' and
Mathieu thought: 'But I am in possession of Form 2.' Suddenly the placard seemed aimed at him personally; as though
his name had been chalked upon the wall, accompanied by
insults and threats. Mobilized. There it was, inscribed on the
wall, and perhaps it was already legible upon his face. He
flushed and hurried off. 'Form 2. That's it. I'm about to
become interesting.' Odette would look at him with suppressed emotion. Jacques would assume his Sunday expression, and say: 'There's nothing I can say to you, old boy.' But
Mathieu felt modest, and didn't want to become an object of
interest. He turned to the left, down to the first side-street, and
quickened his step: on the right-hand pavement stood a
gloomy little group staring at a poster, and muttering to
each other. This was happening all over France. Two by two:
four by four: people stood and stared at placards. And in each
group there would be at least one man conscious of his note-
case and his army book through the stuff of his jacket, aware
that he was now an object of interest. Rue de la Poste. Two
posters; two groups: and still talking about him. He plunged
into a long dark alley, which he felt sure had been passed over
by the bill-posters. He was alone, he could think about himself.
And he thought: 'It has come.' It had certainly come: that full
and rounded day, that should have died of old age, decently
and in peace, was now suddenly prolonged: arrowlike, it
hissed into the night, sped into the darkness and the smoke,
into the deserted countryside, across a turmoil of axles and

engines; and he slid into it all, like a man on a toboggan, which would only stop at the far end of the night, at Paris, on the platform of the Gare de Lyon. Lights began to glimmer in the daylight: the lights-to-be of darkened stations. His eye-sockets had begun to throb with the dry pain of insomnias to come. He was not upset by this, nor anything else; nor amused any longer: it was, in any case, an interesting and rather picturesque turn in his life. 'I must ask about the time of the train to Marseilles,' he thought. The alley, though he had not realized it, led back to the Corniche. He suddenly emerged into a blaze of light, and sat down outside a café that had just opened. 'A cup of coffee, and the railway time-table.' A gentleman with a silvery moustache came and sat down near him, accompanied by a middle-aged lady. The gentleman opened the *Éclaireur de Nice,* the lady turned towards the sea. Mathieu eyed her for a moment and felt depressed. He thought: 'I must put my affairs in order: settle Ivich in my flat, and give her a power of attorney so that she can draw my salary.' The gentleman's head reappeared above his newspaper: 'It's war,' he said. The lady sighed, but did not reply: Mathieu looked at the gentleman's shining, polished cheeks, his tweed jacket, his violet-striped shirt, and he thought: 'It's war.'

It's war. Something that now held him by one sole thread, dropped away from him, and was left behind. It was his life: and it was dead. Dead. He turned and looked at it. Viguier was dead, his hands lay outstretched on the white sheet, there was a live fly on his forehead, and his future extended as far as eye could reach, infinite, unalterable, as fixed as the fixed gaze beneath those dead eyelids. His future: peace, the future of the world, and Mathieu's future. Mathieu's future lay there defencelessly exposed – settled, crystallized, beyond change. Mathieu was sitting at a café table, he was drinking, he was ahead of his future, he eyed it, and he thought: 'Peace.' Madame Verchoux, standing beside the nurse, pointed to Viguier – she had a stiff neck and her eyes were smarting – and said: 'He was a fine man.' She searched for a word, a rather more ceremonious word, with which to describe him: she was his nearest relative, and it was for her to produce the final word. The word 'kindly' came upon her tongue, but it was not sufficiently conclusive. She said: 'He was a man of peace,' and then was silent. Mathieu thought: 'I have had a peaceful future.' Indeed he had: he had loved and hated and suffered, and the future was here and everywhere, overhead and all around him, like an ocean, and every burst of anger, every disaster, every laugh, drew sustenance from that invisible and insistent future. A smile, a mere smile, was a mortgage on tomorrow's peace – on next year's, next century's peace: otherwise I should never have dared to smile. Years and years of peace to come had gathered upon his world of objects, matured them and set them aglow: a man taking out his watch, lifting the latch of a door, grasping a woman's hand, was taking hold of peace. The post-war epoch was a beginning. The beginning of peace. It passed unhurried, as a morning passes. Jazz was a beginning, and the cinema, which I so much enjoy, was also a beginning. Surrealism, too; and Communism. I hesitated, I chose with care. I had time enough. Time, peace – they were the same. And now that future lies at my feet, dead. It was a spurious future, an imposture. He searched those twenty years, like an expanse of sunlit sea, and he now saw them as they had been: a finite number of days compressed between two high, hopeless walls, a period duly catalogued, with a prelude and an end, which would figure in the history manuals under the heading: Between the two Wars. Twenty years: 1918–38. Only twenty years! Yesterday it had seemed both a shorter and a longer period: and indeed no one would have thought to estimate it, since it had not ended. Now it has ended. A spurious future. All the experiences of the last twenty years have been spurious. We were energetic and serious, we tried to understand, and here is the result: those lovely days led to a dark and secret future, they deceived us; today's war, the new Great War, stole them surreptitiously away. Without knowing it we were cuckolds. And now the war is there, my life is dead: *that* was my life: everything must be started afresh. He groped for some random recollection, no matter what – the evening at Perugia, sitting on the terrace, eating an apricot ice, and looking at the calm hills of Assisi far off in the dust. Well, he ought to have seen war in that reddening sunset. If I had discovered, in those red gleams that gilded the table and the balustrade, omens of storm and blood, they would have been with me now, so much would at least have been preserved. But I had no doubts, the ice melted on my tongue, and I merely thought of antique gold, and love, and mystic glory. Now I have lost everything. The waiter made his way between the tables, Mathieu hailed him, paid, and got up, hardly conscious of himself. He was leaving his life behind: I have cast my skin. He crossed the road and stood with his elbows on the balustrade, looking out to sea.

Fateful he felt, and strangely light: naked, robbed of all that he possessed. There is nothing more belonging to me, not even my past. It was a truly spurious past, and I don't regret it. And he thought: 'They have rid me of my life. It was a sorry, ineffectual life, Marcelle, Ivich, Daniel – a squalid life, though that doesn't matter now, since it is dead. As from this morning, since they began to plaster those white notices on to the walls, all lives are ineffectual, all lives are dead. If I had done what I wanted, if I had once, only once, succeeded in being free – well, that would in my case have been an ugly deception, since I should merely have exercised my freedom in this false peace; I should still have been here looking out to sea, with my elbows on the balustrade, and all those placards at my back: those placards on all the walls of France, announcing that my life is dead, and that there never was a peace: there was no sense in all that effort, in those feelings of remorse. The sea, the beach, the tents, the balustrade: all cold and bloodless. They had lost their original future, and not yet acquired a new one: they were adrift in the present. Mathieu was adrift. A survivor, naked on a bench, among heaps of sea-sodden clothes, among shattered crates, and unidentifiable objects cast up by the sea. A sun-burnt youth emerged from a tent, looking calm and blank, as he gazed hesitantly at the sea: a survivor – we are all survivors, the German officers smiled and saluted, the engine revved, the propeller revolved, Chamberlain saluted, turned, and set one foot on the steps.

The Babylonian exile, the curse on Israel, and the wailing wall, the destinies of the Jewish nation had not altered since the time when her sons walked in chains between the red towers of Assyria, under the cruel eyes of their curled and bearded conquerors; Schalom lived his little life among such men, dark-haired, tight-lipped, and cruel. Nothing had altered, Schalom thought of Georges Levy. He thought to himself: 'We have lost our sense of solidarity, and that is the true curse of God!' and he felt rather pathetic, but not ill pleased, having seen those white placards on the walls. He had asked help from Georges Levy, but Georges Levy was a hard man, an Alsatian Jew; and he had refused. He had not exactly refused, he had groaned and wrung his hands, he had talked about his old mother, and the slump. But everybody knew that he detested his old mother, and that there was no slump in the fur trade. Schalom himself had burst into lamentations, he had waved his arms, and talked about the new Exodus, and the poor refugee Jews who had suffered for the rest and in their flesh. Levy was a hard man, a rich man of the rich and nasty type, he propelled Schalom towards the door with his great paunch, puffing in his face. Schalom groaned as he stepped backwards, brandishing his arms, smiling involuntarily as he thought of how the clerks in the next room must be relishing the scene. At the corner of the rue du Quatre-Septembre was a flashy and well-to-do looking pork butcher's: Schalom stopped, quite dazzled: he looked at the jellied chitterlings, the raised pies, the strings of sausages like varnished leather, the stocky, wrinkled *cervelas*, and he thought of the provision-merchants of Vienna. So far as was humanly possible he avoided eating pork, but poor refugees are obliged to feed on whatever comes to hand. When he emerged from the shop, he carried, dangling from his finger by a pink string, a small parcel, so white and delicate that it looked like a parcel of cakes: and he was shocked. And he thought: 'The French are so nastily rich.' The richest nation in Europe. Schalom turned into the rue du Quatre-Septembre, calling down the curse of heaven on such people, and, as though heaven had heard his prayer, he saw out of the corner of his eye a group of French people standing motionless and mute before a white placard. He passed quite close to them, with eyes downcast and lips set, because it was not then expedient that a poor Jew should be caught smiling in the streets of Paris. Birnenschatz, Diamond Merchant; this was the place. He hesitated for a moment, then, before entering the archway, he slipped his parcel of sausage into his portfolio. The engines turned and rumbled, the floorboards quivered, there was a smell of ether and petrol, the coach plunged into the flames,

77

Oh, Pierre, so you're a coward, the aeroplane hovered in the sunlight, Daniel tapped the placard with the ferrule of his stick, and said: 'I'm not worrying; we're not such fools as to go to war without aeroplanes.' The aeroplane flew over the trees, just above them, Dr Schmitt looked up, the engine rumbled, he could see the aeroplane between the leaves, a flash of mica in the sky – *'Bon voyage! Bon voyage!'* he said to himself, and smiled; the wretched Arabs uncomplaining, ghastly pale, lay in a huddle at the back of the coach, a Negro boy came out of the hut, waved his hand, looked long at the departing coach, you saw the little Yid, he bought a pound of saveloy – and I thought they didn't eat pork! The Negro boy, and the interpreter, walked slowly back, their heads still humming with the roar of the engines. It was a round iron table painted green, with a hole in the centre for the shaft of the parasol, and covered with brown patches like a pear; a newspaper, the *Petit Niçois,* was on the table, still unfolded. Mathieu coughed, she was sitting near the table, she had had her early breakfast in the garden; how am I going to tell her? There must be no fuss, above all no fuss, if only she could keep silent – no, silence even would be too emphatic – if she could get up and say: 'Well, I'll make you some sandwiches for the journey.' Something like that. She was wearing a dressing-gown and looking through her letters. 'Jacques isn't down yet,' she said, 'he was working late last night.' Her first words, every time they met again, were always about Jacques, after which he was no longer mentioned. Mathieu smiled and laughed. 'Sit down,' she said: 'there are two letters for you.' He took the letters, and asked: 'Have you read the paper?'

'Not yet. Mariette brought it with the letters, and I haven't had the heart to open it yet. I was never much of a one for reading newspapers, and at the moment I just can't bear them.'

Mathieu smiled, and nodded agreement, but his teeth were still set. All was as before between them. Just a placard on a wall, and all was as before: she was Jacques's wife, and he could find nothing to say to her. 'Raw ham,' he thought: 'that's what I should like for the journey.'

'Do read your letters,' said Odette briskly. 'Don't bother about me: besides, I must go up and dress.'

Mathieu picked up the first letter, which bore the Biarritz

postmark – it was, after all, a moment gained. When she had got up he would say to her, 'By the way, I'm leaving here. . . .' No, that would sound too casual. 'I'm leaving here.' That would be better. 'I'm leaving here . . .' He recognized Boris's handwriting, and thought to himself remorsefully: 'It's more than a month since I wrote to him.'

The envelope contained a letter-card. Boris had written his own address and put a stamp on the left half of the card. On the right half he had written as follows:

My dear Boris,

I am $\left\{ \begin{array}{l} \text{well} \\ \text{not well}^1. \end{array} \right\}$

The reason for my silence is: pardonable or unpardonable; annoyance; illwill; sudden conversion; lunacy; illness; laziness; mere perversity[1].

I will write you a long letter in . . . . days.

Please accept my profound excuses and the expression of my repentant regard.

Signature:
[1] Cross out inapplicable alternatives

'What are you laughing at?' asked Odette.

'It's from Boris,' said Mathieu. 'He's at Biarritz with Lola.' He handed her the letter and she began to laugh too.

'He's charming,' she said. 'Is he . . . Is he of age to . . .?'

'Nineteen,' said Mathieu. 'It will depend on how long the war lasts.'

Odette looked at him affectionately. 'Your pupils do pull your leg, don't they?' she said.

It became more and more difficult to talk to her. Mathieu opened the other letter. It was from Gomez, Sarah's husband. Mathieu had not seen her again since Gomez left for Spain. At present he was a colonel in the Spanish Republican army.

My dear Mathieu,

I am at Marseilles on a service mission, where Sarah has joined me with the boy. I am leaving again on Tuesday, but I must see you first. Expect me by the four o'clock train on Sunday, and book me a room anywhere. I shall manage a brief visit to Juan-les-Pins. We have much to talk about.

Yours,
Gomez

Mathieu put the letter in his pocket, he reflected with some annoyance: 'Saturday is tomorrow – I shall be gone.' He wanted to see Gomez again; at that moment, Gomez was the only friend he did want to see. He must know something of what war meant. 'I might perhaps catch him at Marseilles, between two trains. . . .' He took the crumpled letter out of his pocket: Gomez had not given his address. Mathieu shrugged his shoulders irritably, and threw the letter on to the table: Gomez had remained quite unchanged, Colonel as he now was: brusque, but rather ineffectual. Odette had made up her mind to unfold the paper, and was holding it, with her shapely arms outspread, and reading it intently.

'Oh!' she exclaimed.

She turned to Mathieu, and said to him lightly: 'Are you a Form 2 man?'

Mathieu blushed, and blinked.

'Yes,' he said confusedly.

Odette looked at him severely, as though he were at fault. And he hurriedly added: 'But I'm not leaving today, I shall be staying for another forty-eight hours: I have a friend coming to see me.'

He felt relieved by this abrupt decision: it would postpone any display of emotion for nearly two days: 'It's a good long way from Juan-les-Pins to Nancy, they won't make a fuss over a few hours' delay.' But Odette's look did not relax, he repeated with embarrassment: 'I shall be here for another forty-eight hours, I shall be here for another forty-eight hours,' while Ella Birnenschatz clasped her thin brown arms round her father's neck.

'Papa, you are a darling,' said Ella Birnenschatz.

Odette got up abruptly: 'Well, I'm off,' she said. 'I must go and dress anyway. I think Jacques will be down soon to keep you company.'

She departed, wrapping her dressing-gown closely round her firm, slim hips, and Mathieu thought: 'She did that well – she did that very well,' and he felt deeply grateful. What a fine girl, and what a sexy little piece! – he pushed her away reprovingly, Weiss was standing by the door, dressed apparently in his Sunday best.

'You're making me all wet,' said M. Birnenschatz, wiping

his cheek. 'And you're messing my face up with lipstick.'

She laughed: 'You're afraid of what your typists may think. There!' she said, kissing him on the nose: 'There – and there!' And he felt hot lips on the top of his skull. He caught her by the shoulders, and held her at the length of his long arms. She laughed and struggled, and he thought: 'Grand girl – grand little girl.' The mother was fat and flaccid, with a timid and appealing look in her wide eyes, which got on his nerves, but Ella took after him, or rather she did not take after anybody, she had made herself what she was by her life in Paris; I always say . . . Race? – what do you mean by race, would you take Ella for a Jewess if you met her in the street? Slim as a Parisienne, with the warm complexion of a southern girl, a sensible, passionate, small face, a sedate and restful face, devoid of defect, race, or destiny, a truly *French* face. He released her, took a jewel-case off the desk, and gave it her.

'Here you are,' he said. And he added while she was looking at the pearls: 'Next year, they'll be twice as large, but they will be the last: the necklace will be complete.'

She tried to kiss him again, but he said: 'Get along now. Many happy returns. Hurry! – you'll be late for your lecture.'

She departed, throwing a smile at Weiss; a girl shut the door, went through the secretaries' office, and disappeared. Schalom, sitting on the edge of his chair, with his hat on his knees, thought: 'Pretty little Jewess': she had a little monkeyish head, rather thickset in front, no bigger than could be covered by a hollowed hand, with large, short-sighted, lovely eyes, obviously Birnenschatz's daughter. Schalom got up, and made her a slight bow which she did not appear to notice. He sat down again and thought: 'She looks *too* intelligent; that's how our people are made: our expressions are branded on our faces: it's as though we endured them like a martyrdom.' M. Birnenschatz thought of the pearls, and said to himself: 'Not a bad investment.' They were worth a hundred thousand; Ella had accepted them without excessive rapture and without indifference: she knew the value of things, but she thought it quite natural to have money, to receive handsome presents and to be happy. Good Lord, if, with my sort of wife, and my Cracow background, if this little spit of a girl, daughter of Polish Jews, who doesn't get agitated, nor allow herself to get upset, who finds it natural to be happy, if she had been my sole achievement, I would not have lived in vain. He turned to Weiss: 'Do you know where she's going?' he asked. 'You'll never guess. To a lecture at the Sorbonne. Astounding, isn't it?'

Weiss smiled vaguely, still looking rather sheepish.

'Sir,' he said, 'I've come to say good-bye.'

M. Birnenschatz eyed him over his spectacles.

'Are you mobilized?'

Weiss nodded, and M. Birnenschatz eyed him quizzically: 'I was sure of it! You're fool enough to be in possession of Form 2, eh?'

'It's a fact,' said Weiss with a smile. 'I am.'

'Well,' said Birnenschatz folding his arms, 'you're going to leave me nicely in the lurch. What can I do without you?'

He repeated absentmindedly, 'What can I do without you? What can I do without you?' He tried to remember how many children Weiss had. Weiss glanced at him uneasily.

'Nonsense! You'll find someone to take my place.'

'Not a bit of it! As things stand now, I'm already going to have to pay you for not doing a damned thing. You don't suggest I should take on somebody else into the bargain. Your job will be waiting for you, my boy.'

Weiss looked moved, he rubbed his nose and squinted – he was revoltingly ugly.

'Sir – ' he said.

M. Birnenschatz stopped him: gratitude was loathsome, besides he hadn't a great deal of sympathy for Weiss, because after all he was a fellow who carried his fate in his face, with those furtive eyes of his, and that bulging lower lip that quivered with benevolence and resentment.

'That's all right,' he said. 'That's all right. You aren't leaving the house, you're representing it among the land forces. Are you a lieutenant?'

'I'm a captain,' said Weiss.

'A wash-out of a captain,' thought M. Birnenschatz. Weiss looked happy, his large ears were crimson. A wash-out of a captain – and that's war, that's the military hierarchy.

'What a pack of bloody nonsense it all is,' he said.

'Hum,' observed Weiss.

'Well, isn't it?'

'Of course it is,' said Weiss. 'But I was about to say that, *for us*, it isn't such bloody nonsense.'

'For us?' asked M. Birnenschatz in astonishment. 'For us. Whom are you talking about?'

Weiss lowered his eyes: 'For us Jews,' he said. 'After what they did to the Jews of Germany, we have a reason for fighting.'

M. Birnenschatz took a few steps: he was annoyed.

'What's all this? Us Jews?' he asked. 'Don't know 'em. I'm French myself. Do you feel like a Jew?'

'My cousin from Gratz has been with me since Tuesday,' said Weiss. 'He showed me his arms. They burnt him with lighted cigars from the elbow to the armpit.'

M. Birnenschatz stopped short, he gripped the back of a chair with his great hands, and a black rage set him ablaze up to the eyes.

'The men who did that,' he said, 'the men who did that . . .'

Weiss smiled; M. Birnenschatz cooled down.

'It isn't because your cousin is a Jew, Weiss. It's because he's a man. I can't bear to hear of any man being ill-treated. But what is a Jew? It's a man whom other men take for a Jew. Now look at Ella. Would you take her for a Jew if you didn't know who she was?'

Weiss did not look convinced. M. Birnenschatz marched up to him and tapped him on the chest with his outstretched forefinger: 'Listen, my dear Weiss, I can tell you this: I left Poland in 1910, and came to France. I was well received, I settled down here, and I said to myself: 'Good, France is my country now.' In 1914 the war came. Good. I said to myself – I'm going to fight because this is my country. And I know what war is – I was at the Chemin des Dames, you know. But now, I tell you, I am French. Not a Jew, nor a French Jew: French. The Jews of Berlin and Vienna, the Jews of the concentration camps – I'm sorry for them, and it certainly makes me furious to think of such martyrdom. But mark my words, if there were anything I could do to save a Frenchman, one single Frenchman, from being slaughtered for their sake – I would do it. I feel more akin to the first fellow I shall soon meet in the street than to my Lenz uncles, or my Cracow nephews. The fate of German Jews is not our business.'

Weiss looked sly and obstinate. He said with a sorrowful smile: 'Even if it was true, sir, you shouldn't say so. Those who have to fight must find reasons for fighting.'

M. Birnenschatz felt a flush of embarrassment mounting to his cheekbones. 'Poor fellow,' he thought remorsefully.

'You are right,' he said abruptly. 'I'm nothing but a back number, and it's not for me to talk about this war, as I'm not in it. When do you go?'

'By the half past four train,' said Weiss.

'Today's train? Then what on earth are you doing here? Run along home to your wife at once. Are you in need of money?'

'Not for the moment, thanks.'

'Then get along. Tell your wife to come and see me, I'll settle everything with her. Hurry now. Good-bye.'

He opened the door and pushed him out. Weiss bowed, and babbled some unintelligible words of thanks. Over Weiss's shoulder, M. Birnenschatz noticed a man sitting in the waiting-room, with his hat on his knees. He recognized Schalom, and frowned. He did not like any sort of caller kept waiting.

'Come in,' he said. 'Have you been waiting long?'

'Only half an hour,' said Schalom, with a smile of resignation. 'But what is half an hour? You are such a busy man. And I have all the time there is. What do I do from morning till night? I wait. Life in exile is nothing but a process of waiting, as you know.'

'Come in,' said M. Birnenschatz briskly. 'Come in. They should have told me you were here.'

Schalom went in: he smiled and bowed. M. Birnenschatz went in behind him, and shut the door. He recognized Schalom perfectly well: he had been something in the Bavarian Syndicalist movement. Schalom appeared now and again, touched him for two or three thousand francs, and disappeared for several weeks.

'Take a cigar.'

'I don't smoke,' said Schalom, poking his head forwards. M. Birnenschatz took a cigar, twirled it absentmindedly between his fingers, and then replaced it in the box.

'Well?' he said. 'How are you getting on?'

84

Schalom looked round for a chair.

'Sit down – sit down,' said M. Birnenschatz heartily.

No. Schalom did not want to sit down. He went to the chair, and put his portfolio on it, in order to feel more at ease, and then, turning to M. Birnenschatz, emitted a long, melodious groan.

'I'm not getting on at all,' said Schalom. 'It isn't good for a man to live on other men's territory, it is very hard to bear; he is grudged the bread he eats. And their suspicion – that supremely French suspicion of us! When I get back to Vienna, this is the vision I shall have of France: a long dark staircase, a bell, a door half-opened – 'What do you want?' – and then shut again. The police who check lodgings, the town hall, the queue at the police-station. After all, it's quite natural, we are living in their country. But consider: they might set us to work: I ask no more than to make myself useful. But in order to find a job, you need an employment card, and in order to get an employment card, you need to be in some sort of job. With the best will in the world, I can't earn my living. What I find hardest to bear is to be a charge on others. Especially when they make you feel it so cruelly. And the time I waste! I began to write my memoirs – that would have brought in a little money. But there are so many things to be done in a day: I had to give up the idea.'

He was a short, brisk little man, he had put his portfolio on a chair, and his hands, now free, fluttered round his crimson ears: 'I must say he does look rather Jewy.' M. Birnenschatz moved casually to the mirror, and threw a rapid glance at it: just over five feet tall, a broken nose, American boxer's head behind those large spectacles; no, we are not of the same species. But he did not dare look at Schalom, he felt compromised. He wished the man would go at once, but that was unlikely. It was only by the length of his visits and his cheerful conversation that Schalom could in his own eyes distinguish himself from a beggar. 'I must talk,' thought M. Birnenschatz, Schalom had the right to that. He had the right to his three thousand-franc notes and his quarter of an hour's interview. M. Birnenschatz sat on the edge of his desk. His right hand, which he had thrust into his jacket pocket, was fingering his cigar-case.

'The French are hard,' said Schalom. His voice rose and then broke down prophetically, but a gleam of amusement quivered in his colourless eyes. 'Hard. In their eyes a stranger is a suspect on principle, when he isn't actually guilty.'

He talks to me as if I wasn't a Frenchman. Of course that's true; I am a Jew, a Jew from Poland, who arrived in France on 19 July 1910, no one here remembers that fact, but he hasn't forgotten it. *A Jew who has had a bit of luck.* He turned to Schalom and eyed him with annoyance. Schalom had bent his head in a sort of deferential attitude, but he still looked him in the face from beneath his arched eyebrows. He looked at him, and those great pale eyes *saw him as a Jew.* Two Jews, securely sheltered and secluded in an office in the rue du Quatre-Septembre, two Jews, two accomplices: and all around them, in the streets and houses, nothing but French people. Two Jews, the jovial old Yid who has succeeded, and the ill-nourished little tyke who hasn't had a chance. Laurel and Hardy.

'Hard!' said Schalom. 'Merciless.'

M. Birnenschatz shrugged his shoulders abruptly. 'You must put yourself in . . . in their place,' he said curtly – he could not bring himself to say – 'in our place': 'do you know how many foreigners have come to France since 1934?'

'Yes,' said Schalom, 'I do. And I think it is a great honour for France. But what is she doing to deserve it? You surely know that the young men of Paris comb the Latin Quarter, and if anyone looks like a Jew, they beat him up.'

'Blum did us a great deal of harm when he was Premier,' observed M. Birnenschatz.

He had said – us: he had accepted the complicity of this little blighter. We. We Jews. But it was from compassion that he had done so. Schalom's eyes were fixed on him with respectful insistence. He was small and fragile, they had beaten him up and ejected him from Bavaria, and here he was, lodging in a squalid hotel and spending his days in cafés. And Weiss's cousin, they had burnt him with cigars. M. Birnenschatz looked at Schalom, and felt dirty. *It wasn't sympathy for the man – by no means. It was . . . it was . . .'*

She looked at him and she thought: 'A man of prey. They are marked as what they are, and they are the cause of wars.' But she realized that her old love was not dead.

86

M. Birnenschatz fingered his note-case. 'Ah well,' he said kindly: 'Let us hope it won't last too long.'

Schalom compressed his lips, and jerked up his round head. 'I made my gesture too soon,' thought Monsieur Birnenschatz. *A man of prey. He takes women and kills men. He thinks he is a great man. But it isn't true, he is marked as what he is, that's all.*

'That depends on the French,' said Schalom. 'If once again the French come to understand their historic mission . . .'

'What mission?' asked M. Birnenschatz coldly. Schalom's eyes gleamed with hatred.

'The Germans provoke and insult them in every possible way,' he said in a hard, high voice. 'What do they expect? Do they imagine they can get round Hitler? Each new French concession prolongs the Nazi régime for ten years. And all that time we, the victims, gnaw our nails and wait. Today I saw the white posters on the wall, and I feel faintly hopeful. But even yesterday I thought: the French have no blood left in their veins, and I shall die in exile.'

Two Jews in an office in the rue du Quatre-Septembre. The Jewish standpoint on international events. Tomorrow then will be a statement in *Je suis partout*: 'The Jews are pushing France into war.' M. Birnenschatz took off his spectacles and wiped them with his handkerchief: he was furious. Quietly he said: 'If war comes, will you be in it?'

'Many refugees will join up, I'm sure of that,' said Schalom. 'But look at me,' he added, pointing to his meagre little person, 'I should never be accepted by any medical board.'

'So you're going to mess up the peace for us, are you?' said M. Birnenschatz in a thunderous voice. 'That's what you mean to do, eh? Why the hell do you want to come here and mess up our affairs? I'm French, I'm not a German Jew, and I don't give a damn for German Jews. So go and make your war somewhere else.'

Schalom eyed him for a moment with stupefaction, then he resumed his deferential smile, reached out a hand, picked up his portfolio, and backed towards the door. M. Birnenschatz took his note-case out of his pocket:

'Wait a moment,' he said.

Schalom was already at the door.

'I need nothing,' he said. 'I sometimes ask for help from the Jews. But you are right: you're not a Jew, and I've come to the wrong address.'

He went out, and M. Birnenschatz stood motionless, staring at the door. *He's a hard man, a man of prey, they have a star, and they succeed in everything they do. But they are the cause of wars and of death and pain. They are flame and fire, they do harm, he has done me harm, I carry him like a sliver of wood beneath my finger-nails, like a smouldering cinder under my eyelids, like a splinter in the heart.* That's what she thinks of me. He had no need to go and ask her, he knew her, if he could penetrate that dark and tousled head, he would always find in it that set, inexorable thought, she's a hard woman in her way, she never forgets. He leaned in his pyjamas out over the Place Gélu, the air was still fresh, the sky was pale blue edged with grey, it was the hour when water streams over the flagstones and the fishmongers' stalls, the city smelt of departure and of morning. Morning, open spaces, and down there, a life without remorse, round puffs of bomb-smoke on the cracked soil of Catalonia. But at his back, behind the half-open window, in a room filled with sleep and with darkness, there was a dead thought watching him, judging him; his own remorse. He would set off tomorrow, he would kiss them on the station platform, and she would go back to the hotel with the boy, she would trip down the great staircase, she would think: he has gone off to Spain again. She would never forgive him: it was a dead skin upon her heart. He leaned out over the Place Gélu to postpone the moment when he must return to his room: he needed shouts, shrill songs, swift and violent pains, he loathed the soft atmosphere in which he lived. Water streamed across the square, water, the damp odours of morning, the rustic cries of morning. Beneath the plane-trees lay the square, glistening, white, and vivid like a fish in the sea. And, that night, a Negro had been singing, and the night had seemed sultry and like a Spanish night. Gomez closed his eyes, he felt a stabbing nostalgia for Spain and for the war. She did not understand. Neither night, nor morning, nor the war.

'Bang, bang! Bang, bang, bang, bang!' yelled Pablo.

Gomez turned and went back into the room. Pablo had put on his helmet, he was holding his rifle by the barrel, and brandishing it like a club. He staggered up and down the hotel bedroom dealing violent blows all round him. Sarah watched him with dead eyes.

'It's a positive massacre,' said Gomez.

'I'm going to kill them all,' replied Pablo, continuing his onslaught.

'All whom?'

Sarah in her dressing-gown sat on the edge of the bed darning a stocking.

'All the Fascists,' said Pablo.

Gomez stepped quickly back, and burst out laughing. 'Kill them!' he said. 'Don't leave one alive. You've forgotten that fellow – over there.'

Pablo dashed in the direction of Gomez's outstretched arm, and streaked the air with his rifle.

'Bang, bang,' he cried. 'Bang, bang, bang! No mercy.'

He stopped and turned to Gomez, panting, with a grave, intent look on his face.

'Oh, Gomez,' said Sarah. 'Look – how could you?'

Gomez had just bought Pablo a soldier's outfit.

'He must learn to fight,' said Gomez, stroking the boy's head. 'Otherwise he'll become a coward, like the French.'

Sarah looked up at him, and he saw that he had deeply wounded her.

'I don't understand,' she said, 'why people should be called cowards because they don't want to fight.'

'There are moments when one ought to want to fight,' said Gomez.

'Never,' said Sarah. 'In no circumstances. Fighting means finding myself one day on a road with my house in ruins, and my boy dead in my arms: nothing can justify that.'

Gomez did not answer. Indeed he had no answer. Sarah was right. From her point of view she was right. But Sarah's point of view was one that had to be ignored on principle, otherwise nothing would ever get done. Sarah laughed bitterly: 'When I first knew you, you were a pacifist, Gomez.'

'Yes, because that was the right time to be a pacifist. The aim has not changed. But the means for attaining it are different.'

This baffled Sarah, and she made no comment. She stood

89

with her mouth half-open, and her drooping lip exposed her decayed teeth: Pablo twirled his rifle, and shouted:

'You wait, you dirty Frenchman, you French coward!'

'You see?' said Sarah.

'Pablo,' said Gomez sharply. 'You mustn't abuse the French. The French aren't Fascists.'

'The French are funks,' shouted Pablo. And he dashed the butt of his rifle against the curtains, which bellied backwards into the windows. Sarah said nothing, but Gomez wished he had not seen the look she threw at Pablo. It was not a harsh look – no: it was more of a bewildered look, as though she were seeing her son for the first time. She had laid the stocking on the bed beside her, and was eyeing this little stranger, this lively little brat who slashed off heads and smashed skulls, and was no doubt thinking ruefully: 'This is my fault.' Gomez was ashamed. 'A week,' he thought: 'a week was quite enough.'

'Gomez,' said Sarah brusquely, 'do you really think there's going to be a war?'

'I hope so,' said Gomez. 'I hope Hitler will finally force the French to fight.'

'Gomez,' said Sarah, 'do you know what I've realized recently? – that men are evil.'

Gomez shrugged his shoulders. 'They are neither good nor evil. Everyone pursues his own interest.'

'No,' said Sarah. 'They are evil.' She kept her eyes on little Pablo, as though predicting his destiny. 'Evil; and intent on injuring themselves.'

'I'm not evil,' said Gomez.

'You are,' said Sarah without looking at him. 'You are evil, my poor Gomez, very evil. And you have no excuses: others are unhappy, but you are evil, and happy.'

A long silence fell. Gomez looked at her short, thick neck, and that unlovely body he had once held in his arms, and thought: 'She has no affection for me. No tenderness. No respect. She merely loves me: which of us is the more evil?'

But suddenly remorse laid hold of him again: he had arrived one evening from Barcelona, happy – indeed profoundly happy. He had arranged to stay a week. He left on the following day: 'I am not a good man,' he thought.

'Is the water hot?'

'Tepid,' said Sarah. 'The tap on the left.'

'Good,' said Gomez. 'Well then, I shall shave.' He went into the dressing-room, leaving the door wide open, turned on the water, and selected a blade: 'When I'm gone,' he thought, 'the soldier's outfit won't last long.' When Sarah returned, she would doubtless shut it up in her large medicine cupboard; unless she deliberately mislaid it. 'She teaches him girls' games,' he thought. When would he see Pablo again and what would she have made of him? He certainly looks a stout little lad! He approached the wash-basin, and saw them both in the mirror. Pablo was standing in the middle of the room, panting, flushed, his legs apart and his hands in his pockets. Sarah was on her knees before him, and looking up at him in silence. 'She's wondering if he's like me,' thought Gomez. He felt uncomfortable, and closed the door without a sound.

'. . . has joined me with the boy. Expect me by the half past four train on Sunday, and book me a . . .' A hand was laid heavily on his left shoulder, another hand on his right shoulder. A warm and friendly pressure. So that's that: he replaced the letters in his pocket and looked up.

'Hullo!'

'Odette has just told me . . .' said Jacques, looking deeply into Mathieu's eyes. 'Poor old chap!'

He sat down in the arm-chair which Odette had just vacated, without taking his eyes off his brother: a hand which hardly seemed his own skilfully hitched up his trousers: his legs crossed themselves automatically. He ignored these trifling local incidents: he was simply an embodied look.

'I'm not leaving today, you know,' said Mathieu.

'I know. You aren't afraid of any possible unpleasantness . . . ?'

'Oh – a few hours one way or the other . . .'

Jacques drew a deep breath. 'What shall I say? In other days, when a chap went off, one could say to him: "You are going to fight for your children, your liberty or your property, to fight for France" – indeed one could provide him with various reasons for risking his skin. But today . . .'

He shrugged his shoulders. Mathieu had bent his head, and was scraping the ground with his heel.

'You don't answer,' said Jacques in a penetrating voice.

'You prefer not to speak, for fear of saying too much. But I know quite well what's in your mind.'

Mathieu was still rubbing his shoe against the ground. He said, without looking up:

'As a matter of fact, you don't know.'

A brief silence followed, then he heard his brother's hesitant voice: 'What do you mean?'

'Well, I'm not thinking about anything at all.'

'All right,' said Jacques, with faint irritation. 'You're not thinking about anything, but you're desperate – it's the same thing.'

Mathieu forced himself to look up and smile:

'Neither am I desperate.'

'Look here,' said Jacques. 'You're not asking me to believe that you are resigned to going off, like a sheep to the slaughter-house?'

'Well,' said Mathieu, 'I am rather sheeplike, don't you think? I'm going because I can't do anything else. That being so, the question whether this war is or is not a just war is, for me, quite secondary.'

Jacques tilted his head back, and surveyed Mathieu with eyes half-closed.

'Mathieu, you amaze me. I'm absolutely staggered. I don't recognize you. What happened? I had a turbulent, cynical, sarcastic brother, who would never allow himself to be fooled, who would not lift his little finger without trying to understand why he was lifting his little finger rather than his fore-finger, and the little finger of his right hand rather than his left. Then comes war, he is sent into the front line, and my rebel, my plate-smasher, goes off politely, without any hesitation, merely saying: I'm going because I have no option.'

'It's not my fault,' said Mathieu. 'I have never been able to form an opinion on matters of that kind.'

'But surely,' said Jacques, 'the issue is quite clear: we are confronted by a man – I mean Beneš – who is formally pledged to establish Czechoslovakia as a federation on the Swiss model. He is pledged,' he repeated with emphasis. 'I read it in the Report of the proceedings at the Peace Conference, so you see I can quote my sources. And that promise was equivalent

to giving the Sudeten Germans a genuine ethnographic autonomy. Good. Whereupon the said person ignores his commitments, and places these same Germans under Czech adminis-
tration, law, and police. The Germans don't like it: and they
claim their strict rights. Moreover I know these Czech officials,
I have been in Czechoslovakia, I know what petty tyrants they
can be. Well then – the proposal is that France, the land, so
they say, of liberty, should shed her blood, in order that Czech
officials should continue to torment the German population,
and that is why you, professor of philosophy at the Lycée
Pasteur, are going to spend the last years of your youth ten
feet underground, between Bitche and Wissembourg. And so
you must understand that when you come and tell me that
you are leaving in a spirit of resignation, and that you don't
care a damn whether this war is just or unjust, I do get a bit
hot under the collar.'

Mathieu eyed his brother with perplexity: he thought
'Ethnographic autonomy – I should never have thought of
that.' 'However,' he observed, to salve his conscience, 'it isn't
ethnographic autonomy that the Sudetens now want, it's
union with Germany.'

Jacques winced painfully. 'Please, Mathieu, don't talk like
my concierge, don't call them the Sudetens. The Sudetens are
mountains; say the Sudeten Germans, if you like, or just
Germans. Well, and what then? They want to join Germany?
That's because they have been goaded beyond endurance. If
they had been granted what they asked at the outset, we
shouldn't be in this quandary. But Beneš has practised every
sort of trickery and cunning because the bigwigs here have
been so misguided as to let him believe that he had France
behind him: and this is the result.'

He looked gloomily at Mathieu:

'I can stand all this, if need be; I know what sort of people
politicians are. But that you, a sensible man, a member of the
University, should have so utterly abandoned your most
elementary principles as to assure me that you are going off
to the slaughter because you can't do otherwise – that I really
cannot stand. If there are many like you, it's all up with France,
my poor old chap.'

'But what do you want us to do?' asked Mathieu.

'What? We're still a democracy, Thieu! I imagine there is still such a thing in France as public opinion.'

'Well?'

'Well, if millions of Frenchmen, instead of exhausting themselves in futile quarrels, had closed their ranks, and said to our Government: "So the Sudeten Germans want to return to the bosom of Germania, do they? Then let them: it's their affair!" Not a single politician would have dared to risk war over such a trifle.'

He laid a hand on Mathieu's knee, and continued in a conciliatory tone:

'I know you don't like the Hitler régime. But after all, it is quite possible not to share your prejudices against it: it is a young and energetic régime, which has proved its effectiveness, and exercises an undeniable attraction on the nations of central Europe. Besides, it is in every sense their affair: we are not called upon to interfere.'

Mathieu stifled a yawn, and drew his legs back under his chair: he threw a quizzical look at his brother's rather puffy countenance, and thought that he was beginning to age.

'Perhaps – ' he said, meekly. 'Perhaps you are right.'

Odette went downstairs, and sat down with them in silence. She had the grace and tranquillity of a domestic animal: she sat down, went away, came back, and sat down again, certain that she would pass unnoticed. Mathieu turned to her with annoyance: he did not like to see them together. When Jacques was present, Odette's face did not change, it remained smooth and elusive, like that of a statue without pupils to its eyes. What lay behind it had to be divined.

'Jacques thinks I ought to be more upset about being called up,' he said with a smile. 'He's trying to put death into my soul by explaining that I'm going to get myself killed for nothing.'

Odette returned him a smile. It wasn't the conventional smile that he expected, but a special smile just for him; in one instant the sea had reappeared, the lightly heaving sea, the Chinese shadows speeding across the waves, the streak of sunlight quivering on the water, the green aloes and the green pine-needles that carpeted the ground, the stippled shadows of the tall pines, the dense white heat, the smell of resin, all the richness of a September morning at Juan-les-Pins. Dear Odette.

Mismarried and misloved; but had she wasted her life when she could, with a smile, resuscitate a garden by the water's edge, and the heat of summer on the sea? He looked at Jacques – a sallow, fleshy figure, whose hands trembled as he angrily tapped his newspaper. 'What is he afraid of?' said Mathieu to himself. On Saturday, 24 September, at eleven o'clock in the morning, Pascal Montastruc, born at Nîmes on 6 February 1899, and commonly known as One-eyed Pascal because he had stuck a knife in his left eye on 6 August 1907 while trying to cut the ropes of his little friend Julot Truffier's swing, to see what would happen, was selling, as was his custom every Saturday, irises and buttercups on the Quai de Passy, just by the entrance to the Métro Station; he had his own personal technique, he took some bunches of flowers out of the wicker basket on a camp-stool, and went out into the roadway, the cars drove past him hooting, and he shouted: 'A bunch of flowers, a lovely bunch of flowers for the lady!' brandishing the yellow bouquet; the car dashed at him like a bull in an arena, he did not move, he merely drew in his stomach, flung his head back, and let the car bear down upon him, as he shouted through the open window: 'A bunch of flowers, a lovely bunch of flowers.' The driver usually stopped, he climbed on to the running-board, and the car drew up against the pavement, because it was the 'week-end', and they liked to go back to their fine houses in the rue des Vignes or the rue du Ranelagh with a bunch of flowers for the lady. 'A lovely bunch of flowers,' he jumped back to avoid the car, the hundredth that had passed without stopping. 'Blast them! What's the matter with them all this morning?' They were driving fast, bent over their wheels, deaf and unheeding. They did not turn into the rue Charles Dickens or the avenue de Lamballe, they raced along the quays as though they meant to get as far as Pontoise; One-eyed Pascal was completely baffled: 'Where on earth are they going to?' He trotted back to his basket of yellow and pink flowers, what a shame.

'It's pure lunacy,' he said. 'The worst case of suicide in history. Consider. France has been bled white twice in a hundred years, once in the wars of the Empire, and again in 1914: added to which, the birth-rate is falling every day. Is this the moment to start another war which would cost us three to four million men? Three or four million men whom we could never replace,' he said, rapping out the words. 'Win or lose, the country would decline into a second-class Power: that is quite certain. And then there is something else: Czechoslovakia will be knocked out before we can move a finger. Look at a map: it's like a haunch of meat between the jaws of the German wolf. If the wolf tightens his jaws a bit . . .'

'But,' said Odette, 'that would only be temporary, the Czechoslovak State would be built up again after the war.'

'Indeed?' said Jacques, with a sarcastic laugh. 'You think so? Is it really likely that the English will allow such a storm-centre to be rebuilt? Fifteen million inhabitants, nine distinct nationalities – it's an insult to common sense. Let the Czechs make no mistake,' he added grimly: 'their vital interest is to avoid war at any cost.'

What is he afraid of?' He watched the cars pass, grasping his useless bunch of flowers, it was like the Chantilly road on the evening of a race day, some had trunks, mattresses, perambulators, or sewing-machines piled up on their roofs, and all were full to bursting with suitcases, parcels, and baskets. 'Well, I'm blowed!' said One-eyed Pascal. They sped past, so heavily loaded that at every bump the mudguards rasped against the tyres. 'They're doing a bunk,' he thought. He jumped back a step or two to avoid a Salmson, but he did not get back on to the pavement. They were doing a bunk – these gentlemen with their smoothed, massaged faces, their fat children and their handsome wives, they were running like cats with their tails on fire, they were scuttling from Germans, bombs, and Communism. All his clients gone. But this procession of cars, this wild flight to Normandy, seemed to him so comic that it made up for his losses; he stood in the roadway while the runaway cars brushed past him, and began to enjoy the spectacle.

'And where, I ask you, are we to come to their assistance? Because after all we should have to attack Germany just the same. Well, then: where? In the east, there is the Siegfried Line, we should break our noses on that. In the north, Belgium. Are we to violate Belgian neutrality? Well then – where? Are we to go round by Turkey? That's just fantastic. All that we can do is to wait, with arms at the ready, until Germany has settled

Czechoslovakia's account. After which she will come and settle ours.'

'Well,' said Odette, 'that's just the moment for . . .'

Jacques threw her a warning look: 'For what?' he asked coldly. He leaned towards Mathieu: 'I've spoken to you of Laurent, who was the big noise at Air-France, and stayed on as adviser to Cot and Guy La-Chambre. Well, I'll pass on to you without comment what he told me last July: the French army has, in all and for all purposes, forty bombers and seventy fighters. If that is typical of our condition, the Germans will be in Paris for New Year's Day.'

'Jacques,' said Odette furiously.

What is he afraid of? Pascal laughed and laughed, he had dropped his bunch of flowers so as to laugh in comfort, he jumped backwards, the wheels of a car crushed the flowers. What is he afraid of? She's furious that anyone should even imagine the defeat of France. She is not at all sympathetic: words frighten her. They are afraid of Zeppelins and Taubes, I saw them myself in 1916, they had the wind up then, and it's beginning again: the cars sped over the crushed flowers, and the tears came into Pascal's eyes, he thought it all so funny. Maurice didn't think it was funny at all. He had stood drinks all round to his pals, and his shoulder-blades were still aching from their thumping fists. At the moment, he was alone, and soon he would have to go and tell Zézette. He saw the white notice on the high grey wall of the Penhoët works, and went up to it, he wanted to read it over again alone.

'By order of the Minister of National Defence and War, and of the Minister for Air.' Death wasn't so very terrible, it was an accident of work. Zézette was tough, and young enough to pick up her life again, it's always so simple when there aren't any children. For the rest – well, he would have to go, and then, when it ended, he would keep his rifle, that was an understood thing. But when would the end come? In two years? In five years? The last war had gone on for fifty-two months. For fifty-two months he would have to kowtow to sergeants, and stiffs of that sort – all those swine he had hated so much. Obey them hand and foot, salute them in the street, whereas now he had to keep his hands in his pockets to stop himself from knocking them down. In the line, of course, they have to behave themselves, they're scared of a bullet in the back: but out of it, they were just the same dirty bullies as in barracks. Oh for the first attack, how I shall enjoy knocking out the sergeant ahead of me! He walked on, feeling depressed and limp as he had done as a boxer, when undressing in the changing-room a quarter of an hour before a fight. War was a long, long road, better not think of it too much, otherwise one ended up finding that nothing made sense, not even victory, when they would all come back with their rifles in their hands. A long, long road. And perhaps he would be killed half-way, as though his sole purpose was to lay down his life in defence of the Schneider factories, or Monsieur de Wendel's money-bags. He was walking in the black dust between the wall of the Penhoët works and that of the German building-yard: some distance away on the right he could see the tilted roofs of the repair-shops of the Nord railway, and, still farther off, the tall red chimney of the distillery, and he thought: 'A long, long road.' One-eyed Pascal laughed among the cars, Maurice stumped through the dust, and Mathieu was sitting by the sea, listening to Jacques, and saying to himself: 'Perhaps he is right.' He reflected that he was soon to shed his profession, his clothes, and his identity, and go off naked to the most absurd of wars, to a war lost in advance, he felt submerged by anonymity: he was no longer anything at all, neither Boris's old teacher, nor the former lover of what was formerly Marcelle, nor Ivich's elderly admirer: just a man without a name, without the mark of age, robbed of his future, with days before him that could not be foreseen. At half past eleven, the coach stopped at Safi, and Pierre got out of it to stretch his legs. Flat, yellow huts beside the tarred road: behind him, out of sight, Safi sloped downwards to the sea. Arabs, on an expanse of ochreous earth, crouched stewing in the heat, the aeroplane sped over a yellow-and-grey checkerboard which was France. 'They don't need to care a bugger about all this,' thought Pierre enviously: he was walking among the Arabs, he could touch them, and yet he was not really there: they calmly smoked their hashish in the sunshine, he was going to get his face smashed in Alsace; he tripped over a mound of earth, the aeroplane dropped into an air-pocket, and the old gentleman thought: 'I don't like flying.' Hitler leaned over the table, the

General pointed to the map, and said: 'Five brigades of tanks. A thousand planes will leave Dresden, Tempelhof, and Munich,' and Chamberlain pressed his handkerchief to his mouth and thought: 'It's my second journey by air. I don't like flying.' They can't help me: there they are, squatting in the sunshine, like little saucepans full of steaming water, they are happy, they are alone upon the earth; 'God in heaven,' he thought in desperation: 'if only I were an Arab!'

At a quarter to twelve, François Hannequin, qualified pharmacist, of Saint-Flour, above five feet four inches tall, straight nose, medium forehead, slight squint, short beard, unwholesome breath, malodorous private parts, chronic enteritis up to the age of seven, Oedipus complex liquidated about the age of thirteen, matriculated at seventeen, masturbated two or three times weekly until his military service, subscriber to the *Temps* and the *Matin*, married to Espérance Dieulafoy, no children, practising Catholic – two or three Communions a quarter, went up to the first floor, entered the nuptial chamber where his wife was trying on a hat and said: 'It's just as I told you, they're calling up the No. 2's.' His wife put the hat down on the dressing-table, took the pins out of her mouth, and said: 'So you'll be off this afternoon?' And he said: 'Yes, by the five o'clock train.' 'Oh dear!' said his wife, 'and I'm all upside down, I shall never have time to get things ready for you. What will you want to take? – shirts, of course, and long pants, you've got woollen, cellular, and cotton ones – better take the woollens, and flannel belts, you could take five or six, by rolling them into a bundle.'

'No belts,' said Hannequin, 'they harbour lice.'

'How disgusting – but you won't have any lice. Do take them, just to please me: once you get there, you'll find some use for them. Fortunately I've still got some tinned stuff – I brought it back in '36 at the time of the strikes, though you laughed at me, I've got a tin of cabbage in white wine, but you won't like that.'

'No, it doesn't agree with me. But,' he said, rubbing his hands, 'if you had a small tin of bean-stew . . .'

'A tin of bean-stew,' said Espérance, 'but, my poor dear, how will you manage to heat it?'

'Never mind that,' said Hannequin.

99

'What do you mean? You need a proper saucepan to heat it.'

'Well, there's some jellied chicken, isn't there?'

'Yes, that's the stuff, jellied chicken, and a fine Bologna sausage which the Clermont cousins sent us.'

He pondered a moment, and then said: 'I'll take my Swiss knife.'

'Yes. And where can I have put the thermos for your coffee?'

'Ah, yes, coffee, I shall need something hot to settle the stomach: it will be the first time since our marriage that I shall have dined without soup,' said he, with a dismal smile. 'Put in a few plums while you're about it, and a flask of brandy.'

'Will you take the yellow suitcase?'

He gave a start. 'The suitcase? Not on your life, it's awkward to carry, and besides I don't want to lose it. Everything gets stolen in the army. I'll take my haversack.'

'What haversack?'

'Why the one I used to take when I went fishing, before we were married. What have you done with it?'

'What have I done with it? I really don't know, my poor dear, you confuse me so, I think I put it in the attic.'

'The attic! Good Lord, among the mice! It must be in an awful state by now.'

'You had much better take the suitcase, it isn't very large, you can quite well keep an eye on it. Ah! I know where it is: at Mathilde's. I lent it to her for a picnic.'

'You lent my haversack to Mathilde?'

'No, not the haversack, silly. The thermos, of course.'

'Well, I want my haversack,' said Hannequin firmly.

'Darling, please do think of all the things I've got to do for you, you might try to help me a little, go and look for the haversack yourself; try the attic.'

He went upstairs and opened the door of the attic, it smelt musty, he could hardly see a thing, and a mouse darted between his feet. 'Damn it all,' he thought: 'the rats must have eaten it up.'

There were several trunks, a dress stand, a map of the world, an old oven, a dentist's chair, a harmonium, all of which would have to be moved out of the way. Perhaps she had put it in a trunk, where it would have been safe. He opened the trunks, one by one, and shut them angrily. It was so handy, it was made of leather, with a zip fastener, it had two compartments and would hold a mass of things. It was just the sort of thing that helped a man to get through a bad time: no one realized how precious such things were. 'In any case, I shan't take the suitcase,' he thought angrily. 'I would rather take nothing at all.'

He sat down on a trunk, his hands were black with dust, he felt dust all over his body, like a dry, viscous paste, he held his hands out so as not to dirty his black jacket, and he felt that he would never have the courage to leave the attic – he was sick of it all, he dreaded the night, without even a bowl of hot soup to soothe his stomach, it was all so stupid, and he felt so alone up there at the top of the house sitting on his trunk, and thinking of the noisy, dark railway station that awaited him, two hundred yards below, when a shrill cry from Espérance made him jump: it was a cry of triumph. 'I've got it! I've got it!' He opened the door, and dashed to the staircase:

'Where was it?'

'I've got your haversack, it was downstairs in the storeroom cupboard.'

He came downstairs, took the haversack from his wife's hands, opened it, looked at it, brushed it with the flat of his hand, and then, putting it on the bed, he said: 'Look here, darling, I've been wondering whether I shouldn't do well to buy myself a good pair of shoes?'

Lunch-time! they had entered the blinding tunnel of midday: outside – the sky, white with heat; outside – the dead, white roads, no man's land, and war: behind the closed shutters, they sat stifling in the heat, Daniel put his napkin on his knees, Hannequin tied his napkin round his neck, Brunet took the paper napkin from the table, crumpled it and wiped his lips, Jeannine wheeled Charles into the large and almost empty dining-room with its smudgy windows, and spread a napkin on his chest; this was a truce: the war – well yes, the war, but what about the heat! butter in a bowl of water, a blurred and oily wedge of it at the bottom of the bowl, and over it thick, grey water and scraps of dead butter floating belly upwards, Daniel watched the curls of butter melt in the radish-dish, Brunet wiped his forehead, the cheese sweated on its plate like an honest man at work, Maurice's beer was tepid, he pushed his glass away: 'Pah! It might be piss!' A piece of ice was floating in Mathieu's red wine, he drank – first he felt a cold liquid in his mouth, and then a little pool of musty wine, still slightly warm, which promptly melted into water: Charles turned his head, and said: 'Soup again! It's crazy to serve soup in midsummer.' His plate was laid on his chest, it warmed his skin through the napkin and his shirt, he could see the edge of the plate quite clearly and dipped his spoon into it, then raised it vertically: but a man on his back can't be sure of what is vertical, so part of the liquid splashed back into the plate, Charles moved the spoon to a point above his lips, lowered it, and – Hell! it always happened, the burning liquid trickled on to his cheek, and soaked his shirt collar. The war – ah yes! the war. No, said Zézette, not the radio, I don't want it, I won't think of the war. Well, let's have a bit of music, said Maurice. Chersau, good-b – b-r-r-r – my star – here is the news – sombreros and mantillas – *I Will Wait*, at the request of Huguette Arnal, Pierre Ducroc, his wife and two daughters, Roche Danillac, Mlle Eliane of Calvi and Jean-François Roquette, for his little Marie-Madeleine, and a group of typists at Tulle for their soldier sweethearts, *I Will Wait*, day and night, have some more *bouillabaisse*, no thanks, said Mathieu, something can surely be arranged, the radio crackled, sped over the white, dead squares, smashed the windows, and penetrated into the dim, humid interiors of the houses, and Odette thought: 'Surely something can be arranged, it's so hot.' Mademoiselle Éliane, Zézette, Jean-François Roquet, and the Ducroc family of la Roche-Canillac, thought: 'Surely something can be arranged, it's so hot.' 'What should they do?' asked Daniel. 'It was a false alarm,' thought Charles, 'they'll leave us where we are.' Ella Birnenschatz laid down her fork, tilted her head back and said: 'Well, I don't believe there'll be a war. *I will wait till you come back:* the aeroplane was flying above a flat expanse of dusty glass: at the extremity of that expanse, very far away, a patch of resin could be seen, Henry leaned towards Chamberlain and shouted in his ear: That's England, England and the crowd at the aerodrome gates, *waiting till you come back, darling, waiting till you come back,* he felt slightly faint, it was so hot, he wanted to forget the fly-headed conqueror, and the Hotel Dreesen, and the memorandum, he wanted to believe – he really did – that something could still be arranged, he closed his eyes, *My darling doll*, at the request of Mme Duranty and her little niece, of Decazeville, the war, Good Lord, yes, the war and the heat, and the sad, acquiescent sleep of afternoon: Casa, here we are at Casa, the coach stopped on a white, deserted square, Pierre got out first and scorching tears welled up in his eyes; there was still a feeling of morning in the coach, but outside, in the glaring sunshine, the morning was dead. The end of morning, *my darling doll*, the end of youth and hope – the great catastrophe of noon. Jean Servin had pushed his plate away, he was reading the sports page in *Paris-Soir*, he knew nothing of the Decree of Partial Mobilization, he had been to work, he had come back for lunch, and he would return to work about two o'clock: Lucien Rénier was cracking nuts in the palms of his hands, he had read the white notices, and he thought: 'It's bluff': François Destutt, laboratory assistant at the Institut Derrien, was scouring his plate with a bit of bread, thinking of nothing, his wife was thinking of nothing, René Malleville, Pierre Charnier thought of nothing. Morning – war was a sharp sliver of ice in their heads, which soon melted into a little tepid pool. *My darling doll*, the rich dark savour of *bœuf bourguignon*, the smell of fish, the scrap of meat between two molars, the fumes of red wine, and the heat, the heat! Dear listeners, France, steadfast but peaceful, faces her destiny.

He was tired, he was dizzy, he passed his hand three times over his eyes, the daylight hurt him, and Dawburn, who was sucking the point of his pencil, said to his *Morning Post* colleague: 'He's been given a shock all right.' He raised his hand and said in a faltering voice:

'My first duty, now that I am back, is to report to the French and British Governments on the results of my mission, and until I have done so, it would be difficult for me to say anything more.'

Noon enveloped him in its white shroud, Dawburn looked at him and thought of long, lonely roads curving between red rocks and rusted by the fire of heaven. The old gentleman added, in an even more faltering tone: 'I will say just this: I am confident that all interested parties will continue their efforts to find a peaceful solution to the problem of Czecho-slovakia, because thereby hangs the peace of Europe in our time.'

Slowly she picks up crumbs off the tablecloth. She looks rather off-colour, as though she had hay-fever, and she said: I've got a touch of wind in the stomach, and she cried a little: it would upset all her habits. But I said 'Just at first. Only at first.' She thinks she is unhappy, she fancies that the little shiver in her head must be unhappiness. She sits up straight, she tells herself that she must not give way, all the women of France are as unhappy as she is. Grave and stately, her shapely arms resting on the tablecloth, she looks like the lady enthroned at the cash-desk of a large shop. She does not think, she refuses to think, that she will be much more comfortable when I have gone. What is she thinking about – that fleck of rust on her knife-rest? She frowns, she scratches it off with the tip of a reddened nail. Much more comfortable. Her mother, her friends, the work-room, the great bed all to herself, no meals, she will fry eggs on the side of the stove, the little girl is not difficult to feed, just cornflour all the time, but give me anything you like, I used to say, don't try to make up dinners, I never notice what I eat, but she was obstinate: it was her duty.

'Georges?'

'Darling?'

'Would you like a tisane?'

'No, thank you.'

She drinks her tisane with a sigh, her eyes are red. She looks – not at me, but at the sideboard, because it is there, directly facing her. To me she has nothing to say, except perhaps: Take care not to catch cold. She will in fact picture me this evening, in the train, a small emaciated figure huddled in the corner of a compartment, but that is the limit of what she can imagine: she thinks of her life here – my absence will make a gap. Quite a small gap, Andrée: I make so little noise. I sat in the arm-chair with a book. She was darning stockings; we had nothing to talk about. The arm-chair will always be there. The important item is the arm-chair. She will write to me: three times a week, most conscientiously. She will look very serious, she will hunt for ink and pen and yellow spectacles, and then she will settle down sedately at the rather uncomfortable writing-desk she inherited from her grandmother Vasseur: 'The child is cutting her teeth, my mother will be here for Christmas, Madame Ancelin is dead, Emilienne is going to be married in September, a good match, a middle-aged man in the insurance business. If the child gets whooping-cough, she won't tell me, so as not to cause me any anxiety. 'Poor Georges, it isn't fair, he does worry so.' She will send me parcels – salami, sugar, coffee, tobacco, woollen socks, sardines, meat cubes, salt butter. One of ten thousand parcels, identical with the other ten thousand: if I were given the next man's by mistake, I shouldn't notice – parcels, letters, Jeannette's cornflour, the stains on the knife-rest, the dust on the sideboard, that will be enough for her: in the evening she will say – I'm tired, I can't do any more. She won't read the papers. No more than she does now: she detests them, they make such a lot of waste-paper, which can't be used for two days for the kitchen or the lavatories. Mme Hébertot will come and tell her the news – We have won a great victory; or – Things aren't going well, my dear, not at all well, we aren't making any progress. Henri and Pascal have already agreed with their wives on a cypher to indicate where they are: by underlining certain letters. But that's no good to Andrée: He did suggest it once:

'I can let you know where I am.'

'But isn't that forbidden?' she asked with surprise.

'Well, yes, but it can be done – just as in the '14 War, by reading all the capitals together, for instance.'

'It's very complicated,' she sighed.

'No, you'll see, it's perfectly simple.'

'Yes, and then you'll get caught, your letters will be torn up, and I shall be anxious.'

'It's worth risking.'

'Just as you like, dear, but you know what I am about geography. I shall look at a map, I shall see a circle with a name underneath, and I shall be none the wiser.'

That was that. In one sense it's better, it's much better like that: she will draw my salary . . .

'Have I given you the power of attorney?'

'Yes, darling, I put it away in the desk.'

Much better. It must be trying to have to leave someone

who really does mind, one must feel so vulnerable. I push my chair back.

'No, darling, it's not worth while folding up your napkin.'

'True.'

She does not ask me where I am going. She never asks where I am going. I tell her: I am going to see the child.

'Don't wake her.'

I shan't wake her: even if I wanted to, I couldn't make enough noise to wake her, I'm too light a weight. He went in, one shutter had swung open, a dazzling, chalky afternoon had penetrated the room, quite half of which was still in shadow, while the other half sparkled in a dusty light: the child was asleep in her cradle, Georges sat down beside her. Her fair hair, her innocent little mouth, and her rounded drooping cheeks, gave her an odd resemblance to an English magistrate. She was beginning to love me. The sun was gaining ground, gently he pushed the cradle back. There! That will do. She won't be pretty, she is too like me. Poor little mite, much better be like her mother. Still quite soft; practically boneless. And yet she already bears within her the strict law which has been my law: the cells will multiply, the cartilages will harden, the cranium will ossify, in accordance with my law. A skinny, insignificant little girl, with dull hair, scoliosis in the right shoulder, and very short-sighted, she will glide noiselessly on her way, barely touching earth, and skirting round people and things, too light and weak to handle them. Heavens! The years will come upon her pitilessly, one by one – how futile it all is, her fate is written upon her flesh, and she must live it out minute by minute, the fate she thinks she has discovered herself; but there it is, complete, repellently obvious, I have tainted her, and why must she live, drop by drop, through what I have lived? Why must everything be *repeated* indefinitely? A skinny little girl, a clear-eyed, sensitive small soul, born to suffer sorely in this life. I am going away, I have other things to do: she will grow up, and here, so obstinately and recklessly, she stands for what I was. The whooping-cough, long convalescences, luckless passions for her pretty, plump, pink-fleshed school-friends, and the mirrors in which she will eye herself in passing: Am I too ugly to be loved? Day after day, the hint of something already seen – Good Lord, is it worth what she must endure? She awoke for a moment, and eyed him with solemn curiosity, for this was a moment that seemed wholly new. He lifted her from the cradle, and clasped her in his arms. 'My little one! My little baby! My poor little one!' But she took fright, and began to scream.

'Georges!' came a reproachful voice from the other room. He laid the child gently back in its cradle. She gazed at him again for a moment with a set and surly look, then her eyes closed, opened, blinked, then closed again. She had just begun to love me. In time, had I been constantly with her, she would have got so used to my presence that she could no longer *see* me. How long will it last? Five years, six years? I shall return to a real little girl who will look at me with amazement, and think: 'That's my papa!' and she'll be ashamed of me before her little friends. I have known that too. When my father came home, I was twelve. The afternoon had now invaded almost the whole room. The afternoon; the war. War must be a sort of interminable afternoon. He rose noiselessly, gently opened the window, and pulled down the sunblind.

Cabin 19 – there it was. She did not venture in, she remained outside the door, suitcase in hand, struggling to convince herself that she was still hopeful. And if it did prove to be a really *nice* little cabin, with a bedside rug, and possibly flowers in a tooth-glass on the wash-basin shelf? Such things do happen, one often meets people who say:

'On such and such a boat there's no need to take second-class cabins, the thirds are as comfortable as the firsts.' Then perhaps France would yield and say: 'Ah, this is an exceptional cabin. If the thirds were always like this . . .' Maud imagined herself as France. A conciliatory and rather indecisive France, who would say: 'Oh well . . . we shall be all right here.' But she remained frozen in her inmost self, frozen and resigned. She heard footsteps, she did not like to be caught wandering about the passage-ways by night, there had once been a theft, and she had had to submit to rather unpleasant questions, the poor must be so careful in small matters, people are so merciless: she suddenly found herself in the middle of the cabin; well, this in fact was what she had expected. Accommodation for six: three bunks on her right, three others on her left. 'Well I never!' No flowers on the wash-basin, nor any bedside rug: she wouldn't have believed it. No chairs either, nor a table. Four people would have felt rather cramped there, but the wash-basin was clean. She wanted to cry, but it wasn't worth while: she had foreseen it all. France *could not* travel third-class, that was the plain fact beyond dispute. Just as Ruby could not travel in a train with her back to the engine. One might be tempted to ask why France should persist in taking third-class tickets. But on that point, as on the other, France couldn't be blamed: she took third-class tickets because she had a taste for economy, and because she managed the finances of Baby's orchestra with the utmost care: who could criticise her for that? Maud put her suitcase on the floor, she tried for a moment to strike roots in the cabin, to pretend to have been there for two days. In that event, the bunks, the yellow-painted rivets that dotted the cabin partitions, would all have been familiar, friendly objects. She said to herself in an emphatic undertone: 'But this is a very nice cabin.' Then she felt tired, she picked up her suitcase and remained standing between the bunks not knowing quite what to do; if we stay, I shall have to unpack, but we certainly shan't stay, and if France sees that I have started to make myself comfortable, she is rather perverse, and that would be one more reason for her to refuse to stay. She felt such a transitory being in that cabin, on that ship, and on the earth. The captain was a tall, heavy man with white hair. She shivered and thought: 'We should be quite all right, all four of us, if only there were no one else.' But one look round was sufficient to dispel that hope: baggage had been set down on a right-hand bunk: a wicker basket secured by a rusty rod, and a fibre suitcase – no, not fibre, cardboard – with frayed corners. And then – the last straw – she looked up and saw a woman of about thirty, pallid, with pinched nostrils and closed eyes, outstretched on the upper right-hand bunk. Well, that settled it. He had looked at her legs when she passed him on deck: he was smoking a cigar, she knew that type of man, smelling of cigars and eau de Cologne. Well, they would appear tomorrow, rather flamboyant and heavily made-up, on the second-class deck, when the passengers would be already installed, having got to know each other and chosen their companions for the voyage, Ruby very erect, with her gay, swaying hips and laughing, peering eyes, and Doucette saying in her heady voice: 'No, my pet, come along, since it is what the captain wishes.' Respectable gentlemen, sitting on deck with rugs over their knees, would eye them coldly, the ladies would make offensive comments as they passed, and in the evenings, in the corridors, they would meet sundry more amiable gentlemen with roving hands. How she longed to stay here, within those four yellow-painted iron walls, they would be so comfortable, just the four of them.

France opened the door, Ruby came in behind her.

'Hasn't the luggage been brought down?' asked France in her most impressive voice.

Maud signed to her to be silent, pointing to the sick woman. France raised her wide, clear, lashless eyes to the upper bunk: her face remained imperious and expressionless, as it usually was, but Maud understood that the game was lost.

'We might do worse,' said Maud briskly, 'the cabin is nearly in the middle of the ship; we shall feel the pitching less.'

Ruby's reply was a shrug of her shoulders. France asked nonchalantly: 'How shall we arrange ourselves?'

'Just as you like. Shall I take the lower bunk?' asked Maud eagerly.

France could not sleep if she knew two people were above her.

'We'll see,' she said; 'we'll see.'

The captain's eyes were clear and frosty, his face was red. The door opened and a lady in black appeared. She mumbled a few words, and sat down on the bunk, between the suitcase and the basket. She looked about fifty, very shabbily dressed, with a coarse, dirty furrowed skin, and bulging eyes. Maud looked at her and thought: 'It's no good.' She produced a lipstick from her bag, and began to make up her lips. France looked at her out of the corner of her eye with such an air of majestic satisfaction that Maud, in irritation, let her lipstick drop into her bag. There was a long silence, which Maud recognized as having occurred in another cabin just like this, on the *Saint-Georges* bound for Tangier, and the previous year on the *Théophile Gautier*, when they were on their way for a season at the Polytheion in Corinth. It was suddenly broken by an odd little sniff: the lady in black had produced a handkerchief, opened it right out and placed it against her face: she was crying, quietly but without restraint, like a person preparing for a lengthy ordeal. After a moment or two, she opened her basket and took out a piece of buttered bread, a slice of cold lamb, and a thermos wrapped in a napkin. She began to eat, still crying, she uncorked the bottle, and poured some hot coffee into the cup as she munched, and large glittering tears trickled down her cheeks. Maud looked at the cabin with new eyes: it was a waiting-room, just a waiting-room in a dismal little country railway station. She only hoped he hadn't special tastes. She sniffed, and threw her head back. France glanced at her coldly.

'This cabin is too small,' observed France impressively. 'We shall be very uncomfortable here. At Casablanca they promised me that we should have a six-berthed cabin to ourselves.'

The ritual had begun, there was a feeling of something sinister and a little solemn: Maud said feebly: 'We might pay extra on our tickets.'

France did not reply. She had sat down on the left-hand bunk, and seemed to be reflecting. In a moment or two her face cleared, and she said cheerfully: 'We might suggest to the captain that we should give a free concert in the first-class saloon – then perhaps he would have our luggage moved to a better cabin.'

Maud said nothing: it was for Ruby to reply.

'An excellent idea,' said Ruby brightly.

Maud suddenly shivered, and felt disgusted with herself. She turned to France and said in a pleading voice: 'You go, France! You are our foreman, it's your job to go and see the captain.'

'Not at all,' said France gaily. 'What's the sense in an old woman like me going to see the captain? He'll be much nicer to a pretty young lady like you.'

A large red-faced man with white hair and grey eyes. He would be meticulously neat, they always were. France reached out an arm, and pressed the bell-button.

'It had better be fixed up at once,' she said. The lady in black was still crying. She raised her head abruptly, and seemed to notice their presence.

'Are you thinking of changing your cabin?' she asked anxiously.

France fixed her with an icy look. Maud answered briskly: 'We have a great deal of luggage, madame. We shall be very cramped, and would be in your way.'

'Oh no you wouldn't,' said the lady. 'I like company.'

There was a knock at the door, and the steward entered. 'Now for it,' thought Maud. She produced her lipstick and powder-box, went up to the mirror, and began to make up hastily.

'Would you kindly ask the captain,' said France, 'if he can spare a minute to receive Mademoiselle Maud Dassignies, of Baby's Lady Orchestra.'

'He won't,' he said; 'I bet he won't.'

Wicker arm-chairs in the shade of the plane-trees. Daniel was deep in very old, boring recollections: at Vichy, in 1920, he had sat dozing in a wicker arm-chair, under the great trees in the park, with the same courteous smile on his lips, his mother knitting by his side; now Marcelle was beside him knitting socks for the baby, and dreaming with unseeing eyes of the war. The great fly buzzed and buzzed, much time had passed since Vichy, that fly was still buzzing and the garden smelt of mint: behind them, in the hotel drawing-room, some-one was playing the piano, and had been doing so for twenty years – a hundred years. The hairs on his finger-joints bristled in the sunshine and a flicker of sunshine warmed a drain of coffee, and a little glittering reef of sugar left in the bottom of his cup. Daniel broke up the sugar, for the sheer pleasure of feeling it rasp beneath the spoon. The garden sloped gently down to the sluggish, tepid river; he breathed in the scent of sun-warmed plants, and caught sight of a *Revue des deux mondes,* which M. de Lestrange, a retired colonel, had left on a table beyond the stairway. Death, eternity, not to be escaped – the soft insinuating onset of eternity: green and viscous leaves overhead: the inevitable heap of early dead leaves. Émile, sole living figure in the landscape, was digging beneath the chest-nut trees. He was the son of the hotel-keeper; beside him, at the edge of the ditch, lay a grey tarpaulin sack. In the sack was Zizi, the dead dog. Émile was digging her grave; he was wearing a broad-brimmed straw hat, and the sweat glittered on his bare back. A coarse, commonplace lad, with a brutish face, like a rock with two horizontal, moss-grown fissures in place of eyes, seventeen years old, and already after the girls, he was the local billiards champion, and smoked cigars: but he was the undeserving possessor of a lovely body.

'Ah,' said Marcelle, 'if only I could believe you. . . .'

Of course. Of course she couldn't believe him. And yet what difference could war make to her? She would continue to grow big in some little country retreat. Why on earth doesn't she clear out – she's missing her siesta. The boy put his foot on the spade, and threw all his weight upon it: Daniel longed to lay his hands on the boy's sides and slide them gently upwards, like a masseur, while he went on digging – oh to feel the ripple of those dorsal muscles, to slip his fingers into the moist shadow of the armpits: his sweat smelt of thyme. He swallowed a mouthful of *marc*.

'It would be too lovely,' said Marcelle. 'But you see – mobilization has begun.'

'My dear Marcelle, you mustn't believe all you hear. The Home Fleet will make its usual trip into the North Sea, and two hundred thousand men will be mobilized in France. Hitler will mass four armoured divisions on the Czech frontier. After which these gentlemen, having satisfied their consciences, will have a quiet little talk round a table.'

Women's bodies, like rubber and boned meat, you can always get more than enough to fill your hands. But that lovely body demanded the touch of the sculptor, it ought to be reproduced in clay. Daniel sat up straight in his arm-chair, and fixed a glittering eye upon Marcelle. This won't do – I mustn't drift into that again. I'm too old for it now. I drink a glass of *marc*, I talk gravely about the forthcoming war, and my eyes linger on a bare, youthful back, a sinewy rump, and anything likely to amuse me on a summer afternoon. Let it come! Let war come at last, let it batter at my eyes and fill them with visions of tainted, wrecked, and bleeding bodies, save me from the eternal round, from those endless weak desires, from smiles, and greenery, and buzzing flies; a fiery geyser leaps into the sky, a flame that burns the face and eyes, and seems to tear the cheeks away: let it come at last – the nameless moment that revives no memory.

'But surely,' said Marcelle, in a tone of affectionate tolerance

– she hardly appreciated his political capacities – 'Germany can't draw back, can she? And we have reached the limit of concessions. What then?'

'Don't be afraid,' said Daniel bitterly. 'We shall make all the necessary concessions, there are no limits. So Germany can afford the luxury of a withdrawal – it would, indeed, figure as an act of generosity.'

Émile was now upright, wiping his forehead with the back of his hand, his armpit glistened in the sun, he looked up at the sky with a smile – a young god. A young god! Daniel clawed at the arm of his chair: How often, Oh Lord, how often had he said: A young god – as he looked at a boy in the sunshine. An elderly homosexual's stale patter: I *am* a paederast – he uttered the words, and words they too remained, they passed him by, and suddenly he thought: 'How could the war change anything?' He would find himself sitting on the slope of an embankment during a lull, listlessly eyeing the bare back of a young soldier digging, or searching for lice, and his practised lips would murmur automatically: 'A young god'. A man's self accompanies him everywhere.

'Anyway,' he said abruptly, 'man was born to trouble. Suppose war does come? We should put up with it somehow.'

'Oh Daniel!' Marcelle looked really shocked. 'How can you say such a thing? War would be . . . it would be dreadful.'

Words. Words.

'What is dreadful,' said Daniel with a smile, 'is the fact that nothing is ever very dreadful. There are no extremes.'

Marcelle looked at him with a faint air of surprise, her eyes were dull and red: 'She's getting sleepy,' thought Daniel with satisfaction.

'As regards moral suffering – yes. But, Daniel – there's physical suffering.'

'Ah!' said Daniel, wagging a finger at her. 'You are already thinking of the pain you'll have to bear. Well, wait and see: I fancy that too has been much exaggerated.'

Marcelle smiled at him, stifling a yawn.

'Come,' said Daniel getting up, 'the main thing is not to worry. You have nearly missed your siesta. You don't sleep enough: in your condition you need a lot of sleep.'

'Don't sleep enough!' said Marcelle, yawning and laughing

at the same time. 'On the contrary, I feel quite ashamed, I never read a book, I spend all day on my bed.'

Fortunately, thought Daniel, kissing her finger-tips. 'I bet,' he said, 'you haven't written to your mother.'

'That's true,' she said. 'I'm a bad girl.' She yawned and added: 'I'll do it before I go to sleep.'

'No,' said Daniel briskly. 'You go and rest. I'll drop her a line myself.'

'Oh, Daniel!' said Marcelle with confusion and delight; 'a line from her son-in-law – she'll be so proud.'

She walked rather unsteadily up the stairway; he returned and sat down in his arm-chair. He yawned, time passed, and then he became aware that he was listening to the piano. He looked at his watch: twenty-five minutes past three. Marcelle would come down at six for her walk before dinner. Two and a half hours ahead of me, he said to himself, not without disquiet. The trouble was that his solitude, in other days, was like the air he breathed, he made use of it without noticing. Now that it was allowed to him in spasms, he didn't know what to do with it. Worse still – I'm really less bored in the company of Marcelle. 'Well,' he said to himself, 'the choice was yours.' A little *marc* was left in the bottom of his glass, he drank it up. On that June evening when he had decided to marry her he had been in utter misery, he anticipated every kind of horror. And here was the result: from the wicker arm-chair, the acrid taste of *marc* in his mouth, to that naked back. War would be just the same. Horrors always come next day. Myself married, and a soldier. I come upon nothing but my own self. Scarcely that: a succession of small impulses, darting centrifugally here and there, but no focus. And yet *there is* a focus: that focus is my self, and the horror lies there. He looked up, the fly was buzzing at the level of his eyes, he brushed it away. Another escape. A wave of the hand and it was gone: but why bother about that fly? If I had been an insensible stone figure, incapable of sound and movement, blind and deaf, flies and earwigs and ladybirds would run up and down me, and I should stand, a fantastic, white-eyed statue, without a purpose, without a care: then I might have come face to face with myself. Not so as to accept myself – Heaven forbid! but becoming at last the pure object of my own hatred. A slash in his consciousness –

four notes of a polonaise, the gleam of that back, an itch in his thumb, and then he came down to earth. Why can't I *be* what I am, paederast, villain, coward, a loathsome object that doesn't even manage to exist. He set his knees together, laid his hands on his thighs, and he almost laughed aloud at the thought of how respectable he must look. He shrugged his shoulders: Idiot! He was sick of thinking what he looked like, sick of looking at himself; especially as, when I look at myself, I am two people. I want *to be*: in the unseeing darkness. To extinguish myself. Extinguish the inner eye. 'Extinguish.' To be a paederast, as an oak is an oak. The word rolled like thunder and reverberated through vast empty rooms. Away with words, they produced a swarm of trivial deferments, each proffering an encounter at the far end of himself. . . . Another slash – Daniel found another self, a bored and somnolent fellow with only two hours ahead of him, and trying to kill time. Why can't I be what they see, what Mathieu sees – and Ralph, with his filthy little mind? words should be brushed off like mosquitoes: he began to count, one, two – words came to him: a summer visitor's entertainment. He counted faster, he narrowed the links of the chain, and the words could no longer penetrate. Five, six, seven, eight, depths beneath the sea, an image of something squat and hideous, a denizen of those depths, a spider-crab, it was opening out, twenty-two, twenty-three, Daniel became aware that he was holding his breath, he exhaled, twenty-seven, twenty-eight, the boy was still digging, up above, on the surface: the image was now a gaping sore, an acrid mouth, and it was bleeding, it's myself, I *am* those parted lips, and the blood that bubbles through them, thirty-three, the image was familiar, and yet it had never appeared to him before. Away with images too: a strange, drawn out fear took hold of him. He must let himself slide, as one did when trying to sleep. But *I'm going to sleep!* He shook himself, and came to the surface. What a silence: the crushing, moribund silence, which he sought in vain within himself, was there, outside, and he felt afraid. The meagre sunshine scattering shifting circles on the ground, the river-ripple in the tree-tops, the boy's bare back – so near, so far away! – he felt so terribly alien that he set himself adrift once more, he slipped backwards, he could see the garden from below, like a diver looking upwards at the sky. Noiseless, voiceless – silence all around him, above, below: and himself, a little garrulous hiatus in the centre of that silence. One, two, three – away with words, let the silence of the garden pass, meet again and unify through me, let it steady my breath. Slowly, steadily, let each column of air crash like a piston on to the words struggling to life. Oh *to be*, like a tree, like the boy's back, like the moonlets flickering over the flushed earth. If I shut my eyes: but eyes reach too far, beyond the moment and the self, they are *there*, already, on the leaves, and the boy's back: the hunted, furtive, fleeting gaze, always ahead of itself, peers into the distance. But he dared not lower his eyelids: Émile no doubt was glancing up at him now and again – an elderly gentleman dozing after lunch: he might submit to the spell of an object, let the look linger and browse, absorb it, and then slip into his own depths, freed now from eyes, *in my enveloping night*: he fixed his eyes on the grass border on the left, which lay like a huge embodied motion, green and solidified: a wave poised at the moment of its fall, his distracted look, shifting from leaf to leaf, melted into that turmoil of plant-life. One (breathe in), two (breathe out), three (breathe in), four (breathe out). He spun round as he dropped and met, on his downward passage, a teeming desire to laugh. I'm doing a dervish act, mustn't swallow my tongue, it was overhead already, down he plunged, passing two dishevelled words – Fear, Defiance – re-ascending to the surface. Defiance hurled at the clear sky, he conceived it without a visual image and without words, it appears and opens like the mouth of a drain. Under the blue heaven, a bitter lament, a futile supplication. *Eli, Eli, lama sabacthani*, these were the last words he met, they darted up like dancing bubbles; beyond lay the green abundance of the grass-border, unseen, unnamed, a plenitude of presence in his vision, it comes, *it comes*. It clove him like a scythe, extraordinary, heartbreaking and pleasurable. At long last the husk bursts and opens, I am myself for all eternity, paederast, villain, coward. *I am seen*; no, not even that: *it sees* me. He was *the object* of a look. A look that searched him to the depths, pierced him like a knife-thrust, and was not his own look: an impenetrable look, the embodiment of night, awaiting him in his deepest self, and condemning him to be himself, coward, hypocrite, paederast, for all eternity. Himself, quivering beneath that look, and defying it. The look: and the night. As though the night was a look. I am *seen*. Transparent, transparent, transfixed. But by whom? *I am not alone*, said Daniel aloud. Émile stood up.

'What's the matter, M'sieur Sereno?' he asked.

'I was asking if you would soon have finished,' said Daniel.

'Getting on,' said Émile.

He stood for a moment eyeing Daniel with insolent curiosity. But, after all, it's a human look, a look that can be looked at. Daniel got up, trembling with fear.

'Don't you get tired when you dig in the sun?'

'I'm used to it,' said Émile.

He had an attractive chest, rather fleshy, with two pink points on it, and he leaned on his spade with a provocative air; in three strides . . . But here was this strange, strange joy, more intense than all the pleasures of the flesh; the Look.

'It's too hot,' said Daniel. 'I shall go in and rest for a bit.'

He nodded, and walked up the stairway. His mouth was dry but he had made up his mind: in his room, with curtains drawn and shutters closed, he would begin the experiment afresh.

Five-fifteen at Saint-Flour. Mme Hannequin accompanied her husband to the station; they had taken the steep short cut. M. Hannequin was wearing his sports suit, with the haversack slung over his shoulder: he had his new shoes on, and they pinched him. Half-way up they met Mme Calvé, who had stopped outside the notary's house to get her breath.

'Ah, my poor legs,' she said, as she caught sight of them. 'I'm getting old.'

'You're as active as ever,' said Mme Hannequin. 'I know very few people who can get up this path without stopping for a rest.'

'And where are you off to?' asked Mme Calvé.

'My poor Jeanne,' said Mme Hannequin. 'I'm seeing my husband off. He's been called up.'

'No!' said Mme Calvé. 'I didn't know! Well, well!' Monsieur Hannequin thought she was looking at him with particular interest: 'It must be hard,' she said, 'to have to go on such a lovely day.'

'Pooh, pooh,' said M. Hannequin.

'He's so brave,' said Mme Hannequin.

'That's right,' said Mme Calvé, smiling at Mme Hannequin. 'Just what I was saying yesterday to my husband: our Frenchmen will all go bravely.'

M. Hannequin felt young and bold.

'Well,' he said, 'we must be getting on.'

'We'll be seeing you again soon,' said Mme Calvé.

'I don't know about that,' said Mme Hannequin, shaking her head.

'Certainly you will,' said M. Hannequin emphatically.

They proceeded on their way, M. Hannequin walking briskly, until Mme Hannequin said:

'Gently, François, you know my heart is weak.'

They met Marie, whose son was doing his military service.

'Any message for your son, Marie? Perhaps I shall meet him: I'm a soldier again now.'

Marie looked dumbfounded. 'Jésus!' she said, clasping her hands together.

M. Hannequin waved to her, and they entered the station. Charlot was punching the tickets.

'Ah, Monsieur Hannequin,' said he, 'so it's the big bang this time, eh?'

'The Rum-tum-tum-Rati-da-da bang – drummed out to the rhythm of a rumba,' replied M. Hannequin, handing him his ticket.

M. Pineau, the notary, was on the platform. He shouted from where he stood: 'Off for a spree in Paris, eh?'

'Yes,' said M. Hannequin, 'or another sort of spree on the frontier.' And he added gravely, 'I'm called up.'

'So that's the story, eh?' said the notary. 'But you're a Form 2 man, aren't you?'

'Certainly!'

'Oh well,' said he, 'you'll soon be back: all this is just eyewash.'

'I'm not so sure,' replied M. Hannequin dryly. 'In diplomacy, you know, there are situations that start by being comic, and end in blood.'

'And . . . do you fancy fighting for the Czechs?'

'Czechs or not, it's always a mug's game fighting,' replied M. Hannequin.

They laughed, and waved farewell. The Paris train was just running into the station, but M. Pineau managed to kiss Mme Hannequin's hand.

M. Hannequin climbed unaided into his compartment. He flung his haversack into his reserved corner, came back into the corridor, pulled down the window and smiled at his wife.

'Peep-bo!' said he. 'I'm going to be comfortable. There's plenty of room. I'll be able to lie down to sleep, I hope.'

'A lot of people will get in at Clermont.'

'Yes, I'm afraid so.'

'Write to me,' she said. 'Just a line every day: it needn't be much.'

'Of course I will.'

'Don't forget to wear your flannel belts, just to please me.'

'I promise,' he said with a solemn smile.

He stood up, walked along the corridor, and came down on to the step.

'Give me a kiss, old girl,' he said.

He kissed her plump cheeks. She shed two tears.

'Oh dear!' she said. 'How upsetting it all is! And what's the sense of it?'

'You really mustn't talk like that, darling,' said he. 'Now please –'

They said no more. He smiled at her, she looked at him with a smile, still crying; they had nothing more to say to each other.

Five-fifty-two in Niort. The large clock-hand jerks forward every minute, oscillates, and stops. The train, and the station, are black with coal dust. She insisted on coming, from a sense of duty. I said: 'Don't bother to come.' She looked at me with a shocked expression: 'What do you mean, Georges? You don't know what you're saying.' I said: 'Don't stay too long, you mustn't leave the child alone.' She said: 'I'll ask Mother Cornu to look after her. I'll just see you on to the train and then go back.' And now, there she is, I lean out of the window and look at her. I want to smoke, but I don't like to, it doesn't seem quite decent. She looks towards the end of the platform, shading her eyes against the sunlight. And then from time to time she remembers I am there, and smiles; but she can't think of anything to say. In effect, I have already gone.

'Pillows, rugs, oranges, lemonade, sandwiches.'

'Georges!'

'Darling?'

'Would you like a few oranges?'

My haversack is cram full. But she wants to give me something, just because I'm going away. If I refuse, she'll be upset. I don't like oranges.

'No, thanks.'

'Not?'

'No really. But it's very nice of you.'

A pale smile. I have just kissed those cold, round, pretty cheeks, and the corner of that smile. And she kissed me, which makes me feel a little ashamed: why this fuss, in Heaven's name? Because I am going away? Others are going away too. True, they also are being kissed. Many pretty women stand, in the light of the setting sun, in all the smoke and soot, looking with a painted smile at a man leaning out of a carriage window. And then? We men must look a trifle ridiculous: she is too pretty, and too cold; I am too ugly.

'Write to me,' she said: she had said it before, but one must fill up time – 'as often as you can. It needn't be much. . . .'

It won't be. I shall have nothing to say. Nothing will happen to me, nothing ever does happen to me. Besides, I have already seen her reading letters: her intent, solemn, bored expression as she tilts her spectacles on to the end of her nose, reads to herself in an undertone, and manages to skip a line here and there.

'Well then, my poor darling, I'll say good-bye. Try to get a little sleep tonight.'

Ah well, something had to be said. But she knows I never sleep in trains. She'll soon be repeating all this to Mother Cornu: 'He got off all right, the train was packed. Poor Georges, I hope he'll get some sleep all the same.'

She looks round her with a despondent air: her large straw hat is a little on one side. A young man and a young woman have stopped near by.

'I must go away now: I can't leave the child any longer.' She says this in rather a loud tone, with her eyes on the youthful pair. They are a little awe-inspiring, being both so handsome. But they do not notice her.

'That's right, darling. Good-bye. Hurry back. I'll write as soon as possible.'

One small tear, however. Why – in Heaven's name, why? She hesitates. What if she suddenly reached out her arms and said to me – 'This is all a misunderstanding, I love you – I do love you.'

'Don't catch cold.'

'Of course not. Good-bye.'

She goes. A wave of the hand, a flash of her eyes, and she departs, slowly, swaying her lithe hips, five fifty-five. I don't want to smoke now. The young man and woman are still on the platform. He is carrying a haversack, and they have been talking about Nancy: he too has been called up. They have ceased to talk: they are looking at each other. And I look at their hands, good hands that wear no wedding-rings. The woman pale, tall, and slim, with a mop of black hair: he tall and fair, with a real golden skin, his bare arms emerging from a short-sleeved blue silk shirt. Doors are slammed, they do not hear: they no longer look at each other, they no longer need to, in their inmost selves they are together.

'Take your seats for Paris!'

She shivers, and says nothing. He does not kiss her, he clasps her lovely bare arms at the level of the shoulders, and slowly slides his hands down to the wrists. Thin, frail wrists. He seems to be gripping them with all his strength. She stands impassive, her arms inertly at her side, her face asleep.

'Take your seats.'

The train moves off, he jumps on to the step, and stays there clinging to the bars. She has turned towards him, the sun whitens her face, she blinks, and smiles. A broad, warm smile, confiding, calm, and tender: a man, however handsome and strong, oughtn't to carry away such a smile all to himself. She does not see me, she sees only him, she peers into the sunshine that she may see him for yet another moment. And now I smile at her, I return her smile. Six o'clock. The train has left the station, it comes out into the sunshine, all its windows glittering. She stays, a diminutive dark figure, on the platform. Handkerchiefs are waved all round her. She does not move, she waves no handkerchief, her arms hang down, but she smiles, as though her whole being were dissolving in that smile. She is, no doubt, still smiling, but her smile is no longer visible. She is visible. She is there, for him, for all those who are leaving, for me. My wife is back in our quiet house, sitting by the child, enveloped once more in silence and peace. I'm off now, poor Georges, he's gone, I hope he'll get some sleep, I'm going, I'm escaping into the sunshine, smiling steadily at a small dark figure still standing on the station platform.

Six-ten. Pitteaux was pacing up and down the rue Cassette, he had an appointment at six o'clock, he looked at his wrist-watch, ten minutes past six. I'll go up in five minutes. Five hundred and twenty-eight kilometres south-west of Paris, Georges, leaning on a window-bar, was gliding through the pasture-land, looking at the telegraph poles, sweating and smiling, Pitteaux said to himself: 'What trouble can he have been up to now, the little bastard?' He was suddenly seized by a desire to go up, ring the bell, and shout: 'Well, what's he done now? It's no affair of mine, anyway.' But he forced himself to turn. I'll go as far as that gas-lamp over there; he walked on, the main thing was not to seem too eager, he even reproached himself for having come, he should have replied, on headed paper, Madame – if you want to see me, I am at my office every day from ten to twelve o'clock. He turned his back on the street-lamp, and quickened his step unconsciously. Paris – five hundred and eighteen kilometres, Georges wiped his forehead, he was approaching Paris sideways, like a crab, Pitteaux thought: 'It's a dirty business'; he nearly ran, the length of the train behind him, turned into the rue de Rennes, entered No. 71, walked up to the third floor, and rang the bell: at six hundred and thirty-eight kilometres from Paris Hanne-quin was eyeing the legs of the lady next to him, fleshy, shapely legs in rather coarse rayon stockings. Pitteaux had rung the bell, he was waiting on the landing, wiping his fore-head, Georges was wiping his forehead, amid the clatter of the bogies, what had he been up to now, it's a dirty business, Pitteaux found it difficult to swallow, his empty stomach had begun to rumble, but he stood up straight, his head stiff set upon his shoulders, he dilated his nostrils and assumed his intimidating air, the door opened, Hannequin's train plunged into a tunnel, Pitteaux plunged into a cool and musty darkness, the maid said: 'Please come in,' a plump, perfumed little lady, with soft bare arms – the cool delicious softness of feminine flesh at forty, with a tuft of white in her black hair, dashed out at him, he could smell her ripe odour.

'Where is he?'

He bowed, she had been crying. Hannequin's neighbour uncrossed her legs, he glimpsed a patch of thigh above the garter, he assumed his intimidating air, and said: 'Who do you mean, madame?'

'Where is Philippe?' she said.

He felt quite moved, perhaps she was going to cry, and wave her lovely arms – a woman of her station would be sure to shave her armpits.

A male voice startled him, coming from the far end of the outer room.

'My dear, we are wasting our time. If Monsieur Pitteaux will kindly step into the study, we will tell him what has happened.'

Trapped! He went in, trembling with rage, he plunged into the white heat, the train emerged from the tunnel, a shaft of white light slipped into the compartment. They sat down, with their backs to the window, of course, while I am in the full light. Two of them.

'I am General Lacaze,' said the big man in uniform. He pointed to his neighbour, a very tall man of lugubrious aspect, and added:

'This is Monsieur Jardies, a doctor, and a mental specialist, who has been good enough to examine Philippe, and keep an eye on him during these last few weeks.'

Georges came back into his compartment, and sat down, a short dark-haired man leaned forward, and began to talk, he had a rather Spanish look about him: 'You've got your employer behind you, and very nice too – you clerks and officials don't need to worry. But I've no regular job, I'm a waiter, with nothing but my tips. You tell me it won't last long, that it's just bluff, and I dare say that's true, but supposing it lasts for two months – how is my wife going to live?'

'Philippe, my stepson,' said the general, 'left home without notice in the early hours of the morning. About ten o'clock his mother found this letter on the dining-room table.' He passed it across the writing-table, and said with an imperious air: 'Kindly read it.'

Pitteaux took the letter with repugnance, how well he knew that scraggly handwriting, full of erasures and blots, he would come and wait for hours on end, I used to hear him pacing to and fro, and then go off again, leaving scattered about the room, scraps of crumpled paper covered with that insect scrawl. Pitteaux scanned the writing without reading it, as though it had been a series of tiresome and too familiar comic strips – I wish I'd never met him.

'Darling mamma, this is the age of murder; I choose martyrdom. I suppose you will suffer: I hope I shall. Philippe.'

'The age of murder,' he said. 'Rimbaud's influence has worked appalling havoc.'

The general eyed him: 'We shall return to the question of influences later on,' he said. 'Do you know where my stepson is?'

'How should I know?'

'When did you see him last?'

'Aha,' thought Pitteaux, 'they're interrogating me.' He turned to Mme Lacaze and said in a friendly tone: 'I don't really know. A week ago, perhaps.'

'Did he inform you of his plans?'

'Certainly not,' said Pitteaux, smiling at the mother. 'You know Philippe, he acts on impulse. I am pretty sure that he didn't know yesterday evening what he was going to do this morning.'

'And since,' continued the general, 'did he write or telephone?'

Pitteaux hesitated, but the hand had moved, a docile and obsequious hand that found its way into his breast-pocket, then came the decision, and the hand produced a scrap of paper. Mme Lacaze snatched the paper, I could no longer control my hands. He still controlled his face, assumed his intimidating air, and raised one eyebrow.

'I received that this morning.'

'*Laetus et errabundus*,' read Mme Lacaze laboriously. 'For peace.'

The train rocked, the ship pitched, Pitteaux's stomach rumbled, he rose wearily to his feet. 'That means – the Gay Rover,' explained Pitteaux politely: 'it's the title of a poem by Verlaine.'

The psychiatrist flung a glance at him: 'A rather peculiar poem.'

'Is that all?' asked Mme Lacaze.

She turned the paper over in her fingers.

'Alas, yes, dear madam, that is all.'

He heard the general's rasping voice. 'What more do you want, my dear? The letter is perfectly clear, and I wonder why Monsieur Pitteaux should pretend to be ignorant of Philippe's intentions.'

Pitteaux turned abruptly towards him, looked at the uniform – not the face, the uniform – and the blood surged into his head.

'Sir,' said he, 'Philippe wrote me notes like this three or four times a week, until finally I decided to ignore them. Forgive me for saying that I have many other matters on my mind.'

'Monsieur Pitteaux,' said the general. 'Since 1937 you have been the editor of a review entitled the *Pacifist*, the policy of which is not merely antagonistic to war, but also to the French Army. You became acquainted with my stepson in October '37 in circumstances unknown to me, and you converted him to your ideas. Under your influence, he adopted an attitude which I, as an officer, could not accept, nor could his mother, because she is married to me; he took part in public demonstrations of a definitely anti-militarist character. And now he has left home, at the height of an international crisis, merely informing us in the note that you have read that he proposes to become a martyr in the cause of peace. You are thirty years old, Monsieur Pitteaux, and Philippe is not yet twenty, so you will not be surprised if I tell you that I hold you personally responsible for all that may happen to my stepson as a result of this escapade.'

'Well,' said Hannequin to the lady beside him, 'the fact is I have just been called up.' 'Oh dear,' said she. Georges glanced at the waiter, who looked a pleasant fellow, and he wanted to say to him: I have been called up too, but refrained, from a sort of modesty, the train vibrated terribly. 'There must be wheels just underneath me,' he thought.

'I *can't* take any sort of responsibility,' said Pitteaux in a categorical tone. 'I sympathize with your feelings, but for all that I refuse to figure as a scapegoat. Philippe Grésigne came to the office of the review in October '37 – that I shall not attempt to deny. He offered us a poem which we thought very promising, and we published it in our December issue. Since then he has often come to see us, and we did all we could to discourage him: he is much too highly strung for our work, and – to tell you the truth – we didn't know what to do with him.' (Sitting erect in his chair, he fixed a blue, embarrassing gaze on Pitteaux, he watched him drink and smoke, he watched his lips move, he did not smoke, he did not drink, from time to time he put a finger into his nose or a nail between his teeth, still eyeing him.)

'But where can he be?' exclaimed Mme Lacaze abruptly. 'Where can he be? And what is he doing? You talk about him as though he were dead.'

A silence followed. She was leaning forward, with a distraught, disdainful look upon her face: Pitteaux could see the base of her throat through the open-work blouse; the general, stiff-set in his chair, waited, allowing a few minutes' silence to a mother's natural distress. The psychiatrist looked at Mme Lacaze with an air of attentive, if slightly professional, sympathy. Then he wagged his large, melancholy head, turned to Pitteaux, and resumed hostilities.

'I will admit, Monsieur Pitteaux, that Philippe did not grasp all your ideas. Still, it is a fact that he was a very impressionable youth, and an ecstatic admirer of yours.'

'Is that my fault?'

'Perhaps it isn't. But you abused your influence.'

'Really!' said Pitteaux. 'In fact, since you have examined Philippe, you know he was a sick person.'

'I wouldn't go so far as that,' smiled the doctor. 'His family history was certainly not all that could be desired – on his father's side,' he added, with a glance at the general. 'But he wasn't altogether a psychopathic case. He was a solitary, maladjusted, lazy, self-absorbed young man. All sorts of tics and phobias, of course, with sexual obsessions

126

predominant. He came to see me fairly often latterly, and in the course of our talks he admitted – how can I put it? – you will excuse a doctor's bluntness,' he said to Mme Lacaze. 'Briefly – frequent and systematic masturbation. I am aware that many of my colleagues regard it merely as an effect, I consider it a cause, following Esquirol on this point. In short, he was going through the rather painful stage which M. Mendousse calls so aptly the crisis of adolescent eccentricity: he needed a guide. You have been a bad shepherd, Monsieur Pitteaux, a bad shepherd.'

Mme Lacaze appeared to be looking quite accidentally at Pitteaux, but that gaze was more than he could bear. Pitteaux turned frankly to the psychiatrist:

'I apologize for this in front of Madame Lacaze,' he said, 'but since you press me, I had better say quite plainly that I have always regarded Philippe as a complete degenerate. If he needed a guide, why didn't you take charge of him? It's your business.'

The psychiatrist smiled sadly, licked his lips, and sighed. She smiled, she was leaning against the cabin door, she shivered, and she smiled an alluring smile.

'Well, my dear,' said the captain. 'Come and see me again at nine, and I'll have some news for you and your friends.' He had clear, expressionless eyes, he was very red in the face, he stroked her breasts and neck, and added: 'Don't forget: this evening, nine o'clock sharp.'

'General Lacaze was kind enough to send me a few pages of Philippe's diary, and I thought it my duty to go through them. Monsieur Pitteaux, I gathered from what I read that you practised a sort of blackmail on this unhappy lad. Knowing how much he wanted to gain your esteem, you took advantage of that fact apparently, to ask certain services of him, not specified in his diary. During these latter weeks he had decided to rebel, and you treated him with such crushing contempt that you reduced him to despair.'

How much did they know? But anger prevailed, he smiled in response. Maud smiled and bowed, she was backing out into the corridor, as, with head and shoulders still in the warm and scented air of the cabin, she replied: 'Certainly, captain. At nine o'clock, then, I'll be here, captain.'

'Who reduced him to despair? Who was it that humiliated him every day? Was I the one who boxed his ears last Saturday at the dinner-table? Did I pretend he was ill, send him to a psychiatrist, and force him to answer humiliating questions?'

'Have you been called up too?' asked the waiter.

Georges smiled at him ruefully, but he ought to have talked, he ought to have answered the two young women's questions.

'No,' said he, 'I'm going to Paris on business.'

Mme Lacaze's shrill voice made him start: 'I won't hear another word. How you must despise him! A lad of twenty – whom you have deliberately corrupted – can't you even respect his mother? He may have drowned himself in the Seine, and you sit there trying to shift your responsibility on to someone else.'

'We are all to blame,' he said. 'You must not goad me in this way, that's what we all did to him.'

The general was red in the face: so was Maud:

'It's all right,' she said, 'they'll fetch our luggage into the second-class tonight.'

'Darling,' said France. 'Well, there you are, you made a lot of fuss, but it wasn't so difficult as all that.'

'Rose!' said he, without raising his voice, and fixing wooden eyes upon her. She shuddered, and looked at him with her mouth open:

'It's . . . loathsome,' she said, 'I feel utterly ashamed.'

He reached out a powerful hand, and clasped his wife's bare arm: again he said 'Rose' in a toneless voice. Mme Lacaze settled herself in her chair, she set her lips, shook her head, and seemed suddenly to awaken: she looked at the general, smiled: order was restored.

'I do not share my wife's apprehensions,' he said. 'My stepson left after stealing ten thousand francs from his mother's bureau. I don't think he is likely to make an attempt on his own life.'

A silence followed. The steamer was already beginning to roll; Pierre was feeling rather clammy, as he stood beside his bunk and opened his suitcase; it released the smell of lavender, dental cream, and American tobacco, which made him feel rather sick, and he remembered that the steward had said the crossing would be rough. The general pondered, the General's wife looked like a well-behaved child, Pitteaux was nonplussed, his stomach rumbled, and his head ached; up, and then down-wards, the planking quivered underfoot, the air was hot and sticky, he looked at the general, and didn't feel equal to hating him any more.

'Monsieur Pitteaux,' said the general, 'in concluding this interview, I consider that you can and *ought* to help us to find my stepson. Until now I have confined myself to notifying the various police-stations. But if, within forty-eight hours, Philippe has not been traced, my intention is to place the matter in the hands of my old friend the Public Prosecutor, and ask him at the same time whether the legal authorities would not do well to make some inquiry into the sources from which the *Pacifist* is financed.'

'I . . . of course I'll help you,' he said. 'Anyone can investi-gate the accounts of the *Pacifist*, we have nothing whatever to conceal.'

The steamer pitched heavily, with a sort of switchback motion: and he added, getting his words out with some difficulty: 'But I . . . I am not refusing to help you. On the single ground of humanity, general.'

The general bowed slightly: 'That is what I meant,' he said.

Gently, gently, almost imperceptibly, it rose, then fell, one couldn't help looking at the bunks or the wash-basin in the effort to catch the motion of something as it rose or fell, but nothing could be seen, except, from time to time, a slightly tilted dark blue band, level with the lower edge of the port-hole, which then vanished; it was a vivid, timid little move-ment, like the beating of a heart, and Pierre's heart beat in unison: for hours and hours it would continue thus – up, then down: Pierre's tongue felt like a large and juicy fruit inside his mouth; at each swallowing he could hear a faint cartilagi-nous crackle somewhere in his ears, there was an iron crown about his temples, and he kept on wanting to yawn. But he was not uneasy: no one really need be seasick. He had only to get up and take a turn on deck; he would recover, and this faint sense of nausea would be dispelled. 'I'll go and see Maud,' he said to himself. He dropped the suitcase, stood up straight beside his bunk, as though awakening from sleep. Just then the steamer rose and fell beneath his feet, but his stomach and his head were steady: Maud's disdainful eyes reappeared, and, with them, fear: and shame. I shall tell her I was ill – a touch of sunstroke, too much to drink. I *must* explain myself; he would talk, she would transfix him with those implacable eyes of hers – how wearisome it all was. He swallowed his saliva with an effort – it slid down his throat like a horrid silky ooze, a stale liquid had gathered in his mouth – so very wearisome, his ideas fled, his consciousness was possessed by a sense of something large and soft and out of reach, a desire to rise and fall rhythmically, to gently vomit, to fall back on to the pillow, ho-hup, ho-hup, without a thought in his head, adrift on this great heaving world: he saved himself in time: no one need be seasick. He recovered his whole self – stiff, unsympathetic, a coward, a despised lover, a forthcoming war-casualty, he recovered his clear, icy fear. He lifted his second suitcase from the upper bunk, put it on the lower one, and began to open it. He stood erect, not bending down, nor even looking at the suitcase, his numbed fingers fumbling blindly at the lock: is it worth the trouble? Is it worth putting up a fight? He would relapse into something large and soft, unvisited by thought or fear, he had merely to give way. 'I must go and see Maud.' He raised a hand and moved it through the air with a kind of soft and hesitant solemnity. Soft gestures, soft flutterings of my eyelashes, a soft taste at the back of my mouth, soft smells of lavender and dental paste, softly the steamer rises, softly she descends; he yawned, time slowed down, and melted into a syrupy haze: he need only pull himself together, and take a few steps in the fresh air. But *what for*? To feel his fear upon him once again? He swept the suitcase on to the floor and collapsed on the bed. Syrup: viscous, sticky, sugary syrup; he was no longer afraid, nor ashamed, it was delightful to be seasick.

He sat on the edge of the quay, his legs dangling above the water, he was tired, and he said: 'Marseilles wouldn't be so bad if there weren't so many houses.' Below him the boats stirred ever so slightly – small boats, lots of them, some with flowers, or adorned with rich red curtains and naked statues. He watched the boats, some pranced like goats, others lay motionless, he looked at the deep blue water and a great iron bridge in the distance: it is pleasant to look at distant objects, they soothe the mind. His eyes were smarting: he had slept under his truck, and men had come with lanterns, shone their lights on him, cursed him, and driven him away: after which he found a heap of sand, but sleep would not return. 'Where,' he asked himself: 'am I going to doss down tonight?' Surely there must be some nice spot with a bit of grass that would do. But one had to know them: he ought to have asked the Negro. He felt hungry, and got up, his knees were stiff, and creaked as he moved. 'I've got no more food,' he said to himself. 'I must find a restaurant.' He resumed his walk, he had walked all day, going in here and there to ask: 'Got a job for me?' and so on again: the Negro had said there were no jobs to be had. It is tiring to walk about in towns, the pavements are so hard. He crossed the quay slantwise, walking very slowly, looking to right and left to avoid the trams, their tinkling bells always made him jump. There were a lot of people about – quayside derelicts, hurrying along, and looking at their feet as though in search of something: when they bumped into him they apologized without even looking at him: he would have liked to speak to them, but they looked so brittle that he was nervous. He stepped on to the sidewalk, and eyed the cafés with their fine terraces, and then some restaurants, but did not go in: there were tablecloths on the tables, and tablecloths have a way of getting stained. He turned down a dark alley which smelt of urinals, and said to himself: 'But where on earth am I going to get something to eat?' and, at that very moment, he found what he wanted: in front of a small low-built house, stood a dozen or so wooden tables: each of them laid for two or four, and each with a small round lamp not intended to give much light, and no tablecloths. At one of these tables a gentleman was at dinner with a pleasant-looking lady. Gros-Louis sat down at the next table, and smiled at them. The lady eyed him gravely and shifted her chair back. Gros-Louis called the waitress, a pretty slim young girl, with a plump and distinctly gay behind.

'What can I have to eat, my dear?'

She was pretty, and smelt nice, but she didn't seem pleased to see him. She eyed him dubiously:

'There's the menu,' she said, pointing to a sheet of paper on the table.

'Thank you,' said Gros-Louis.

He picked up the paper and pretended to read it, but was afraid of holding it upside down. The waitress had moved off, she was talking to a man in the doorway. The man listened, nodding his head and looking at Gros-Louis. Then he left her, and approached Gros-Louis with a gloomy air.

'What do you want, my friend?' he asked.

'I want something to eat,' said Gros-Louis with astonishment. 'I expect you've got some soup and a bit of bacon.'

The gentleman shook his head gloomily: 'No,' he said, 'we have no soup.'

'I've got money,' said Gros-Louis. 'I'm not asking for credit.'

'I'm sure of that,' said the gentleman. 'But I think you've made a mistake. You won't be comfortable here, and you would be in the way.'

Gros-Louis looked at him: 'But isn't this a restaurant?' he asked.

'Of course,' said the landlord. 'But we have a certain sort of customer. . . . You had much better go to the other side of the Canebière, you will find all sorts of little restaurants that will be just what you want.'

Gros-Louis had got up. He looked perplexed, and scratched the top of his head. 'I've got money,' he said: 'I can show it to you.'

'Don't trouble,' said the man briskly: 'I'll take your word for it.'

He grasped him amicably by the arm, and led him a few steps along the street. 'Go in that direction; when you come out on to the quay, turn to the right, you can't go wrong.'

'You're very kind,' said Gros-Louis, touching his hat. He felt himself in fault.

He found himself back on the quay, among the little black men who ran against his legs, he walked very slowly for fear of overturning them, and felt sad: at that hour, he used to come down from the Canigou towards Villefranche, his flock trotting along in front of him, which made for company: he often met M. Pardoux on his way up to the Vétil farm, and M. Pardoux never passed without giving him a cigar and a couple of hearty thumps in the ribs, the mountains were crimson now and silent, at the far end of the valley rose the smoke of Villefranche. He was lost, all these people moved too fast, he could only see the tops of their heads or the crowns of their hats, they were a puny race. An urchin darted against his legs, grinned up at him, and said to his small companion: 'Look at him – he must be pretty bored up there all by himself.'

Gros-Louis watched them run, and felt at fault once more: he was ashamed of being so tall. 'Well,' he said to himself, 'I suppose they have their little ways', and leaned against the wall. He felt sad, and rather subdued – almost as sad as on the day when he had been ill. He thought of the Negro, so polite and cheerful, his only friend, and he said: 'I oughtn't to have let him go.' Then, suddenly, a bright idea came into his head: a Negro can be seen from far away, and can't be difficult to find: he set off once more, feeling less solitary, and looking out for the Negro. 'I'll stand him a drink,' he said to himself.

All the women were out on the square, their faces reddened by the setting sun; Jeanne, Ursule, the Clapot sisters, Marie, and all the rest. They had begun by waiting at home, and then as the hours passed they had returned to the square, one by one, and stood waiting. Through the smudged windows they saw the first lamps lit in the widow Tremblin's café, three nebulous patches against the upper panes. And they felt depressed: Mother Tremblin had lit the lamps in her deserted café, she had sat down at a marble-topped table, she had put her workbasket on the said table, and, being a widow, was darning her cotton stockings quite composedly. But they – they stayed outside waiting for their men, they felt behind them the lengthening shadows of their empty houses and kitchens, and in front of them that long, hazardous road, leading to Caen. Marie looked up at the church clock, and said to Ursule:

'It will soon be nine o'clock, perhaps they've been kept there all the same.' The mayor had said that couldn't have happened, but what did he know, he was just as ignorant of what went on in towns as they were. Was it likely that a lot of strapping lads come to join up would be sent back home? Perhaps the reply had been: 'Well, since you *are* here – ' and they had been told to stay. Little Rose ran up, out of breath, crying: 'Here they are! Here they are!' and all the women began to run too: they ran as far as the Darbois farm, from which a stretch of road was visible; they saw the men on the white road, between the meadows, on their carts in single file, as they had gone, returning slowly, singing, Chapin was at their head, huddled on his seat, asleep, barely grasping the reins, the horse was walking on mechanically. Marie noticed he had a black eye; he had been fighting again. Behind him, standing on his cart, the Renard boy was singing at the top of his voice, but not looking particularly merry, the others came behind, black now against the clear sky. Marie turned to one of the Clapot sisters and said: 'They're drunk – that's all we need.' Chapin's cart creaked slowly on, and the women fell back to let it pass. As it came by Louise Chapin shrieked: 'My God, he's only brought one animal back, what has he done with the other – he must have sold it to buy drink.' The Renard boy was singing at the top of his voice, zigzagging his cart from one ditch to the other, and others behind him were standing in their carts and singing, whip in hand. Marie saw her husband, he did not look drunk, but when she saw his surly face near to she realized that he was fighting drunk. 'Worse than a beast,' she thought despondently. But she was glad he had come back, the work on the farm was heavy, and it was better that he should beat her up now and again, on Saturdays, and be there to do his job. He had dropped on to a chair outside a small café and asked for red wine, he was given white in a small glass, he became conscious of his legs, stretched them out under the table and began to wriggle his toes inside his shoes: 'It's a fair do,' he said. He drank, and said: 'I've looked for him everywhere.' He would have sat him down opposite, just for the pleasure of looking at his genial black head: they had enjoyed some good laughs together – the Negro had the confiding, gentle look of an animal. 'I'll stand him smokes and wine.'

His neighbour eyed him: thinks me odd because I'm talking to myself; a stunted, sickly-looking lad of about twenty, with a girlish skin, and beside him a dark-haired, rather handsome fellow with a broken nose, hairy ears, and an anchor tattooed on his left forearm. Gros-Louis realized that they were talking about him, in a lingo of their own. He smiled at them and called the waiter.

'Another glass of the same, my lad. And if you've got any bigger glasses, you can bring one.'

The waiter did not move, nor did he say anything, but he

eyed Gros-Louis with a knowing look. Gros-Louis took out his pocket-book and laid it on the table.

'What's the matter, my lad? Think I can't pay? Here!'

He produced three thousand-franc notes, and held them under the man's nose.

'What about that? Now go and get me another glass of that muck of yours.'

He replaced his pocket-book and noticed that the curly-haired lad was smiling at him politely.

'You're flush,' said the lad.

'Eh?'

'Everything all right?'

'Quite all right. I'm looking for my Negro.'

'You don't come from hereabouts?'

'No,' laughed Gros-Louis. 'I don't. Have a drink?'

'I don't mind if I do,' said curly-hair. 'Can I bring my pal?'

He said a few words to his companion, in their own lingo. The man smiled, and got up in silence. They came and sat down opposite Gros-Louis. The lad smelt of scent.

'You smell like a tart,' said Gros-Louis.

'I've just had my hair cut.'

'So that's it. What's your name?'

'Mario,' said the lad: 'my pal's an Italian. His name's Starace: we're sailors.'

Starace laughed, and nodded.

'He doesn't know any French, but he's a scream,' said Mario. 'Do you know Italian?'

'No,' said Gros-Louis.

'Never mind, you'll see: he's a scream.'

They spoke to each other, in Italian. It was a very pretty language, they sounded as though they were singing. Gros-Louis was glad of their company, but he still felt solitary.

'What will you have?'

'*Pastis,* I think,' said Mario.

'Three *pastis,*' said Gros-Louis. 'What is it – wine?'

'No – much better than wine; you'll see.'

The waiter poured some liquid into three glasses, Mario added water, and the liquid was transformed into a white, swirling mist.

'Here's to you,' said Mario.

He drank noisily and wiped his mouth with his sleeve. Gros-Louis drank also: not bad – it smelt of aniseed.

'Watch Starace, he'll make you laugh,' said Mario.

Starace squinted, screwed up his nose, thrust out his lips, and waggled his ears like a rabbit. Gros-Louis did laugh, but he felt shocked and uneasy: he did not like Starace. Mario laughed till the tears came into his eyes.

'I warned you,' he said, still laughing. 'He's a scream, that's what he is. Now he'll do the saucer trick for you.'

Starace set his glass on the table, grasped his saucer in his broad palm, and three times in succession slid his left hand over his right hand. At the third time the saucer vanished. Taking advantage of Gros-Louis's surprise, Starace slipped a hand between his knees, Gros-Louis felt something scrape against his legs, and the hand reappeared holding the saucer. Gros-Louis laughed in moderation, while Mario slapped his thighs, weeping with delight.

'You old bastard,' said Mario between two hiccups. 'And he'll make you laugh a few times more before he's done.'

Gradually he grew calmer: when he had recovered his composure, a heavy silence fell on the three men. Gros-Louis found them tiresome, he wanted them to go away, but reflected that it would soon be dark, he would have to take to his wanderings again through the long, shadowed streets, searching forever for a place to eat in, and another place to sleep in, he felt depressed, and ordered another round of *pastis*. Mario leaned towards him, Gros-Louis inhaled his scent.

'So you don't come from here?' asked Mario.

'I don't, and I know no one here,' said Gros-Louis.

'The only chap I know I can't find. Unless you know him,' he said after a moment's reflection. 'It's the Negro.'

Mario shook his head vaguely.

Suddenly he bent across to Gros-Louis, and looked at him with half-closed eyes: 'Marseilles is a place where you can have some fun,' he said. 'If you don't know Marseilles, you've never had any fun in your life.'

Gros-Louis did not answer. He had often had some fun at Villefranche. And in the brothels at Perpignan, during his military service: and he had enjoyed it. But he could not imagine having any fun in Marseilles.

'Don't you want a bit of fun?' asked Mario. 'Don't you like a turn with the girls?'

'That's not it,' said Gros-Louis. 'Just now I would sooner eat. If you know a restaurant, I'll stand you a meal.'

As night fell solids tended to evaporate, leaving vague gaseous masses, sombre mists: she walked quickly, with head bent and hunched shoulders, afraid of bumping into a coil of rope, she kept close to the wall: she longed to let the night consume her, to dissolve into a drifting patch of vapour in that enveloping haze, and slither overboard. But she knew that her white dress was a beacon-light. She crossed the second-class deck, she heard no sound except the endless lamentation of the sea: but on every side of her, still, silent men stood out against the flat shadow of the sea, and they had eyes: from time to time a shaft of fire pierced the night, reddened a face, the eyes gleamed, looked at her, and vanished – she longed to die.

She had to go down a stairway, cross the third-class deck, climb another stairway, steep as a ladder and painted white: if I'm seen, there can't be any doubt, his cabin is up there, quite isolated: the man has his job to do, he can't keep me all night. She was afraid he might get a taste for the amusement, and send a steward to look for her every evening in the saloon, as the Greek captain had done, but no, I'm much too thin for a fat old fellow like that, he'll be disappointed with such a bag of bones. She didn't need to knock, the door was ajar, he was waiting in the dark, and said:

'Come in, little lady.'

She paused, with a choking sensation in her throat: a hand drew her into the cabin, and the door closed. She was suddenly crushed against a great paunch, and an elderly mouth that smelt of cork fastened on to hers. She did not resist, she thought with proud resignation: 'It's my job, it's part of my job.' The captain pressed the switch, and a head emerged from the shadow, the whites of his eyes were moist and bluish, there was a red speck in the left eye. She drew back with a smile: it was all much more difficult now the lights had been turned on: hitherto she had pictured him in the mass, but now he existed down to the minutest details, she was going to make love with a unique individual, as were all individuals, and this night would be unique, as were all nights, a night of unique and irreparable love, irreparably lost. Maud smiled and said: 'Wait a bit, captain, you're in such a hurry: we must get to know each other first.'

What's this? He raised himself uneasily on one elbow: the ship seemed still. He gave three or four belches, one of them extremely violent, passing through his nose, he felt limp and exhausted, but clear in the head. 'What's happening?' he thought. And suddenly he found himself sitting on his bunk, his head encircled with an iron band, and the already too familiar anguish eating at his heart. Time, a relentless, jerky mechanism, had resumed its progress, every second rent him like the tooth of a saw, every second brought him nearer to Marseilles, and the grey land where he was going to die. Again the world was there, around his cabin, the terrible world of railway stations, smoke, uniforms, devastated countryside, a world where he could not live, and which he could not leave; and a muddy hole awaiting him in Flanders. A coward, son of an officer, and afraid of war: he loathed himself. And yet he clung desperately to life. Which was even more repellent: it's not for what I stand for that I want to live; it's – for nothing: just to be alive. He would do anything to save his skin – run away, plead for mercy, or betray his cause, and yet he didn't attach so much importance to his skin. He got up: what am I to say to her? Tell her I had a touch of sunstroke, an attack of malaria: that I wasn't normal. He walked unsteadily up to the mirror: he was as yellow as a lemon. That settles it: I can't even depend on my face. And I suppose I smell of vomit into the bargain. He dabbed some eau de Cologne on his face and gargled with Bottot water. What a business, he thought with irritation. It's certainly the first time I've worried about what a tart might think of me. A semi-prostitute, a dance-hall violinist; and I've had married women, mothers – most of them. But she's got me, he thought, as he slipped on his jacket: she *knows*.

He opened the door and went out: the captain was stark naked, his skin was waxen and glossy, hairless except for some on his chest, the rest must have dropped out from old age, and when he laughed, he looked like an overgrown, mischievous baby. Maud touched his great polished thighs with the tips of

138

her fingers, he quivered and said: 'You're tickling me.'

He knew the number of the cabin: 27 – down one corridor on the right, another on the left, a sound of heavy rhythmic knocking against the bulkhead: ah, here was No. 27. A young woman lay prostrate on her back, as pallid as a corpse; an old lady was sitting on a bunk, her eyes red and swollen, and eating a cheese sandwich.

'Oh!' said she, 'the three ladies? They were so nice. But they've gone – they moved to the second-class: I shall miss them.'

He eyed her with surprise, and he laid a hand on her hip: 'You've a nice figure, with a pretty little face, but you're so thin!'

She laughed: when anyone touched her hip it made her laugh. 'Don't you like thin women, captain?'

'I wouldn't say I disliked them – not by any means,' he hurriedly replied.

He ran up the companionway: he *must* see Maud. At the moment he was in the second-class corridor, a pleasant carpeted corridor, the doors and walls ripolined in blue-grey. He had a bit of luck: Ruby suddenly appeared, followed by a steward carrying her suitcases.

'Hullo,' said Pierre. 'Are you travelling second?'

'Yes,' said Ruby. 'France is afraid of being ill. So we agreed to move: when it's a matter of health, one must make sacrifices.'

'Where's Maud?'

Maud was lying on her side, the captain was stroking her behind with absent-minded courtesy: she felt dreadfully humiliated: 'If I'm not his type, he mustn't feel any obligation.' She slid a hand over his side by way of returning the compliment: it was old man's skin.

'Maud?' said Ruby in a shrill tone. 'I couldn't say. You know what she's like. I expect she felt she'd like to go and see the trimmers, or the captain, she adores sea-crossings, she always runs all over the ship.'

'Inquisitive little girl,' said the captain. He laughed, and gripped her wrist. 'I'll take you on a personally conducted tour,' said he. And his eyes lit up for the first time. Maud acquiesced, she was rather upset by the change of cabins, but after all he must get his due, she bitterly regretted that she was so thin, she felt she had cheated him: the captain smiled, dropped his eyes, looking quite modest and domestic, he grasped Maud's wrist and gently but firmly guided her hand: Maud didn't mind, she thought: 'It would be mean to refuse the one thing he wants, after all the trouble we have made, especially as he doesn't like thin women.'

'Thank you! Thank you very much!'

He bowed and resumed his journey – he *must* find Maud: she would be on deck. He climbed on to the second-class deck, it was dark and almost impossible to recognize people without looking right in their faces. I'm an idiot, I should have waited for her here: wherever she comes from, she must take this stairway. The captain had closed his eyes, with a calm and pious expression on his face that much appealed to Maud, her wrist was getting tired but she was glad to be giving him pleasure, besides she felt quite alone as she used to do when she was a little girl, and Grandpa Theveneur took her on his knees, and suddenly nodded off to sleep. Pierre looked at the sea, and thought, 'I'm a coward.' A fresh wind streamed over his cheeks, and ruffled his hair, he watched the sea rise and fall: he considered himself with astonishment and thought: 'Coward. I could never have believed it.' Coward beyond redemption. One day had been enough for him to discover his true character: but for these threats of war he would never have known it. If I had been born in 1860, for instance. He would have made his way through life with calm conviction: he would have been extremely severe on cowardice in others, and nothing – nothing would ever have revealed his true nature to him. No luck. One day, just one day. Now he knew, and he was alone. Cars and trains and boats forged ahead through that clear, resonant night, all converging in the direction of Paris, carrying young men like himself, unsleeping, peering out to sea, or flattening their noses against dark windows. It isn't fair, he thought. There are thousands, perhaps millions, of people who have lived in happier times, and never known limitations: they got the benefit of the doubt. Alfred de Vigny might have been a coward. And what about Musset, Sainte-Beuve, Baudelaire? They were lucky. Whereas I – he muttered, stamping his foot. She would never have known, she would have continued to look at me with her air of adoration, she would have lasted no longer than the rest, I should have got rid of her in three months. But now she knows: she knows. The bitch – she's got me.

It was dark outside, but the bar was so bright that Gros-Louis was dazzled. It looked particularly gay, being lit invisibly. A long red tube all round the ceiling, and another – a white one, provided the light: there were mirrors all round the room; in the mirror opposite Gros-Louis could see his own entire head, and the top of Starace's skull, but he couldn't see either Mario or Daisy, they were too short. He had paid for the meals and four rounds of *pastis*: he ordered brandies. They were sitting at the far end of the bar, opposite the counter, an excellent seat, enveloped in a loud and rather soothing restaurant din. Gros-Louis felt expansive, he wanted to get on the table and sing. But he couldn't sing. Then his eyes closed, he seemed to drop into a hole, and he felt overwhelmed, as though something awful had happened to him, opened his eyes again, and tried to remember what it was, the upshot being that nothing had happened to him at all. He was, in fact, feeling pretty well all right, a little annoyed, perhaps, but quite at ease: he had to make an effort to keep his eyes open. He had stretched his long legs out under the table, one between Mario's, the other between Starace's, his reflection in the mirror made him laugh, he tried to imitate Starace's grimace, but he couldn't squint or waggle his ears. Under the mirror sat a very nice little lady, smoking meditatively, she must have thought the grimace was meant for her, she put her tongue out at him, gripped her right wrist in her left hand, clenched her right hand, and turned it round and back again, grinning all the while. Gros-Louis felt abashed and looked away, he was afraid he had hurt her feelings.

Daisy, a plump and warm little person, was sitting at his side. But she paid no attention to him. She smelt nice, she was plastered with paint, and her breasts were alluring, but he liked girls who laughed a bit and teased you – blew in your ear, and looked demure while they whispered dirty stories that you didn't quite understand. Daisy was rather intense: she was talking earnestly to Mario about the war.

'Well,' she said: 'we shall fight. If we must, we shall.'

Starace was sitting very straight in his chair, opposite Daisy; he seemed to be listening, but that was mere politeness, as he could not understand her. Gros-Louis rather liked him, because he kept quiet and never lost his temper. Mario looked at Daisy with a knowledgeable air, nodded his head, and said: 'I dare say you're right.' But he did not look convinced.

'I prefer war to strikes,' said Daisy. 'Don't you? Remember what the dockers' strike cost – it made a difference to everybody.'

'I wonder,' said Mario.

Daisy was talking eagerly, and looking despondent: she wagged her head as she went on: 'There won't be any strikes during the war,' she said severely. 'Everybody will work. Aha! You ought to have seen the ships in '17, but you were a kid then. I was a kid too, but I can remember them. It was a grand spree, you could see lights as far as the Estagne. And all the faces in the streets – it might have been anywhere in the world, and how proud we all were: and the queues in the rue Boutherille – English, Americans, Italians, Germans, even Hindu, I tell you! My old mother made a pretty packet.'

'There weren't any Germans,' said Mario; 'we were at war with Germany.'

'I tell you there were Germans,' said Daisy. 'And still in uniform, with a badge on their caps. You don't think I saw them?'

'We were at war with them,' said Mario.

Daisy shrugged her shoulders. 'Of course we were, but up in the north. These fellows didn't come from the trenches; they came by sea, to do business.'

A tall girl passed, as fat and fair as butter, but she also looked far too serious. Gros-Louis thought: 'It's living in a town that makes them look like that.' She leaned over Daisy in apparent indignation: 'Well, I don't like war, let me tell you. I'm fed up to here with the war, and my brother fought in the '14 War, do you want him to fight again? And my uncle's farm was burnt down. What about it, eh?'

Daisy was disconcerted for a moment, but promptly recovered herself.

'So you prefer strikes?' she said. 'Then you should say so.'

Mario eyed the tall blonde, and she departed in silence,

shaking her head as she went. She sat down near by, and began to talk eagerly to a gloomy little man who was chewing a straw. She pointed to Daisy, and went on talking with astonishing speed. The little man did not reply, he went on chewing and did not even look as if he heard what she said.

'She comes from Sedan,' explained Mario.

'Where's that?' asked Daisy.

'Up north.'

She shrugged her shoulders. 'Well, then, what's she making such a fuss about? They're used to it up there.'

Gros-Louis yawned heavily, and tears trickled down his cheeks. He was bored, but quite contented at the moment, he liked yawning. Mario threw a rapid glance at him. Starace yawned too.

'Our chum's getting restive,' said Mario, indicating Gros-Louis. 'Be nice to him, Daisy.'

Daisy turned to Gros-Louis and put an arm round his neck. She no longer looked serious.

'Getting bored, ducky – with a fine strapping lass beside you?'

Gros-Louis was just about to reply when he caught sight of the Negro. He was standing at the counter, drinking a yellow liquid out of a large glass. He was wearing a green suit, and a straw hat with a multicoloured ribbon. 'Aha,' said Gros-Louis. He looked at the Negro and was happy.

'What's the matter,' asked Daisy in astonishment.

He turned his head towards her, then towards Starace, and looked at them with amazement. He was ashamed to be in their company. He shook his shoulders to rid himself of Daisy's arm. The Negro was drinking, and Gros-Louis laughed with pleasure. Daisy said sharply across his back: 'What's up with the old stick? He hurt me.' But Gros-Louis didn't care: he was rescued from Mario and Starace. He raised his right hand over the Negro, and give him a great thump between the shoulder-blades. The Negro nearly choked: he coughed and spat, and then turned upon Gros-Louis with a look of fury.

'It's me,' said Gros-Louis.

'Who the hell do you think you are?' yelled the Negro.

'Don't you see it's me?' repeated Gros-Louis.

'I don't know you,' said the Negro.

Gros-Louis looked sadly at the Negro: 'Don't you remember? We met yesterday, you'd been swimming.'

The Negro was still coughing and spitting. Starace and Mario had got up, and were standing on each side of Gros-Louis. 'Aren't they ever going to let me alone?' thought Gros-Louis wrathfully. Mario tugged him gently by the sleeve.

'Come along,' he said. 'You see he doesn't like you.'

'It's my Negro,' said Gros-Louis, in a threatening tone.

'Take him away,' said the Negro, 'and put him to bed.'

Gros-Louis looked at the Negro, and felt unhappy: it was certainly him, looking very festive in his fine straw hat. Why was he so forgetful and so rude?

'I stood you a drink,' he said.

'Come on,' repeated Mario. 'It isn't your Negro: they all look alike.'

Gros-Louis clenched his fists and turned to Mario: 'Get out of this. It's no business of yours.'

Mario stepped back.

'All Negroes look alike,' he said uneasily.

Gros-Louis had raised his fist when the door opened and a second Negro appeared, exactly like the first, in a stiff straw hat and a pink suit. He glanced at Gros-Louis, crossed the room with rather a mincing gait, and sat down with his elbows on the counter. Gros-Louis rubbed his eyes, looked at the two Negroes in turn, and burst out laughing.

'Looks like the same chap twice,' he said.

Mario approached him. 'You see – I was right.'

Gros-Louis was bewildered. He didn't much like Starace, nor Mario, but he felt he had been unfair to them. He took them by the arm: 'I thought it was my Negro,' he explained.

The Negro turned his back, and took another drink. Mario looked at Starace, then they both turned towards Daisy. Daisy was standing up, her hands on her hips waiting for them. She didn't look too pleased.

'Ha!' said Mario.

'Ha!' said Starace.

They swung round, each seized Gros-Louis by an arm, and led him away.

'We'll go and look for your Negro,' said Mario.

The street was narrow and empty, and smelt of cabbage. Stars were visible above the rooftops. 'They're all alike,' thought Gros-Louis gloomily. 'Are there many of them in Marseilles?' he asked.

'Many what, mate?'

'Negroes.'

'A good few,' said Mario with a nod. 'I must be drunk,' thought Gros-Louis. I'll help you, said the captain, I'll be your lady's maid. Mario put his arm round Gros-Louis's waist, the captain had picked up the cami-knickers by a suspender. Maud couldn't help laughing: 'You're holding them upside down!' Mario leaned forward, he gripped Gros-Louis by the waist, rubbed his head against his stomach, and said: 'You're my pal, isn't he, Starace? – you're my little old pal, and we love each other very much.' Starace laughed silently, his head turned round and round, his teeth gleamed, it was a nightmare, his head echoed with cries and lights, he was on his way to more noise and lights, they would stick by him all night, Starace's laugh, his brown face heaving up and down, Mario's weasel-mask, he felt sick, the sea rose and fell in Pierre's stomach, he knew that he would never find his Negro. Mario pushed him, Starace pulled him, the Negro was an angel, and I'm in hell. He said aloud: 'The Negro was an angel', and great tears rolled down his cheeks, Mario pushed, Starace pulled, they turned the corner of the street, Pierre closed his eyes, and nothing remained but the flicker of the street lamp on the pavement, and the foaming hiss of the water against the ship's side.

Shutters closed, windows closed, the place reeked of bugs and formalin. He bent over the passport, the candlelight shone on his crisp grey hair but the shadow of his skull fell across the table. 'Why doesn't he turn on the electric light, he'll ruin his eyes.' Philippe cleared his throat: he felt swamped in silence and anonymity. Back there I exist, I really do exist, I am secure, necessary, she can't swallow a mouthful – she's got a lump in her throat from so much crying, he is stunned; the menacing hand collapses, he wouldn't have believed me capable of such a thing, back there I have just come to life, and yet here I am, confronting this sedate little old man with the grey moustache, so utterly unaware of me. Here; *here!* Here – a humdrum presence amid the blind and deaf, I melt into the shadows: back there, under the lights of the candelabra, between the arm-chair and the sofa, I exist, I am a person. He tapped his foot on the floor, and the old man peered at him short-sightedly with dull, watering, tired eyes.

'Have you ever been to Spain?'

'Yes,' said Philippe. 'Three years ago.'

'This passport is no longer valid. It ought to have been renewed.'

'I know,' said Philippe impatiently.

'It's all the same to me. Can you speak Spanish?'

'Just as well as French.'

'If you get taken for a Spaniard you'll be lucky, with that straw-coloured hair of yours.'

'There are blond Spaniards.'

The old man shrugged his shoulders. 'I'm just telling you, you know . . .'

He turned the passport over absentmindedly, '*I* am *here*, visiting a forger.' It didn't seem true. Since that morning nothing seemed true. The forger looked more like a gendarme.

'You look like a gendarme.'

The old man did not reply: Philippe felt ill at ease. Insignificance: it had reappeared *here* – the transparent insignificance of yesterday, when I was passing through their looks, when I was a jolting sheet of glass on a glazier's back, and I was passing through the sunshine. *Back there* – now that I am as blank as a corpse, she will be saying: 'Where is he? What has he done? Is he thinking about me?' But this old creature doesn't look as if he knew that there's a place upon the earth where I am a precious possession.

'Well?' said Philippe.

The old man fixed his weary eyes upon him. 'I suppose it was Pitteaux who sent you?'

'That's the third time you've asked that question. Yes, it was Pitteaux,' said Philippe coolly.

'Right,' said the old man. 'I usually do the job for nothing: for you it will be three thousand francs.'

Philippe assumed Pitteaux's expression. 'I should hope so. I wasn't asking you to do a job for nothing.'

The old man grinned. My voice has a false ring, thought Philippe irritably. I haven't yet acquired a *natural* insolence. Especially towards older people. There's an old score of smacks in the face between them and myself which I must wipe out before I can speak to them on equal terms. But the last – he thought excitedly – the last to date is cancelled.

'There,' said he.

He produced his pocket-book, and laid three notes on the table.

'You young fool!' said the old man. 'Now I shall take them, and refuse to do the job.'

Philippe eyed him uneasily, and reached out a hand as though to pick them up again. The old man burst out laughing.

'I thought . . .' said Philippe.

The old man was still laughing, Philippe snatched his hand away, and smiled: 'I know my fellow-men,' he said. 'I *know* you wouldn't have done such a thing.'

The old man stopped laughing. He looked cheerfully malicious.

'You do, do you? Poor little sucker, you come here, having never seen me before, you produce the lolly and put it on the table – why you're fairly asking to be murdered! Go away, and leave me to get on with it. I'll take a thousand francs off you at once, in case you change your mind. Bring me the rest when you come for the papers.'

One more smack in the face, I shall pay them all back. Tears came into his eyes. He had the *right* to lose his temper, but his real feeling was astonishment. Why are they all so tough, they always have their weapons ready, they're always on the alert, at the slightest slip they're on to you. What have I done to this man or to the people back there in the blue drawing-room? I'll learn the rules of the game, I'll be tough too, I'll make them tremble.

'When will it be ready?'

'Tomorrow morning.'

'I thought . . . I didn't think it would take so long.'

'Indeed?' said the old man. 'What about the stamps – do you think I just invent them? Go away, and come back tomorrow morning, it will take me all night to do your job.'

Outside – the night, the loathsome, tepid night with all its monsters, footsteps pattering behind you, so you dare not turn

your head; night, at Saint-Ouen: a dangerous district.
'When may I come back?' said Philippe in a toneless voice.
'Any time after six o'clock.'
'Are there . . . are there any hotels round here?'
'Plenty in the avenue de Saint-Ouen. Now go.'
'I'll be back at six,' said Philippe decisively.

He picked up his suitcase, shut the door and went down-stairs. His tears gushed down on to the third-floor landing, he had forgotten to bring a handkerchief, so he wiped his eyes with his sleeve, sniffing once or twice; I'm not a coward. The old ruffian upstairs took him for a coward, his contempt pursued him like a stare. They're looking at me. Philippe hurried down the last flight. 'Door, please,' The door opened into murky tepid grey mess. Philippe plunged into the dishwater. I am not a coward. Only that loathsome old man thinks so. And he doesn't think so now – he said to himself emphatically. He's not thinking about me at all, he has started work. The look vanished. Philippe quickened his step. 'Well then, Philippe, you've got the wind up?' – 'I haven't got the wind up, I just *can't* . . .' 'You can't, Philippe, you can't . . .?' He had recoiled against the wall. Pitteaux stroked his chest and sides, fingered his nipples through his shirt, then tapped him on the mouth with two fingers of his right hand: 'Good-bye, Philippe, go away. I don't like cowards.' The street was alive with nocturnal statues – men leaning silently against the wall – they do not smoke, they stand motionless and watch you pass with eyes dimmed by the night. He was almost running now, his heart throbbing. 'With a face like that? Nonsense, you're a coward.' They'll see, they shall all see, he'll come there like the rest, he'll read my name and say: 'Well, for a little rich boy, that's not so bad.'

A slash of light on his right; a hotel. A waiter standing in the doorway, he had a squint: is he looking at me? Philippe slowed down, but took one step too many, and passed the door, now the waiter must be squinting at his back: he *could no longer* decently retrace his steps. The squinting wine-waiter, or the duel of the Cyclops. How's this for a Cyclops story? The Cyclops looks at himself in the glass one fine morning, feeling an itch above his cheekbones: another eye is growing beside the first! How appalling! The two eyes won't work simultaneously, of course, his first eye having got so used to functioning by itself. On the opposite pavement there was another hotel, the Hôtel de Concarneau, a small one-storied building. What about that? Suppose they ask for my papers, he thought. He didn't dare cross the road, he went straight on. I need guts for this sort of thing, and tonight the old man has taken all I've got: suddenly he caught sight of a hotel sign: 'Café: wines, liqueurs.' A drink would be a good idea. He pushed open the door.

It was a very small café, with a zinc counter and two tables, and the sawdust stuck to the soles of his shoes. The landlord eyed him dubiously. 'I'm too well dressed,' thought Philippe with annoyance.

'Brandy, please,' he said, walking up to the counter.

The landlord picked up a bottle with a small tin spout in its cork, and poured out the brandy, Philippe put down his suitcase and watched him with amusement: a thread of alcohol trickled from the spout: he looked as though he were watering vegetables. Philippe sipped a little, and thought: 'It *must* be bad stuff.' He never drank spirits, they tasted like burnt wine, and scorched his throat: he hurriedly set down the glass. The landlord looked at him. Was there irony in those placid eyes? Philippe picked up the glass again and raised it to his lips with a nonchalant air: his gullet was on fire, his eyes were moist, and he emptied the glass at a gulp. When he put down the glass he felt unconcerned, and a bit merry. 'Here,' he thought, 'is an opportunity for observation.' A fortnight before he had discovered that he had no powers of observation – I'm a poet, I don't analyse. From then on he tried to make inventories wherever he went – reckoning up the objects displayed in a shop window for instance.

He glanced round him – I'll begin with the top row of bottles behind the counter. Four bottles of Byrrh, one of Goudron, two of Noilly, and a pot of rum.

Someone had just come in. A workman in a cap. 'A proletarian,' thought Philippe. He had seldom had a chance of meeting one, but he thought about them a great deal. A strong but rather clumsy man of about thirty with long arms and bandy legs – obviously distorted by manual labour – with bristly yellow hairs under his nose: he was wearing a tricolour badge in his hat, and seemed distressed and agitated.

'A glass of white wine, quick, please.'

'We're closing,' said the landlord.

'You wouldn't refuse a drop of wine to a man just called up?' said the workman.

He spoke with a strained and husky voice, as though he had been shouting all day. And he added, blinking his right eye: 'I'm off tomorrow morning.'

The landlord picked up a glass and a bottle: 'Where are you going?' he asked, putting the glass down on the counter.

'Soissons,' said the man. 'I'm in Tanks.'

He raised the glass with a shaky hand, and some wine trickled on to the floor.

'We'll knock them out properly,' he said.

'Hm!' said the landlord.

'Like that,' said the man. He slammed his left fist twice on to the palm of his right hand.

'Well,' said the landlord. 'The brutes are pretty tough, you know.'

'Just like that, I tell you.'

He drank, clicked his tongue and began to sing. He seemed excited and weary: now and again his features sagged, his eyes closed, his lips drooped: but some relentless force seemed to lift his eyelids, and raise the corners of his mouth: he looked like the exhausted victim of a too prolonged celebration. He turned towards Philippe: 'Have you been called up?'

'I . . . not yet,' said Philippe, drawing back.

'What are you waiting for? We must smash them, you know.'

He was a proletarian: Philippe smiled, and forced himself to take a step towards him.

'I'll stand you a glass of white,' said the proletarian. 'Landlord – two glasses, one for yourself, and one for him: it's my round.'

'I'm not thirsty,' said the landlord severely. 'Besides, it's closing-time: I have to get up at four o'clock.'

But he pushed a glass towards Philippe.

'Here's to us all,' said the proletarian.

Philippe raised his glass. A few minutes ago in a forger's room, now clinking glasses at a zinc counter with a proletarian. If they could only see me!

'Your health,' said he.

'To victory,' said the proletarian.

Philippe looked at him with surprise: he was surely joking: workers stand for peace.

'You say it too,' said the worker: 'Say: To victory.' He looked sober and dissatisfied.

'I won't,' said Philippe.

'Why not?' said the man.

He clenched his fists. A belch cut short his words; he rolled his eyes, his jaw dropped, and his head swayed feebly.

'Go on,' said the landlord.

The proletarian had recovered himself, he thrust his face into Philippe's, he stank of wine. 'I won't drink to victory.'

'You won't? You're saying that to me? – to a soldier of '38?'

The proletarian grabbed him by the necktie and thrust him against the counter: 'You don't want to drink to it?'

What would Pitteaux do in my place?

'Look here,' said the landlord sternly. 'Do what he tells you: I don't want a row: and then get out: I have to get up at four o'clock.'

Philippe picked up his glass: 'To victory,' he muttered.

He drank, but his throat had so contracted that he could scarcely swallow. The man released him, and grinned complacently as he wiped his moustache with the back of his hand.

'He wouldn't drink to victory,' he explained to the landlord. 'I had to twist his necktie for him – by gosh, a little tyke like that shan't insult a '14 veteran.'

Philippe flung a two-franc piece on to the counter, picked up his suitcase and hurried to the door. The man was a soaker, he had to give in, Pitteaux would have given in: I'm not a coward.

'Hi, young fellow!'

The man had followed him out. Phillippe heard the landlord shutting the door and turning the key in the lock. He shivered: he felt as though he were shut in somewhere with this man.

'You aren't going to get away like that,' said the man. 'We're going to smash them, and we'll have another drink on it.'

He came up to Philippe and put an arm round his neck, Mario had taken Gros-Louis's arm and was squeezing it affectionately, it was hell, they marched along dark alleys, never stopping, Gros-Louis was exhausted, he felt sick, and his ears were buzzing.

'The fact is I'm in rather a hurry,' said Philippe.

'Where are we going?' said Gros-Louis.

'We're going to look for your Negro.'

'And no heel-taps next time. When I stand drinks, you've got to drink them, see?'

Gros-Louis looked at Mario and he was frightened. 'Tired, are you, mate?' said Mario. But his face had changed. Starace had taken his left arm, it was hell. He tried to free his right arm, but he felt a sharp pain in the elbow.

'Look here – you're breaking my arm,' he said.

Philippe dashed away and began to run. The man was a drunkard, there was no discredit in escaping from him. Starace suddenly dropped his arm, and stepped back. Gros-Louis half-turned to see what he was up to, but Mario clutched his arm, Philippe heard a voice behind him gasp: 'You dirty whore, dirty little bugger – afraid of me, are you? I'll give you something to be afraid of!' – 'What's the matter, old pal, what's the matter – aren't we friends any more?' 'They're going to kill me,' thought Gros-Louis, and fear froze him to the marrow, he seized Mario by the throat with his free hand and lifted him off the ground: but, at the same moment, his head was cloven to the chin, he let go of Mario and fell on to his knees, blood pouring over his eyebrows. He tried to steady himself by grabbing Mario's coat, but Mario jumped backwards, and Gros-Louis saw no more of him. He saw his Negro skimming over the ground, not looking in the least like other Negroes, approaching him with extended arms, laughing, Gros-Louis reached out his hands, a vast pain rang like a gong inside his head, he shouted – 'Help!' a second blow on the skull flung him face downwards in the gutter, Philippe ran and ran, Hôtel de Canada, he stopped, recovered his breath and looked behind him, he had shaken the man off. He retied his necktie, and walked with measured steps into the hotel.

Pitch and roll, pitch and roll. The oscillations of the ship ascended in spirals into his calves and thighs, and died away in dull vibrations into the pit of his stomach. But his head was clear. He belched sourly once or twice, and gripped the railing with both hands. Eleven o'clock; the sky swarmed with stars, a red glow flickered over the horizon: perhaps that is the vision that will visit me, and remain for ever, when I'm lying in a shell-hole with my jaw shot away, under a blinking sky. A dark, unruffled vision, a rustling of palms, and these presences of men, so far beyond that red glow in the darkness. He saw them, all in uniform, packed like herrings behind their beacon-light, gliding silently towards death. They looked at him in silence, the red glow slid over the waters, they slid with it, filed past Pierre and eyed him as they passed. He hated them, he felt solitary and defiant beneath the contemptuous eyes of night: and he shouted to them: I am right, I am right to be afraid, I am born to live, to *live*! and not to die: there's nothing worth dying for. She did not come: where could she be? He leaned over the empty between-decks. You bitch, I'll make you pay for keeping me waiting. He had slept with artists' models, mannequins, women with the loveliest figures, but this skinny little drab was the first woman he had desired so violently. It was nice to stroke her neck – and she adored it – just where the hair begins to grow, to watch the thrill rising from her belly to her head, to confuse those prim ideas of hers – I'll fuck you, I'll fuck you; I'll get inside your contempt and shatter it like a bubble; when you are full of me, when you cry, 'Darling Pierre,' and turn your eyes up, you won't look at me in that contemptuous way, nor call me coward.

'Good-bye, my dearest, dearest girl, good-bye, come back, come back!'

It was a whisper, and the wind scattered it. Pierre turned his head, and the air whistled into his ear. On the fore-deck a small lamp above the captain's cabin shone on a white dress ballooning in the wind. The white-clad woman walked slowly down the ladder holding the rail to steady herself against the wind and the motion of the ship; her dress, bellowing out, then flattening against her, looked like a striking clock. Then she vanished, she must be crossing the between-deck, the ship plunged into a trough, the sea towered above him, a heaving black and white expanse, then the ship laboured upwards again and the woman's head reappeared, she was climbing the companion-way on to the second-class deck. So that's why their cabin was changed. She was moist with perspiration and her hair rather dishevelled, she passed Pierre without seeing him, with her usual frank and grave expression.

'Bitch!' muttered Pierre. He felt engulfed in an absolute indifference, he no longer wanted her, nor did he want to live. The ship fell, fell to the bottom of the sea, Pierre fell, a limp and flaccid figure, fell with it, he hesitated for a moment, then his mouth filled with bile, he leaned over the black water and vomited.

'And now the registration form,' said the waiter.

Philippe put his suitcase down, picked up the pen and dipped it in the ink. The waiter watched him, his hands clasped behind his back. Was he stifling a yawn or a laugh? 'Just because I'm decently dressed,' thought Philippe angrily. Clothes was what caught their eyes, they saw no further. He wrote with a firm hand: Isidore Ducasse. Commercial Traveller.

'Show me my room,' he said to the waiter, looking him straight in the eye.

The waiter unhooked a large key from the board and they went upstairs one behind the other. The staircase was dark, lit by blue bulbs at infrequent intervals: the waiter's slippers flapped against the stone stairs. Behind one door a baby was crying: the place smelt of lavatories. 'It's a boarding-house,' thought Philippe. Boarding-house was a melancholy phrase which he often met with in realistic novels, and it always filled him with disgust.

'Here we are,' said the waiter, slipping the key into a lock.

It was a vast room with tiled floor: the walls were painted brown to half way, and from there a faded yellow up to the ceiling. One chair, one table, marooned in the centre of the room: two windows, a wash-basin that looked like a sink, a large bed against the wall. 'The nuptial bed has been moved into the kitchen,' thought Philippe.

The waiter did not go away. He said with a smile: 'That will be ten francs. I must ask you to pay for the room now.'

Philippe gave him twenty francs. 'Keep the change,' he said. 'And call me at half past five.'

The waiter did not seem impressed.

'Good night, monsieur, sleep well,' he said as he went out. Philippe stood for a moment listening. When the shuffle of slippers had died away on the stairs, he turned the key twice in the lock, shot the bolt, and set the table against the door. Then he put his suitcase on the table, and looked at it listlessly. The candelabra in the drawing-room was out, out too was the forger's candle: darkness had devoured everything. Darkness without a name. Only the long, bare room gleamed in the darkness, impersonal as night. Philippe looked at the table with a sort of numbed indifference. He yawned. And yet he was not sleepy: he felt drained. A forgotten fly awakening in winter when all the other flies are dead, and now without the strength to move. He looked at the suitcase and told himself he must open it, and get out his pyjamas. But his intentions froze inside his head, he could not even raise his arm. He looked at the suitcase, and at the wall, and thought: 'What's the use? What's the use of preventing myself from dying because that wall exists and faces me with its vile overbearing colours?' He was not even afraid now.

Hop – she rises! Hop – she falls! He was no longer afraid. The wash-basin, brimming with frothy liquid, rose and fell, he rose and fell, prostrate on his back, and he was no longer afraid. The steward will be furious because I've been sick on the floor, but I don't care. Everything around him was so soft – the liquid in his mouth, the smell of vomit, the lump in his throat, and his whole prostrate body; and the wheel that revolved and crushed his forehead, he saw it and was glad to see it – it was a taxi-wheel with a worn grey tyre. The wheel revolved, familiar thoughts revolved, but he didn't care – after all, he didn't need to care, in a week I shall be under fire in the Argonne, but I don't care, she despises me, she thinks me a coward, I don't care, what difference can that make to me *today*? I don't care, I think of nothing, I'm afraid of nothing, I blame myself for nothing.

Hop – she rises! Hop – she falls! It's a good feeling to give up caring.

Eleven o'clock, eleven strokes amidst silence. He reached out a hand, opened the suitcase, his right cheek was burning him like a torch; eleven o'clock, the candelabra had been relit, she was sitting in the arm-chair, a plump little person with

lovely bare arms, his cheek was burning, the torture was renewed, the hand lifted, the cheek burned, I'm not a coward –
I'm not a coward, he unfolded his pyjamas: eleven o'clock,
good night, mamma, I kissed the general's concubine on her
perfumed cheeks, I looked at her arms, I bowed to him; good
night – Father; good night – Philippe; good night – Philippe.
Only yesterday he thought with amazement: that was yesterday. But what have I done? What has happened since? I put
my pyjamas in my suitcase, I went out as on all other days, and
everything was changed: a rock has fallen on the road behind
me, and cut off my retreat. But when – *when* did this happen?
I took my suitcase, opened the door quietly, and walked
downstairs. . . . That was yesterday. She is sitting in the arm-
chair, he is standing in front of the fireplace, *yesterday*. The air
in the drawing-room is soft and limpid, I am Philippe Grésigne,
General Lacaze's stepson, Bachelor of Letters, poet-to-be,
yesterday, yesterday, yesterday and for ever. He had undressed
and slipped into his pyjamas: in a boarding-house these were
unfamiliar and tentative gestures which he had to learn. The
Rimbaud was in his suitcase, and he left it there, he did not
want to read. Only once – if she had only once believed me,
if she had put her lovely arms round my neck, and said: I
trust you, you are brave and will be strong, I should not have
gone away. She's a concubine, she used to bring the general's
fossil words into my room, and drop them there, they were
too heavy for her, they rolled under the bed, and I let them
accumulate there for five years: when the bed is shifted, they
will all be found – country, honour, virtue, family, all there in
the dust, I have not exploited one of them. He stood barefooted on the tiled floor and sneezed, I shall catch cold, the
switch was beside the door, he turned off the light and groped
his way into bed, he was afraid of treading on insects like the
enormous spider with tentacles as big as fingers that looked
like a severed hand, the trap-door spider, if there was one
here – was there one? He slipped between the sheets and the
bed creaked. His cheek burned like a torch in the night, a
crimson flame, he pressed it against the pillow. They were
going to bed, she has put on her pink lace nightdress. This
evening Philippe pictured the scene with less distress: this
evening he won't dare to touch her, he'll be ashamed, and she,

the concubine, certainly wouldn't allow him to, while her boy was dying of cold and hunger on the streets; she thinks of me, she pretends to sleep, she sees me, pale and resolute, with set lips and dry eyes, she sees me walking through the night beneath the stars. He isn't a coward, my boy isn't a coward, my little darling boy. If only I could be there, visible only to her, and drink those tears that trickle down her cheeks, and stroke those lovely arms – Mamma, my dear little Mamma.

The General is Chancellor said an eerie voice in his head. A small green triangle fell off the wall and began to revolve, the General is Chancellor.

The triangle revolved, it was Rimbaud, he expanded like a mushroom into a dry and scabby pustule, a boil on the cheek – to victory, *to victory*, TO VICTORY. I'm not a coward, cried Philippe, awakened with a start. He was sitting on the bed, bathed in sweat and looking straight in front of him, the sheet smelt of sulphur, what right have they to watch me? Clods! They judge me by their rules, and I will admit none but my own. Here's to my splendid orgies – Here's to my pride! I belong to a race of heroes. 'Alas,' he thought savagely: 'Not yet.' In time to come they will put a marble tablet on the wall of this hotel – Here Philippe Grésigne spent the night of 24-25 September 1938. But I shall be dead. A soft confused murmur passed beneath the door. The night faded away. He looked at it from the far future, through the eyes of the black-coated gentry who would be making speeches beneath the marble tablet. Every minute sped through the darkness, each a precious sacred minute, and already past. A time would come when this night would belong to a glorious past, like the nights of Maldoror, the nights of Rimbaud. My night, 'Zézette,' said a man's voice. Pride wavered; the past was shattered; behold the present. A key turned in the lock, his heart leapt within him. 'No, it's next-door.' He heard the door of the next room creak. 'There are two of them at least,' he thought: 'a woman and a man.'

They talked. Philippe could not hear all they said, but he gathered that the man's name was Maurice, which reassured him a little. He lay down again, stretched out his legs, and drew the sheet away from his chin for fear of catching the clap. A little flute-like chant began: a singular little chant.

'Don't cry,' said the man affectionately: 'don't cry, it's no good.'

He had a hot rasping voice, he attacked his words abruptly in jerks, they emerged from his gullet, sometimes in a rush, sometimes slowly, with a harsh and grating intonation: but together producing a gentle, melancholy hum. The flute-like chant gurgled into silence. He leans over her, he takes her by the shoulders. Philippe felt two strong hands upon his shoulders, and saw a face bent over his. A thin, brown, almost black, face, blue cheeks, a boxer's nose, a shapely, rather sardonic mouth, a Negro's mouth.

'Don't cry,' repeated the voice: 'darling, don't cry: take it easy.'

Philippe was now quite calm. He heard them moving to and fro – almost as though they're in my room. They dragged a heavy object across the floor. The bed, perhaps, or a trunk. Then the man removed his shoes.

'Next Sunday,' said Zézette.

Hers was a coarser but more attractive voice. He could visualize her less well: blonde, perhaps, with a pallid face, like Sonia in *Crime and Punishment*.

'Ah well . . .'

'Oh, Maurice, you have forgotten. We were to go to Corbeil, to see Jeanne.'

'You must go without me.'

'I shouldn't have the heart.'

They lowered their voices, Philippe could not understand what they were saying, but he felt happy because they were sad. These were proletarians. Genuine proletarians. The other had been just a sot and an oaf.

'Have you ever been to Nancy?' asked Zézette.

'Yes – a while ago.'

'What's it like?'

'Not a bad sort of place.'

'You must send me a lot of postcards. I want to be able to picture where you are.'

'They won't leave us there long, you know.'

A genuine proletarian. He didn't want war, and he wasn't thinking of victory: he went, with death in his soul, because he couldn't help it.

'Dear old boy,' said Zézette.

They fell silent. Philippe thought to himself: 'They are miserable', and soft tears moistened his cheeks. Sad, gentle angels. I'll go in, I'll hold out my hands to them, and say: 'I'm miserable too, for your sake. It's for your sake that I left my parents' house. For your sake, and for the sake of all those who must go and fight.' Maurice and I will stand on either side of her, and I shall say: 'I am the martyr of peace.' He closed his eyes contentedly: he was no longer alone, two sad angels peered over his shoulders. The recumbent martyr, like a stone effigy with two sad angels at his head, bearing palms in their hands. And they murmured – Dear old boy, don't go away, I love you; and another word, too, a sweet and precious word, which he had forgotten already, the most loving of all loving words, it revolved and burst into flame like a catherine wheel, and Philippe carried it off into his sleep.

'Gosh!' said Gros-Louis. 'Gosh!' He was sitting on the pavement: the pain in his head was unimaginable, every throb of it aroused fresh disbelief. 'Oh,' he exclaimed. 'Oh the dirty sods!' He lifted his hand to his cheek, it was moist and tingling – that must be blood. 'Well,' he said: 'I'd better bandage it. What's become of my bag?' He groped around him, and his hand came upon a hard object – a pocket-book. 'One of them must have dropped his pocket-book.' He picked it up and opened it – empty. He fumbled in his pocket, produced a sulphur match and struck it on the tarred road: it was his own pocket-book. 'Well,' he observed, 'that's a bit of all right.' His army book was still in the pocket of his jacket, but his pocket-book was empty. 'What's to be done now?' He was still groping round him, and he said: 'I shan't go to the police. That's not the thing to do.' He closed his eyes, and began to gasp: his head was hurting him so much that he wondered whether it hadn't been split. He fingered his skull cautiously, it seemed intact, but the hair had matted into sticky tufts, and if he pressed it he felt as though he were being pounded with a mallet. 'I won't go to the police,' he said. 'But what should I do?' His eyes were becoming accustomed to the half-light, he made out a dark mass a few yards away in the road. 'It's my bag.' He crawled towards it, unable to stand upright. 'What's this?' He had put his hand into a pool of liquid. 'They've broken my bottle,' he thought in utter misery. He picked up the bag; the canvas was soaked, the bottle was in fragments. 'That's the limit,' said Gros-Louis. He dropped the bag, sat down in the puddle of wine, and burst into tears: his sobs came through his nose and shook him, his skull felt as though it were bursting: he hadn't cried like this since the old woman died. Charles was quite naked, with his legs in the air, confronting six staff nurses, the greenest of whom flapped her wings and champed her jaws, which meant: Passed for service: Mathieu dwindled into a kind of globe, Marcelle was waiting for him, legs apart, Marcelle was a throwing-board, when Mathieu had become quite globular, Jacques threw him, he fell into the black rocket-hole, he fell into the war: war was raging, a bomb shattered the tiled floor and rolled to the foot of the bed, Ivich sat up again, the bomb blossomed into a bouquet of roses, from which Offenbach emerged. 'Don't go,' said Ivich, 'don't go and fight, or what will become of me?' Victory, Philippe charged with bayonet fixed and he shouted – victory! victory! here's to Victory! the twelve Tsars decamped, the Tsarina was rescued, he unloosed her bonds, she was naked, small, and plump, and she squinted: shrapnel and hand-grenades scurried full-speed at his colonel, Pierre grabbed them and put them in his knapsack, that was the order, but the fourth tried to fly away, and he caught it by the wing-sheath as it buzzed and struggled, the colonel looked at him, he lay prostrate, the shrapnel had blown his cheeks and gums away but his eyes remained, his wide, contemptuous eyes, Pierre fled at top speed, he was a deserter, a deserter, he ran through the desert, Maud said: 'Can I clear away?', Viguier was dead and stinking; Daniel took off his trousers, and thought: 'There are eyes upon me': he stood up to confront them, coward, paederast, and villain. They see me, they see me as I *am*. Hannequin could not sleep, he thought to himself: 'I've been called up', which seemed somehow odd – his neighbour's head weighed heavily on his shoulder, she smelt of hair and brilliantine, he dropped his arm and felt her thigh, which was pleasant, if a little tiring. He had fallen on his stomach, he no longer had any legs. 'Darling!' she cried – 'What are you talking about?' said a sleepy voice. 'I was dreaming,' said Odette. 'Go to sleep, darling, go to sleep.'

Philippe awoke with a start – no – it wasn't the crow of a cock, it was a soft and feminine moan, ah-h-h-h; he thought at first that she was crying, but no, he was familiar with that sound, he had often listened to it, with his ear glued to the door, pale with rage and cold. But this time it did not disgust him. It seemed quite novel and attractive: an angel's chant.

'Ah-h-h! – how I love you,' said Zézette, in a throaty voice. 'Ah-h-h . . . Oh . . . oh – oh!'

A silence followed. The dark-haired angel with the bitter mouth lay upon her with the full weight of his body. She was crushed, satiated. Philippe sat up abruptly, a sneer on his lips and his heart distraught with jealousy. None the less, he rather liked Zézette.

'Ha-a-a-h!'

He drew a deep breath: that was the sharp acknowledgement of consummation: they had finished. He heard some damp splashes: naked feet pattered over the tiled floor, the tap twittered like a bird on a branch, and the water-pipes began to gurgle. Zézette had returned to Maurice, fresh and clean, if rather chilly about the legs: the bed creaked, she had lain down in the hot damp bed, cuddled up close to him, and was inhaling the russet odour of his sweat.

'If you died, I should just kill myself.'

'Don't say that.'

'I should, Momo.'

'That would be a pity. You've knocked about a bit, and you're a worker; you enjoy your food, and making love; think of all that you would lose.'

'Only with you. With you,' said Zézette passionately. 'But you don't care, you're going away, you're perfectly happy.'

'No, I'm not happy,' said Maurice. 'I hate to go.'

He's going away! He'll take the train to Nancy, I shall never see them again, I shall never see his face, he will never know who I am. His feet clawed at the sheet: I must see them.

'If only you didn't have to go. . . .'

'Don't be silly,' said Maurice gently.

I must see them. He jumped out of bed. The spider was watching him, crouched beneath the bed, but he ran faster than the spider, pressed the switch, and it vanished in the light. I must see them. He put on his trousers, slipped his bare feet into his shoes and went out. The passage was lit by two blue bulbs. A sheet of grey paper had been pinned on to the door of No. 18, inscribed: 'Maurice Gounod.' Philippe leaned against the wall, his heart was pounding in his chest, and he was as breathless as if he had been running hard. *What can I do?* He reached out a hand and lightly touched the door: they were there, on the other side. *I don't ask anything, I simply want to see them.* He bent down, and peered through the keyhole. A breath of cold air on his eyeball made him blink, and he saw nothing: they had put out the light. *I must see them*, he said to himself, knocking on the door. No answer. His throat contracted, and he knocked louder.

'What is it?' said the voice: an abrupt, harsh voice, but it would change. The door would open and the voice would change. Philippe knocked: he could not speak.

'Well?' said the voice impatiently. 'Who's there?'

Philippe stopped knocking. He was out of breath. He drew a deep breath, and forced his voice through his tight throat.

'I want to speak to you,' he said.

A long silence. Philippe had almost gone away when he heard the sound of footsteps, then of breathing, just behind the door, and a click: the light had been switched on. The steps moved off, *he is putting on his trousers.* Philippe drew back, and stood with his back against the wall; he was afraid. The key turned in the lock, the door opened, and in the gap appeared a red and hairy head, with broad cheek-bones and a rather wrinkled skin. The man's eyes were clear and lashless: he looked at Philippe with comical amazement.

'You've come to the wrong room,' he said.

It was his voice, but in passing through that mouth it became unrecognizable.

'No I haven't,' said Philippe.

'Well, what do you want?'

Philippe looked at Maurice, and he thought: 'It's no good now.' But it was too late. He said: 'I want to speak to you.'

Maurice hesitated: Philippe realized that he was going to shut the door again, and leaned heavily against it.

'I want to speak to you,' he repeated.

'I don't know you,' said Maurice. His pale eyes were hard

and sly. He looked rather like a plumber come to repair the bathroom.

'What is it, Maurice? What does he want?' said Zézette's uneasy voice.

The voice was *real*: real too was the gentle unseen face. But Maurice's fleshy countenance was a vision in a dream. A nightmare. The voice was extinguished, and so was the mild face: Maurice's head emerged from the shadow massive, hard, and real.

'It's a bloke I've never seen,' said Maurice. 'I don't know what he wants.'

'I can be of use to you,' stammered Philippe.

Maurice surveyed him doubtfully. He *sees* my flannel trousers, thought Philippe, he sees my calf-leather shoes, he sees my black Russian pyjama-jacket.

'I ... I was in the next room,' he said, setting his back against the door. 'And I – I swear I can be of use to you.'

'Come back, Maurice,' cried Zézette. 'Tell him to go away.'

Maurice was still looking at Philippe. He pondered for a moment, then his surly face cleared a little: 'Did Émile send you?' he asked in a lowered voice.

Philippe averted his eyes. 'Yes,' he said, 'he did.'

'Well?'

Philippe shivered. 'I can't talk out here.'

'How did you get to know Émile?' asked Maurice dubiously.

'Let me come in,' pleaded Philippe. 'Why not let me in? I can't talk in this corridor.'

Maurice opened the door. 'All right,' he said. 'But not for more than five minutes, I'm sleepy.'

Philippe entered. The room was exactly like his own. But there were clothes on the chairs – stockings, and a pair of trousers, and a woman's shoes on the red-tiled floor near the bed, and on the table a gas-ring with a saucepan on it, smelling of cold fat. Zézette was sitting up in bed, she had thrown a fleecy mauve shawl round her shoulders. She was plain, with small, deep-set, sparkling eyes. She stared at Philippe with hostility. The door closed and he shivered.

'Well? What does Émile want?'

Philippe threw an agonized look at Maurice: he could no longer speak.

'Look here – be quick,' said Zézette angrily. 'He's going off tomorrow morning, this isn't the time to come and pester people.'

Philippe opened his mouth, and made a violent effort, but no sound came. He saw himself with their eyes, and he couldn't bear it.

'Don't you understand French?' said Zézette. 'I tell you he's going off tomorrow.'

Philippe turned to Maurice, and said in a strangled voice: 'You mustn't go.'

'Go where?'

'To the war.'

Maurice looked dumbfounded.

'He's a copper,' said Zézette shrilly.

Philippe stood limply looking at the red tiles, and felt almost pleasantly benumbed. Maurice gripped his shoulder and shook him.

'Look here – do you know Émile?'

Philippe did not answer. Maurice shook him roughly.

'Answer! I asked you if you knew Émile.'

Philippe raised despairing eyes to Maurice. 'I know an old man who produces false papers,' he said in a low quick voice.

Maurice released him abruptly. Philippe bent his head, and added, 'He'll make you some.'

There was a long silence, then Philippe heard Zézette's triumphant voice: 'What did I tell you – he's a police agent.'

He managed to raise his eyes, Maurice was looking at him savagely. He raised a large hairy hand, and Philippe leapt backwards.

'It's not true,' he said, lifting his elbow: 'it's not true. I have nothing to do with the police.'

'Then what the hell are you doing here?'

'I'm a pacifist,' said Philippe, on the point of tears.

'A pacifist!' repeated Maurice with stupefaction. 'Listen to the boy!' He scratched his head, then burst out laughing. 'A pacifist!' he said. 'Do you hear that, Zézette?'

Philippe shook. 'You mustn't laugh,' he said hoarsely. He bit his lips to hold back the tears, then added painfully, 'Even if you aren't a pacifist, you ought to respect me.'

'Respect you?' repeated Maurice. 'What on earth for?'

'I'm a deserter,' said Philippe with dignity. 'I suggest you should get some false papers, as I have done. I shall be in Switzerland the day after tomorrow.'

He looked Maurice straight in the face: Maurice was frowning, there was a Y-shaped wrinkle on his forehead, he seemed to be thinking.

'Come with me,' said Philippe. 'I've got enough money for two.'

Maurice eyed him with disgust. 'You little bastard!' he said. 'Look at his clothes, Zézette! I'm sure war revolts you, I'm sure you don't want to fight the Fascists. Oh no! – They keep your money safe, you rich little pimp.'

'I'm not a Fascist,' said Philippe.

'No – I suppose I am, eh?' said Maurice. 'Get out of here before I kick you out.'

It was Philippe's legs and feet that itched to run away. But he wouldn't run away. He forced his legs forward, he approached Maurice, he lowered the elbow that had risen in boyish self-defence. He eyed Maurice's chin: but he did not venture to look at those pale, lashless eyes. And he said: 'I shan't go away.'

They stood for a moment confronting each other, and then Philippe burst out: 'You're such brutes – the whole lot of you. I happened to hear you talking, and I hoped ... But you're just like the rest, you're unreachable. You damn everybody without even trying to understand: do you know who I am? It's *for your sake* I deserted: I could perfectly well have stayed at home, where I'm well fed and warm and comfortable, with servants to wait on me, but I threw it all up for your sake. And you are being packed off to the slaughter, you don't mind, you don't lift a finger, a rifle is shoved into your hands and you think you're heroes, and if anyone protests, you call him a plutocrat, and a Fascist, and a coward, because he doesn't do as everybody else does. I'm not a coward, that's where you're wrong. I'm not a Fascist, and it isn't my fault if I'm rich. After all it's much easier to be poor.'

'You'd better get out,' said Maurice in a toneless voice: 'I don't much like this kind of claptrap, and I might get angry.'

'I won't go away,' said Philippe stamping on the floor. 'I'm sick of the whole thing. I'm sick of all these people who pretend not to see me, or look down their noses at me – what right have they, I'd like to know? I exist, don't I? – I'm as good as you are! I won't go away, I shall stay all night if I like, I'm going to explain what it all means.'

'Oh! So you won't go away, won't you?' said Maurice.

He gripped him by the shoulders and pushed him towards the door: Philippe tried to resist, but in vain: Maurice was as strong as an ox.

'Let me go!' cried Philippe. 'Let me go! If you put me out, I shall stay outside your door and make a row, I'm not a coward, you must listen to me. Let me go, you bully,' he said, and kicked him several times.

He saw Maurice's lifted hand, and his heart stopped:

'No!' he cried, 'no!'

Maurice struck him twice with his clenched fist.

'Go easy,' said Zézette. 'He's only a boy.'

Maurice released Philippe, and looked at him with a kind of surprise.

'You . . . I hate you,' muttered Philippe.

'Look here, my lad . . .' said Maurice uncertainly.

'You'll see,' said Philippe: 'you'll all of you see. And you'll be ashamed.'

He ran out, went back into his room and double-locked the door. The train rumbled on, the ship rose and fell, Hitler slept, Ivich slept, Chamberlain slept, Philippe flung himself on his bed and wept, Gros-Louis staggered along, houses and still more houses, his skull was ablaze but he couldn't stop, he had to make his way through the dreadful whispering night, Philippe wept, his strength had left him, he wept, he heard their whispers through the wall, he could not even hate them, he wept, an exile in the cold and squalid night, in the grey night of cross-roads, Mathieu had awakened, he got up and stood at the window, he could hear the whisper of the sea, and he smiled at the lovely, milky night.

Sunday, 25 September

A DAY of shame, a day of rest, a day of fear, the day of God, the sun rose upon a Sunday. The light-house, the lanterns, the cross, the cheek, the CHEEK, God carries the cross inside the churches. I carry my cheek through the Sunday streets, dear me! – what a nasty boil you've got – No; the fact is they've smacked me on the cheek, poor little wretch with his buttocks on his face, a huge top-heavy head, a split and bandaged head, a head like a pumpkin or a gourd, they struck from behind, one – two, there were footsteps in his head, tramp-tramp inside his head, it's Sunday, where on earth am I going to get a job, the doors were shut, great iron doors, nail-studded rusty doors, enclosing darkness, emptiness, smelling of sawdust, oil and old iron, earthen floors strewn with rusted junk; the menacing little wooden doors were closed too, closed upon rooms filled to bursting with furniture, knick-knacks, children, hatred, the dense smell of burnt onions, the starched collar shining on the bed, women brooding behind the windows, he walked on between the windows, between the peering eyes, stiffened, petrified by all those eyes. Gros-Louis walked between brick walls and iron doors, he walked on and on – not a penny in his pocket, nothing to eat, his head throbbing like a heart, and as he walked his footsteps hammered in his head – tap-tap, they tramped, already sweating, through the Sunday-murdered streets, his cheek shone up the avenue, and he thought: 'War streets already.' Again he thought: 'How am I to get something to eat?' Again he thought: 'Isn't there anyone to help me?' But the small brown men, the tall workmen with their rocky faces were shaving and thinking about the war, thinking that they would have a whole day in which to think about the war, a whole empty day in which to trail their anguish through those murdered streets. War: closed shops, deserted streets, three hundred and sixty-five Sundays in the year; Philippe was called Pedro Cazarès, he bore his name on his chest. Pedro Cazarès, Pedro Cazarès, Pedro Cazarès, Pedro Cazarès was leaving for Switzerland that very evening, he was taking to Switzerland a swollen, florid cheek bearing the marks of five knuckles; women peered down on him from their high windows.

God looked at Daniel.

Shall I call him God? One solitary word and everything changes. He stood with his back to the grey shutters that protected the saddler's shop, the people were hurrying towards

the church that stood out black against the pink street;
and those people were eternal. Everything was eternal. A
young woman passed, a blonde lithe figure, her hair in elaborate disorder, she lived in the hotel, her husband, a manufacturer at Pau, visited her on two days every fortnight, she hadn't
bothered with her face because it was Sunday, her little feet
were pattering towards the church, her soul was a pool of
silver. The church was a dismal hole: a Romanesque façade,
and a recumbent stone effigy in the second chapel on the right
as you went in. He smiled at the draper's wife and at her little
boy. Shall I call him God? He wasn't astonished – it was
bound to happen. Sooner or later. I felt sure there was something. Indeed I've always done everything for the benefit of
an eye-witness. A man evaporates without an eye-witness.

'Good morning, Monsieur Sereno,' said Nadine Pichou.
'Are you going to mass?'

'Yes, and I must hurry,' said Daniel.

He watched her, she was limping more than usual, two little
girls ran gaily round her. He looked at them – but wait, the
looker was now looked at. My look is but a shell, God's look
has pierced it. 'Oh, this is literary stuff,' he thought with
irritation. God was here no longer. Last night, as he lay
sweating in his bed, he had been conscious of God's presence,
and had felt like Cain: Here am I, as thou hast made me,
cowardly, futile, and a paederast. And then? The look was
there, and everywhere, silent, transparent, and mysterious.
At last Daniel had gone to sleep, and when he awoke, he was
alone. Merely the memory of a look. A throng poured out of
all the gaping doors, black gloves, starched collars, rabbit-
skins, hands clasping family missals. Ah! said Daniel to
himself: a method is essential. I am tired of this constant drifting towards an empty sky, I want a roof. The butcher passed,
a large and florid man who wore spectacles of a Sunday to
dignify the occasion; a missal in his hairy hand: he will be
seen, the look will reach him through the stained-glass windows: they will all be seen: half humanity lives beneath a look.
Does he feel that look upon him when a joint splits under his
hatchet and discloses a round bluish bone. An eye sees him –
sees his hard heart, as I see his hands, sees his greed, as I see
his straggling hair, and the patch of pity that gleams through

his avarice, as his skull gleams through his hair: all this he knows as he turns the thumbed pages of his missal, and says with a groan: 'Lord, Lord, I *am* a miser.' The Medusa's petrifying gaze will fall upon him from above. Stone virtues, stone voices: how restful! Those people's technique is sound, said Daniel resentfully to himself, watching their black backs steering into the darkness of the church. Three women trotted side by side in the clear, russet air of morning: three sad, sedate women, natives of the place. They had lit fires, swept floors, poured milk into the coffee, merely arms at the end of a broom, hands clasping the teapot handle, as insubstantial as that haze that creeps upon visible things, percolates through walls, and broods over fields and woods. Now, in that dim light, they will soon be what they really are. He eyed them from a distance – suppose I joined them? Nonsense! here am I. Here am I as thou hast made me, a vile coward, irredeemable. Thou lookest at me, and all hope departs: I am weary of my efforts to escape myself. But I know that, beneath thy eye, I *can* no longer escape myself. I shall enter, I shall stand among those kneeling women, like a monument of iniquity. I shall say: ' I *am* Cain. Well? Thou hast made me, now sustain me.' Marcelle's look, Mathieu's look, Bobby's look, my cats' look: they always stopped short at my skin. Mathieu, I *am* a paederast. I am, I am, I *am* a paederast, God help me! The old man with the wrinkled face and a tear in his eye, peevishly chewing a tobacco-stained moustache, entered the church – shabby, broken, senile, and Daniel entered, behind him. It was the hour when Ribadeau would appear on the bowling-alley, whistling, and the boys cried: 'Hullo, Ribadeau – on form today?' Ribadeau thought of that as he rolled a cigarette, his hands felt hollow, he looked gloomily at the trucks and rows of casks, and was conscious of something missing in his hand, the weight of a nail-studded globe, nicely adjusted in his palm; he looked at the casks and he thought: 'Sunday – blast it!' Marius, Claudio, Remy had gone off one by one, they were playing soldiers: Jules and Charlot did their best, they rolled the casks along the rails, and hoisted them together into the trucks; they were powerful men but getting on in years, Ribadeau could hear them panting as the sweat poured down their naked backs: it was an endless job. A tall fellow with a bandage round his head, who had been prowling round the depot for the last quarter of an hour, came up to Jules, and Ribadeau saw his lips move. Jules listened to the man with his usual crabbed air, then he half-rose, laid the palms of his hands on his hips, and jerked his head in the direction of Ribadeau.

'What is it?' said Ribadeau.

The man approached rather diffidently: he walked with a duck-like gait, his feet turned outwards: a ghastly-looking creature, who touched his bandage by way of salutation.

'Got a job for me?' he asked.

'A job?' repeated Ribadeau. He eyed the man: a ruffian, his head swathed in a dirty bandage; he looked strong, but his face was ghastly pale.

'A job?' said Ribadeau.

They stared at each other, Ribadeau thought the man was going to collapse where he stood.

'A job,' he said, scratching his head. 'There's no lack of jobs.'

The man blinked. From close at hand he didn't look so bad.

'I can work,' he said.

'You don't look healthy,' said Ribadeau.

'How do you mean?' said the man.

'You look ill.'

The man eyed him with astonishment. 'I'm not ill,' he said.

'You're quite white. And what's that bandage?'

'That's where they hit me on the head,' the man explained. 'It's nothing.'

'Who hit you on the head? The cops?'

'No. It was some chaps I met. I can work all the same.'

'That remains to be seen,' said Ribadeau.

The man bent down, grasped a cask, and lifted it with arm outstretched.

'Son of a bitch!' said Ribadeau with admiration. And he added: 'What's your name?'

'Gros-Louis.'

'Have you got your papers?'

'I've got my army book.'

'Give it here.'

Gros-Louis felt in the inner pocket of his jacket, produced

the booklet cautiously and handed it to Ribadeau. Ribadeau opened it and began to whistle.

'Well!' he said. 'Well!'

'It's all in order,' said Gros-Louis with an anxious air.

'In order! Can you read?'

Gros-Louis gave him a crafty look: 'I can shift casks, even if I can't read.'

Ribadeau handed him his book. 'You're a Form 2 man, my boy. You're due at Montpellier, at the barracks. You'd better get busy or you'll be posted as a defaulter.'

'Montpellier?' said Gros-Louis in amazement. 'Why should I go to Montpellier?'

Ribadeau lost his temper. 'I tell you you're called up,' he said. 'You're a Form 2 man; you're called up.'

Gros-Louis put the book in his pocket. 'So you won't take me on?' he said.

'I can't employ a deserter.'

Gros-Louis bent down and lifted a cask. 'That'll do, that'll do,' said Ribadeau briskly. 'You're a tough fellow, certainly. But I should look silly if they came and arrested you within forty-eight hours.'

Gros-Louis had hoisted the cask on to his shoulder: he looked steadily at Ribadeau, contracting his heavy eyebrows. Ribadeau shrugged his shoulders: 'I'm sorry,' he said.

There was nothing more to be said. As he moved away, he thought, 'I don't want a defaulter, anyway.' 'Hi! – Charlot!' he cried.

'Hullo!' said Charlot.

'Keep an eye on that chap, he's a defaulter.'

'Pity,' said Charlot, 'he might have given us a hand.'

'I can't take on a defaulter.'

'Of course not,' said Charlot.

They both turned round: the tall man had put down the cask, and was gloomily turning the pages of his army book.

The crowd enclosed them and carried them along – thickening as it circled round them. René no longer knew if he were stationary, or moving with the crowd. He looked at the French flags floating above the entrance to the Gare de l'Est: over there was the war, at the far end of the railway lines, but it did not trouble him, he felt threatened by a much more imminent catastrophe: crowds are always in some sort of peril. *Gallieni's funeral, trailing a small white garment between the black roots of the crowd, beneath the horror of the sun, the scaffolding collapses, don't look, they have carried the woman out, a stiff and lifeless figure, with a red lace foot sticking out of a burst shoe*; the crowd enveloped him, beneath a clear and empty sky, I hate crowds – eyes upon him everywhere, suns that made flowers blossom on his back and belly, suns that set his long pale nose alight – a trip into the suburbs on the first Sunday or two in May, and next day, in the papers: 'Red Sunday': a few left lying where they fell. Irène protected him with her plump little person, *don't look, she grabs my hand and pulls me away, and the woman passes behind me, gliding over the crowd like a corpse on the Ganges*. She looked disapprovingly at the raised fists in the distance, beneath the tricolour flags, above the caps.

'Fools!'

René pretended not to hear: but his sister continued in a voice of slow conviction: 'Idiots. They're being packed off to the shambles, and they're happy.'

She was disgraceful. In buses, at the cinema, in the underground, she behaved badly, she always said what ought not to be said, and made the most scandalous remarks in her full rich voice. He glanced behind him – that weasel-headed fellow with the goggling eyes and corroded nose was looking at them. Irène put a hand on his shoulder with a thoughtful air. She had just remembered she was his elder sister – no doubt she was about to give him some tiresome advice; anyway, she had insisted on accompanying him to the station, and at the moment she was alone among all these men, just as when he took her to a boxing match at Puteaux, and he must consider her feelings. She read and smoked, lying on her divan, and produced her own opinions, as well as her hats. She said: 'Listen to me, René, you mustn't behave like all these fools.'

'No,' said René, in a low voice. 'No; of course not.'

'Listen,' she continued. 'You mustn't do more than your duty.'

When she had made up her mind, her voice became resonant. She said: 'What's the good of it? You are going because you must, but don't attract attention when you get there by doing more or less than you need: it comes to the same thing. And for God's sake keep your head down.'

'Yes, of course,' he said.

She held him firmly by the shoulders, eyed him earnestly but without affection. She was pursuing her idea.

'I know you, René, you love to throw your weight around, and you'll do anything to get talked about. Now I warn you that if you come back with a mention in dispatches, I'll never speak to you again; it's too silly. If you come back with a game leg, or a hole in your face, don't expect me to be sorry for you, and don't tell me it happened by accident: with a little care, those are things that can be perfectly well avoided.'

'Yes,' said he. 'Yes.'

She was right, but it wasn't the kind of thing to say. It ought to happen naturally, and without discussion, by the force of events, so that afterwards there can be no need for self-reproach. Caps; a sea of caps, the caps of Monday morning and of every day, caps of factory yards, of Saturday meetings, Maurice felt happy in the thickest of the crowd. The tide swayed the lifted fists, and carried them, with a few halts, hesitations, and fresh starts, slowly to the tricolour flags, *Comrades, Comrades, the fists of May, the blossoming fists surge towards Garches, towards the red stands on the Garches meadow, my name is Zézette and the Falcons are singing in honour of the lovely month of May, and the world now coming to birth.* There was a smell of corduroy and wine, Maurice was everywhere, he was everyone, he smelt the corduroy and wine, he rubbed his sleeve against the rough tweed of a jacket, a curly-haired boy thrust a haversack into the small of his back, the shuffle of countless feet thrilled up his legs to his stomach, something buzzed in the sky above his head, he looked up at the plane, then down again, and saw beneath him an expanse of upturned faces, reflections of his own, and smiled at them. Two clear pools in a tanned skin, tousled hair, a scarred cheek – and he smiled. He smiled too at the earnest fellow in pince-nez, at the thin, pallid, bearded man with set lips, who did not smile. A shout echoed in his ears, a shout and a burst of laughter – Well, I'm blowed, so it's you, Jojo, there had to be a war for us to meet. It was Sunday. When the factories are closed, when men assemble and wait, empty-handed, in railway stations, with packs on their backs, at the behest of an iron destiny, then it is Sunday, no matter whether they are going off to a war, or on a trip to Fontainebleau. Daniel standing at a *prie-dieu* breathed a suave cellar-like odour laden with incense, eyed the array of bald skulls beneath the violet light, the solitary standing figure among those kneeling men, Maurice, enclosed by standing men, men without women, in a hectic smell of wine, coal, and tobacco, looked at the caps beneath the light of morning, and thought: 'It's Sunday.' Pierre was asleep; Mathieu pressed the tube, a cylinder of pink paste emerged with a faint hiss, broke, and dropped on to the bristles of the brush. A boy jostled Maurice, laughed, and shouted: 'Hullo, Simon! Simon!' Simon turned, his cheeks were red, he laughed and said: 'Well! This is what you might call a black Sunday, eh?' Maurice laughed too, and repeated: 'Black Sunday,' a handsome youth returned the smile, he had a slim and rather flamboyant woman with him: she clung to his arm and looked up at him plaintively, but he did not look at her; otherwise they would have merged into a single person. Even so, an isolated pair. He was enjoying himself, he looked at Maurice, the woman did not count, Zézette did not count, *she's gasping now, and how she smells, she's quite limp underneath me*, darling, darling, come! – there was still an hour or two of night left, like a veil of sweat between her body and her nightdress, just a little sweat, a little stale and amorous anguish, but he was enjoying the fresh air, women were out of place: here was war – war, revolution, and victory. We shall keep our rifles. All these men: curly-haired, bearded, bespectacled – they will all return, rifles in hand, singing the *Internationale,* and it will be Sunday. Forever Sunday. He raised his fist.

'He's raising his fist. That's the idea.'

Maurice turned, his fist in the air: 'What do you mean?' he said.

It was the bearded man. 'Do you want to die for the Sudetens?' demanded the bearded man.

'Shut up!' said Maurice.

He of the beard eyed him with a malignant but rather hesitant air, rather as though he were trying to remember something. Suddenly he shouted: 'Down with the war!'

Maurice recoiled, and bumped his haversack into someone's back. 'Keep your mouth shut, you bloody fool!'

'Down with the war!' shouted the other. 'Down with the war!'

His hands quivered and his eyes rolled, he went on shouting because he couldn't help it. Maurice eyed him with disgusted astonishment, but without anger, he thought of knocking him out just to keep him quiet – as one thumps a hiccuping child; but he could still feel flesh beneath his finger-joints, and he was ashamed: he had struck a boy: never again! He thrust his hands into his pockets: 'You silly sod!' he said.

The bearded man went on shouting, in a cultured, weary voice – a rich man's voice: and Maurice suddenly had an unpleasant feeling that the whole performance was put up. He looked round him, and his good humour vanished: it was those other people's fault, they didn't know how to react. At meetings, when a chap made himself a nuisance, the crowd surged upon him and submerged him, his arms waved for a moment, then he disappeared. But these fellows had recoiled and left the bearded man isolated: the young woman eyed him curiously, she had dropped her man's arm, the boys were turning round, they looked shifty, and pretended not to hear.

'Down with the war!' shouted the bearded man. Maurice was aware of an odd thrill of disquiet in the centre of his back; the sunshine, the man shouting, and the crowd all looking at the ground. .... His disquiet increased into a pain, he shouldered the crowd aside, and made his way towards the station entrance, towards the genuine comrades who stood with lifted fists beneath the flags. The Boulevard Montparnasse was deserted. Sunday. Outside the Coupole five or six people were sitting over drinks: the lady from the scarf-shop was standing in her doorway: on the first floor of No. 99, above the *Kosmos*, a man in shirtsleeves appeared at the window, and laid his elbows on the railing. Maubert and Thérèse uttered a cry of joy – there was one over there, on the wall between the Coupole and the chemist's shop, a large yellow, red-edged notice – *Frenchmen!* – still quite damp. Maubert charged, his neck hunched between his shoulders, his head outthrust, Thérèse after him, in high glee: they had torn down six, under the astonished gaze of many worthy citizens, it was

175

wonderful to have a young and sporting employer, a fine fellow who knew his mind.

'Rubbish!' said Maubert.

He looked round him: a small girl, about ten years old, had stopped, and twisted her plaits as she stood watching them: Maubert repeated at the top of his voice: 'Rubbish!'

Thérèse said loudly, addressing Maubert's back: 'I can't think how the Government can allow such rubbish to be put up on the walls.'

The seller of scarves did not reply: she was a large, somnolent woman, with a vague professional smile lingering between her cheeks.

Frenchmen!
The German demands are unacceptable. We have done everything possible to preserve peace, but no one can expect France to go back on her commitments and decline into a second-class power. If today we abandon the Czechs, tomorrow Hitler will claim Alsace. . . .

Maubert seized the notice by one end and tore off a long ribbon of yellow paper, like a strip of flesh from a duck's breast. Thérèse took the notice by the right-hand corner, pulled, and a large fragment came away:

France to
ments and
a second-class power
if today
will claim

A yellow, jagged, star-shaped patch of paper remained upon the wall. Maubert took a step back to inspect his handiwork: a yellow star, just a yellow star, displaying a few innocuous, truncated words. Thérèse smiled and looked at her gloved hands, a fragment of the notice, a thin sliver of paper, was still sticking to her right glove: 'Repu . . .' She rubbed her thumb against her forefinger, and the yellow scrap coagulated into a pellet as hard as a pin-head. Thérèse opened her fingers, the pellet dropped, she had an intoxicating sense of power.

'A piece of steak, Monsieur Désiré, something about a pound and a half, a really nice piece, please to cut it carefully: yesterday your assistant served me, and gave me a very stringy bit. By the way, what has been happening across the street. At No. 24, I mean – the black curtains? Is someone dead?' – 'I don't know,' said the butcher. 'I haven't any customers at No. 24, they get their meat from Berthier's. Now this is a really special bit, pink and tender, sparkles like champagne, it'll melt in your mouth – wouldn't mind eating it raw.'

'No. 24,' said Mme Lieutier, 'I know, it's Monsieur Viguier.' 'Monsieur Viguier? Don't know him. He must be a new tenant?' – 'No indeed, it's the little old gentleman, you know him quite well, he used to give Thérèse sweets.' – 'Oh, that old chap? What a pity. I shall miss him; Monsieur Viguier – fancy that!' – 'Well, he was pretty old, you know.' – 'Oh,' said Mme Lieutier: 'and then, as I said to my husband, the little old fellow died just at the right time, he knew what he was about, I dare say in six months we shall all be sorry we aren't where he is. You've heard of what they've invented?' – 'Oh? Who have?' – 'The Germans: kills people like flies, in awful agony.' – 'Good God, you don't say so! The monsters! But what is it?' – 'A kind of gas, I believe, or ray, if you like – I have had it explained to me.' – 'Ah, that would be the death-ray,' said the butcher, wagging his head. – 'Yes, something of that kind. I begin to think it would be much better to be below ground.' – 'You're quite right, that's what I always say. No more housekeeping, no more troubles; that's how I should like to die: go to sleep at night, and not wake up in the morning.' – 'Well, that's how he did die, apparently.' – 'Who!' – 'The little old chap.' – 'Some people have all the luck, we women always get the worst of everything, you saw what happened in Spain. No, a bit of rib, and have you got any scraps for my cat? When I just think – another war! My husband served in '14, and now it's my son's turn; I tell you men are crazy. Is it so difficult to come to an understanding?' – 'But Hitler doesn't want an understanding, Madame Bonnetain.' – 'Hitler, you say – he wants his Sudetens, doesn't he? Well, let him have them. I don't even know whether they're men or mountains, and my son is to be killed for a matter of that sort. I would hand them over, so I would. You want them? Here they are. He would be nicely caught. Tell me,' she continued more seriously: 'Is the funeral today? You don't happen to know at what time? I would like to be at the window to watch it pass.' – What's all this about a war? He was still clutching his army book, he couldn't make up his mind to put it back in his pocket: it was his sole possession. He opened it as he walked on, saw his photograph, and felt a little reassured: those little black lines that described him – while he looked at them, they didn't seem so formidable. But he said to himself: 'All the same, it's a nuisance not to be able to read!' A deserter – the thin exhausted youth who made his way up the avenue de Clichy, trailing his reflection from window to window, this emaciated youth with no hatred in his heart, was a rebel, a deserter, a terrible personage with a shaven crown, living at Barcelona in the Barrio Chino, and kept in hiding by an adoring mistress. But how can one *be* a deserter? What is the true vision of a man's own self?

He was standing in the nave, the priest was chanting for him: and he thought: 'Rest and peace – rest and peace.' *In himself eternity shall transform him at last.* Thou hast created me even as I am, and thy purpose is inpenetrable: I am the most shameful of thy thoughts, thou seest me and I serve thee, I set myself against thee, I insult thee, and in so insulting thee I serve thee. I am thy creature, thou lovest thyself in me, thou maintainest me, thou who hast created monsters. A bell tinkled, the faithful bowed their heads, but Daniel remained erect, looking steadily before him. Thou seeest me, thou lovest me; he felt calm and sanctified.

The hearse stopped at No. 24. 'Here they are, here they are,' said Mme Bonnetain. – 'It's the third floor,' said the concierge. She recognized the undertaker's man, and said: 'Good morning, Monsieur René, I hope you're well.' – 'Good morning,' said M. René: 'It's an odd notion to get buried on a Sunday.' – 'Ah,' said the concierge: 'that's because the gentleman was a freethinker.' Jacques looked at Mathieu, drummed on the table, and said: 'And even if we win this infernal war, do you know who will profit by it? Stalin.' – 'And if we do nothing, Hitler will,' said Mathieu quietly. – 'Well, and what then? Hitler – Stalin, it's all the same. Except that an understanding with Hitler will save us two million men, and spare us a revolution.' – Ah well. Mathieu got up, walked to the window and looked out. He wasn't even irritated, he thought: 'What is the sense of it all?' He was a deserter, and the sky retained the genial air of Sunday, the streets smelt of rich dishes, frangipani, fowls, and domesticity. A couple passed, the man was carrying some pastry done up in fancy paper, and hanging by a loop of pink string from his little finger. Like every other Sunday. *It's all bluff, it makes no difference, see how quiet everything is, not a ruffle on the surface, the miniature death called Sunday in the domestic circle, try again, the sky exists, the grocer's shop exists, the pie exists; deserters don't.'* Sunday, Sunday, the first queue outside the urinal on the Place Clichy, the first warmth of the day. He saw himself entering the lift which had just come down, inhaling in the dim lift cage the perfume of the blonde lady on the third floor, and pressing the white button: a faint tremor, a smooth upward glide, and he would slip his key into the lock as he did every Sunday, hang his hat on the third peg, settle his tie before the mirror in the hall, open the drawing-room door, and say: 'Here I am!' What would she do? Would she run to meet him, as she did every Sunday, murmuring: 'Darling!' It was so lifelike, so stiflingly like life. And yet all that had gone for ever. If only I could get angry! He struck me – he thought. He stopped, he had a stitch in his side, he leaned against a tree, but he wasn't angry. 'Oh dear,' he thought desperately. 'Why did I have to grow up?' Mathieu returned and sat down opposite Jacques. Jacques was talking, Mathieu looked at him, it was all so tedious, the bureau in the half-light, the snatches of band-music from beyond the pines, the curls of butter in the little dish, the empty bowls on the tray: so futile an eternity. He too wanted to speak: not to say anything in particular, but merely to break that eternal silence on which his brother's voice made no impression. And he said: 'Don't worry. War, or peace – it's all the same.'

'All the same?' said Jacques in astonishment. 'Go and tell that to the millions of men who are preparing to be killed.'

'And what then?' said Mathieu genially. 'They have carried their death within them since the day they were born. And even if they are massacred to a man, humanity will still be up to strength: not an empty place, not one person missing.'

'Except for a loss of twelve to fifteen millions,' said Jacques.

'It isn't a question of numbers,' said Mathieu. 'Humanity replenishes itself, none are missed and none awaited. Humanity will continue on its futile journey, the usual people will ask themselves the usual questions, and wreck their lives in the usual way.'

Jacques eyed him with a knowing smile.

'And what does it all come to?'

'Well, just to nothing,' said Mathieu.

'There they are – there they are,' exclaimed Madame Bonnetain brightly, 'they're just going to put the bier in the hearse. The war doesn't matter, the train moved out, bristling with lifted fists, Maurice had found his old friends once more. Dubech and Laurent flattened him against the window, as he yelled the *Internationale*. 'You can't sing for nuts,' said Dubech. – 'I dare say not,' said Maurice. He was hot, his temples throbbed, it was the finest day in his life. He felt chilly, he had a stomach-ache, he rang for the third time: he heard the sound of hurried footsteps in the corridor, doors slammed, but no one came: 'Where are they – I shall make a mess in my bed.' Someone pounded past his door.

'Hi!' yelled Charles.

The noise in the corridor continued, and then died away; then came a sound of knocking overhead. Curse them – that would be the little Dorliac woman, who slips them five-thousand-franc notes every month, just in tips, they'd fight to get on to her floor. He shivered, there must be windows open somewhere, an icy draught came from underneath the door, they must be airing the place, we haven't gone yet, and they're airing the place already: what with the noise, the draught, and the shouting, I might be in a windmill, or on a public square. He hadn't felt so wretched since his first X-ray was taken.

'Hullo there! Hi!' he yelled.

Ten minutes to eleven, Jeannine had not come, he had been alone all the morning. When are they going to stop that row overhead? The hammer-blows thudded in his eye-sockets – they might be nailing down my coffin. His eyes were dry and painful, he had awakened with a start at three in the morning, after a bad dream. Indeed it was scarcely a dream: he was left alone at Berck, beach, hospitals, clinics, all were deserted; no patients nor nurses, darkened windows, empty wards, grey, bare sands as far as eye could reach. But the emptiness was of the kind seen only in dreams. The dream continued: his eyes were open, and the dream continued: he was on his trolley in the centre of his room, and yet his room was empty; no longer any up or down, nor any right or left. Only four walls, four walls that met at right angles, just some sea-air caught between four walls. A heavy object was being dragged into the corridor, a rich patient's trunk, no doubt.

'Hi!' he yelled. 'Hi!'

The door opened and Mme Louise came in.

'At last,' he said.

'Now, please,' said Madame Louise. 'There are a hundred patients to be dressed: all must wait their turn.'

'Where's Jeannine?'

'She hasn't time to attend to you now – she is dressing the Pottier girls.'

''Give me the pan, quick,' said Charles. 'Quick – quick!'

'What's the matter? It isn't your time.'

'I'm in pain,' said Charles. 'That's why.'

'Yes, but I must get you ready. Everybody has to be ready by eleven o'clock. So hurry up.'

She undid the cord of his pyjamas, and pulled down his trousers, then she lifted him by the small of his back, and slipped the pan underneath him. The enamel surface felt chilly and harsh. 'I've got diarrhoea,' thought Charles with vexation.

'How am I going to manage if I have diarrhoea on the train?'

'Don't you worry. Everything has been thought of.'

She looked at him, jingling her bunch of keys.

'You'll have a fine day for the journey.'

Charles's lips began to quiver: 'I hate to be going away.'

'Nonsense!' said Madame Louise. 'Well – finished?'

Charles made a last effort: 'Yes, I've finished.'

She felt in her pocket and produced a sheet of paper, and a pair of scissors. She cut the paper into eight sections.

'Up with you,' she said.

He heard the crackle of the paper, and felt it rub against his skin.

'Ouf!' said he.

'There,' she said. 'Now turn over so that I can get the pan away: and I'll finish you off.'

He turned over, he heard her walking about the room, then

he felt the touch of expert fingers. That was the moment he most enjoyed. A mere object: a forlorn little object.

Mme Louise turned him over like a parcel: she looked down and began to laugh: 'A last little joke, eh?' she said, 'Well, we shall miss you, Monsieur Charles, you were the life and soul of the party.'

She threw back the bedclothes, and took off his pyjamas. 'A little eau-de-Cologne on your face,' she said, rubbing it accordingly. 'You won't get much of a wash today, I'm afraid. Lift your arms. Good. Now the shirt. Drawers next – don't wriggle like that, I can't get your socks on.'

She drew back to contemplate her handiwork, and said with satisfaction: 'There you are, as neat as a new penny.'

'Will it be a long journey?' asked Charles huskily.

'Probably,' she said, putting on his jacket.

'And where are we going?'

'I don't know. I believe you'll stop at Dijon first.'

She looked round her: 'I must just see I haven't forgotten anything. Ah,' she said: 'of course. Your cup. Your blue cup. You've been so fond of it.'

She took it from the shelf, and bent over the suitcase. It was a blue china cup decorated with red butterflies. A very handsome cup.

'I'll put it between the shirts so that it won't break.'

'Give it me,' said Charles.

She eyed him with surprise and handed him the cup. He took it, raised himself on one elbow, and hurled it against the wall.

'You vandal!' exclaimed Mme Louis indignantly. 'You should have let me keep it, if you didn't want to take it with you.'

'I didn't want to give it away, or take it with me,' said Charles.

She shrugged her shoulders, walked to the door, and flung it open.

'Are we going now?' he asked.

'Certainly,' she said. 'You don't want to miss the train?'

'It's so sudden,' said Charles.

She came back and began to wheel the trolley out of the room: he stretched out a hand to touch the table as they passed, he caught sight of the window for an instant, and a section of wall reflected in the mirror above his head, and then nothing more, he was in the corridor, behind some forty trolleys ranged in Indian file against the wall: his heart contracted.

The funeral procession moved off. 'They're just starting,' said Mme Bonnetain. 'I say, there aren't many people to see him to his last home.' Progress was slow, a turn of the wheels and then a stop, the dark pit waited at the journey's end, the nurses wheeled the trolley towards it, two by two, but there was only one lift and progress was slow.

'It's a long business,' said Charles.

'You won't be left behind,' said Mme Louise.

The hearse passed underneath the window: the small lady in mourning – she must be 'the family', the concierge had locked up the lodge, was walking behind the hearse, side by side with a buxom woman in a grey dress and a blue felt hat – the nurse. M. Bonnetain stood beside his wife with his elbows on the balcony. 'Old Viguier was a Three Point Brother,' said he. 'How do you know?' 'Aha!' he said complacently: and he added after a moment's pause: 'He used to make a triangle with his thumb inside my hand when he shook hands with me. A surge of anger rose into Mme Bonnetain's temples, at hearing her husband speak so lightly of a dead man. She watched the little procession and thought: 'Poor man.' He lay there prostrate, they were carrying him feet foremost to the pit. Poor man: it is sad to have no family. She made the sign of the cross. Prostrate in a lightless pit, he would soon feel the lift sink down beneath him.

'Who is going with us?' he asked.

'No one from here,' said Mme Louise. 'The three nurses from the Norman Chalet, and Georgette Fouquet, a tall brown-haired girl whom you must know, she's at Dr Robertal's clinic.'

'Ah, yes,' said Charles, as she pushed him slowly towards the pit. 'A dark-hair girl with pretty legs. She doesn't look very amiable.'

He had often noticed her on the beach, in charge of a throng of rickety children, cuffing them impartially as might be needed: she had bare legs, and wore straw sandals. Fine,

183

sinewy legs they were, veiled in soft down – he often used to wish she were nursing him. They will lower him into the pit and no one will lean over him, except that rather dowdy little female – how sad to die like that: Mme Louise pushed him into the lift, there was already a trolley standing in the dim light against the wall.

'Who is that?' said Charles blinking.

'Petrus,' said a voice.

'Aha, you old devil,' said Charles, 'So we're off, eh?'

Petrus did not answer, there was a faint jerk, Charles felt as though he were hovering a few inches above his trolley, then they plunged, the floor of the third storey was already above his head, he was quitting life downstairs, through a hole in a sink.

'But where is she?' he said with a convulsive sob: 'Where is Jeannine?'

Mme Louise did not seem to hear, and Charles swallowed his tears on account of Petrus. Philippe walked on and on, he could not stop: if he did, he would faint: Gros-Louis went on walking, he had hurt his right foot. A man passed along the deserted street, a short fat man with a moustache and wearing a straw boater. Gros-Louis reached out a hand:

'Can you read?' he said to him. 'Can you read?'

The man stepped sideways, and hurried on.

'Don't run away,' said Gros-Louis. 'I shan't eat you.'

The man walked faster, Gros-Louis limped after him, holding out his army book: the man finally took to his heels and fled, with a squeal like a frightened animal. Gros-Louis stopped, and watched him go, scratching his head above the bandage: the man, now dwindled into the small round semblance of a ball, rolled to the corner of a street, rebounded, turned, and vanished.

'Oh dear!' said Gros-Louis. 'Oh dear!'

'Don't cry,' said Mme Louise.

She dabbed his eyes with her handkerchief, I didn't even know I was crying. He felt rather moved: it was rather pleasant to bewail one's own troubles.

'I was so happy here.'

'No one would have believed it,' said Mme Louise. 'You were always grumbling.'

She shot back the iron gate of the lift, and wheeled him into the vestibule. Charles raised himself on his elbows, he recognized Totor, and the Gavalda boy. The Gavalda boy was as pale as a sheet: Totor had huddled himself into his bed-clothes, and lay with eyes closed. Men in caps received the trolleys as they emerged from the lift, propelled them through the doorway of the clinic, and disappeared with them into the park. A man came up to Charles.

'Well, good-bye, and a good journey,' said Mme Louise. 'Send us a postcard when you arrive. And don't forget: the little case with the toilet articles is by your feet, under the bedclothes.'

The man was already bending over Charles.

'Hi!' cried Charles. 'Take care. You may do me a serious injury if you aren't used to this sort of thing.'

'That's all right,' said the man. 'Don't you worry. What with the barrows at Dunkirk station, the trucks at Lens, and the trolleys at Anzin, there's nothing I don't know about this job.'

Charles said no more, he was afraid: the lad who was pushing the Gavalda boy's trolley swung it round a corner on two wheels, and rasped the wooden ledge against the wall.

'Stop!' said Jeannine. 'Stop! I'm taking him to the station.'

She ran down the stairs, quite out of breath.

'Monsieur Charles!' she cried.

She looked at him with a sort of sad intensity; her throat heaved violently, and she fumbled with his bedclothes merely that she might touch him: well, there was one thing that was his wherever he might be, and that was a woman's loving, loyal heart, it would beat for him, in a deserted clinic, at Berck.

'Well,' he said. 'You've let me down.'

'Oh, Monsieur Charles, I was so rushed; I just couldn't make it, as Madame Louise must have told you.'

She bustled rather sadly round the trolley on her two sturdy legs, and he quivered with hatred: she was a *stand-up,* she had vertical recollections, he would not long remain in the shelter of that heart.

'Well, well,' he said dryly. 'We must hurry: take me along.'

'Come in,' said a feeble voice.

Maud opened the door, and a smell of vomit took her by the throat. Pierre lay stretched full length on the bunk. He was pale, his eyes were unnaturally large, but he seemed composed. She had a moment of repulsion, but forced herself to walk into the cabin. On a chair, beside Pierre's head, stood a pan filled with turbid, frothy liquid.

'I'm only vomiting phlegm now,' said Pierre in a level voice. 'I brought up everything in my stomach long ago. Take the pan away and sit down.'

Maud took away the pan, holding her breath as she did so, and put it down by the wash-basin. She sat down: she had left the door open to air the cabin. A silence followed: Pierre looked at her with embarrassing curiosity.

'I didn't know you were ill,' she said, 'or I would have come sooner.'

Pierre raised himself on one elbow. 'I'm feeling a bit better,' he said: 'but I'm still very weak. I've been sick continuously since yesterday. Perhaps I'd better eat something at lunch-time – what do you think? The wing of a chicken, perhaps.'

'How can I say?' said Maud pettishly. 'You must know if you feel hungry.'

Pierre stared uneasily at the coverlet.

'Of course,' he said, 'there's the risk of overloading the stomach, but food may settle it, and from another standpoint, if I start being sick again, I had better have something to bring up.'

Maud eyed him with amazement. 'Well,' she thought: 'it does take time to get to know a man.'

'Right – I'll tell the steward to bring you some vegetable soup, and white of chicken.' She laughed a little constrainedly, and added: 'If you are thinking of food, you can't be very ill.'

A silence fell. Pierre had raised his eyes, and was observing her with a disconcerting blend of attention and indifference.

'Now tell me: you're in the second-class now.'

'Who told you?' said Maud pettishly.

'Ruby. I met her yesterday in a corridor.'

'Well yes,' said Maud. 'Yes, we're in the second-class.'

'How did you manage that?'

'We suggested giving a concert.'

'Ah,' said Pierre.

He continued to look at her. He laid his hands on the sheets, and said nonchalantly: 'And then you slept with the captain?'

'What nonsense is this?' said Maud.

'I saw you come out of his cabin,' said Pierre: 'there couldn't be any doubt about it.'

Maud was uncomfortable. In one sense, she no longer owed him any account of what she did: at the same time it would have been more straightforward to tell him. She dropped her eyes and coughed: her sense of guilt restored a little of her affection for Pierre.

'Look here,' she said, 'if I had refused, France wouldn't have understood.'

'But what on earth had France got to do with it?' said Pierre's placid voice.

She raised her head abruptly: he smiled, he still wore his expression of nonchalant curiosity. She felt insulted: she would have preferred him to abuse her.

'If you want to know,' she said dryly: 'When I'm on a ship, I always sleep with the captain, so that Baby's orchestra can travel second-class. That's how it is.'

She waited for him to protest, but he did not speak. She bent over him, and added forcibly: 'I'm not a tart.'

'Who said you were? You do what you like, or what you can. I see no harm in that.'

He felt as though he were lashing her across the face. She rose abruptly: 'Oh, so you see no harm in it!' she said. 'You see no harm in it, don't you?'

'Certainly not.'

'Well, you are wrong,' she said hotly. 'You are completely wrong.'

'So there is harm in it?' said Pierre with amusement.

'Don't try to confuse me. No, there's no harm in it: why should there be? Who has the right to tell me I shouldn't do such things? Not the men who are always after me, nor my friends who get the benefit, nor my mother who can't earn her living now, so I have to send her what I can. But you ought to think there's harm in it, because you are my lover.'

Pierre had clasped his hands on the coverlet: on his face

was a sick man's malicious, shifty look. 'Don't shout,' he said quietly: 'I've got a headache.'

She controlled herself and eyed him coldly: 'Don't be afraid,' she said in a low tone: 'I won't shout. But I might as well tell you now that it's all over between us. I hate to have to let myself be messed about by that old soup-tureen, and if you'd bawled me out or been sorry for me, I would have thought that you cared a bit about me, and I should have felt better. But if I can sleep with anyone I please, and no one – not even you – cares tuppence either way, then I'm just a mangy little bitch, a whore. Well, chum, whores run after men who pay, and don't have to waste their time on down and outers like you.'

Pierre did not answer: he had closed his eyes. She kicked her chair across the cabin, went out and slammed the door.

He glided, reclining on one elbow, between villas, clinics, and pensions: all empty, the hundred and twenty-two windows of the Hôtel Brun were open: in the hall of the Villa Mon Désir, in the garden of the Villa Oasis, patients were waiting, lying in their coffins, with heads uplifted; they looked silently at the procession of trolleys on its way towards the railway station. No one spoke, nothing could be heard but the creaking of springs, and the dull thud of wheels dropping from the sidewalk on to the road. Jeannine walked quickly: they overtook a large, elderly, red-faced lady propelled by a little old man in tears, they overtook Zozo, it was his mother who was taking him to the station, the lame attendant of the public lavatory.

'Hi!' yelled Charles.

Zozo gave a start, lifted himself a little and looked at Charles with his clear, vacant eyes.

'We're out of luck,' he sighed.

Charles dropped flat on his back: he was conscious, on his right and on his left, of all those horizontal presences, ten thousand miniature entombments. He reopened his eyes, and saw a patch of sky, and then hundreds of people leaning out of the windows of the Grande Rue waving handkerchiefs, Bastards! Bastards! This isn't July 14. A flight of gulls whirled screaming overhead, and Jeannine, behind him, blew her nose. She wept beneath her veils of crêpe; the nurse stared fixedly at

the solitary wreath dangling from the rear of the hearse, but
she heard the woman weep, she couldn't have regretted him
much, it was more than ten years since she had seen him –
still, somewhere in the depths of ourselves we all harbour an
ashamed, unsatisfied melancholy that quietly awaits a funeral,
a first communion, or a marriage, to evoke those latent tears:
the nurse thought of her paralysed mother, the war, her
nephew recently called up, the hard, hard life of a nurse, and
she too began to cry, glad to be crying in the little lady's
company; behind her the concierge had begun to sniff, poor
old gentleman, so few people to go with him, we must try to
look mournful: Jeannine wept as she wheeled the trolley.
Philippe walked on and on, I'm going to faint, Gros-Louis
walked on and on – war, illness, death, departure, misery: it
was Sunday, Maurice sang out of the window of his compartment, Marcelle went into the confectioner's to buy a cake.

'You haven't got much to say,' said Jeannine. 'I thought
you would be sorry to leave me.'

They had turned into the station road.

'Haven't I got enough to worry about as it is?' said
Charles. 'They pack me up, they send me off I don't know
where, whether I like it or not, added to which you want me
to be sorry to leave you.'

'You've got no heart!'

'All right,' he said severely, 'I wish you were in my place.
You wouldn't have much of a heart either.'

She did not reply, he saw a dark ceiling overhead.

'Here we are,' said Jeannine.

Was there no help? No one to whom he could say – for
God's sake leave me behind, she'll look after me, she'll take
me out in the evening, she'll caress me with those soft hands
of hers . . .

'Ah well,' he said to her: 'I believe I shall die on the
journey.'

'You're crazy,' said Jeannine frantically. 'You're completely
crazy – how can you say such things!'

She came from behind the trolley, and bent over him, he
could feel her warm breath.

'Now then,' he said, laughing in her face. 'No scenes,
please. You won't need to worry if I die. It will be the pretty

189

dark-haired girl, you know who I mean – Dr Robertal's nurse – who will have all the bother.'

Jeannine stiffened abruptly. 'She's a nasty bit of work,' she said. 'You can't imagine the trouble she gave Lucienne. You'll soon see what she's like,' she added through her clenched teeth. 'It isn't worth while making eyes at her, she isn't such a mutt as I am.'

Charles raised himself and looked uneasily around him. There were more than two hundred trolleys lined up in the hall. The porters pushed them on the the platform, one after the other.

'I don't want to leave,' he muttered.

Jeannine eyed him with a distraught look.

'Good-bye,' she said to him. 'Good-bye – little doll.'

He was about to reply, but the trolley had started. A tremor ran up from his feet to his neck: he tilted his head back, and saw a flushed face bent over his own.

'Write to me,' cried Jeannine. 'Do write to me.'

He was already on the platform, amid a din of whistles, and shouts of good-bye.

'But that can't be our train?' he asked frantically.

'Why not? What sort of train do you expect? The Orient Express?' said the porter ironically.

'But they're goods vans!'

The porter spat between his feet: 'A passenger train wouldn't do for you folks. The seats would need to be taken out, and that would be too much of a job.'

The porters grasped the stretchers at each end, lifted them off the trolleys, and carried them to the train. In the compartments there were railwaymen in caps, who received the stretchers as best they could, and transported them into the darkness. The handsome Samuel, the Don Juan of Berck, who owned eighteen suits of clothes, passed quite close to Charles, in the arms of two porters, and vanished, with his legs up-tilted, into the van.

'There are hospital trains, aren't there?' said Charles indignantly.

'Sure. But you don't suppose they're going to send hospital trains to Berck, just before the war starts, to pick up crocks.'

Charles was about to reply, but his stretcher dipped, and he was slung into the van feet upmost.

'Keep level!' he yelled.

The porters laughed, the pit came nearer and expanded, they released the ropes and the coffin fell with a soft thud on to the fresh earth. Leaning over the edge of the excavation, the nurse and the concierge were now sobbing whole-heartedly.

'You see,' said Boris. 'You see. They'll all doing a bunk.'

They were sitting in the vestibule of the hotel, not far from an elderly gentleman with a ribbon in his buttonhole, reading a newspaper. The porter had just brought down two pigskin suitcases, and deposited them near the entrance, beside some others.

'Five departures this morning,' he observed dispassionately.

'Look at those suitcases,' said Boris; 'they're pigskin. Those people don't deserve them,' he added severely.

'Why, my lovely?'

'They ought to be covered with labels.'

'But in that case one couldn't see the pigskin,' said Lola.

'That's the point. Luxury should conceal itself, and labels would do that. If I had a pigskin suitcase I wouldn't be here.'

'Where would you be?'

'No matter where: in Mexico, or China,' and he added, 'with you, of course.'

A tall woman in a black hat, walked excitedly across the hall, crying: 'Mariette! Mariette!'

'That's Madame Delarive,' said Lola. 'She's leaving this afternoon.'

'We shall be left alone in the hotel,' said Boris. 'What a scream! We'll change our room every evening.'

'There were only ten in the audience yesterday at the Casino, so I just made them sit together at the centre tables, and I whispered my songs at them.'

Boris got up to look at the suitcases. He examined them discreetly, and came back to Lola.

'Why are they going away?' he asked, sitting down again. 'They would be just as comfortable here. Their house may be bombed the day after they get back.'

'Yes,' said Lola. 'But it's *their* house. Don't you understand that?'

'No.'

'Well that's how it is. After a certain age one likes to meet trouble at home.'

Boris began to laugh, and Lola stiffened uneasily: it was a habit of hers from old days: when he laughed, she always thought he was laughing at her.

'Why are you laughing?'

'Because I admire your nerve. There you sit explaining what middle-aged people feel. But you don't understand anything about it, Lola: you've never had a home.'

'No,' said Lola sadly.

Boris took her hand and kissed the hollow of the palm.

Lola blushed.

'How nice you are to me – you aren't like you used to be at all.'

'Are you complaining?'

Lola squeezed his hand. 'Indeed I'm not. But I should like to know why you're so nice.'

'It's because I'm getting older,' he said.

She let her hand rest in his: and she smiled, lying back in her chair. He was glad that she should be happy: he wanted to leave her pleasant memories. He stroked her hand and thought: a year: we've only a year left together: he felt quite moved: their affair already possessed the charm of something past. He used to treat her roughly, but that was because their lease was unlimited: that upset him, he liked definite commitments. One year: he would give her all the happiness she deserved, he would make up for all he had done to hurt her feelings, then he would leave her, but decorously, not for another woman, nor because he was tired of her: it would happen naturally, by the force of events, because he would be of age and due to be called up. He glanced at her: she looked young, her lovely bosom was heaving with satisfaction and he thought despondently: 'I shall have been one woman's man.' Mobilized in '40, killed in '41 – no, in '42, because he would have to finish his course at the University; that made one woman in twenty-two years. Three months ago, he was still dreaming of sleeping with women in high society, it's because

I was just a kid, he thought, though not in self-excuse. He would die without having known any duchesses, but he regretted nothing. In one sense, he might, during the months to come, make the most of any opportunities that offered, but he didn't really want to: I should waste my energies. When a man has no more than two years to live, he ought to concentrate on serious matters. Jules Renard had said to his son: 'Study one woman only, but study her well, and you will know the race of women.' He must study Lola carefully, in restaurants, in the street, and in bed. He slid his finger along Lola's wrist and thought: 'I don't know her very well yet.' There were corners of her body of which he was ignorant, and he did not always know what was passing in her mind. But he had a year before him. And he was going to begin at once. He turned his head and eyed her attentively.

'Why are you looking at me like that?' asked Lola.

'I'm studying you,' said Boris.

'I don't like you to look at me too long, I'm always afraid you'll think I'm getting old.'

Boris smiled: she was still suspicious, she had not accustomed herself to her new-found happiness.

'Don't you worry,' he said.

A widow bowed curtly as she passed them, and sank into a chair beside the beribboned gentleman.

'Well, dear lady,' said the gentleman. 'We are to have a speech from Hitler.'

'Oh – and when?' asked the widow.

'He's speaking tomorrow, at the Sportpalast.'

'Br-r,' she said with a shiver. 'Then I shall go to bed early, and put my head under the bedclothes. I shan't listen. I don't suppose that he can have anything pleasant to say to us.'

'I'm afraid not,' said the gentleman.

There was a silence, and he went on: 'Our great mistake, you see, was in '36, at the time of the remilitarization of the Rhine Zone. We ought to have sent ten divisions there. If we had shown our teeth, the German staff had their withdrawal orders in their pockets. But Sarraut had to defer to the Popular Front, and the Popular Front chose to hand our arms over to the Spanish Communists.'

'England wouldn't have joined us,' observed the widow.

'She wouldn't have joined us!' repeated the gentleman impatiently. 'Well, I'll ask you one question, Madame: do you know what Hitler would have done if Sarraut had mobilized?'

'No,' said the lady.

'He would have *committed suicide*, my dear lady: I had it from an unimpeachable source: I have an officer friend in the 2nd Bureau, whom I have known for twenty years.'

The widow shook her head despondently.

'What lost opportunities,' she said.

'And whose was the fault, madame?'

'Ah,' she said.

'Yes,' said the gentleman: 'yes. That's what comes from voting red. The Frenchman is incorrigible: with war at the door, he clamours for paid holidays.'

The widow looked up: she looked genuinely uneasy. 'So you think there will be war?'

'War?' said the gentleman, rather abashed. 'Don't let us go too fast. No: Daladier is no fool: he will certainly make all appropriate concessions. But there's trouble coming.'

'Bastards!' said Lola between her teeth.

Boris smiled at her sympathetically. For her, the question of Czechoslovakia was very simple: a small country was attacked, France must defend it. She was rather summary in her political views, but they were at least generous.

'Let's have some lunch,' she said. 'These people are getting on my nerves.'

She got up. He looked at her fine strong hips, and he thought of woman as a type. It was woman, as such, that he was to possess that night. His ears throbbed in a sudden flush of passion.

Behind his back, the railway station, and Gomez, in the train, with his feet up on the cushions. He had rather scamped his good-byes: 'I don't like embraces on the platform.' She went down the great station staircase while the train was still in the station, Gomez was reading and smoking, his feet upon the cushions, he was wearing a pair of fine new calfskin shoes. She saw the shoes against the grey cloth of the seat: he was in a first-class compartment: war was rather a paying game. I hate him, she thought. She felt arid and empty. For one more moment she saw the glittering sea, the harbour and the ships, and then a vista of dismal hotels and roofs and trams.

'Pablo, don't walk so quickly! You'll fall.'

The boy stopped with one foot in the air. He is going to see Mathieu. He might have stayed one more day with me, but he preferred Mathieu. Her hands were burning. While he was here, I was in torment: now he has gone, I don't know what to do.

Little Pablo eyed her gravely. 'Has my papa gone away?' he asked.

A clock over the way indicated thirty-five minutes past one. The train had left seven minutes ago.

'Yes,' said Sarah. 'He has gone away.'

'Is he going to fight?' asked Pablo, with shining eyes.

'No,' said Sarah. 'He's going to see a friend.'

'Yes, but afterwards, is he going to fight?'

'Afterwards,' said Sarah, 'he is going to make other people fight.'

Pablo had stopped on the last step but one: he bent his knees and jumped with feet together on to the pavement, then turned and eyed his mother with a smile of pride. The little show-off, she thought. She did not smile, she turned and looked up at the great staircase. The trains rumbled, stopped, and started overhead. Gomez's train was rolling eastwards between chalk cliffs or rows of houses. Overhead, the deserted station, a great grey bubble filled with sunlight and with smoke, smells of wine and sweat, and gleaming railway lines. She bent her head, it wasn't pleasant to think of that desolate station in the white heat of afternoon. In April '33 he had gone off by the same train, he was wearing a grey tweed suit, Mrs Simpson was awaiting him at Cannes, they had spent a fortnight at San Remo. I liked that even better, she thought. A small groping fist touched her hand, and she clasped it, dropped her eyes and looked at Pablo. He was wearing a sailor-shirt and a straw hat.

'Why are you looking at me like that?' asked Pablo.

Sarah turned her head away and looked at the street. She was rather horrified to find herself so unrelenting. He's only a child, she thought. Only a child. She looked at him again, and tried to smile, but could not, her jaws were clenched, and her mouth set. The boy's lips began to quiver, and she realized that he was going to cry. She pulled him to her, and strode away. The boy, in his surprise, forgot his tears, and pattered along beside her.

'Where are we going, mamma?'

'I don't know,' said Sarah.

She turned down the first street on the right. It was quite deserted: all the shops were shut. She quickened her pace again, and turned into another street on the left, between tall, dark, squalid houses. Not a soul in sight.

'Don't go so fast,' said Pablo.

Sarah squeezed his hand without replying, and dragged him along. They came out into a broad straight street, with tram-lines. Not a car nor a tram was in sight, nothing but lowered iron shutters, and the tram-lines to the harbour. She tugged at Pablo's fist.

'Mamma,' whimpered Pablo. 'Oh, mamma!'

He was running now in order to keep up with her. He was not crying, he was very white, with dark rings under his eyes: he looked up at her with a puzzled and mistrustful air. Sarah stopped: tears were trickling down her cheeks.

'Poor kid,' she said. 'Poor innocent baby.'

She crouched down in front of him: it mattered little what he might turn into later on. For the moment he was there, an innocent, ugly little boy with a diminutive shadow at his feet, alone in the world, and with all those horrors in his eyes, but, after all, he had not asked to be born.

'Why are you crying?' asked Pablo. 'Is it because papa has gone away?'

Sarah's tears dried up, and she wanted to laugh. But Pablo eyed her with an anxious air. She rose and said, turning her head away: 'Yes. Yes, it's because papa has gone away.'

'Shall we be going home soon?' he asked.

'Are you tired? We're still quite away from home. Come along,' she said. 'We'll walk on slowly.'

They walked on a few steps and then Pablo stopped: he held out a finger: 'Look!' he said in almost agonized entrancement.

It was a poster, on the door of a blue-painted cinema. They went up to it. A smell of formalin emerged from the dark, cool auditorium. The poster showed cowboys pursuing a masked horseman and firing their revolvers. More firing, more revolvers. Pablo panted as he looked: he would get his helmet and his rifle, when he got home and run about the room pretending to be a masked bandit. She hadn't the courage to take him away. She simply averted her eyes. The cashier was fanning herself in her glass cabin. She was a large, dark-haired woman, with a pallid complexion and a glitter in her eyes. On the pay-desk, behind the glass stood a vase of flowers: and a photo of Robert Taylor was affixed to the wall with drawing-pins. A middle-aged man came out of the hall and walked up to the cashier.

'Well?' he asked through the ticket window.

'Fifty-three admissions,' she said.

'Just about what I guessed. Sixty-seven yesterday. And such a good film, full of galloping horsemen.'

'People are staying at home,' said the cashier, with a shrug of her shoulders.

A man had stopped near Pablo, and stood breathing heavily as he looked at the poster, but did not seem to see it. He was a tall, pallid fellow, with torn clothes, a blood-stained bandage round his head, and dried mud on his cheeks and hands. He must have come from far away. Sarah took Pablo's hand.

'Come along,' she said.

She was walking very slowly, on account of the child, but she wanted to run, for she felt someone was looking at her from behind. In front of her the tram-lines glittered, the tar melted gently in the sun, the air quivered round a street lamp, it was no longer the same Sunday. 'People are staying at home.' Only a little while ago she could see, behind those blocks of houses, a vision of cheerful crowded boulevards smelling sweet of face powder and American cigarettes: she was walking along a quiet suburban street, accompanied by an unseen throng. One word had been enough to clear the boulevards. Now they led towards the harbour, white and deserted: the air danced between blind walls.

'Mamma,' said Pablo, 'the man is following us.'

'No he isn't,' said Sarah. 'He's just taking a walk, like we are.'

She turned to her left; it was the same street, interminable, unaltered: there was now only one street straying through Marseilles. And Sarah was in that street, out of doors, with

197

a child: all the inhabitants of Marseilles were indoors. Fifty-three admissions. She thought of Gomez, and of Gomez's laugh: of course, all Frenchmen are cowards. And what then? They stay at home, which is quite natural: they are afraid of war, and they are quite right. But she remained uneasy. She noticed she was walking faster again, and tried to slow down on account of Pablo. But the boy dragged her on.

'Quick – quick!' he said in a choking voice. 'Oh, mamma!'

'What's the matter?' she said curtly.

'He's still there, you know.'

Sarah turned her head slightly and saw a hobbling figure, clearly following them. Her heart began to throb.

'Let's run!' said Pablo.

She thought of the blood-stained bandage, and turned abruptly round. The man stopped dead, and looked at them with rheumy eyes as they approached. Sarah was afraid. The boy had clutched her with both hands, and was trying to drag her backward. 'People are staying at home.' It would be no use to cry out or call for help, no one would come.

'Do you want anything?' she asked, looking straight at the limping figure before her.

He smiled pitifully, and Sarah's fears vanished.

'Can you read?' he asked.

He held out a tattered booklet. She took it – it was an army book. Pablo was now clasping her legs, she could feel his warm little body.

'Well?' she said.

'I want to know what's written there,' said the man, pointing to a page.

He looked a decent fellow, despite his purple, half-closed eye. Sarah looked at him for a moment, then at the printed page.

'It's awful,' the man muttered ruefully. 'It's awful not to be able to read.'

'Well, you've got the white page,' said Sarah. 'You'll have to go to Montpellier.'

She handed him the book, but the man did not take it. 'Is it true there's going to be war?'

'I don't know,' said Sarah.

'He'll go,' she thought. Then she thought of Gomez. 'Who made that bandage?' she asked.

'I did,' said the man.

Sarah felt in her bag, and produced some pins and two clean handkerchiefs.

'Sit down on the pavement,' she said authoritatively. The man sat down rather painfully. 'My legs have gone to sleep,' he said with a rueful laugh.

Sarah tore up the handkerchiefs. Gomez was reading the *Humanité* in a first-class carriage, with his feet up on the cushions. He would see Mathieu, and then go on to Toulouse, where he could get a plane for Barcelona. She untied the blood-stained bandage and jerked it gradually off his forehead; the man moaned faintly as she did so. A black, sticky scab extended half across his head. Sarah handed a handkerchief to Pablo.

'Go and get some water at a fountain.'

The boy ran off, glad to get away. The man looked up at Sarah and said: 'I don't want to fight.'

Sarah laid a hand gently on his shoulder. She would have liked to beg his pardon.

'I'm a shepherd,' he said.

'What are you doing at Marseilles?'

He shook his head. 'I don't want to fight,' he repeated.

Pablo had returned. Sarah washed the wound roughly, and bandaged it again.

'Now get up,' she said.

He got up, and looked at her with vacant eyes. 'So I've got to go to Montpellier?'

She felt in her bag and produced two hundred-franc notes.

'For your journey,' she said.

The man did not take them at once: he looked at her intently.

'Take them,' said Sarah in a low, quick tone. 'Take them. And don't fight if you can help it.'

He took the notes. Sarah shook his hand vigorously.

'Don't fight,' she repeated. 'Do anything – go home, go into hiding: but don't you fight.'

He looked at her blankly. She seized Pablo's hand, swung round, and they walked on. In an instant or two, she turned: he was looking at the bandage and the wet handkerchief which Sarah had thrown into the roadway. Then he bent down, picked them up rather unsteadily, and put them in his pocket.

Beads of sweat stood out across his forehead, and trickled across his cheeks from the nostrils to the ears, he had thought at first that they were insects and clapped a hand to his face, only to find that he had crushed his own warm tears.

'My God, it's hot,' said his left-hand neighbour.

He recognized the voice, it was that detestable fellow Blanchard.

'They do it on purpose,' said Charles. 'They leave the carriages in the sun for hours together.'

There was a silence, then Blanchard said: 'Is that you, Charles?'

'It is,' said Charles.

He was sorry he had spoken. Blanchard was addicted to practical jokes, he squirted people with a water-pistol, or steered his trolley past them and dabbed a cardboard spider on to their bedclothes.

'It's odd that we should meet like this.'

'Yes.'

'It's a small world.'

A jet of water hit Charles full in the face. He wiped it off, and spat. Blanchard was delighted.

'You bloody fool,' said Charles.

He produced a handkerchief, and wiped his neck, doing his best to laugh.

'It's your water-pistol, I suppose.'

'Sure,' said Blanchard. 'Got you that time, didn't I? Right in the mug! And I've got all sorts of gadgets in my pockets: we'll have some fun on this trip.'

'You bloody fool,' said Charles with a laugh: 'You bloody young fool.'

Blanchard alarmed him: their trolleys were touching, if he wants to pinch me, or put itching powder under my bed-clothes, he's only got to reach out a hand. I have no luck, he thought: I shall have to be on the look-out during the whole journey. He sighed, and found himself looking at the ceiling, a large dark expanse studded with rivets. He had tipped his mirror backwards, and its surface was as dark as a plate of smoked glass. Charles raised himself slightly, and glanced round him. They had left the sliding door wide open: a yellow light frothed through the compartment, hovering over the bed-clothes and bleaching the patients' faces. But the illuminated space was exactly delimited by the frame of the door: on the left and right the darkness was almost complete. Lucky devils, no doubt they had been careful to tip the porters: they will have all the air and all the light: now and again, if they raise themselves on one elbow, they will see a green tree go past. He fell back, exhausted: his shirt was soaked. If only the train would start. But the train remained at a standstill in that merciless sunlight. A strange smell of rotten straw and Houbigant scent hung about the floor. He found it nauseating, and tried to raise his head above it, but the sweat burst out all over him, he sank back, and the smell gathered once more above his nose. Outside – railway lines and sunshine, empty trucks on the sidings, bushes white with dust: desolation. And then, farther off – Sunday. Sunday at Berck: children playing on the beach, families drinking coffee in the restaurants. What a scream, he thought, what a scream. A voice came from the far end of the carriage: 'Denis! Hi! Denis!'

No one answered.

'Maurice, are you there?'

There was a silence, then the voice concluded, mournfully 'The swine!'

The silence was broken. Someone groaned near Charles: 'How hot it is!'

And a voice answered, the pallid, wavering voice of someone gravely ill: 'It will be better soon, when the train starts.'

They were talking blindly, not knowing to whom they spoke: and someone said with a short laugh: 'That's how soldiers travel.'

The silence fell once more. Heat, silence, misery. Charles suddenly caught sight of two shapely legs in white cotton stockings, his eyes travelled up them to a white blouse: the pretty nurse. She had just got into the carriage. She was carrying a suitcase in one hand, and a camp-stool in the other: and she surveyed the scene with an air of vexation.

'It's crazy,' she said. 'It's just crazy.'

'What – what?' said a harsh voice from outside.

'If you had thought for a moment, you might have realized that the men mustn't be put with the women.'

'We put them just as they came in.'

'And how do you suppose I'm to attend to men and women together?'

'You should have been there when they were put into the train.'

'I can't be everywhere at once. I was getting the luggage registered.'

'What a mess,' said the man.

'It certainly is.'

There was a silence, then she continued: 'Kindly get some more porters: the men will be transferred into the rear coaches.'

'Yes, I don't think! Who's going to pay for the extra work?'

'I shall make a complaint,' said the nurse curtly.

'Complain away, my girl.'

The nurse shrugged her shoulders and turned away. She stepped cautiously between the bodies, and sat down on her camp-stool, not far from Charles, on the edge of the rectangle of light.

'Hi, Charles!' said Blanchard.

'Well,' quavered Charles.

'There's females around.'

Charles did not reply.

'And what am I to do,' said Blanchard at the top of his voice, 'if I want to shit?'

Charles flushed with rage, but he thought of the itching powder, and emitted a collusive little laugh.

There was a shuffling noise at the level of the floor – no doubt some of the men straining their necks to see if they had feminine neighbours. But a general sense of uneasiness brooded over the compartment. Some scattered whispers faded into silence. 'What shall I do if I want to shit?' Charles felt dirty, he was aware, inside himself, of a mass of damp and sticky innards: how ghastly to have to ask for a pan in the presence of all these young women. He held himself in, and thought: 'I'll stick it out.' Blanchard was breathing hard, his nose emitted an ingenuous little chant – Oh God, if he could only sleep! Charles had a moment of hope, he took a cigarette out of his pocket, and lit it.

'What's the matter?' asked the nurse. She had a bunch of

knitting on her knees. Charles saw her angry face, in a blue shadow, far away above him.

'I'm lighting a cigarette,' he said: and his voice sounded oddly intrusive.

'You mustn't smoke here,' she said.

Charles blew the match out, and groped round him with the tips of his fingers. Between two sets of bedclothes, he came upon a damp rough plank which he scratched with a finger-nail before he dropped the scrap of half-carbonized wood; then suddenly the contact revolted him, and he brought his hands back to his chest: I'm level with the ground, he thought. Level with the ground. On the floor. Under the tables and the chairs, under the heels of the nurses and the porters, prostrate among the mud and straw, all the insects that swarm in the cracks of floor-boards could dart on to his stomach. He shook his legs and arms, he scraped his heels on the toe of the stretcher – but softly: so as not to wake Blanchard. The sweat poured over his chest: he drew his knees up beneath the bedclothes. These uneasy tinglings in his thighs and legs, these violent, vague revulsions in his whole body had in-cessantly tormented him since his earliest days at Berck. And then it had all passed away: he had forgotten his legs, he had found it quite natural to be pushed and wheeled and carried, he had developed into an object. 'It won't start again,' he thought with anguish, 'surely it won't start again?' He stretched his legs and closed his eyes. He must say to himself: I am just a stone. His clenched hands opened, he felt his body gradually petrifying beneath the bedclothes. A stone among stones.

He sat up suddenly, with open eyes and stiffened neck: a jerk, then a grinding sound that promptly merged into a monotonous rumble, as soothing as the fall of rain: the train had started. It was passing *alongside something*: outside, solid objects soaked in sunshine slid past the coaches: fleeting shadows, slowly at first and then with increasing speed, crossed the luminous wall opposite the open door; like a screen in a cinema. The light, on the wall, paled a little and grew grey – then a sudden blaze: 'We're coming out of the station.' Charles had a pain in his neck, but he felt calmer: he lay back, raised his arms and tilted his mirror at an angle of ninety degrees. Now he could see in the left corner of the glass a section of the illuminated rectangle. That was enough: that shining surface was alive, it embodied a whole country-side: sometimes the light flickered and faded, as though it were about to vanish, sometimes it hardened and set into the semblance of a patch of yellow wash: then from time to time it quivered, slanting undulations shot across its surface, as though a wind had stirred it. Charles looked at it for a long while: in a moment or two he felt almost as free as though he were sitting with his legs dangling on the step of the carriage, watching the trees, the fields and the sea pass by.

'Blanchard!' he murmured.

No answer. He waited a moment, and whispered: 'Are you asleep?'

Blanchard did not answer. Charles heaved a little sigh of satisfaction, and relaxed, stretching himself out full length, his eyes still on his mirror. He sleeps; he sleeps, when he came in he could hardly stand, he dropped on to the seat, but his eyes were hard and what they said was: 'You won't get me.' He ordered his coffee with a very truculent air, there are certainly some customers who treat the waiters as enemies: mostly half-baked youths who think of life as a battle, they have read as much in books, so they make trouble in cafés, order a grenadine with a look fit to kill.

'One coffee here,' said Felix, 'and two ports on the terrace.'

She pressed the buttons and swung the crank. Felix winked at her and pointed to the short young man who had fallen asleep. It wasn't a conflict: it was a morass, try to move and you get stuck, but they don't realize it at once, and get sucked down all the quicker: I've been there, I've been there; now I'm getting old, I keep calm and quiet, I don't move, at my age one is scarcely likely to get stuck again. He was asleep, his mouth was open and his jaw sagging on to his chest, he didn't look at all inviting, his red and swollen eyelids and red nose gave him an oddly sheep-like air. I guessed at once, when I saw him come into the empty café, with that blind look on his face, so hot outside and all those customers on the terrace, I said to myself: he's got a letter to write, or he is waiting for a woman, or something has gone badly wrong. He lifted a long, pale hand, and brushed the flies away without opening his eyes: there wasn't a fly. He is suffering even in his sleep: indeed, troubles pursue us everywhere, I was sitting on a bench looking at the railway lines and the tunnel, a bird was singing, I was down and out. I was pregnant and had just been sacked, I had no more eyes to cry with, no more money in my bag, just my ticket, and I went to sleep, I dreamt I was being killed, that someone was pulling my hair and calling me a tart and then the train came and I got into it. Sometimes I think he'll get his allowance – as a working-man in bad health, they can't refuse it to him, sometimes I think they'll wriggle out of it, they're such a grasping lot: here I am, I'm old, I don't budge now, but I get ideas into my head. He's well dressed, I'm sure he has a mother to look after his clothes, but his shoes are very dusty: what has he been doing? Where has he come from? The blood gets into young folks' heads, if he'd told me to kill my father and mother, I'd have done it, a girl can be so besotted sometimes: perhaps he has murdered an old woman like me: they'll catch him all right, he can't look after himself: I dare say they'll come here to pinch him, and his photograph will appear in the *Matin*, a nasty little tyke, not in the least like him, and people will say as usual: Aha, he looks just the sort of chap to do such a thing: well, I always say that if you wanted to think the worst of a man, better not see him close to, because when you watch him getting stuck a little deeper you think it's all just hopeless and in the end there's no differ-ence between drinking a cup of café crême outside a café, saving up to buy a house, or murdering one's mother. The telephone rang, and she gave a start.

'Hullo?'

'I want to speak to Madame Cazin.'

'Speaking,' she said. 'Well?'

'They've refused it,' said Julot.

'What?' she said. 'What – what?'

'They've refused it.'

'You don't mean it.'

'They've refused it.'

'But an old worker like you, and sick too: what did they say?'

'They said I hadn't any claim.'

'Oh!' she said. 'Oh!'

'See you this evening,' said Julot.

She hung up the receiver. So they've refused it. And him an old man, in bad health, and they've told him he hasn't any claim. Now I'm going to get angry, she thought. The young man was snoring, he looked silly and pompous. Felix went out, carrying the two ports and the coffee on his tray: he pushed the door open and the sunlight came in, the mirror glittered above the sleeper, then the door closed once more, the mirror grew dim, and the two of them were left alone. What has he done? Where has he come from? What has he got in his suitcase? Well, he'll pay: and go on paying, for twenty, thirty years, unless he's killed in the war, poor lad, he is of an age to fight. There he is, asleep and snoring, and in trouble, while people on the terrace are talking about the war, and my husband can't get his allowance. 'Poor, poor wretches that we are,' she said.

'Pitteaux!' exclaimed the young man.

He had awakened with a start: for an instant he looked at her, with reddened eyes and open mouth, then he clicked his jaws, bit his lips, and assumed an air of brisk ill-humour.

'Waiter!'

Felix did not hear: she could see him on the terrace, as he came and went, taking orders. The young man looked annoyed and tapped on the marble table, peering to right and left with a hunted expression on his face. She took pity on him.

'It's a franc,' she said, from the elevation of the cashier's desk.

He glanced venemously at her, flung a five-franc piece on to the table, picked up his suitcase and limped away. The mirror flashed, a blast of talk and heat came into the room: solitude came in too. She looked at the tables, the mirrors, the door, all those too familiar objects that could no longer hold her thought: She said to herself, 'I'm going to get angry.'

A splash of light fell upon him – it was an electric torch pointed at him from the side. He turned his head and grunted. The torch flashed across the floor: he blinked. Behind that flash a calm implacable eye observed him, and it was more than he could bear.

'What's the matter?' he said.

'Yes – it's him,' said a lilting voice.

A woman. The oblong package beside me is a woman. After a brief moment of satisfaction he reflected angrily that she had flashed a light on him as though he were an object: he might have been a wall: 'I don't know you,' he snapped.

'We have often met,' she said.

The light went out. He was still dazzled, violet circles revolving within his eyes.

'I can't see you.'

'I can see you,' she said. 'Even without the torch I can see you.'

The voice was young and pretty, but he felt suspicious. He said again: 'I can't see you: I was dazzled by your torch.'

'I can see in the dark,' she said proudly.

'Are you an albino?'

She laughed. 'Albino? I haven't got red eyes, and white hair, if that's what you mean.'

She had a marked accent, which lent a questioning intonation to all she said.

'Who are you?'

'Guess!' she said. 'It shouldn't be difficult: you saw me the day before yesterday, and looked at me as if you hated me.'

'Hated you? I don't hate anybody.'

'Oh yes you do,' she said. 'Indeed I think you hate everybody.'

'Wait! Weren't you wearing a fur?'

Again she laughed. 'Reach out a hand,' she said: 'feel!'

He stretched out an arm, and felt a large soft mass – a fur. Underneath the fur there would be blankets, then layers of clothing, then a soft white body, like a snail in its shell. How hot she must be! He stroked the fur, which exhaled a warm, heavy odour. That was what he had noticed a little while ago. He stroked the fur against the nap, and felt quite pleased.

'You have fair hair,' he said triumphantly: 'And you wear gold ear-rings.'

She laughed, and switched on the torch again: this time she pointed it at her own face: the rocking of the train made the torch quiver in her hand: the light moved from her chest to her forehead, skimmed over the painted lips, gilded a faint, yellow down at their corners, and reddened the nostrils. The curved and darkened eyebrows stood out like two little paws above the swollen eyelids: they looked like two insects on their backs. Her fair hair frothed in a light cloud round her head. His heart turned over. He thought to himself, She's beautiful: and abruptly withdrew his hand.

'I recognize you now. There was always an old gentleman wheeling you about: and you never looked at anybody.'

'I looked at you carefully, through my eyelashes.'

She lifted her head, and he recognized her.

'I couldn't have believed you would notice me,' he said. 'You looked so rich, so much above us all: I thought you were at the Pension Beaucaire.'

'No,' she said. 'I was at Mon Chalet.'

'Well, I didn't expect to meet you again in a cattle truck.'

The light went out: 'I'm very poor,' she said.

He stretched out a hand, and laid it lightly on the fur: 'How about this?'

She laughed. 'It's all I've got left.'

She had receded into shadow, and lay there, a large, dark, shapeless package. But the vision of her lingered in his eyes. He clasped his hands across his stomach, and stared at the ceiling. Blanchard was snoring gently: the patients had begun to talk among themselves, in twos and threes: the train rumbled on. She was poor and ill, she was lying on her back in a cattle-truck, she had to be dressed and undressed like a doll. And she was beautiful. As beautiful as a film star. Beside him lay all that humiliated beauty, that slim, pure, tarnished body. She was beautiful. She sang in music-halls, she had looked at him through her eyelashes, and she had wanted to make his acquaintance: he felt as though he had been lifted on to his two feet.

'You are a singer?' he asked abruptly.

'Singer? Why, no. I can play the piano.'

'I took you for a singer.'

'I'm Austrian,' she said. 'All my money is there, in German hands. I left Austria after the Anschluss.'

'Were you ill then?'

'I was already on my back. My parents took me away by train. It was just like today, except that we weren't in the dark and I was on a seat in a first-class compartment. There were German planes overhead, we kept on imagining they were going to bomb us. My mother was crying, I lay with my nose in the air, I could feel the weight of the sky upon me through the ceiling. It was the last train that got through.'

'And then?'

'Then I came here. My mother is in England: she has to keep us all.'

'And the old gentleman who was with you?'

'Just an old fool,' she said harshly.

'So you are quite alone?'

'Quite.'

He repeated: 'Quite alone in the world,' and felt as strong and enduring as an oak.

'When did you realize it was me?'

'When you struck that match.'

He would not indulge his delight: it loomed in the background, almost out of view: but it lent an acid quiver to his voice. He would reserve it for the night-time, he wanted to savour it in solitude.

'Did you see the light on the partition?'

'Yes,' she said. 'I've been looking at it for the last hour.'

'Look – look. There's a tree passing.'

'Or a telegraph pole.'

'The train isn't going fast.'

'No,' she said. 'Are you in a hurry?'

'No. We don't know where we're going.'

'Indeed we don't,' she said gaily. Her voice was trembling too.

'After all,' he said, 'this train isn't so bad.'

'It's not stuffy,' she said. 'And I love to watch the passing shadows.'

'Do you remember the myth of the cave?'

'No. What is it?'

'It's about some slaves imprisoned in a cave, who see shadows on a wall.'

'Why were they imprisoned?'

'I don't know. Plato wrote it.'

'Ah yes – Plato,' she said vaguely.

'I'll explain to her who Plato was,' he thought rapturously. He had a slight stomach-ache, but he found himself wishing that the journey might never end.

Georges shook the door-handle. Through the window he could see a tall moustachioed fellow and a young woman with a napkin knotted round her head, washing cups and glasses behind a wooden counter. A soldier sat dozing at a table. Georges tugged violently at the handle, and the window shook. But the door did not open. The woman and the man did not seem to hear.

'They won't open.'

He turned: a large, florid man was eyeing him with a smile. He wore a black jacket over a pair of army trousers, puttees, a soft hat and a winged collar. Georges pointed to the notice: 'The canteen opens at five o'clock.'

The other shrugged his shoulders. 'It's ten past five,' he said. A capacious haversack hung against his left hip, a gas-mask against his right hip: he flung his arms out, with his elbows in the air.

'They open when they feel inclined.'

The barrack yard was filled with men of middle age who looked very bored. Some strolled about alone staring at the ground. Some wore a military tunic, others khaki trousers, others were still in civilian clothes, with brand-new clogs, which clattered against the tarred surface of the yard. A tall red-haired fellow who had been lucky enough to get hold of a complete outfit was pacing pensively up and down, his hands in the pockets of his tunic; but he had a bowler hat cocked truculently over one ear. A lieutenant shouldered his way through the little groups and made for the canteen.

'Haven't you got your uniform?' asked the short fat man. He tugged at the straps of his haversack in an effort to slew it round to his back.

'There are none left.'

The man spat between his feet. 'I've been issued with this little lot, and I'm about stifling on a day like this. What a bloody mess-up!'

Georges indicated the officer. 'Do we have to salute him?'

'How? I can't very well take my hat off to him.'

The officer passed but did not look at them. Georges eyed his skinny back, and felt utterly despondent. It was hot, the windows of the barrack buildings were painted blue: behind the white walls lay white roads, and aerodromes, green beneath the sunshine as far as eye could reach: the barrack walls had cut from the turf of the countryside a small, level, dusty section of land, on which weary men walked up and down as they did in a street. It was the hour when the shutters were opened at home: the sun came into the dining room: the sun was everywhere, in houses and barracks, and the country. He said to himself: 'It's always the same.' But he didn't quite know what was always the same. He thought of the war, and realized that he wasn't afraid to die. A train whistled in the distance; and he felt as though someone had smiled at him.

'Listen,' he said.

'To what?'

'To the train.'

The small fat man eyed him uncomprehendingly, then produced a handkerchief and began to dab his forehead. The train whistled again, and moved off with its load of civilians, pretty women, and children: the fields slid innocuously past the windows. The train whistled and slowed down.

'It's going to stop,' said Charles.

The train creaked to a standstill; all sense of movement was drained out of Charles, he was left arid and empty as though purged of all his blood; it was a sort of death in miniature.

'I don't like it when a train stops,' he said.

Georges thought of the trains packed with travellers moving southwards, towards the sea, and the white villas by the seaside; Charles was conscious of the green herbage growing under the floor-boards and between the rails, his vision penetrated the iron walls, and he could see the luminous rectangle outlined on the partition, green fields as far as eye could reach; the train was embedded in the countryside like a ship in an ice-floe, the grass was climbing up the wheels, thrusting through the gaping planks, the country was flooding into the motionless train. The trapped train whistled mournfully: the whistle faded into a romantic cadence and then died away: the train rumbled gently on, the head of Maurice's neighbour lolled to and fro on its yellow collar, he was a big man smelling of garlic, he had been singing the *Internationale* since the start, and had drunk two litres of raw wine. At last he collapsed with a gurgle on to Maurice's shoulder. Maurice was very hot, but he did not dare to move – what with the heat, the white wine, and the white sunshine pouring through the grimy windows, he felt quite sick, and thought: 'I wish we were there.' His eyes smarted, swelled, and hardened, he closed his eyelids, and heard the blood buzzing in his ears, the sun stabbed through his eyelids: a white, sweaty, blinding slumber came upon him, the man's hair tickled his neck and chin, it was a ghastly afternoon. The tall man produced a photo from his pocket book:

'That's my wife,' he said.

It was the nondescript type of female usually depicted on photographs, and Georges could find nothing to say about her.

'She looks healthy,' said Georges.

'She eats enough for four,' said the man.

They remained face to face, irresolute: Georges rather disliked this large, florid fellow, who gasped when he talked, but he wanted to show him his daughter's photograph.

'Married?'

'Yes.'

'Any children?'

Georges looked at him and grinned. Then he thrust a hand into his pocket, produced his pocket-book, and took out a photograph, which he handed to the other with eyes averted.

'That's my daughter.'

'You've got a grand pair of boots,' said the man, taking the photograph. 'They'll last you a long while.'

'I suffer from corns,' said Georges with a deprecating air. 'Do you think they'll let me keep those boots?'

'They'll be only too glad. I dare say they haven't got boots enough to go round.'

He surveyed Georges's boots for another moment or two, then regretfully raised his eyes to the photo. Georges felt that he was blushing: 'What a fine child,' said the man. 'How much does she weigh?'

'I don't know,' said Georges.

He looked with amazement at the large man as he held the photograph between his fingers, and fixed his chilly gaze upon it. And he said: 'When I come back, she won't recognize me.'

'Quite probable,' said the man. 'Unless . . .'

'Yes,' said Georges. 'Unless . . .'

'Well,' asked Sarraut. 'Am I to go?'

He turned the paper over in his fingers. Daladier had trimmed a match with a knife, and thrust it between two of his teeth. He did not answer, he sat, a creased and huddled figure in his chair.

'Am I to go?' repeated Sarraut.

'It's war,' said Bonnet quietly. 'And we shall lose the war.'

Daladier started, and fixed Bonnet with a heavy look. Bonnet returned it with a guileless expression in his clear, shallow eyes. He looked like an ant-eater. Champetier de Ribes and Reynaud stood a little in the background, two silent, disapproving figures. Daladier sank back and blurted out, 'Go,' with a limp wave of his hand.

Sarraut rose and went out of the room. He walked downstairs, conscious of an ache in the top of his head. They were all there, they fell silent at the sight of him and assumed their professional expressions. 'Fools,' thought Sarraut.

'I will now read the communiqué,' he said.

The responding murmur gave him a moment in which to wipe his spectacles; then he read as follows:

'The Cabinet Council has heard the observations of the President of the Council and of Monsieur Georges Bonnet on the memorandum communicated to Monsieur Chamberlain by the Chancellor of the Reich.

'The Council has unanimously approved the statement which Messieurs Edouard Daladier and Georges Bonnet propose to take to London for communication to the British Government.'

'I thought so,' said Charles to himself. 'I want to shit.' It had happened quite suddenly: his belly was brimful.

'Yes, yes,' he said. 'I agree with you. Yes.'

The voices rose placidly, side by side. He would have liked to merge himself into his voice, to be just a grave voice beside the lilting blonde voice of his neighbour. But, *first of all* – the heat, the throbbing urgency within him, the mass of moist matter that gurgled in his intestines – all this was himself. A silence fell: she lay dreaming at his side, a cool and snowy presence: he cautiously lifted a hand and passed it over his damp forehead. 'H-r-r-m,' he ejaculated.

'What's the matter?'

'Nothing,' he said. 'It's my neighbour snoring.'

It had caught him in the stomach like a laugh beyond control – a dark and violent desire to open and dissolve into a fall of rain: a frantic butterfly between his buttocks. He clenched them, the sweat poured down his forehead, oozed into his ears and tickled his cheeks. 'I'm going to let it all go,' he thought in terror.

'You are very silent,' said the blonde voice.

'I . . .' he said, 'was wondering . . . why did you want to know me?'

'You have such nice arrogant eyes,' she said. 'And I wanted to find out why you hated me.'

He shifted his back slightly, to help himself to hold out. He said: 'I hated everyone because I was poor. I am an unpleasant sort of fellow.'

The words escaped him under pressure of his need: he had evacuated upwards: upwards or downwards, he had to do it.

'An unpleasant sort of fellow,' he gasped. 'I'm envious.'

He had never talked so frankly to anyone. She touched his hand with the tips of her fingers.

'Don't hate me: I'm poor too.'

A quiver shot through his penis: not because of those warm, slender fingers on the back of his hand, it came from further away, from the large, bare room at the edge of the sea. He rang the bell, Jeannine came in, folded back the covers and slid the bedpan under him, she watched him pee and sometimes she held John Thomas between her finger and thumb – he loved that. Now, his flesh had stiffened, it had become a habit: all his urges to shit were poisoned by a sour languor, a swooning desire to let himself go with someone looking on, to stink under professional eyes. 'That's what I am,' he thought. His heart stopped. He despised himself, he shook his head and the sweat stung his eyes. 'So the train won't leave?' It seemed to him that if the carriage started up again, he would have been torn out of himself, his dubious, miserable longings left behind, and he would have been able to hold out a bit longer. He smothered another groan: pain tore through him like a rag; he shrank in silence, his hand on the soft, slim one beside him. *Almond cream hands, deftly take hold of John Thomas, triumphant John Thomas, lazy, head drooping a little, as a butcher's maid takes a chitterling on its bed of jelly between her fingers. Quite naked. Split. Seen. A burst pod, it's spring. Hell! He hated Jeannine.*

'How hot your hands are,' said the voice.

'I'm feverish.'

Someone whimpered in the sunlight; one of the patients near the door. The nurse got up and went to him, stepping across the intervening bodies. Charles raised his right arm and manoeuvred his mirror: the glass suddenly caught the nurse, bending over a large red-cheeked youth with prominent ears. She looked contemptuous and annoyed. Then she got up and returned to her place. Charles watched her search in her suitcase. She faced them, holding a bed-pan. And she said in ringing tones: 'Does anyone want this? If so, please speak up while the train is not moving – it's more convenient then. Above all don't restrain yourselves, don't feel ashamed. There are no men nor women here: only sick people.'

She surveyed them sternly, but no one responded. The large boy grabbed the bed-pan and slipped it under the bedclothes. Charles squeezed his friend's hand. He had only to raise his voice and say, 'Here, please.' The nurse bent down and removed the bed-pan. It flashed in the sunshine, now filled with a frothing yellow liquid. The nurse went to the door and leaned out: Charles saw her shadow on the partition, her lifted arm outlined in the rectangle of light. She tipped the bed-pan, a shadow spurted out of it.

'Madame . . .' said a quavering voice.

'Ah!' she said. 'You've decided to be sensible. I'm coming.'

They will give way one by one. The women will hold out longer than the men. The men will inflict their odours on the women beside them: how they dare to speak to them afterwards! 'Bastards,' he thought. There was much bustling at floor level: whispered, shamefaced appeals from every corner. Charles recognized some of the feminine voices.

'You must wait,' said the nurse. 'One at a time.'

Only sick people. They think they may do anything because they are patients. Not men nor women: sick people. He was suffering, but proud to suffer: I won't give way; I'm a man. The nurse went from one to the other, her shoes creaked across the floorboards, then came the rustle of paper. A stale, tepid odour filled the compartment. 'I won't give way,' he said to himself, writhing in his agony.

'Madame,' said the blonde voice.

He thought he had misheard, but the lilting voice repeated, in accents now of shame, 'Madame! Madame! – Here!'

'I'm coming,' said the nurse.

The hot, slim hand slipped out of Charles's grasp. He heard the creak of shoes: the nurse towered over them, like a stern archangel.

'Turn round,' said the pleading voice. And again she whispered: 'Please turn round.'

He turned his head, wishing he could plug his ears and nose. The nurse swooped, like a flight of blackbirds, darkening his mirror. He could see nothing more. 'She's a sick person,' he thought. She had had to throw off her fur: for an instant the scent of it drowned everything, then gradually a strong and rancid odour filled his nostrils. Well, she was a sick person: that taut and silky skin enclosed liquid vertebrae, and purulent intestines. He hesitated, torn between disgust and foul desire. Then, suddenly, his entrails closed up like a fist, and he was no longer conscious of his body. A sick person. All needs and all desires were extinguished, he felt clean and fresh, like a man who has regained his health. A sick person. 'She held out as long as she could,' he thought tenderly. There was a rustle of paper, the nurse got up, several voices already beckoned her to the other end of the compartment. He would not call her: he was hovering a few inches from the floor, above them. He was not an object: nor a helpless infant. 'She couldn't hold out,' he thought, with so warm a feeling that the tears came into his eyes. She didn't dare speak to him: 'She's ashamed. I'll look after her,' he thought affectionately. Standing up, and leaning over her, and gazing at her gentle, haggard face. She was panting faintly in the shadows. He reached out a hand and groped over her fur. The young body recoiled, but Charles found a hand and took it. The hand resisted, he drew it close to him, and squeezed it. A sick person. And there he was, compact and dry, a man delivered: he would look after her.

'What is your name?' he asked.

'Well, read it,' said Chamberlain impatiently.

Lord Halifax took Masaryk's message and began to read:

'He needn't put all that expression into it,' thought Chamberlain.

'My Government,' read Halifax, 'has now studied the document and the map. It is a *de facto* ultimatum, such as is commonly presented to a conquered nation, and not a proposal to a sovereign State which has shown every possible readiness to make sacrifices for the pacification of Europe. Monsieur Hitler's Government has shown not the faintest trace of a similar disposition. My Government is astonished by the contents of the memorandum. The proposals go far beyond what we agreed to in the so-called Anglo-French plan. They deprive us of all safeguards for our national existence. We are to yield large sections of our carefully prepared fortifications, and allow the German armies to penetrate deeply into our territory before having been able to organize it on a new basis, or make the smallest preparations for defence. Our national and economic independence would automatically disappear with the adoption of Monsieur Hitler's plan. The whole procedure of the transfer of population will be reduced to a mere stampede for those who will not accept the German Nazi régime. They will have to leave home without even the right to take their personal possessions with them, not even, in the case of peasants, their cow.

'My Government wishes me to declare with all possible solemnity that Monsieur Hitler's demands under their present form are absolutely and unconditionally unacceptable to my Government. Against these new and cruel demands, my Government feels constrained to offer a supreme resistance, and with the help of God, will do so. The nation of Saint Wenceslas, of Jan Hus, and Thomas Masaryk, will not be a nation of slaves.

'We rely on the three great Western democracies, to whose wishes we have deferred against our own judgement, to stand beside us in our hour of need.'

'Is that all?' asked Chamberlain.

'That is all.'

'More trouble,' he replied.

Lore Halifax did not answer: he stood erect like an embodied conscience, respectful and reserved.

'The French Ministers will arrive in an hour,' said

Chamberlain dryly. 'I find this document . . . inopportune, to say the least.'

'Do you think it is calculated to influence their decisions?' said Halifax with a sting of irony.

The old gentleman did not reply: he took the paper, and began to read it with muttered comments.

'Cows!' he ejaculated with annoyance. 'What's all this about cows? So very uncalled-for.'

'I don't find it so. I was rather touched,' said Lord Halifax.

'Touched?' said the old gentleman with a curt laugh. 'My dear fellow, we are conducting a negotiation. If we allow ourselves to be touched, we shall lose the game.'

Red and pink and mauve fabrics, mauve dresses, white dresses, bare throats, lovely bosoms, scarves, flickers of sunshine on tables and hands, sticky golden liquids, more hands, thighs emerging from shorts, gay voices, red-pink-white frocks, gay voices whirling in the air, thighs, the *Merry Widow* waltz, the smell of pines, warm sand, the vanilla-fragrance of the open sea, all the islands of the world unseen and present in that sunlight, the Leewards, Easter Island, the Sandwiches, the luxury shops along the sea front, ladies' raincoats at three thousand francs, jewelled clips, red-pink-white flowers, hands, thighs, 'Here's the band,' gay voices whirling in the air, Suzanne – what about your diet? Oh never mind – let's forget it just for once. Sails on the sea, skiers leaping with outstretched arms from wave to wave, pine-scented breezes; peace. Peace at Juan-les-Pins. There it still lurked, forlorn, forgotten, turning sour. People get caught in it; they mask their petty, accustomed agony behind thickets of music and colours: Mathieu strolled past the cafés and the shops, the sea on his left: Gomez's train did not arrive until six-seventeen: he looked mechanically at the women, eyeing their peaceful thighs and peaceful bosoms. But he was a defaulter. Since three-twenty-five he had been a defaulter. At three-twenty-five a train had left for Marseilles. 'I am no longer here. I am in Marseilles, in a café on the avenue de la Gare, I am waiting for the Paris train, I am in the Paris train. I am in Paris on a drowsy early morning, I am in barracks, I am pacing round and round the barrack yard, at Essey-lès-Nancy.' At Essey-lès-Nancy Georges stopped talking because he could not make himself heard; they all looked up, the plane was skimming over the roofs, Georges watched it, over the walls, over the roofs, over Nancy – at Niort, he was in Niort, in his room with that girl of his, with a hint of dust in his mouth. What is he going to say to me? He will dash out of the train, as gay and sunburnt as a holiday maker at Juan-les-Pins, I am as sunburnt as he is, but I've got no answers for him. I was at Toledo, at Guadalajara; what were you doing? I was living ... I was at Malaga, one of the last to leave the place; what have you done? I have lived. 'Well, well,' he thought irritably, 'it's a friend I'm going to meet, not a judge.' Charles laughed, she said nothing, she was still a little ashamed, he held her hand and laughed: 'Catherine – that's a lovely name,' he said to her affectionately. He has been lucky after all, he was in the Spanish war, he *was able* to be in it, no weapons, hand-grenades versus tanks, eagles' nests in the Sierra, love-making in desolate Madrid hotels, smoke-clouds in the plain, hand-to-hand fighting, Spain hasn't lost her savour: mine is going to be a dreary war, a ceremonious and boring war: anti-tank guns versus tanks, a collective, technical war, a sort of epidemic. There was Spain, a big flat fish afloat on the blue water. Maud stood with her elbows on the railing, looking at Spain. They're fighting over there. The ship glided past the coast: there, the sound of guns; here, the sound of waves, the splash of flying-fish. Mathieu was walking towards Spain, the sea on his left, France on his right. Maud glided past the coast, with Algeria on her left, voyaging towards her right, towards France; that scorching breath, that hovering haze, was Spain. Maud and Mathieu thought of the Spanish war, which kept them from brooding on the other war, the verdigris war preparing on their right. They must crawl as far as the ruined wall, round it, and back, then their mission will be done. The Moroccan clambered over the blackened rocks, his nails and toe-nails clogged with earth, he was afraid, he was thinking of Tangier: at the peak of Tangier there was a yellow one-storied house from which could be seen the eternal glitter of the sea, the home of a white-bearded Negro who swallowed snakes to amuse the English tourist; he must not forget that yellow house. Mathieu thought of Spain, Maud thought of Spain, the Moroccan clambered over the cracked soil of Spain, he thought of Tangier, and he felt alone. Mathieu turned into a dazzling street, Spain swung round, blazed, then dwindled into a smudge of fire on his left. Nice on the right, and beyond Nice, a gap – Italy. Before him lay the railway station, France and war, the *real* war; Nancy. He was at Nancy: beyond the station, he was making his way to Nancy. He wasn't thirsty, he wasn't hot, nor tired. His body swung beneath him, but seemed no longer his: colours, sounds, sunshine, smells, buried themselves in that body: it no longer concerned him. 'It's like the start of an illness,' he thought. Philippe slipped his suitcase into his left hand: he was exhausted, but he must last out until the evening. Until the evening: I shall sleep on the train. The terrace of the Tour d' Argent hummed like a beehive, red-pink-mauve frocks, rayon stockings, painted cheeks, caramel drinks, a syrupy, sticky crowd; pity stabbed his heart: they would be snatched out of their cafés and their rooms, and the war would be waged with their bodies. He pitied them, and he pitied himself: they sweltered in the light – clammy, satiated, desperate. Philippe was suddenly possessed by an access of weariness and pride: I am these people's conscience.

Another café. Mathieu eyed these handsome, sunburnt men, so smooth and perfectly composed, and felt like someone from another world. The casino on their right, the post-office on their left, and the sun behind them: and that's all: France, Spain, Italy are lamps they do not see. Here they are, solid and compact, and the war is a phantom. 'I am a phantom,' he thought. They would be lieutenants and captains, they would sleep in beds, they would shave every day, and many of them would know how to wangle themselves out of active service. Why not? What should prevent them? Loyalty to their fellows in this filthy business. But I'm one of them. And I ask no loyalty from any man. Why am I going to the war? he asked himself abruptly. 'Look out!' exclaimed Philippe to a man who bumped into him. He bent down to pick up his suitcase: the tall man in shabby shoes did not even turn. 'Brute!' muttered Philippe. He faced the café, and glared at the occupants. But nobody had noticed the incident. A little boy was crying, his mother dabbed his eyes with a handkerchief. At the adjoining table three men were sitting huddled in their chairs, with glasses of orangeade in front of them. 'Not so innocent as they look,' he thought, surveying them all with the insolent air that he assumed at times. Why should they go? They have only to refuse. The car sped onwards. Daladier lying back on the cushions sucked at an extinct cigarette, and eyed the passers-by. It bored him to go to London, no decent drinks, disgusting food, a hatless woman was laughing with her mouth wide open, he thought to himself: 'They don't realize the situation,' and shook his head. Philippe thought: 'They are being taken to the slaughter-house, and they don't realize it. They regard war as an illness. War is not an illness,' he thought emphatically. 'It's an abomination, because it's caused by men.' Mathieu swung the barrier open: 'I'm coming to meet a friend,' he said to the ticket-collector. The station looked cheerful, though deserted, and as silent as a cemetery. Why am I going? He sat down on a green bench. Some will refuse to go. But that's not my business. I might refuse and damn the consequences, or slip into Switzerland. Why don't I? Well, I just *can't*. And the war in Spain wasn't my business either. Nor the Communist Party. But what is my business? – he asked himself, almost in desperation. The railway lines gleamed in the sunshine, the train would arrive at the platform on the left. To his left, that little shimmering pool in the distance, where the lines rejoined – that was Toulon. Marseilles, Port-Bou, Spain. An absurd and futile war. Jacques says it is already lost. War is an illness, he thought: my business is to bear it like an illness. Merely from a sense of decency. I shall be a brave patient, anyway. Why make war? I can't approve of war. And, equally, why not? My skin isn't even worth saving. Well – he thought – there it is: I'm for it. I'm an official. And his sole resource was the dismal stoicism characteristic of officials, who endure everything – poverty, illness, and war – from motives of self-respect. He smiled as he reflected that he didn't even respect himself. A martyr – they need a martyr, thought Philippe. He was adrift and utterly exhausted; not a disagreeable sensation, but not to be resisted: in point of fact he couldn't see very much, two shutters to the right and left blocked his view of the street. The crowd swallowed him up, people were coming at him from every direction, children ran against his legs, faces blinking in the sunshine slid above his head, below his head, the same face swaying back and forth – Yes-yes-yes. Yes, we accept these starvation salaries, yes, we will fight, yes, our husbands shall fight, yes, we will queue up at the bakers' shops with our children in our arms. It was the crowd – the vast, silent acquiescence called a crowd. And if you try to explain anything to them, they hit you in the eye, thought Philippe, whose cheek still smarted, they trample you underfoot, and they still shout: Yes. As he looked at those dead faces, he measured his own impotence: one can't say a thing to them, a martyr is what they need: a man who stands up on tiptoe and shouts – No. They would fall upon him and tear him to pieces. Blood shed for them, and by them, would inject fresh force into their hearts: the spirit of the martyr would enter into them, they would lift their heads and their unblinking eyes, and a thunderous roar of refusal would roll from one end of the crowd to the other. I am that martyr, he thought. The victim's ecstasy took hold of him and he bowed his head, dropped the suitcase, and fell on his knees, engulfed in that universal consent.

'Hullo!' said Mathieu.

Gomez ran towards him, bareheaded, and still handsome. His eyes were blurred, he blinked, and said Where am I? Voices above him muttered: 'What's the matter? – He has fainted – what's your address?' A head bent over him, the head of an old woman – is she going to bite me? Your address! Mathieu and Gomez grinned at each other – your address, *your address*, YOUR ADDRESS, he made a violent effort, and got up. Then he smiled and said: 'It's nothing, madame, it's the heat. I live quite near, I'll go straight home.'

'Someone must go with him,' said a voice behind him, 'he can't go home alone.' And the voice was lost in a rustle of leaves: 'Yes, *yes*, YES, someone must go with him – go with him – go with him.'

'Let me alone!' he exclaimed; 'Let me alone, don't touch me! No! *No!* No!' He looked them in the face, he looked at their weary, shocked eyes, and he cried: 'No.' No to the war, No to the general, No to guilty mothers, No to Zézette and Maurice. No – leave me in peace. They fell back, and he began to run with leaden feet. He ran and he ran, someone laid a hand on his shoulder and he nearly burst into tears. It was a young man with a small moustache, who handed him his suitcase.

'You have forgotten your suitcase,' he said with a laugh. The Moroccan stopped: it was a snake that he had taken for a dead branch. A small snake: he needed a stone to crush its head. But the snake wriggled, streaked over the ground like a flash, and vanished into the ditch. A lucky omen. Nothing stirred behind the wall. I'll come back, he thought.

Mathieu laid both hands on Gomez's shoulders.

'Well,' he said. 'Well, colonel!'

Gomez smiled a high, mysterious smile: 'A General,' he said.

Mathieu dropped his hands. 'General? Promotion must be rapid in your part of the world.'

'They're short of officers,' said Gomez, still smiling. 'How sunburnt you are, Mathieu.'

'It's luxury-tan,' said Mathieu, rather irritably. 'You pick it up at these seaside places, by doing nothing.'

He scanned Gomez's hands and face for any mark of what he had gone through: he was prepared for any amount of self-reproach. But Gomez, a slim and lively little figure in a flannel suit, was not yet giving himself away: for the moment, he looked like a summer visitor.

'Where shall we go?' he asked.

'We'll find some quiet little restaurant,' said Mathieu. 'I'm staying with my brother and my sister-in-law, but I won't ask you to dine with them: they are not amusing.'

'Let's go to a place where there's music and women.' He looked quizzically at Mathieu. 'I've just spent a week with my family.'

'Right,' said Mathieu. 'We'll go to the Provençal.'

The orderly watched them approach with a not unkindly and rather professional air. He stood motionless, and slightly bent, between two automatic ticket machines: his rifle and helmet gleamed in the sunshine. He hailed them as they passed.

'Where for?'

'Essey-lès-Nancy,' said Maurice.

'When you get outside, take the tram on the left, and go on to the terminus.'

They came out into the usual dismal railway station square,

223

with its cafés and hotels. There were puffs of smoke in the sky.

'It does one good to stretch one's legs,' said Dornier with a sigh.

Maurice looked up, smiled, and winked. 'I wonder where that lousy tram has got to,' said Bébert.

A woman eyed them sympathetically. 'It hasn't arrived yet. Where do you want to go?'

'To Essey-lès-Nancy,' said Maurice.

'You've got a good quarter of an hour yet. They go every twenty minutes.'

'Time for a drink,' said Dornier to Maurice.

It was cool, the train rolled on, the air was red: a thrill of joy swept over him, and he tugged at his bedclothes. 'Catherine!' he said; she did not reply. But something birdlike brushed against his chest and slowly slid up to his neck, then flew up and alighted on his forehead. It was her hand, her soft, perfumed hand, it glided on to Charles's nose, the light fingers fluttered against his lips, and tickled him. He seized the hand and pressed it against his mouth. It was warm: he slid his fingers along it to the wrist, and felt the pulse throb. He closed his eyes, kissed the slender hand, and the pulse throbbed beneath his fingers like the heart of a bird. She laughed: 'It's as though we were blind: we must get to know each other through our fingers.' He reached out an arm in his turn, he was afraid of hurting her: he touched the iron mirror-rod, and then a strand of hair outspread on the coverlet, fair hair, then a temple, then a cheek, delicately rounded like a woman's body, then a warm mouth breathed against his fingers, teeth nibbled them, and countless needles tingled up his back and neck: 'Catherine!' he said: 'This,' he thought, 'is making love.' She let go his hand and sighed, Maurice blew the froth off his beer on to the floor. He drank, and she said: 'What are those boats where people lie side by side?' Maurice licked his upper lip and said: 'It's nice and cool.' – 'I don't know,' said Charles: 'gondolas, perhaps.' – 'No, not gondolas – anyhow it doesn't matter: we might be in a boat like that.' He took her hand, they glided side by side downstream, she was his mistress, a star with pale gold hair, he was another man, and he was looking after her. He said: 'I wish the train would never get there.' Daniel nibbled his fountain-pen, there was a knock at the door, and he held his breath, he looked unseeing at the white paper on the blotting-pad. 'Daniel!' said Marcelle's voice. 'Are you there?' He did not answer: Marcelle's heavy footsteps moved away, she went downstairs, the stairs creaked one by one. He smiled, dipped his pen in the ink, and wrote: 'My dear Mathieu.' A clasped hand in the darkness, the scratch of a pen, Philippe's face emerges from the darkness and comes to meet him, pale in the shadowed mirror, a pitching ship, the iced beer gurgles in his throat and half-chokes him, the train covers thirty-three yards between Paris and Rouen in a human second, the three-thousandth second of the twentieth hour of 24 September 1938. A second gone speeding between the rails after Charles and Catherine through the sweltering country-side, left behind by Maurice in the sawdust of a dark, cool café, afloat in the wake of a steamer, immersed in a pool of ink, glistening and drying in the downstrokes of the M in Mathieu, while the pen scratches at the paper, and Daladier, recumbent on the cushions of his car, sucks an extinct cigarette and watches the passers-by. He loathed London: he kept his eyes fixed on the door so as not to see Bonnet's ugly mug, and that blasted Englishman's wooden face: 'They don't realize what's up,' he thought. He noticed a hatless woman, laughing with her mouth wide open. They all looked vacantly at the car, two or three of them shouted: 'Hurrah!' but clearly they did not realize what was happening, they did not understand that the car was carrying war and peace to Downing Street, war or peace, heads or tails – that black car hooting along the road to London. Daniel continued to write. The captain stopped outside the first-class saloon, and read: 'This evening at nine o'clock, Baby's Ladies' Orchestra will give a sym-phonic concert in the first-class saloon. All passengers, re-gardless of class, are cordially invited.' He puffed at his pipe and thought: 'She's much too thin.' Just at that moment, he smelt a warm perfume, and heard a faint flutter of wings, it was Maud, and he turned round: in Madrid the setting sun gilded the ruined façades of the university city; through the debris, the Belgian aimed, Maud and the captain eyed each other. The Moroccan raised his head and saw the Belgian: they eyed each other, and then, abruptly, Maud smiled an acid smile, and turned her head away, the Belgian pressed the

trigger, the Moroccan fell dead, the captain stepped towards
Maud, then thought: 'She's too thin', and stopped. 'Bloody
bastard,' said the Belgian. He looked at the dead Moroccan,
and repeated: 'Bloody bastard!'

'Well,' said Gomez, 'and Marcelle? Sarah told me it was over?'

'It is,' said Mathieu. 'She has married Daniel.'

'Daniel Sereno? That's odd,' said Gomez. 'Still, it's a
let-out for you.'

'Let-out?' said Mathieu. 'From what?'

'Marcelle wasn't your sort,' said Gomez.

'Nonsense!' said Mathieu.

The dinner-tables were arranged in a semicircle round a
sanded dance-floor strewn with pine needles. The Provençal
was deserted: a solitary guest was eating the wing of a chicken
and drinking Vichy water. The bandsmen climbed wearily on
to their stage, sat down with much clattering of chairs and
began to whisper to each other, as they tuned their instru-
ments; the sun was still visible, a dark disc between the
pines, Mathieu stretched his legs under the table and sipped
a glass of port. For the first time in a week he felt at home:
he had suddenly collected himself, he was completely at ease
in this strange place which combined the atmosphere of a
private room with that of a magic grotto. The pines looked
like cardboard trees, and in the soft outdoor darkness the
lamps shed a sort of boudoir radiance on the tablecloths: a
spotlight flashed through the trees, suddenly whitening the
dance-floor into a semblance of cement. But overhead hovered
the shadow of what was not there, the stars flickered in the
sky, vague persistent little insects: a smell of resin, and the
sea-wind, insistent and uneasy like an anguished soul, flutter-
ing the tablecloths, and suddenly thrusting its cold muzzle
into one's neck.

'Let's talk about you,' said Mathieu.

Gomez seemed surprised: 'Have you had no adventures?'
he asked.

'None,' said Mathieu.

'Not during the last two years?'

'No. I am exactly as you left me.'

'Oh you damned Frenchmen!' laughed Gomez. 'You're all
eternal.'

The saxophonist laughed, as the violinist said something into his ear. Ruby leaned towards Maud, who was tuning her violin: 'Play at the old chap in the second row,' she said.

Maud giggled: the old chap was as bald as an egg. She look round the auditorium, there were quite five hundred people present. She noticed Pierre standing near the door, and stopped laughing. Gomez eyed the violinist gloomily, then glanced at the empty chairs.

'For a quiet little corner – one couldn't do better,' he said in a voice of resignation.

'There's a band,' said Mathieu.

'So I see,' said Gomez.'

He looked at the players with an air of disapproval. Maud read disapproval in all their eyes, her face was rather flushed, as always on these occasions: and she thought: 'Oh dear what's the good of it all?' But France, an erect and sparkling figure in a tricolour sash, displayed every sign of happiness; she smiled, she beat time in advance: she held the bow with her little finger lifted, as though it were a fork.

'You promised me women,' said Gomez.

'I know I did,' said Mathieu despondently. 'I don't know what's the matter: at this time last week all the tables were booked, and there were plenty of lovelies, I assure you.'

'It's the news,' said Gomez in his quiet voice.

'I expect so.'

Events: it was still true: events existed for them too. They fought, with their backs to the Pyrenees and their eyes on Valencia, Madrid, and Tarragona: but they read the papers and they think of the men and weapons swarming at their backs, and they have their views on France, Czechoslovakia, and Germany. He shifted a little on his chair: a fish had approached the window of the aquarium, and was goggling at him. He threw a shrewd grin at Gomez and said in a hesitant tone:

'People are beginning to understand.'

'They understand nothing,' said Gomez. 'A Spaniard may understand, a Czech also, and perhaps even a German, because they're in it. The French aren't; they understand nothing: they're just afraid.'

Mathieu felt hurt, and said curtly: 'They are not to be

blamed for that. I personally have nothing to lose, and I don't particularly mind joining up: it's a change for me. But anyone who is really keen about something can't find it easy to change over from peace to war.'

'I did it in an hour,' said Gomez. 'Do you think I wasn't keen on painting?'

'You're different,' said Mathieu.

Gomez shrugged. 'You talk like Sarah.'

They fell silent. Mathieu did not think very highly of Gomez. Less than Brunet, and less than Daniel. But he felt guilty in the company of a Spaniard. He shivered. A fish against the window of the aquarium. And that look made him feel abysmally French. Guilty. Guilty, and French. He wanted to say: 'But damn it all! – I was an interventionist.' But that was not the point. His personal views did not count. He was French, it would have served no useful purpose to disavow his solidarity with other Frenchmen. I decided on non-intervention in Spain, I sent no arms, I closed the frontier to the volunteers. He must defend himself with all the rest, or suffer condemnation with them, together with the *maître d'hôtel*, and the dyspeptic gentleman drinking Vichy water.

'It's very silly,' he said: 'but I had imagined that you would appear in uniform.'

Gomez smiled. 'In uniform? Would you like to see me in uniform?'

He produced a packet of photographs from his pocket-book, and handed them to Mathieu one by one. 'There!' A trim, imperious officer on the steps of a church.

'You don't look very amiable.'

'That's the intention,' said Gomez.

Mathieu looked at him and burst out laughing. 'Yes,' said Gomez. 'It's a farce.'

'I wasn't thinking that,' said Mathieu. 'I was wondering whether I should look as unpleasant as you do in uniform.'

'Are you an officer?' asked Gomez with interest.

'No, a private.'

'All Frenchmen are privates,' said Gomez with a gesture of annoyance.

'Just as all Spaniards are generals,' said Mathieu sharply.

Gomez laughed. 'Look at that,' he said, holding out a photograph.

A girl, dark-haired and rather sad, but very pretty. Gomez had an arm round her waist, and was smiling with the self-complacent air he always assumed in photographs.

'Mars and Venus,' said he.

'That's as I know you,' said Mathieu. 'You seem to like them rather young.'

'She's fifteen: but war matures them. Here's one of me in action.'

Mathieu saw a little man squatting under a section of ruined wall.

'Where is that?'

'Madrid. The university city. Fighting's still going on there.'

He had fought. He had really crouched behind that wall under fire. He was a captain at the time. Perhaps he was short of cartridges, and cursing the French. Gomez sat back in his chair, he had finished his glass of port, he took out his box of matches with a suave, deliberate gesture, lit his cigarette, his fine, rather humorous features leapt out of the shadow, and were again extinguished. He had fought: no sign of it is visible in his eyes. The falling night enveloped him, his face looked blue above the pink lamp, the band was playing *No te quiero mas*, the wind fluttered the tablecloth, a woman entered, a luxurious, solitary figure, and sat down at the next table, her perfume drifted to their noses. Gomez inhaled it, dilating his nostrils, his face hardened, and he turned his head with an inquisitive air.

'To your right,' said Mathieu.

Gomez fixed a wolfish look upon her, he had become serious now. 'That's a pretty girl,' he said.

'She's an actress,' said Mathieu. 'She owns a dozen pairs of beach pyjamas. Kept by a Lyons manufacturer.'

'Hum!' said Gomez.

She returned his look, and averted her eyes with a half-smile.

'You won't waste your evening,' said Mathieu.

He did not reply. He had laid his forearm on the table, Mathieu looked at the hairy, ringed hand, pink beneath the radiance of the lamp. There he is, a blue-chinned male with pink hands, inhaling the fair-haired lady's perfume, and summoning her with a look. He has fought. Behind him lie scorched villages, eddies of red dust, bare hill-ridges, bursting flames that do not even glimmer in his eyes. He has fought: he is going back to fight, and he is there, he sees the same white tablecloths that I see. He tried to look at the pines, the dancing-floor, the woman, with the eyes of Gomez, eyes burnt by flames of war: he succeeded for a moment, and then the restless, parched splendour of the vision vanished. He has fought, he has . . . how romantic he is! 'I am not romantic,' thought Mathieu. 'No,' said Odette: 'only two places, M. Mathieu won't be back to dinner.' She went to the open window, she could hear the band at the Provençal playing a tango. They listened to the music: and Mathieu thought: 'He is only passing through.' The waiter brought the soup. 'No,' said Gomez: 'no soup.' They played the *Tango du chat*: France's violin leapt into the light, then suddenly dived into shadow like a flying-fish. France smiled, her eyes half-closed, she dived behind her violin, the bow scraped across the strings, the violin squeaked, Maud heard the violin squeaking against her ear, she heard the bald gentleman cough, and Pierre looked at her, Gomez began to laugh, there was a rather unamiable expression on his face.

'A tango,' he said: 'a tango. If a French band played a tango like that, in a Madrid café . . .'

'They would be pelted with potatoes, eh?' said Mathieu.

'Stones!' said Gomez.

'We aren't popular in those parts?' said Mathieu.

'What do you think?' said Gomez.

He pushed the door open: the Bar Basque was deserted. Boris had gone into it one evening because of its name: 'Bar Basque' was reminiscent of *barbaque*, which was a word he could never say without laughing. Then he realized that the bar was a nice place, and he had come back there every evening, while Lola was at work. Through the open windows could be heard the distant band of the Casino: once, even, he had thought he recognized Lola's voice, but not again.

'Good day, Monsieur Boris,' said the landlord.

'Good day,' said Boris. 'I'll have a white rum.'

He felt in high spirits. He would drink two white rums while he smoked a pipe; then, about eleven o'clock, he would have a sausage sandwich. About midnight, he would call for Lola. The landlord bent over him and filled his glass.

'The Marseillais isn't here?' asked Boris.

'No,' said the landlord. 'He's got a business dinner.'

'Ah yes – I forgot.'

The Marseillais was a traveller in corsets, and there was another constant visitor called Charlier, a printer. Boris sometimes played cards with them, sometimes they talked politics and sport, or sat in silence at the bar-counter, or at a table at the back. Now and again Charlier would observe: 'Yes, yes, yes. Just so,' nodding his head: and thus the time passed pleasantly.

'Not many people today,' said Boris.

The man shrugged his shoulders.

'They're all doing a bunk. I usually keep open until All Saints,' he said, making his way back to the counter. 'But if this goes on, I shall shut down on 1 October, and go to my place in the country.'

Boris stopped drinking, he felt startled. In any case, Lola's contract expired on 1 October, they would have gone. But he did not like to think of the Bar Basque closed behind their backs. The Casino would close too, and all the hotels in Biarritz would be deserted. One had just the same feeling about death: if one was certain that other men would still be drinking white rum, bathing in the sea, and listening to jazz bands, one could feel a little comforted: but if everyone had to die at the same time, and humanity closed shop, the prospect would certainly be bleak.

'When do you reopen?' he asked, to reassure himself.

'If there's a war,' said the landlord, 'I shan't reopen at all.'

Boris counted on his fingers: 26, 27, 28, 29, 30, I shall come back five more times, and that will be the end: I shan't see the Bar Basque again. How funny! Five times. He would drink white rum at that table five more times, and then there would be war, the Bar Basque would close, and, in October '39, Boris would be mobilized. Oak candelabra shed a mellow reddish light over the tables. And Boris thought: I shall never see that light again. Not just that light: red against black. He would of course see many others, flares by night above the battlefields – not a bad sight, so people said. But that light would go out on 1 October, and Boris would never see it again. He looked with respect at a white reflection on the table; it was his own fault. He had always treated objects like forks and spoons as though they had been indefinitely renewable: a profound mistake: there was a finite number of bars, cinemas, houses, towns and villages, and one and the same individual could not go to each of them more than a finite number of times.

'Shall I turn on the wireless?' asked the landlord. 'It might entertain you.'

'No thanks,' said Boris. 'I'm quite all right.'

At the moment of his death, in '42, he would have lunched 365×22 times, 8,030 times in all, counting his meals in infancy. And assuming that he had had an omelette once out of every ten occasions, he would have eaten 803 omelettes. 'Only 803 omelettes?' he said to himself with astonishment. Oh no; there are the dinners too, that makes 16,060 meals, and 1,606 omelettes. Anyway, for a man partial to omelettes, that was not a considerable total. And what about cafés? – he continued. The number of times that I shall go to a café after today can be calculated: suppose I go twice a day, and that I am called up in a year, that makes 730 times. 730 times! – that's not very often. It gave him a shock all the same, but he was not particularly surprised: he had always known he would die young. He had often told himself that he would die of consumption, or be murdered by Lola. But in his inmost self he had never doubted that he would be killed in war. He worked, he prepared for his school certificate or his degree, but it was more or less by way of passing the time, just as girls go to lectures at the Sorbonne, while waiting to get married. How funny it all is, he said to himself: there were periods when men read law or philosophy, thinking they would have a good solicitor's practice by the time they were forty, or a professor's pension at sixty. One wondered what was really inside their heads. People who could look forward to 10,000, 15,000 evenings at cafés, 4,000 omelettes, 2,000 nights of love. And, if they left a place they liked, they would say quite definitely to themselves: we will come back here next year, or in ten years. They must do a lot of idiotic things, he said austerely to himself. One can't conduct one's life forty years ahead. For himself, he was much more modest: he had plans for two years, after which all would be over. One must restrict oneself. A junk passed slowly down the Blue River, and Boris suddenly felt despondent. He would never go to India, nor China, nor Mexico, nor even to Berlin, his life was even more restricted than he could have wished. A few months in England, Laon, Biarritz, Paris – and there are people who have gone round the world! One woman only. It was quite a small life: indeed it had an air of already being concluded, since he knew in advance all that it would not contain. One *must* restrict oneself. He sat up straight, drank a little rum, and thought: 'It's much more sensible, then there's no risk of waste.'

'Another rum.'

He raised his head, and gazed intently at the electric bulbs.

The clock opposite, above the mirror, began to strike: he could see his face in the mirror. 'Nine-forty-five,' he thought. 'At ten o'clock!' he thought: and called the waitress.

'The same again.'

The waitress went away and returned with the bottle of brandy and a saucer. She poured the brandy into Philippe's glass, and laid the saucer on the three others. She was smiling rather ironically, but Philippe looked her calmly in the eyes: he picked up the glass with a steady hand, and lifted it without spilling a drop: he drank a little, and put the glass down, still looking at the waitress.

'How much?'

'Do you want to pay now?' she asked.

'Yes.'

'Twelve francs.'

He gave her fifteen francs, and waved her away. 'Now,' he thought, 'I don't owe anything to anyone.' And he laughed to himself. Again he thought: 'Not to anyone.' He saw himself laughing in the mirror, and that made him laugh still more. On the last stroke of ten, he would get up, tear his reflection out of the glass, and his martyrdom would start. For the moment, he felt cheerful, and considered the situation in a nonchalant sort of way. A café was a hospitable place – a sort of Capua; his seat was as soft as a feather mattress, so soft that he sank into it, a faint sound of music came from behind the counter, and a clatter of crockery that reminded him of the cow-bells at Seelisberg. He saw himself in the glass, and he could have sat looking at himself and listening to the music for an eternity. At ten o'clock, he would get up, take his reflection in his hands and rip it off the glass like a dead skin, or like a speck flicked out of an eye. *Mirrors operated on for cataract.* . . . .

Cataracts of day.
In mirrors operated on for cataract.
Or, alternatively,
Cataract obliterates day in the mirror operated on for cataract.
Or again:
Niagara of day cataracts in the cataract operated mirror.

The words fell into powder, he clung to the cold marble, the wind is carrying me away, there was a sticky taste of alcohol in his throat. THE MARTYR. He looked at himself in the glass, he was looking at a martyr: he smiled a salutation at himself. 'Ten minutes to ten, aha!' he thought with satisfaction, I find *time so long.* Five minutes gone – an eternity. Two more motionless eternities, devoid of thought or pain, passed in contemplating the martyr's handsome, emaciated face, and then time will plunge with a roar into a taxi, into the train, on to Geneva.

Ataraxia.
Niagara of time.
Niagara of day.
In mirrors operated on for cataract.
I'm going off in a taxi.
To Gauburge, to Bibracte.
Whence an act! Whence an act!
Whence, too, cataract.

He laughed, he stopped laughing, he looked round him, the café smelt of railway station, train, and hospital; he longed to call for help. Seven minutes. Which would be most revolutionary? he asked himself. To go or not to go? If I go I revolt against others: if I don't go, I revolt against myself, and that is the nobler deed. Make every preparation, steal some money, procure false papers, break all his contacts, and then, at the last moment – pfftt! – I'm not going after all – good night! Freedom in the second degree; freedom contesting freedom.

At three minutes to ten he decided to toss heads or tails whether he should go or not. He had a clear vision of the entrance hall of the Gare d'Orsay, desolate and ablaze with light, and the stairway plunging underground, the smoke of the loco-motives, there was already a taste of smoke in his mouth: he picked up the two-franc piece and he flung it into the air – tails I go! tails I go. It came down tails. Very well, I go! – he said to his reflection. Not because I hate the war, not because I hate my family, not even because I have decided to go: but by pure *chance*: because a coin turned one side up rather than the other. Admirable – he thought: I am at the extremest point of freedom. A martyr without motive: if only she had seen me spinning that coin! One more minute. A throw of dice. Ding – never – ding, ding – will a throw – ding – of dice – ding ding – abolish – ding, ding, ding – luck – *Ding!* He got up, he walked quite straight, he placed his feet one after the other on a strip of floorboard, he felt the wait-ress's eyes upon his back, but he would not give her any cause to laugh at him.

'Monsieur!'

He turned, trembling.

'Your suitcase.'

Blast! He ran across the room, picked up his suitcase, and tottered with difficulty back to the door amid a burst of laughter, went out, and hailed a taxi. He held his suitcase in his left hand, in his right hand he was clutching the two-franc piece. The cab stopped in front of him.

'Where to?'

The driver had a moustache and a wart on his cheek.

'Rue Pigalle,' said Philippe. 'To the Cabane Cubaine.'

'We have lost the war,' said Gomez.

Mathieu knew it, but had thought that Gomez didn't know it yet. The band was playing *I'm Looking for Sally*, the plates gleamed beneath the table-lamp, and the spotlights shed a sort of monstrous moonlight on to the dancing-floor, a Honolulu-poster moonlight. Gomez was seated there, the moonlight on his right, and on his left a woman with a half-smile on her face: he was on his way back to Spain, and he knew that the Republicans had lost the war.

'You can't be sure,' sid Mathieu. 'No one can be sure.'

'Yes, they can,' said Gomez. 'We, in fact, are sure.'

He did not seem cast down: he was merely stating a fact. He looked at Mathieu with the calm expression of a man whose task is finished. He said: 'All my soldiers are sure the war is lost.'

'And they're fighting all the same?' said Mathieu.

'What would you have them do?'

Mathieu shrugged his shoulders. 'Obviously.'

I pick up my glass, I drink a little Chateau-Margaux, and someone says to me: they are fighting to the last, there's nothing else they can do. I drink a little Chateau-Margaux, I shrug my shoulders, and I say: Obviously. Bastards!

'What's that?' asked Gomez.

'*Tournedos Rossini*,' said the head waiter.

'Ah, yes,' said Gomez. 'Give me the dish.'

He took it and laid it on the table.

'Not bad,' he said, 'not bad.'

The *tournedos* are on the table: one for him, one for me. He has the right to enjoy his steak, to chew it with those fine white teeth of his, he has the right to look at that pretty girl, and think: That's a nice bit of stuff! But I haven't. If I eat, a hundred dead Spaniards leap at my throat. I haven't paid.

'You aren't drinking,' said Gomez. He took the bottle and filled Mathieu's glass...

'I will, since you invite me to,' said Mathieu with a short laugh. He picked up his glass and emptied it. A *tournedos* suddenly appeared on his plate. He picked up his knife and fork: 'I eat, since Spain invites me,' he muttered.

Gomez did not seem to hear. He had poured out a glass of wine, drank it and smiled: '*Tournedos* today, dried peas tomorrow. It's my last evening in France,' he said. 'And it's the only good dinner that I've had here.'

'What!' said Mathieu. 'Not at Marseilles?'

'Sarah is a vegetarian,' said Gomez. He looked straight in front of him with a genial expression: and he said: 'When I went on leave, there had been no tobacco in Barcelona for three weeks. Can you imagine an entire city where no one smokes?' He turned his eyes on Mathieu, and seemed suddenly to see him. His face resumed his rather unpleasantly meaning look.

'You'll go through all that,' he said.

'It isn't certain,' said Mathieu. 'War may still be avoided.'

'Oh, of course,' said Gomez. 'War can *always* be avoided.'
He laughed curtly and added: 'You have only to go back on
the Czechs.'

'No, old boy,' thought Mathieu: 'No! Spaniards may
lecture me about Spain, that's their department. But at
lectures on Czechoslovakia I demand the presence of a Czech.'

'Frankly, Gomez,' he asked, 'ought they to be backed up?
It isn't so long since the Communists claimed autonomy for
the Sudeten Germans.'

'Ought they to be backed up?' said Gomez, mimicking
Mathieu's voice. 'Ought we to have been backed up? Or the
Austrians? And what about you? Who will back you up when
your time comes?'

'We don't come into question,' said Mathieu.

'But you do,' said Gomez. 'Of course you do.'

'Gomez,' said Mathieu. 'Eat your *tournedos*. I quite understand that you hate us all. But anyway this is your last evening
of leave, your food is getting cold, there's a woman smiling
at you, and – after all – I was an interventionist.'

Gomez had recovered himself. 'Yes,' he said with a smile:
'I know.'

'Besides,' said Mathieu, 'you must realize that in Spain the
situation was clear-cut. But when you begin to talk to me
about Czechoslovakia I no longer follow you, because the
issue seems to me much less obvious. There is a question of
right that I find I cannot determine: after all – what if the
Sudeten Germans don't want to be Czechs?'

'Never mind questions of right,' said Gomez shrugging
his shoulders. 'You want a reason for fighting. There's only
one: if you don't, you're done for. What Hitler wants isn't
Prague, or Vienna, or Dantzig: it's Europe.'

Daladier looked at Chamberlain, he looked at Halifax, then
he averted his eyes and looked at a gilt clock on a bracket:
the hands pointed to thirty-five minutes past ten: the taxi
stopped outside the Cabane Cubaine. Georges turned over on
his back, and groaned a little, his neighbour's snores were
keeping him awake.

'Well,' said Daladier, 'I can only repeat what I have already

237

stated: the French Government has undertaken certain commitments toward Czechoslovakia. If the Prague Government maintains its refusal of the German proposals, and if in consequence of that refusal it becomes the victim of an aggression, the French Government will regard itself as under an obligation to fulfil its commitments.'

He coughed, looked at Chamberlain, and waited.

'Yes,' said Chamberlain. 'Yes, obviously.'

He seemed inclined to add a few words: but no words came. Daladier waited, describing circles on the carpet with the toe of his shoe. At last he looked up and said wearily: 'What, in that eventuality, would be the position of the British Government?'

France, Maud, Doucette, and Ruby got up and bowed. From the front rows came a little limp applause, then the crowd dispersed with much clattering of chairs. Maud looked round for Pierre, but he had disappeared. France turned towards her, her cheeks were flushed, and she smiled.

'It was a good evening,' she said. 'A *really* good evening.'

The war was there, on the white dancing floor, in the dead glare of the artificial moonlight, in the rasping falsetto of the muted trumpets, on the cool table-cloth, in the smell of wine, and in the old age lurking behind Gomez's features. Halifax looked at Bonnet, Bonnet looked at Daladier: they were silent, and Mathieu looked at the war on his plate, and in the black eyes of the caviare on his *tournedos*.

'And supposing we too lost the war?'

'Then Europe would go Fascist,' said Gomez lightly. 'It's not a bad preparation for Communism.'

'What will become of you, Gomez?'

'I imagine their cops will track me down in some boarding house, or I shall go and starve in America. What does it matter? I shall have lived.'

Mathieu looked at Gomez with curiosity: 'And you regret nothing?' he asked.

'Nothing at all.'

'Not even painting?'

'Not even painting.'

Mathieu shook his head sadly. He liked Gomez's pictures. 'You used to paint good pictures,' he said.

'I shall never paint again.'

'Why?'

'I don't know. It's physical. I've lost patience. I should find it boring.'

'But patience is needed in war too.'

'Not the same sort of patience.'

They were silent. The *maître d'hôtel* brought the *crêpes* on a pewter dish, sprinkled them with rum and Calvados, then he held a lighted match over the dish. A spectral flame hovered a moment in the air.

'Gomez,' said Mathieu suddenly, 'you are a solid sort of man: you know what you are fighting for.'

'You mean you wouldn't know?'

'Not at all. I think I should know. But I wasn't thinking of myself. There are men who have nothing but their lives, Gomez. And no one does a thing for them. No one. No government, no régime. If the Fascio took the place of our Republic, they wouldn't even notice. Take a shepherd in the Cevennes. Do you think he would know why he was fighting?'

'In my country it's the shepherds who are the most militant,' said Gomez.

'Why are they fighting?'

'That depends. I've known some who are fighting for the opportunity to learn to read.'

'In France everyone can read,' said Mathieu. 'If I came across a shepherd from the Cevennes in my regiment, and saw him die beside me in defence of my Republic and my liberties, I assure you I should feel extremely uncomfortable. Gomez, don't you feel ashamed sometimes? – don't you think of all those people who have died for you?'

'It doesn't worry me,' said Gomez. 'I risk my skin just as they do.'

'Generals die in their beds.'

'I haven't always been a general.'

'In any case it isn't the same,' said Mathieu.

'No, I'm not sorry for them,' said Gomez. 'I don't pity them.' He moved a hand across the tablecloth and grasped Mathieu's arm. 'Mathieu,' he said in a slow undertone, 'war is fine.'

239

His face blazed. Mathieu tried to disengage himself, but Gomez gripped his arm, and went on: 'I love war.'

There was nothing more to say. Mathieu laughed a short, embarrassed laugh, and Gomez took his hand away.

'You have made a strong impression on our neighbour.'

Gomez flashed a glance to his left.

'Indeed?' he said. 'Well, one must strike while the iron is hot. Is that a dancing-floor?'

'Of course.'

Gomez rose, and buttoned his jacket. He approached the actress, and Mathieu saw him bend over her. She looked up at him with a mechanical smile, then they moved away and began to dance. They danced: she had no Negroid smell, she must be a Martiniquaise, Philippe thought: 'Martiniquaise,' but it was the word Malabaraise that came to his lips. He muttered: 'My lovely Malabaraise.'

'You dance well,' she answered.

There was a fife-like cadence in her voice which was not at all unpleasant.

'You speak French well,' he said.

She looked at him indignantly: 'I was born in France.'

'That doesn't matter,' he said. 'You speak French very well all the same.' – 'I'm tight,' he thought, and laughed. She said to him, quite without anger: 'You're tight.'

'Y-e-e-s,' said he.

His weariness had left him: he could have danced till morning: but he had decided to sleep with the Negress, which was a more serious business. The attraction of being drunk was the power it gave you over objects. No need to touch them: just a look, and you possess them: he possessed that forehead and that dark hair: his eyes caressed that polished face. Farther off, the scene was rather blurred: a large man drinking champagne, and beyond him, a sprawling throng of people whom he could not clearly distinguish.

'How well you dance,' she said. 'A handsome boy like you must have had lots of women.'

'I'm a virgin,' said Philippe.

'You little liar.'

He lifted a hand: 'I swear I'm a virgin. I swear it by mother's head.'

'Ah?' she said disappointedly. 'I suppose you aren't interested in women.'

'I don't know,' he said. 'We shall see.'

He looked at her, he possessed her with his eyes, grimaced at her, and said: 'So I'm relying on you.'

She puffed some cigarette-smoke into his face: 'You'll see what I can do.'

He grasped her hair and drew her towards him: from close to she did smell faintly of grease. He kissed her lightly on the lips. She said: 'A virgin, eh? So I'm going to win first prize.'

'Win?' he said. 'One always loses.'

He did not desire her in the least. But he was glad she was pretty, and didn't make him nervous. He felt quite at ease, and thought: 'I know how to talk to women.' He released her, she sat up straight: Philippe's suitcase fell on to the floor. 'Look out,' he said. 'You're tight.'

She picked up the suitcase: 'What's inside it?'

'Ssh! Don't you touch it: it's a diplomatic bag.'

'I want to know what's inside,' she said, with a childish pout. 'Darling, tell me what's inside.'

He tried to snatch the suitcase away from her, but she had already opened it. She saw the pyjamas and the toothbrush.

'A book,' she said as she picked up the Rimbaud. 'What is it?'

'That,' he said, 'is by a fellow who went away.'

'Where to?'

'You wouldn't be interested,' he said. 'He went away.'

He took the volume from her and put it back in the suitcase.

'He was a poet,' he said ironically. 'Does that help you to understand?'

'Sure,' she said. 'You ought to have said that at once.'

He closed the suitcase, and thought: 'But I haven't gone away,' and his drunkenness fell from him. 'Why? Why haven't I gone?' Now he could clearly distinguish the large gentleman opposite: he wasn't particularly large, and his eyes were rather sinister. The human clusters fell apart: there were women, black and white: men also. People seemed to be continually looking at him. 'Why am I here? How did I get here? Why haven't I gone?' There was a gap in his recollections: he had spun the coin, he had hailed a taxi, and here he was: at present he was sitting at this table, over a glass of champagne, in the company of a Negress who smelt of fish paste. He visualised the Philippe who had spun the coin, and tried to make him out: but he thought: 'I'm someone else': he thought: 'I don't recognize myself.' He turned to the Negress.

'Why are you looking at me?' she asked.

'I don't quite know.'

'Do you think I'm pretty?'

'So-so.'

She cleared her throat and her eyes glittered. Leaning her hands on the table, she rose a few inches from the seat.

'If you don't fancy me, I can go: we aren't married.'

He felt in his pocket and produced three crumpled thousand-franc notes. 'Here,' he said. 'Take those, and stay.'

She took the notes, unfolded them, smoothed them out, laughed, and sat down again.

'You're a bad boy,' said she. 'A very bad little boy.'

An abyss of shame had opened right in front of him: he had only to drop into it. He had been knocked about and thrown into the street, and even so he had not gone. He leaned over the pit, and felt dizzy. Shame awaited him at the bottom of it: he had but to *choose* that shame. He closed his eyes, and the day's exhaustion surged back upon him. Exhaustion, shame, and death. Shame, self-chosen. Why didn't I go? Why did I *choose* not to go? He felt like a man with the world on his shoulders.

'You're not very chatty,' she said.

He laid a finger under her chin. 'What's your name?'

'Flossie.'

'That's not a Malabar name.'

'I tell you I was born in France,' she said irritably.

'All right, Flossie. I've given you three thousand-franc notes. You don't want me to make conversation into the bargain, do you?'

She shrugged her shoulders and turned her head away. The black pit was still there, and at the bottom of it – shame. He peered down into it, suddenly he understood, and anguish wrung his heart: it was a trap, if I fall into it I could never face myself again. Never. He sat up straight, and said firmly to himself: 'I didn't go, because I was tight!' the abyss closed:

he had chosen. He had come too near to shame: he had been too frightened: he had chosen never to feel shame again. Never again.

'I ought to have caught a train, you see. But I got too tight.'

'You'll catch it tomorrow,' she said good-humouredly.

He started: 'Why do you say that?'

'Well,' she said in astonishment. 'When you miss a train, you take the next.'

'I'm not going after all,' he said with a frown. 'I've changed my mind. Do you know the meaning of a sign?'

'A sign?' she repeated.

'The world is full of signs. Everything is a sign. They need to be interpreted. You were due to go, you got tight, and you didn't go: why didn't you go? It was because you oughtn't to have gone. It's a sign: you had a job to do here.'

She nodded. 'That's true,' she said. 'What you say is quite true.'

A job to do. Those sticky crowds in the Bastille district – that's where I must testify. On the spot. And be torn to pieces on the spot. Like Orpheus. *Down with the war*. No one can call me a coward then? I'll shed my blood for all of them, for Maurice and Zézette, for Pitteaux, for the General, for the men whose nails will tear my flesh. He turned to the Negress and looked at her with affection: one night, only one night. My first night of love. My last night.

'You're a pretty girl, Flossie.'

She smiled. 'You could be a nice boy if you liked.'

'Come and dance,' he said to her. 'I'll be nice till cock-crow.'

They danced. Mathieu looked at Gomez, and thought: 'His last night,' and he smiled: the Negress liked dancing, and half-closed her eyes: Philippe danced, and thought: 'My last night, and my first night of love.' He no longer felt shame: he was tired, and it was hot: tomorrow I shall shed my blood for peace. But dawn was far away. He danced, his mind at rest, his honour vindicated: indeed, he thought himself rather romantic. Lights slid along the wall of the compartment: the train slowed down, jerked forward twice, then stopped, light splashed into the compartment, Charles blinked, and let go Catherine's hand.

'Laroche-Migenne,' cried the nurse. 'We've arrived.'

'Laroche-Migenne?' said Charles. 'But we didn't go through Paris.'

'We must have gone round by another route.'

'Get your things together,' cried the nurse. 'You're going to be taken off the train.'

Blanchard had awakened with a start. 'What – what?' he said. 'Where are we?'

No one answered. The nurse explained: 'We shall take the train again tomorrow. We are spending the night here.'

'My eyes are smarting,' said Catherine with a laugh: 'it's this light.'

He turned his head towards her, she laughed as she laid a hand over her eyes.

'Get your things together,' cried the nurse. 'Get your things together.'

She bent over a bald man's gleaming cranium: 'Finished?'

'Do wait a minute, please!' said the man.

'Hurry up,' she said. 'The porters are just coming.'

'All right now,' said he. 'You can take it away – I no longer want to.'

She rose, carrying the pan in her outstretched arms, stepped over the rows of prostrate forms, and made her way to the door.

'We needn't worry,' said Charles. 'There are about a dozen men on the job, and twenty coaches to unload. They'll be some time before they get to us. . . .'

'Unless they start with the tail end.'

Charles put his forearm over his eyes: 'Where are they going to put us? In the waiting-rooms?'

'I suppose so.'

'I wish we didn't have to leave this compartment. I'd begun to feel at home here – hadn't you?'

'Oh well,' she said, 'as long as I'm with you . . .'

'Here they are,' cried Blanchard.

Some men entered the compartment, black figures against the light. Their shadows were outlined on the carriage wall: they seemed to have come in from both sides at once. Silence fell; and Catherine said in a low tone: 'I told you they would begin with us.'

Charles did not reply. He saw two of the men bend over a

patient, and his heart contracted. Jacques was asleep, his nose betrayed the fact: she would not sleep: she would not sleep until he got back. In a line with his feet Charles saw an enormous shadow bending double, they're taking the fellow in front, it will be my turn next, night and smoke and cold, the swaying stretcher, the deserted platforms – how he dreaded it all. There came a shaft of light underneath the door, she heard a noise on the ground floor – here he was. She recognized his step on the stairs, and peace descended on her: he is here, beneath our roof, I've got him. Another night. The last. Mathieu opened the door, then closed it, opened the window and closed the shutters; she could hear the sound of running water. He is going to bed. Beyond the wall; beneath our roof.

'It's my turn,' said Charles. 'Tell them to take you next.'

He squeezed her hand, while the two men bent over him and a puff of vinous breath came full in his face.

'Hah!' said the man behind him.

He felt suddenly afraid, and swung his mirror as they lifted him, so that he could see whether she was coming next, but could see nothing but the porter's shoulders and his owlish head.

'Catherine!' he cried.

No reply. He was swaying through the doorway, the man behind him shouted directions, his legs dipped and he thought he was falling.

'Gently!' he said. 'Gently.'

But he could see stars in a black sky; it was very cold.

'Will she be next?' he asked.

'Who?' asked the owl-headed porter.

'My neighbour. She's a friend of mine.'

'The women will be taken out later,' said the man. 'You won't be in the same place.'

Charles began to tremble: 'But I thought . . .' he said.

'You wouldn't want ladies to relieve themselves in front of you, would you?'

'I thought . . .' said Charles. 'I thought . . .'

He passed a hand over his forehead, and suddenly began to yell: 'Catherine! Catherine! Catherine!'

He was swinging from the porters' outstretched arms, he glimpsed the stars, then a lamp splashed a glare into his eyes, the stars again, then another lamp, and he yelled: 'Catherine! Catherine!'

'He's cracked,' said the rear porter. 'Keep your mouth shut, can't you!'

'I don't even know her surname,' said Charles in a voice choked by tears. 'I shall never see her again.'

They put him down, opened a door, lifted him again, he saw a ghastly yellow ceiling, he heard the door close; he was in the trap.

'Bastards!' he said, as they laid him down. 'Bastards!'

'Who do you think you are!' said the owl-headed man.

'That's all right,' said the other. 'Can't you see he's dotty?'

He heard their footsteps die away, the door opened, and then closed.

'Well!' said Blanchard's voice. 'We meet again.' And at the same moment Charles received a jet of water full in the face. But he remained silent and motionless, like a corpse, he stared up at the ceiling, while the water trickled into his ears and down his neck. She could not sleep, she lay motionless in the darkened room: he's going to bed, he'll soon be asleep, while I watch over him. He is a fine brave fellow, he heard this morning that he was to be called up, and he did not blink an eyelid. But now he is disarmed: he'll soon be asleep, it's his last night. 'How romantic he is,' she thought.

A warm and scented room, with gleaming lights, and flowers everywhere.

'Come in,' she said.

Gomez went in. He looked round him, caught sight of a doll on a divan, and thought of Teruel. He had slept in just such a room, with lamps and dolls and flowers, but no scent, and no ceiling: and there was a hole in the middle of the floor.

'Why are you smiling?'

'This is a charming place,' he said.

She came up to him and said: 'If you like it, you can come here as often as you wish.'

'I'm off tomorrow,' said Gomez.

'Tomorrow?' she said. 'Where to?'

She looked at him with lovely, inexpressive eyes.

'To Spain.'

'To Spain? But then – '

'Yes,' he said. 'I'm a soldier, on leave.'

'On which side?' she asked.

'On which side would you like me to be?'

'On Franco's side?'

'Do I look it?'

She put her arms round his neck. 'My handsome soldier.'

Her breath was exquisite: he kissed her.

'Only one night,' she said. 'It isn't much. Just when I've met a man I could really love.'

'I'll come back,' he said. 'When Franco has won the war. . . .'

She kissed him again, then softly let him go. 'Wait for me. There's gin and whisky on the sideboard.'

She opened the door into the dressing-room and disappeared. Gomez went to the sideboard and poured himself a glass of gin. The lorries rumbled past, the windows shook, Sarah, awakened with a start, sat up in bed. 'How many can there be?' she asked herself. 'There's no end to them.' Heavy lorries, already camouflaged, roofed with grey tarpaulins, their bonnets painted green and brown, packed with men and weapons. She thought: 'This means war,' and began to cry. *Catherine! Catherine!* She had been dry-eyed for two years: and when Gomez had got into the train, she couldn't produce a single tear. And now the tears were pouring down her cheeks. *Catherine!* Shaken by sobs, she sank back on the pillow, and bit into it, so as not to awaken the boy. Gomez drank a little gin, and found it good. He took a few steps into the room, and sat down on the divan. In one hand he held his glass, with the other he picked up the doll by the back of the neck, and set it on his knee: he could hear the sound of running water from a tap in the dressing-room, a familiar sense of well-being thrilled up his sides, like two smooth hands. He was happy, he drank, and he thought: 'I'm a strong man.' The lorries rumbled past, the windows quivered, water spouted from the tap, and Gomez thought: 'I'm strong, I love my life and risk it, I expect death tomorrow, or sometime soon, and I'm not afraid, I love luxury, and I'm going back to squalor and starvation, I know what I want, I know why I am fighting, I give orders and am obeyed, I've sacrificed everything – painting, and success: and I am perfectly happy.' He thought of Mathieu and said to himself: 'I wouldn't be in his skin.' She opened

the door, naked under her pink wrap. And she said: 'Here
I am.'

'Okay, then,' she said. 'Okay, okay. Oh shit!'

She had spent half an hour in the dressing-room, washing
and scenting herself, because white people didn't always like
her smell, she approached him smiling and with open arms,
and there he lay asleep, naked in the bed, his head buried
in the pillow. She grasped his shoulder and shook him
indignantly:

'Wake up!' she hissed. 'You little bastard, wake up!'

He lifted his eyelids, and looked at her with wondering eyes.
He put the glass on the table, the doll on the divan, got up,
and took her in his arms. He was happy.

'Can you read that?' asked Gros-Louis.

The porter pushed him away.

'That's the third time you've asked me. You've got to go
to Montpellier.'

'And where's the train for Montpellier?'

'It doesn't leave till four in the morning: it isn't made up
yet.'

Gros-Louis eyed him uneasily. 'Then what am I to do?'

'Go and shake down in the waiting-room, and take a nap
until four o'clock. Have you got your ticket?'

'No,' said Gros-Louis.

'Well, go and get it. No – not there. At the ticket office, you
old dope!'

Gros-Louis made his way to the office. A spectacled clerk
was dozing behind the window.

'Hi!' shouted Gros-Louis.

The clerk gave a start.

'I'm going to Montpellier,' said Gros-Louis.

'To Montpellier?' The clerk looked surprised: no doubt
he was barely awake yet. A suspicion flickered through Gros-
Louis's mind.

'Is that Montpellier written there?' He produced his army
book.

'Montpellier,' said the clerk. 'Quarter-fare – fifteen francs.'

Gros-Louis handed him the kind lady's hundred francs.

'And now,' said he, 'what am I to do?'

'Go to the waiting-room.'

'When does the train start?'

'Four o'clock. Can't you read?'

'No,' said Gros-Louis. He paused before turning away. 'Is there going to be war?'

The clerk shrugged his shoulders. 'How should I know? You won't find it on the indicator, anyway.'

He got up, retired to the back of his office, pretended to consult some papers, but after a moment or two sat down with his head in his hands and continued his doze. Gros-Louis looked round him. He wished he could find someone who would tell him about the war, but the hall was deserted. 'All right,' he said: 'I'll go to the waiting-room.' And he shuffled across the hall: he was sleepy, and his legs ached.

'Let me sleep,' moaned Philippe.

'No you don't,' said Flossie. 'You told me you were a virgin, so you must do something; it'll bring me luck.'

He opened the door, and entered the waiting-room. It was packed with people sleeping on benches, and suitcases and parcels strewn over the floor. The light was dim: a glazed door at the far end opened on to darkness. He walked across to a bench and sat down between two women. One was sweating as she slept; her mouth was open, the sweat had trickled down her cheeks, and left pink streaks on them. The other woman opened her eyes and looked at him.

'I'm called up,' explained Gros-Louis. 'I've got to go to Montpellier.'

The woman drew away from him, and glared. Gros-Louis supposed she didn't like soldiers, but added:

'Is there going to be war?'

She did not reply: her head had fallen back, and she had gone to sleep again. Gros-Louis was afraid of going to sleep. 'If I go to sleep,' he said to himself, 'I shan't wake up.' He stretched his legs: he ached for something to eat, a bit of bread and sausage: he had some money left, but it was late now and all the shops would be shut. 'Who are we going to fight?' he asked himself. The Germans no doubt: possibly over Alsace-Lorraine. There was a newspaper lying on the floor, he picked it up, then he thought of the kind lady who had bandaged his head, and said: 'I oughtn't to have reported. But what was I to do, I hadn't any money left. Might try the barracks – they would give me a bit of food. But he didn't like barracks. Nor waiting-rooms either. Suddenly he felt miserable and exhausted. They had got him drunk and beaten him up, and now they were going to send him to Montpellier. 'God Almighty,' said he: 'what's it all about? I wish I could read.' All these sleeping people knew more than he did: they had read the paper, they knew all about this war. He was alone in the night, so small and solitary, he knew and understood nothing, like a man about to die. Then he became conscious of the newspaper in his hand: everything was written down in it – all about the war, tomorrow's weather, the prices of goods, and the times of trains. He unfolded the paper and inspected it. What he saw were thousands of black specks, like pianola rolls with the perforations that produce the sounds when the crank is turned: he felt quite dizzy if he looked at them for long. There was also a photograph of a spruce and smiling man with plastered hair. He dropped the paper and burst into tears.

Monday, 26 September

FOUR-THIRTY. Everybody looks at the sky, and I look at the sky. 'They're not late,' says Dumur. He has his Kodak ready, he looks up at the sky, and blinks in the blazing sunshine. The plane is a black speck that glitters now and again, it grows larger but the sound of it remains – a fine rich sound, very satisfying to the ear. 'Don't push,' I say. They are all there, jostling round me. I turn: they tilt their heads back, they blink too. They look green in the sunlight, and they move with a sort of jerky indecision rather like decapitated frogs. Dumur said: 'One day we'll be standing like this in a field with our noses in the air: but we'll be in khaki, and the plane will be a Messerschmitt.' And I reply, 'And pretty soon too, with such fatheads to look after our affairs.' The plane circles round, then drops, bumps on the ground, rises, bumps again, runs jerkily over the grass, and comes to a standstill. We run towards it, fifty of us, Sarraut ahead of the rest, bent nearly double: a dozen gentlemen in bowler hats scurry across the turf, everybody stands still, the plane is lifeless, we eye it in silence, the cabin door stays shut, the occupants might be dead. A man in a blue tunic brings a ladder and puts it against the plane, the door opens, one man comes down the ladder, then another, then Daladier. My heart throbs inside my head. Daladier lifts his shoulders and lowers his head. Sarraut goes up to him and I hear him say: 'Well?'

Daladier takes a hand out of his pocket and waves it vaguely. He hurries forward with head bent, and the crowd throngs round him. I don't move, I know he will say nothing. General Gamelin jumps out of the plane, a brisk little man in elegant field-boots and with a bulldog head. He looks at the scene with a fresh and lively eye.

'Well?' said Sarraut. 'Well, general? Is it war?' My mouth dries up: I can't bear it. I shout to Dumur: 'I'm going, you must take your photographs alone.' I dash to the exit and out on to the road, I hail a taxi: 'To the *Humanité* office!' The driver smiles, I smile too, and he says: 'Well, comrade?'

'It's come!' I reply. 'They've got it in the pants: they couldn't dodge it this time.'

The taxi rattles along, I look at the houses and the people: they know nothing, they ignore the taxi, and the taxi rattles past them carrying a man who does know. I look out of the window, I want to shout – The day has come! I jump out of the taxi, I pay, I dash upstairs. There they all are – Dupré, Charvel, Renard, and Chabot: in shirt-sleeves, Renard smoking, Charvel writing, Dupré looking out on to the street. They look at me with astonishment. I say to them: 'Come along out, boys, the drinks are on me.'

They are still looking at me: Charvel lifts his head and looks at me. 'This is it! This is it!' I say: 'It's war! Let's all go out, and I'll stand you drinks.'

'That's a pretty hat of yours,' said the landlady.

'Isn't it?' said Flossie. She contemplated herself in the hall mirror and said with satisfaction: 'Such lovely feathers.'

'Yes, indeed,' said the landlady. And she added: 'There's someone in your room: Madeleine couldn't tidy it.'

'I know,' said Flossie. 'It doesn't matter: I'll do it myself.'

She went upstairs and opened the door. The shutters were closed, and the room smelt of the previous night. Flossie closed the door gently, went out and knocked at No. 15.

'Who is it?' said Zou's hoarse voice.

'Flossie.'

Zou opened the door, she was in her knickers.

'Come in quick.'

Flossie went in. Zou flung her hair back, planted herself in the middle of the room, and began to tuck her capacious bosom into a brassière. Flossie reflected that she ought to shave her armpits.

'Have you just got up?' she asked.

'I didn't get to bed till six,' said Zou. 'What's the matter?'

'Come and see my boy-friend,' said Flossie.

'What do you mean, you little nigger-girl?'

'Come and see my boy-friend.'

Zou slipped on a wrap, and followed her into the corridor. Flossie preceded her into her room, laying a finger on her lips.

'I can't see a thing,' said Zou.

Flossie pushed her towards the bed, and whispered: 'Look.'

They leaned over the bed, and Zou laughed silently.

'Shit,' she said. 'Why he's just a kid.'

'His name's Philippe.'

'He's very handsome.'

Philippe slept, lying on his back: he looked positively angelic. Flossie eyed him with an expression of mingled admiration and resentment.

'He's fairer than I am,' said Zou.

'He's a virgin,' said Flossie.

Zou eyed her with a quizzical smile. '*Was*,' she said.

'What?'

'You said: he is a virgin. I said: he *was*.'

'Ah, yes. Well, as a matter of fact, I think he still is.'

'Nonsense!'

'He has been asleep like that since two o'clock this morning,' said Flossie acidly.

Philippe opened his eyes, he looked at the two women leaning over him, grunted, and turned over on his face.

'Look,' said Flossie.

She pulled down the bedclothes, and revealed a white and naked body. Zou rolled two large eyes.

'Yum-yum!' she exclaimed. 'Cover it up, or I might do something silly.'

Flossie slid a light hand over the boy's narrow hips, his youthful, slim buttocks, and then drew up the bedclothes with a sigh.

'Bring me,' said M. Birnenschatz, 'a Noilly-cassis.'

He sank on to the seat, and wiped his brow. Through the glass of the revolving door, he could keep an eye on the entrance to his office.

'What will you have?' he said to Neu.

'The same,' said Neu.

The waiter went away, Neu called him back: 'Bring me the *Information*.'

They eyed each other in silence, then Neu suddenly raised his arms in the air: 'Alas, alas! My poor Birnenschatz!'

'Yes,' said M. Birnenschatz.

The waiter filled their glasses, and handed the paper to Neu. Neu looked at the day's quotations, made a wry face, and laid the paper on the table.

'Shocking,' he said.

'Of course. What do you expect? They are waiting for Hitler's speech.'

M. Birnenschatz looked morosely round at the walls and the mirrors. Normally, he rather liked this cheerful, cosy little café: today he was annoyed that he felt so ill at ease there.

'We can only wait,' he said. 'Daladier has done what he could: so has Chamberlain. There's nothing to do now but wait. We shan't enjoy our dinner, and at half past eight we shall switch on the wireless to listen to this speech. And wait for what?' he said abruptly, thumping on the table. 'One man's good pleasure. One man. Business is at a standstill, the Bourse is collapsing, my clerks can't settle down to work, poor See is called up: all on account of one man: war and peace are in his hands. It's a disgrace to humanity.'

Brunet got up: Mme Samboulier looked at him. He rather appealed to her: he would make love well, with no needless noise or fuss, and a sort of countryfied deliberation.

'Won't you stay and dine?' she said, and pointing to the radio, she added: 'I can offer you Hitler's speech by way of a digestive.'

'I've got an appointment at seven o'clock,' said Brunet. 'Besides, I don't give a damn for Hitler's speech.'

Mme Samboulier looked puzzled.

'If capitalist Germany is to live,' said Brunet, 'she needs all the European markets: she must therefore forcibly eliminate all her industrial competitors. Germany *has to* make war,' he added with emphasis: 'and she *has to* lose it. If Hitler had been killed in 1914, we should be exactly where we are today.'

'So,' said Mme Samboulier, speaking with an effort: 'this Czech business isn't a bluff?'

'Hitler may think it is,' said Brunet, 'but what Hitler thinks is of no importance whatever.'

'He can still stop it,' said M. Birnenschatz. 'If he wishes, he can still stop it. All the trumps are in his hand: England doesn't want war, America is too far off, Poland will stand in with him: if he wished, he could be master of the world tomorrow without firing a shot. The Czechs have accepted the Franco-English plan; he has only to accept it too. If he gave that proof of moderation . . .'

'He can't draw back now,' said Brunet. 'The whole of Germany is behind him and pushing him on.'

'But we can draw back,' said Mme Samboulier.

Brunet looked at her and laughed. 'True,' he said, 'you are a pacifist.'

Neu turned the box upside down and the dominoes dropped on to the table.

'Oh dear,' he said, 'I fear Hitler's moderation. Do you realize the prestige he would get out of it?'

He leaned towards M. Birnenschatz and whispered in his ear. M. Birnenschatz moved aside irritably. 'Neu can't say three words without a lot of conspiratorial whispering and gesticulations.'

'If he accepted the Franco-English plan, in three months Doriot would be in power.'

'Doriot . . .' said M. Birnenschatz, shrugging his shoulders.

'Doriot, or someone like him.'

'And what then?'

'What about us?' asked Neu in a still lower tone.

M. Birnenschatz looked at his friend's large melancholy mouth, and felt his ears flush with anger:

'Anything is better than war,' he said acidly.

'Give me your letter, the girl will post it.'

He put the envelope on the table, between a saucepan and a pewter plate: Mlle Ivich Serguine, 12 Rue de la Mégisserie, Laon. Odette glanced at the address, but made no comment: she was tying up a large parcel.

'Now don't be impatient,' she said. 'It will soon be finished.'

The kitchen was white and clean, like a room in a sanatorium. It smelt of resin and the sea.

'I've put in two wings of chicken,' said Odette, 'and a little jelly, which I know you like, a few slices of brown bread, and some raw ham sandwiches. There's wine in the thermos. It will keep, of course, you may want some when you get there.'

He tried to catch her eye, but she appeared to be intent upon the parcel. She hurried to the dresser, snipped off a long piece of string and hurried back.

'Well,' said Mathieu, 'it's an admirable parcel.'

The little maid laughed, but Odette did not reply. She put the string between her teeth, and deftly turned the parcel over. The smell of resin suddenly filled Mathieu's nostrils, and for the first time since the evening before last, he felt immersed in an atmosphere that he might soon regret: the peace of that afternoon in the kitchen, these quiet domestic tasks, the sunlight filtering through the roller-blind and scattering on to the floor, and, beyond all that perhaps, his childhood, and a certain kind of placid, busy life that he had once and for all rejected.

'Put your finger there,' said Odette.

He leaned over her bent head, and pressed a finger on the string. He would have liked to say a few affectionate words to her, but Odette's voice did not invite affection. She looked up at him. 'Would you like a few hard-boiled eggs? You could put them into your pockets.'

She looked quite girlish. He did not regret her. Perhaps because she was Jacques's wife. He would soon forget that demure face of hers. But he could have wished her to feel a little upset at his departure.

'No, thank you,' he said. 'No hard-boiled eggs.'

She put the parcel into his arms: 'There,' she said. 'A fine parcel.'

'Will you come with me to the station?' he asked.

She shook her head. 'I think not. Jacques will go with you. I fancy he would sooner be alone with you for the last few minutes.'

'Good-bye then,' he said. 'Will you write to me?'

'I just couldn't: mine are little girl's letters, full of spelling mistakes. No: I'll be sending you parcels.'

'I wish you would write to me,' he said.

'Well then, from time to time you may find a little note between a box of sardines and a packet of soap.'

He held out his hand and she pressed it hurriedly. Her hand was hot and dry. Vaguely he thought: 'It's a pity.' The long fingers slipped through his like warm sand. He smiled and went out of the kitchen. Jacques was on his knees in the drawing-room in front of his radio set, twisting the knobs. Mathieu passed the door and walked slowly upstairs. He was not sorry to be going. As he approached his room, he heard a faint sound behind him and turned: it was Odette. She was standing on the top step, she was pale and her eyes were on him.

'Odette!' he said.

She did not reply, she was looking at him with a set expression on her face. He felt embarrassed, and slipped the parcel under his left arm to keep himself in countenance.

'Odette!' he repeated.

She approached him, her face wore an unguarded and prophetic look that he had never seen on it before.

'Good-bye,' she said.

She was quite near him. She closed her eyes, and suddenly laid her lips on his. He tried to take her in his arms but she eluded him. She had resumed her demure expression; and she went downstairs without looking round.

He entered his room, and put the parcel in his suitcase, which was so full that he had to kneel on the lid to close it.

'What is it?' said Philippe.

He had started up, and was looking at Flossie with terror-stricken eyes.

'It's only me, darling,' she said.

256

He fell back again, lifting a hand to his forehead.

'I've got such a headache.'

She opened the drawer of the bedside table, and produced a tube of aspirin: he pulled out the drawer in the sideboard, took out a glass and a bottle of Pernod, put them on the presidential desk, and sank back on his chair. The aeroplane engine was still hammering in his head. He had a bare quarter of an hour in which to pull himself together.

He poured some Pernod into the glass, picked up a carafe of water, and tilted it some distance above the glass. The liquid splashed about and bit by bit turned silvery. He unstuck a cigarette-end from his lower lip, and threw it into the waste-paper basket. I've done all I could. He felt exhausted. 'France,' he said to himself: 'France . . .' and drank a mouthful of Pernod. 'I've done all I could: the word is now with Hitler.' He took another sip, clicked his tongue, and thought: 'The position of France is clearly defined. And now I can only wait.' He was exhausted: he stretched his legs out under the table, and thought with something resembling satisfaction: 'I can do nothing but wait.' Like everyone else. The stakes are set. He had said: 'If the Czech frontiers are violated, France will keep her commitments.' And Chamberlain had answered: 'If, in consequence of those obligations, the French forces become actively engaged in the hostilities against Germany, we shall feel it our duty to support them.'

Sir Nevile Henderson came forward, Sir Horace Wilson stood stiffly erect behind him: Sir Nevile Henderson handed the message to the Chancellor of the Reich; the Chancellor took the message and began to read it. When he had finished, the Chancellor said to Sir Nevile Henderson:

'Is this message from Mr Chamberlain?'

Daladier drank a little more Pernod, sighed, and Sir Nevile Henderson replied concisely: 'Yes; from Mr Chamberlain.' Daladier got up, and locked the bottle of Pernod in the sideboard drawer: the Chancellor said in his rasping voice: 'You can consider my speech this evening as a reply to Mr Chamberlain's message.'

'Bloody fool!' thought Daladier. 'What is he going to say?' His temples were faintly flushed from what he had drunk, and he thought: 'Things are slipping out of my grasp.' It was a kind of relief. 'I have done everything,' he thought, 'to avoid war: and now, war and peace are out of my hands. There was no further decision to take, nothing to do but wait; like everybody else, like the loafer at a street-corner.' He smiled, he *was* that loafer, he had been stripped of his responsibilities: the position of France is clearly defined. ... A relief. He stared at the dark flowers on the carpet, and felt a little dizzy. Peace – war. I have done all I could to preserve peace. But he now wondered whether he didn't actually want to be swept away like a straw in this vast torrent, whether he didn't long for that tremendous holiday – war.

He looked about him in bewilderment, and exclaimed: 'I haven't gone.' She had opened the shutters and was now back beside the bed, leaning over him. He felt her warm body, and inhaled her fishy odour.

'What have you been up to, you bad boy?'

She had laid one of her sinewy black hands upon his chest. The sunlight made an oily patch on her left cheek, Philippe looked at her and felt profoundly humiliated: she had wrinkles at the corners of her eyes and mouth. 'She was so pretty in the light,' he thought. She breathed in his face, and slipped her pink tongue between his lips. 'I haven't gone,' he thought. And he said to her: 'You're not quite so young as all that.'

She made an odd grimace, closed her mouth and said: 'Not so young as you are, you bad boy.'

He tried to get out of bed, but she held him firmly: he was naked and defenceless: and he felt miserable.

'You bad boy,' she said. 'You bad little boy.'

The black hands slid slowly down his sides. After all, he thought, it isn't given to everybody to lose his virginity with a Negress. He sank back, and a whirl of black and grey garments approached within a few inches of his face. The man made less noise now: the sounds he uttered were more like gasps and gurgles. A shoe appeared above his head, he saw a pointed sole, with a clod of earth still sticking to the heel: the sole descended with a creak beside his stretcher: it belonged to a large black buttoned shoe. He raised his eyes, saw a cassock and high up in the air two hairy nostrils above the twin neckbands of a cleric. Blanchard whispered in his ear: 'The chap must be pretty bad or they wouldn't have sent for a priest.'

'What's the matter with him?' asked Charles.

'I don't know, but Pierrot says he's on the way out.'

Why not me? thought Charles. He considered his life and thought: Why not me? Two railwaymen passed close to him, he recognized the fabric of their trousers: he heard behind him the priest's calm, unctuous voice: the sick man had stopped groaning. 'Perhaps he's dead,' he thought. The nurse passed, holding a basin in her hands: 'Madame,' he said timidly, 'you couldn't go now, could you?'

She looked down at him, and flushed with anger: 'It's you again, is it? What do you want?'

'You couldn't send someone to the women's place? Her name is Catherine.'

'For God's sake keep quiet,' she replied. 'That's the fourth time you've asked me.'

'It's only to ask her surname, and tell her mine: it wouldn't be much trouble.'

'There's a man dying,' she said roughly. 'Do you suppose I've got time to bother about such nonsense?'

She departed and the man began to moan again. Charles felt quite unnerved: he swung his mirror round and observed an array of bodies stretched out side by side, and, beyond them, the vast posterior view of the priest kneeling beside the sick man. Above them, a mantelpiece with a mirror in a frame. The priest got up, the porters leaned over the body and carried it away.

'Is he dead?' asked Blanchard.

Blanchard's stretcher had no rotating mirror.

'I don't know,' said Charles.

The procession passed close to them raising a cloud of dust. Charles began to cough, then he saw the bent backs of the porters making their way towards the door. A skirt swirled up to him, and suddenly hung motionless. He heard the nurse's voice:

'We are completely cut off here, we get no news. How are things going, M. *le curé*?'

'Badly,' he said. 'Badly. Hitler is going to speak this evening, I don't know what he'll say, but I believe it will be war.'

His voice dropped in layers on to Charles's face. Charles burst out laughing.

'What's the joke?' asked Blanchard.

'The joke is that the parson said there's going to be a war.'

'I don't think that's a joke,' said Blanchard.

'I do.'

'They'll get their war – right in the pants.' He will still be laughing. Five and a half feet or so above his head, it was war, tempest, outraged honour, patriotic duty: but on the floor, there was neither war nor peace: nothing but the misery and shame of the submen, stricken and laid upon their backs. Bonnet didn't want it: Champetier de Ribes did: Daladier looked at the carpet, it was a nightmare, he could not shake off that sense of dizziness behind his ears: let it break out at last: let the big bad wolf of Berlin declare for war that very evening. He scraped his shoe against the floor, Charles felt a qualm rise from his stomach to his head: shame, a pleasant and comforting sense of shame, that was all the feeling that remained. The nurse had nearly reached the door, she stepped over a body, and the *abbé* stood back to let her pass.

'Madame!' cried Charles. 'Madame!'

She turned – a tall and buxom female, with a handsome face, a faint moustache, and angry eyes.

'Madame! Madame! Give me the pan – quick.'

Here he is! The thrusting crowd surged forward on to the policeman, who stepped back a pace and stretched out his arms. 'Hurrah! Here he is!' they shouted. He walked with stiff unhurried steps, arm in arm with his wife. Fred was touched – just like Father and Mother on a Sunday outing to Greenwich – and he too shouted – 'Hurrah!' it was nice to see them there, so placid, who could possibly feel afraid after seeing them there, taking a little afternoon walk like an amicable old married couple? He gripped his attaché-case, brandished it, and shouted: 'Hurrah for peace!' They both turned in his direction and Mr Chamberlain smiled at him: Fred felt a sense of ease and peace moving right down into his heart, he was safe ... protected, governed, fortified, and old Chamberlain still found it possible to walk quietly through the streets, just like anybody else, and smile at him personally. Everybody was cheering all round him. Fred watched Mr

Chamberlain's gaunt back, as he walked away with his rather ecclesiastical stride, and thought: 'It's England,' and the tears came into his eyes. Little Sadie bent down and took a photograph from beneath the policeman's arm.

'Queue up, madame, you must queue up like everyone else.'

'Queue up for a *Paris-Soir*?'

'Certainly! And I shall be surprised if you get a copy.'

She could not believe her ears. 'What do you take me for? I'm not going to queue up for the *Paris-Soir*: I've never queued up for a newspaper in my life!'

She turned her back on them as the cyclist arrived with his bundles of papers. He put them down on the table beside the kiosk, and they began to count them.

'Here they are! Here they are!'

The crowds eddied round the table. 'Look here,' said the newspaper-lady, 'are you going to let me count them?'

'Don't push, please,' said a rather posh lady. 'Don't push, I tell you.'

'I'm not pushing, madame,' said a short, fat man. 'I'm being pushed, which is not the same thing.'

'I won't have my wife insulted,' said a short and skinny individual.

The lady in mourning turned to Émile. 'That's the third row I've seen this morning.'

'Yes,' said Émile, 'everyone is so jumpy at the moment.'

The plane was nearing the mountains: Gomez looked at them, and then he looked down at the rivers and the fields beneath him, there was a little round town on his left, it was all so absurd and diminutive, it was the green and yellow land of France, with its spreading pastures and its quiet rivers. 'Good-bye. Good-bye.' They would plunge between the mountains, good-bye to *tournedos Rossini*, Coronas, lovely women, he would soon be gliding down towards the red and naked earth, towards the land of blood. Good-bye: good-bye. All the Frenchmen of France were there beneath him, in the little round town, in the fields, by the seashores: six-thirty-five, they were scurrying about like ants, waiting for Hitler's speech. Three thousand feet below me they are waiting for Hitler's speech. I am not waiting for anything. In a quarter of an hour he would no longer see those pleasant meadows; vast rocks would stand between him and that land of fear and avarice. In a quarter of an hour he would alight among a race of lean men with vivid gestures and hard eyes, *his own* men. He was happy, and indeed there was a lump in his throat. The mountains were approaching, they were brown by now: 'What's Barcelona going to be like when I get there?' he thought.

'Come in,' said Zézette.

It was a rather stout and handsome lady in a straw hat, and a Prince of Wales check costume. She looked round her, dilating her nostrils, and smiled a ready, friendly smile. 'Madame Suzanne Tailleur?'

'Yes,' said Zézette, rather puzzled.

She had got up. She remembered that her eyes must be rather red, so she stood with her back to the window. The lady looked at her and blinked. At a closer view, she appeared older: and she looked exhausted.

'I hope I'm not disturbing you.'

'Not at all,' said Zézette. 'Do sit down.'

The lady bent over the chair and eyed it, then sat down. She sat up very straight, and did not touch the chair-back.

'I must have walked up forty flights of stairs since this morning. And people don't always think of offering you a chair.'

Zézette noticed that her thimble was still on her finger. She took it off and threw it into her workbox. At that moment the steak began to sputter in the frying-pan. She dashed to the stove and turned out the gas: but the smell remained.

'I'm afraid you were just going to have your lunch.'

'Oh, I'm not in a hurry,' said Zézette. She looked at the lady and felt torn between embarrassment and a desire to laugh.

'Is your husband called up?'

'He went yesterday morning.'

'They are all going,' said the lady. 'It's so dreadful. You must be in rather a difficulty ... financially....'

'I think I shall go back to my old job,' said Zézette. 'I was a flower-seller.'

The lady shook her head. 'It's too, too dreadful!' She looked so woebegone that Zézette felt a twinge of sympathy.

'Has your husband gone too?'

'I'm not married.' She looked at Zézette and added quickly: 'But I have two brothers who may be called up.'

'What is it you want?' asked Zézette rather curtly.

'Well,' said the lady, 'I'll tell you.' She smiled: 'I don't know what your views are, and what I'm going to ask you is quite outside politics. Do you smoke? Have a cigarette?'

Zézette hesitated: 'I don't mind if I do,' she said.

She was standing beside the gas-oven, and her hands were grasping the edge of the table behind her back. The smell of the steak was now blended with the visitor's perfume. The lady handed her case to Zézette, who took a step forward. The visitor had slim white fingers and manicured nails. Zézette took a cigarette. She looked at her fingers and the lady's fingers and wished she would go away soon. They lit their cigarettes and the lady said:

'Don't you think this war ought to be stopped at any price?'

Zézette stepped back to the stove, and looked at her suspiciously. She felt uneasy. She noticed some suspenders and a pair of briefs lying on the table.

'Don't you think,' said the lady, 'that if we combined forces . . .'

Zézette walked nonchalantly across the room: when she reached the table, she said: 'Who do you mean by – we?'

'We women!' said the lady with emphasis.

'We women,' repeated Zézette. She hurriedly opened a drawer, threw the suspenders and briefs into it, then turned to the lady with a look of relief.

'We women? But what can we do?'

The lady was smoking like a man, ejecting the smoke from her nose: Zézette looked at her tailored suit, her jade necklace and felt odd at saying 'we' to her.

'You can't do anything alone,' said the lady amiably. 'But you are not alone: at this moment there are five million women afraid for the life of someone dear to them. On the floor below, it is Madame Panier, whose brother and husband have just gone, and who has six children. On the other side of the street it's the baker's wife. At Passy it's the Duchesse de Cholet.'

'Oh – the Duchesse de Cholet. . . .' murmured Zézette.

'Well?'

'It's not the same thing.'

'What isn't the same thing? Because some women go about in cars, while others do their marketing themselves? Ah, madame, I'm a strong supporter of a better social organization. But do you imagine that war will give it us? Class questions count so little in the face of the danger that now threatens us. We are women first of all, madame, women attacked in what they hold most dear. Suppose we all joined hands and shouted all together, "We won't have war." Come now – you surely want him to come back?'

Zézette shook her head: it seemed to her absurd that this lady should be addressing her as madame. 'War can't be stopped,' she said.

The lady flushed: 'And why not?' she asked.

Zézette shrugged her shoulders. So she wanted to stop war. Others, like Maurice, wanted to abolish poverty. And in the end nobody stopped anything.

'Because,' she said, 'it can't be stopped.'

'Oh, but you mustn't say that,' said the visitor reproachfully. 'It is people who say that sort of thing who are responsible for wars. Besides, you must think a little of other people. Whatever you do, you must be loyal to your sex.'

Zézette did not answer. She was clipping her cigarette, which had now gone out, rather nervously between her fingers, and felt as though she had gone back to school.

'You can't refuse to sign it, madame,' said the lady. 'You really can't.'

She had taken a sheet of paper out of her bag, and held it under Zézette's nose.

'What's that?' asked Zézette.

'It's a petition against the war,' said the lady. 'We are collecting supporters by the thousand.'

Zézette read in an undertone:

'The women of France, signatories of the present petition, declare that they rely on the Government of the Republic to safeguard peace by every possible means. They affirm their absolute conviction that war, whatever may be the circumstances in which it breaks out, is always a crime. Negotiations, exchanges of views – yes! – recourse to violence – No! For universal peace, against war in all its forms, this 22 September 1938. The League of French Mothers and Wives.'

She turned the page over: the back of it was covered with signatures, squeezed one below the other, horizontal, oblique, sloping up and sloping down, in black ink, violet ink, and blue ink. Some bold and sprawling, in large angular letters, others in a miserly elongated script, squeezed sheepishly into a corner. Against each signature there was an address: Mme Jeanne Plémeux, 6 rue d'Aubignac: Mme Solange Péres, 142 avenue de Saint-Ouen. Zézette surveyed the names of all these madames. They had all bent over that sheet of paper, some with children yelling in the next room, others had signed in a boudoir with a gold fountain-pen. Here were all their names side by side, and looking all alike. Mme Suzanne Tailleur: she had only to borrow a pen from the lady, and she too would become a madame, her name would take its place, looking equally forbidding and important, underneath the others.

'What are you going to do with that?' she asked.

'When we have got enough signatures, we shall send a delegation of women to take them to the Prime Minister's office.'

Mme Suzanne Tailleur. She was Mme Suzanne Tailleur. Maurice kept on lecturing her on class solidarity. And now it seemed that she had obligations in common with the Duchesse de Cholet. She thought to herself: 'I can't refuse to sign.'

Flossie laid her elbows on the pillow: 'Well, you bad boy, what do you think of it?'

'Quite nice,' said Philippe. 'It would have been nicer if I hadn't got a headache.'

'I must get up,' said Flossie. 'I'll get a bite somewhere, and then go along to the night club. Are you coming?'

'I'm too tired,' said Philippe. 'You must go without me.'

'You'll wait for me here, won't you? Promise me you'll wait!'

'Certainly,' said Philippe with a frown. 'Hurry along now, I'll wait.'

'Well,' said the lady: 'will you sign?'

'I haven't got a pen,' said Zézette.

The lady handed her a fountain-pen. Zézette took it and signed at the bottom of the page. She wrote her name in a copybook hand, and her address beside it, then looked up at the lady: she felt as though something was going to happen.

Nothing happened at all. The lady got up. She took the paper and eyed it attentively.

'Excellent,' she said. 'Well, my day's work is finished.'

Zézette opened her mouth: she felt she had a mass of questions to ask. But the questions did not come. She merely said: 'So you are going to take that to Daladier?'

'Yes, of course,' said the lady.

She waved the paper for a moment, then folded it up and slipped it into her bag. Zézette's heart turned over when the bag was shut. The lady raised her head and looked her straight in the eyes.

'Thank you,' she said: 'Thank you for his sake. Thank you for us all. You are a noble woman, Madame Tailleur.'

She held out her hand. 'And now,' she said, 'I must run away.'

Zézette shook her hand, after having wiped her own on her apron. She felt bitterly disappointed.

'Is . . . is that all?' she asked.

The lady laughed. She had teeth like pearls. Zézette repeated to herself: 'Class solidarity.' But the word had no longer any meaning.

'Yes, for the moment, that's all.'

She walked briskly to the door, opened it, threw a farewell smile at Zézette, and disappeared. Her scent still pervaded the room. Zézette listened while the sound of her footsteps died away, and sniffed two or three times. She felt as if she had been robbed of something. She went to the window, opened it and leaned out. A car stood by the pavement. The lady emerged from the house, opened the door of the car, got in, the car started. 'I've made a bloody fool of myself,' thought Zézette. The car turned into the avenue de Saint-Ouen and disappeared, carrying off her signature and the lovely perfumed lady, never to be seen again. Zézette sighed, shut the window, and relit the gas. The fat began to sputter, the smell of hot meat drowned the perfume, and Zézette thought: 'If ever Maurice gets to hear of this, I'll be in for something.'

'Mummy, I'm hungry.'

'What is the time?' the child's mother said to Mathieu.

She was a good-looking, buxom Marseillaise with a shadow of a moustache.

Mathieu glanced at his wrist-watch: 'Twenty minutes past eight.'

The woman produced from between her legs a basket secured by an iron rod: 'All right, you little horror, you shall have something to eat.'

She turned towards Mathieu: 'She would make a saint swear.'

Mathieu responded with a vaguely affable smile. 'Twenty minutes past eight,' he thought. 'In ten minutes Hitler is going to speak. They are in the drawing-room, Jacques will have been fiddling with the knobs on the wireless for the last half-hour.'

The woman had set the basket on the seat: she opened it, Jacques exclaimed: 'I've got it – I've got Stuttgart!'

Odette was standing near him with her hand on his shoulder. She heard a confused hum – as though a blast of air from a long vaulted hall seemed to strike her in the face. Mathieu edged along the seat to make room for the parcel: he had not left Juan-les-Pins. He was near Odette, in contact with Odette, but blind and dead, the train was carrying his ears and eyes to Marseilles. He felt no love for her, his feeling was something quite different: she had looked at him as though he was not wholly dead. He wanted to give expression to the formless affection that weighed upon him: he tried to recall Odette's face, but it eluded him. Jacques's face appeared twice instead of hers, Mathieu finally caught a glimpse of a motionless form in an arm-chair, an inch or two of neck bent forward, and an expression of attention on a face devoid of mouth and nose.

'Just in time,' said Jacques, turning round towards her. 'He hasn't started yet.'

My eyes are here. He saw the basket: the contents were wrapped in a handsome red and black striped napkin. Mathieu eyed the sunburnt neck for another moment or two, then let it go: so little for so deep an affection. It vanished into the shadows, and the napkin assumed a capacious existence, occupying his eyes, and scattering all other ideas and thoughts. *My eyes are here.* A muffled buzz made him start.

She turned to Mathieu with a deprecating laugh. 'It's the alarm clock. I always set it at half past eight.'

The little girl hurriedly opened a suitcase, thrust her hands into it, and the buzz ceased. Half past eight, he is just entering the Sportspalast. I am at Juan-les-Pins. I am at Berlin, but *my eyes are here. Somewhere* a long, black car had stopped at a door, and brown-shirted men were getting out of it. *Somewhere* to the north-east, on his right and behind him: but *here*, a small checked cloth blocked the view. Plump ringed fingers deftly pulled at its corners, and it disappeared, Mathieu observed a thermos lying on its side and a packet of bread and butter: he was hungry. I am at Juan-les-Pins, I am at Berlin, I am in Paris, I have no life left, nor any future. But *here*, I am hungry. Here, beside this large, dark-haired lady, and this little girl. He got up, lifted his suitcase down from the rack, and felt for Odette's parcel. Then he sat down again, took out his knife and cut the string: he ate hurriedly, as though he wanted to have finished in time to listen to Hitler's speech. He entered: a tremendous clamour shook the windows, and died away, he raised a hand. *Somewhere* there were ten thousand weaponed men, heads erect, arms uplifted. *Somewhere*, at his back, Odette was leaning over a radio set. He speaks, he says: 'Fellow citizens,' and his voice has already ceased to be his own, it has become an international voice; heard at Brest-Litovsk, Prague, Oslo, Tangiers, Cannes, Morlaix, and on the great white steamer plying between Casablanca and Marseilles.

'Are you sure you've got Stuttgart?' asked Odette. 'I can't hear a thing.'

'Hush – ' said Jacques. 'Yes, I'm sure.'

Lola stopped outside the entrance to the Casino.

'See you soon, then,' she said.

'Sing your best,' said Boris.

'Sure. Where are you off to, darling?'

'To the Bar Basque,' said Boris. 'There are some fellows there who don't know any German, and have asked me to translate Hitler's speech.'

'B-r-r-r,' said Lola with a shudder, 'that won't be very amusing.'

'I rather like translating,' said Boris.

He speaks! Mathieu made a violent effort to *hear* him, then he

suddenly felt hollow, and switched his mind off. He ate: the
little girl opposite was munching a jam sandwich: nothing
could be heard but the rhythmic panting of the bogies, it was a
honeyed evening, softly intimate. Mathieu turned his head and
looked at the sea through the carriage window. The pink arc
of dusk was closing down upon it. And yet a voice was pierc-
ing that sugar-coated egg. An all-pervading voice; the train
thrusts into it, and it is in the train, under the child's feet, in
the lady's hair, in my pocket, and if I had a radio set I could
make it burst forth from the luggage rack or under the seat. It
is there, enormous, it drowns the rumble of the train, it shakes
the windows – and I do not hear it. He was tired, he noticed
a sail far away over the sea, and he could think now of
nothing but that sail.

'Listen!' said Jacques triumphantly. 'Listen!'

A vast din suddenly burst forth from the radio. Odette
drew back a step, it was almost unendurable. 'What a lot of
them there are,' she thought, 'and how they admire him!'
Thousands of kilometres away, tens of thousands of damned
souls. Their voices filled the placid, family drawing-room –
and it was her own destiny that was there at issue.

'Here he is,' said Jacques. 'Here he is!'

The uproar gradually died down: a few harsh and nasal
voices came through, then silence fell, and Odette realized that
he was about to speak. Boris swung open the door of the bar,
and the landlord signed to him to hurry.

'Come along,' he said. 'It's just going to begin.'

There were three of them, with their elbows on the zinc
counter: Charlier from Marseilles, a compositor from Rouen,
and a tall, powerful, clumsily built man who travelled in
sewing-machines and whose name was Chomis.

'Evening,' said Boris in an undertone.

They threw him a cursory greeting as he approached the
radio. He respected them for cutting short their dinner to listen
to what would certainly be an unpleasant performance. They
were stout fellows, who looked things in the face.

He was standing with his two hands on the table,
he looked at the expanse of sea, and he could hear the sound
of the sea. He raised his right hand, and the sea grew calm.
He said:

'Fellow citizens,

'There is a limit beyond which it is not possible to yield, because to do so would be culpable weakness. Ten millions of Germans situated outside the Reich in two great organized territories, wanted to re-enter the Reich. I should not have the right to appear at the bar of German history if I had been willing merely to ignore their claims. Nor should I have the moral right to be the Führer of this people. I have made sufficient sacrifices and renunciations. That was the limit that I could not pass. The plebiscite in Austria has shown how well founded was this feeling. That was a testimony not expected by the rest of the world. But we have already seen that, for the democracies, a plebiscite becomes useless and even deleterious when it does not produce the result they had expected. None the less this problem was settled in a way that satisfied the great German people.

'And now we have before us the last problem that has to be settled, and one *that will be settled*.'

The sea surged into a heaving mass of waters, and he remained for a moment without speaking, surveying its enormous waves. Odette pressed a hand against her chest – the roaring of a crowd always made her heart leap. She leaned over Jacques's ear, he was still frowning and listening with extreme attention, although Hitler had ceased speaking for some seconds. She said to him, without much hope:

'What is he saying?'

Jacques pretended to understand German, having spent three months at Hanover, and for the last ten years had assiduously listened to all the Berlin orators, he even subscribed to the *Frankfurter Zeitung* for its financial articles. But the information he gave about what he had read or heard always remained extremely vague. He shrugged his shoulders:

'Always the same thing. He talked about sacrifices and the happiness of the German people.'

'He agrees to make sacrifices?' asked Odette eagerly. 'Does that mean that he would make concessions?'

'Yes – no. It was left very much in the air.'

He reached out a hand and Karl stopped shouting: it was a command. He turned to his right and left, muttering: 'Listen! Listen!' he felt as though the Führer's unuttered command had transfixed him and was taking shape in his mouth. 'Listen!' he said. 'Listen!' He was merely an instrument, a sounding-board: he was quivering with ecstasy. Everybody was silent, the entire hall was engulfed in silence and darkness; Hess, Göring, and Goebbels had disappeared, there was no longer anyone in the world but Karl and his Führer. The Führer was speaking in front of a huge red swastika'd standard, he was speaking to Karl, and to him alone. One voice, one sole voice in all the world. He speaks to me, he thinks for me, he decides for me. My Führer.

'This is the last territorial claim that I have to formulate in Europe, but it is a claim from which I shall not deviate, and which I shall realize, if God wills.'

He paused. Then Karl understood that he had permission to shout, and he shouted with all his might. Everybody began to shout, Karl's voice swelled, rose to the vaulted ceiling and rattled the very windows. He was ablaze with joy, he had ten thousand mouths, and he felt himself historic.

'Oh chuck it!' shouted Mimile into the radio. He turned to Robert and said: 'What a gang! These fellows are never happy except when they can yell in company. Apparently they do it to amuse themselves. There are huge thingamigs in Berlin holding twenty thousand people, they meet there on a Sunday, and sing in chorus and drink beer.'

The instrument continued to bellow: 'Look here,' said Robert, 'let's cut it off.'

They twisted the knob, the voices died away, the room seemed suddenly to emerge from shadow, and enclosed them once again, a small and quiet room, the brandy on the table; they had only needed to turn a knob and all those clamours of the damned had gone back into their box, a lovely placid evening had come through the window, a French evening: they were among Frenchmen.

'This Czech state was established on the foundation of a lie. The author of that lie was called Beneš.'

Tumult from the radio.

'This M. Beneš appeared at Versailles and began by affirm-ing the existence of a Czechoslovak nation.'

Laughter from the wireless. The rasping voice continued: 'He was obliged to invent that lie in order to confer more weight and importance on the meagre total of his fellow-citizens. And the Anglo-Saxon statesmen, who have never been sufficiently familiar with ethnical and geographical questions, did not then think it necessary to verify M. Beneš's affirmations.

'As this state did not appear likely to survive, three and a half million Germans were simply included in it, in contravention of their right to self-determination and of their desire to exercise that right.'

The wireless shouted: 'Shame! Shame!' and M. Birnenschatz exclaimed: 'Liar! Those Germans were not taken from Germany!' She looked at her father, now quite red with indignation, smoking a cigar in his armchair, she looked at her mother and her sister Ivy and almost hated them: 'How *can* they listen!'

'As though that were not enough, a million Magyars had also to be included, together with a mass of Sub-Carpathian Russians, and finally several hundred thousand Poles.

'Such is the state that was later called Czechoslovakia, in contravention of the national right of self-determination, and of the clearly expressed will of the peoples whose rights were thus violated. In speaking to you thus, I naturally sympathize with the fate of all these oppressed peoples: I sympathize with the fate of the Slovaks, the Poles, the Hungarians, and the Ukrainians: but I am of course speaking only of the destiny of my Germans.'

A vast clamour flooded the great hall. How can they listen to this stuff? The yells of '*Heil! Heil!*' made him feel positively sick. 'After all, we are Jews,' she reflected with annoyance, 'we don't have to listen to our executioner. It's all right for him, I have always heard him say that the Jews no longer existed. But she,' she reflected, looking at her mother, '*she*, she knows she is a Jewess, she feels it and she stays and listens.' Mme Birnenschatz, who rather enjoyed prophesying, had exclaimed two days before: 'It's war, my children, and a lost war, the Jewish nation will have to trail round with the begging bag again.' At the moment she was dozing through the uproar, her painted eyes closed from time to time, and her great head, crowned with jet black hair, nodded. The voice continued, dominating the storm:

'And here is this truly cynical outcome. This state, which is governed by a minority, obliges its nationals to pursue a policy that will compel them one day to fire upon their brothers.'

She got up. These raucous words, wrenched from a congested throat, were knife-thrusts. This man has tortured Jews: even while he speaks, thousands of them are suffering in concentration camps, and here we are, allowing that voice to bellow in the very room in which, only yesterday, we received our cousin Dachauer, whose eyelids had been burned.

'Beneš says to the Germans, "If I make war on Germany, you will have to fire on Germans. And if you refuse, you will be traitors, and I will have you shot." And he makes the same demand of the Hungarians and the Poles.'

The voice was there, enormous, the very voice of hatred: this one man versus Ella. The great plain of Germany, the mountains of France, had dissolved, he confronted her as an absolute enemy, outside space, he was threshing about in that box of his – he's looking at me, he sees me. She turned to her mother, to Ivy: but they had suddenly receded. She could still see them but not touch them. Paris also had drifted out of reach, the light from the windows fell dead upon the carpet. Contacts between people and things were imperceptibly disintegrating, she was alone in the world with that voice.

'On 20 February of this year I declared to the Reichstag that the conditions in which ten million Germans outside our frontiers now live must be changed. But Beneš has acted in the opposite direction. He started a régime of even more total repression.'

He was addressing her as though they two were alone, his eyes glaring into hers, his temper rising, intent upon terrifying and injuring her. She stood fascinated, her eyes fixed on the mica plaque. She could not hear his words, but his voice flayed her.

'A still greater terror . . . an era of dissolution. . . .'

She turned abruptly, and left the room. The voice pursued her into the hall, now blurred and flat, but still venomous: Ella darted into her room and locked the door. In the drawing-room, the threats continued: but she could hear no more than a confused murmur. She sank on to a chair: was there no one, the mother of a tortured Jew, the wife of a murdered Communist, who would pick up a revolver and shoot the man? She clenched her fists – had she been a German, she was sure she would have killed him.

Mathieu got up, took one of Jacques's cigars out of his weatherproof pocket, and slid back the door of the compartment.

'If that's on my account,' said the lady from Marseilles: 'don't bother; my husband smokes a pipe and I'm used to it.'

'Thank you,' said Mathieu. 'But I want to stretch my legs a bit.'

He was, in fact, tired of looking at her, the child, and the basket. He strolled along the corridor, stopped, and lit his cigar. The sea was blue and calm, he was gliding alongside it, and he thought: 'What is happening to me?' *This man's reply was always the same – All those he does not favour shall be shot, arrested, or imprisoned.* Mathieu wanted to try to understand. Nothing had ever happened to him that he did not understand: it was his only strength, his sole defence, his ultimate pride. He looked at the sea, and thought: 'I do not understand – *then came my Nuremberg demand. That demand was absolutely clear: for the fir—*and here I am, off to the war.' Nothing very odd about that, and yet it baffled him. In regard to what concerned him personally, everything was plain and simple: he had played and lost, his life lay behind him, wasted. I am leaving nothing; I regret nothing, not even Odette, not even Ivich, I am nobody. Remained the event itself. *I declared that the right of self-determination ought at last, twenty years after President Wilson's declarations, to be applied for the benefit of these three and a half millions,* all that had befallen him up to date had been within his compass as a man, the little setbacks and catastrophes, he had seen them coming, and he had faced them. When he took the money from Lola's room he had seen the notes, he had touched them, he had inhaled the perfume hovering in the room, and when he had thrown Marcelle over, he had looked her in the eyes while he was talking to her: his difficulties had been solely with himself: he could say to himself: there I was right, or there I was wrong: he could judge himself. This had now become impossible *and again M. Beneš has given his reply: more dead, more imprisonments, more* – He thought to himself: I am going to join the army, and that means nothing. Something had happened that puzzled him. And that was the war. Not so much that it puzzles me, as that it *isn't there*. Where is it? Everywhere: it turns up everywhere, the train plunges into war, Gomez comes down into war, those summer visitors in white linen suits are walking up and down in war, there isn't a heart-throb that doesn't lend it vigour, nor a consciousness that isn't transfixed by it. And yet, like Hitler's voice, it fills this train though I can't hear it. *I stated categorically to M. Chamberlain that what we now consider the sole prospect of a solution:* from time to time it seemed almost within touch, no matter where – in, say, the sauce on a *tournedos*, but try to touch it, and it isn't there: nothing remains but a dish of meat covered with sauce. 'Ah well,' he thought, 'one would have to be everywhere at the same time.'

My Führer, my Führer, you talk and I am changed into stone, I have no thought nor will, I am nothing but your voice, I would wait for him on the way out and aim at his heart, but I am primarily the mouthpiece of the Germans, and it is for these Germans that I have spoken, making plain that I am not disposed to remain a calm and inactive spectator while this madman from Prague thinks he can, I shall be that martyr, I did not start for Switzerland, at present I can do nothing now but endure that martyrdom, I swear I'll be that martyr, I swear, I swear, I swear, hush, said Gomez, we are listening to the buffoon's speech.

'This is Radio-Paris: in a minute or two we shall be transmitting the French translation of the first part of Chancellor Hitler's speech.'

'You see,' said Germain Chabot. 'You see. It wasn't worth while going out and running around for two hours in search of an *Intransigeant*. I told you so: they always do that.'

Mme Chabot put her knitting in the workbasket, and drew up her chair.

'So we shall know what he said. I hate listening to this sort of thing,' she said: 'it gives me a sinking feeling in the stomach. Don't you feel that way?'

'I do indeed,' said Germain Chabot.

The wireless burst into a roar, then died away in rumblings, and Chabot grabbed his wife's arm: 'Listen,' he said to her.

They leaned slightly forward, listening intently, and some-one began to sing the *Cucaracha*.

'You're sure that you're on Radio-Paris?' asked Madame Chabot.

'Sure.'

'Then we must just be patient.'

The voice sang three verses, then the record stopped.

'Now for it – ' said Chabot.

There followed a faint crackling sound, and a Hawaiian orchestra started to play *Honey Moon*.

One would have to be everywhere. Gloomily he surveyed the end of his cigar: everywhere, otherwise one gets fooled. I have been fooled. I *am* a soldier going off to the war. That is what one ought to *see*: the war, and the soldier. The stump of a cigar, white villas by the seashore, the monotonous glide of the carriages along the rails, and the too familiar traveller, Fez, Marrakesh, Madrid, Perugia, Siena, Rome, Prague, London, smoking for the thousandth time in the corridor of a third-class carriage. No war, no soldier: one would have to be everywhere, I would have *to be seen from everywhere*, from Berlin as a three-millionth part of the French Army, and with the eyes of Gomez, as one of those French hounds that have to be kicked into battle with the eyes of Odette. I would have to be seen *with the eyes of war*. But where are the eyes of war? I am *here* – large, clear surfaces glide past my eyes, I am preter-naturally clear-sighted, I see – and yet I grope blindly for my whereabouts, and each of my movements lights a bulb, or sets a bell ringing in a world I do not see. Zézette had closed the shutters, but the fading daylight still filtered through the crevices, she felt worn out, she threw her vest and knickers on to a chair and slipped naked into bed, I always sleep so well when I'm worried: but, when she got between the sheets, it was in that bed that Momo had made love to her two nights ago, as soon as she began to drop off, he took her and he crushed her, and if she opened her eyes she was no longer there, he was asleep far way in his barracks, and then there was that blasted radio blaring away in a foreign language, it was the set belonging to the Heinemanns, the refugee Ger-mans on the first floor, a raucous, viperine voice that rasped the nerves, it will not stop – Oh will it never stop! Mathieu envied Gomez and then said to himself: Gomez doesn't see more of it than I do, he is struggling against what he cannot see – and he ceased to envy him. What does he see? Walls, a telephone on his desk, his orderly officer's face. He *makes* war, he does not see it. And indeed, in making war, we all join in making it: I raise my hand, I draw at my cigar, and I *make* war: Sarah curses men's folly, she clasps Pablo in her arms: she *is making* war. Odette is making war when she wraps ham sandwiches in a piece of paper. The war takes and embraces everything, war preserves every thought and every gesture, and no one can see it, not even Hitler. No one. He repeated: No one – and suddenly he caught a sight of it. It was a strange entity, and one indeed beyond the reach of thought.

'This is Radio-Paris: in a few moments we shall be transmitting the French translation of the first part of Chancellor Hitler's speech.'

They did not move. They looked at each other out of the corners of their eyes, and when Rina Ketty began to sing *J'attendrai* they smiled at each other. But at the end of the first verse, Mme Chabot burst into a laugh.

'*J'attendrai!*' she said. 'Very appropriate. They're just guying us.'

A vast entity, a planet, in a space of a hundred million dimensions: three-dimensional beings could not so much as imagine it. And yet each dimension was an autonomous consciousness. Try to look directly at that planet, it would disintegrate into tiny fragments, and nothing but consciousnesses would be left. A hundred million free consciousnesses, each aware of walls, the glowing stump of a cigar, familiar faces, and each constructing its destiny on its own responsibility. And yet, each of those consciousnesses, by imperceptible contacts and insensible changes, realizes its existence as a cell in a gigantic and invisible coral. War: everyone is free, and yet the stakes are set. It is there, it is everywhere, it is the totality of all my thoughts, of all Hitler's words, of all Gomez's acts: but no one is there to make that total. It exists solely for God. But God does not exist. And yet the war exists.

'And I have made quite plain that henceforward German

patience has a limit. I have made plain the fact that it is a characteristic of the German people to be very patient, but that when the moment comes, a decision must be made.'

'What is he saying?' asked Chomis.

'He is saying that German patience has its limits,' explained Boris.

'So has ours,' said Charlier.

The world began to bellow from the wireless.

'Hullo!' said he, catching sight of Gomez. 'Well? Had a good leave?'

'So-so,' said Gomez.

'The French are still . . . cautious, I suppose?'

'You don't know how cautious. But I fancy they're going to get it in the pants.' He pointed to the wireless: 'The Berlin buffoon is loose!'

'Are you serious?' Herrera's eyes sparkled. 'I say, that would make a big difference.'

'It would indeed,' said Gomez.

They smiled at each other for a moment. Tilquin, who was at the window, came towards them:

'Turn it a bit lower, I can hear something.'

Gomez turned the knob, and the noise diminished.

'Do you hear?'

Gomez listened: he caught a dull humming sound.

'Ah!' said Herrera. 'An alarm. The fourth since this morning.'

'The fourth!' said Gomez.

'Yes,' said Herrera. 'Things have changed since you went away.'

Hitler was speaking again: they bent over the instrument. Gomez was listening to the speech with one ear, and with the other to the hum of aeroplanes. Then followed the dull thud of a distant explosion.

'What is he doing? He has not ceded any territory, and he is now expelling the Germans. Monsieur Beneš had scarcely spoken when his military measures of repression were resumed with greater intensity. The following terrible figures are authentic: in one day ten thousand persons were ejected, twenty thousand on the following day. . . .'

The hum diminished, then suddenly grew louder: two reverberating explosions.

278

'The harbour's getting it,' whispered Tilquin.

'The next day thirty-seven thousand, two days later forty thousand, then sixty-two thousand, then seventy-eight thousand: now this process is continuing at the rate of ninety thousand, a hundred and seven thousand, a hundred and thirty-seven thousand. And today – two hundred and fourteen thousand. Entire districts have been depopulated, towns burnt down, and the Germans expelled by the use of gas and artillery. Monsieur Beneš, for his part, is safe in Prague, and saying to himself: "I run no risk, in the last resort I can depend on the support of England and France."'

Herrera pinched Gomez's arm.

'Listen,' he said: 'listen: he's going to let them have it now.'

His face had flushed, he was gazing at the radio with something like approval. The thunderous, harsh voice burst forth once more:

'And now, my fellow-citizens, I think the hour has come when it is necessary to speak without reserve.'

A string of explosions, gradually approaching, drowned the applause. But Gomez paid little attention to them: he stared at the radio, listened to that threatening voice, and felt within him the revival of an emotion long since buried, something that resembled hope.

> You who pass without a greeting,
> You who ever scorn a meeting,
> Give me but a faint and fleeting
>   Breath of hope before I sleep,
>   Nor let me always weep.

'I understand,' said Germain Chabot. 'This time I understand.'

'Well, what is it?' said his wife.

'It's a link-up with the evening Press. They won't broadcast the translation before it is published in the papers.'

He got up and took his hat. 'I'm going out,' he said. 'I shall find an *Intran* on the Boulevard Barbès.'

The moment had come. He swung both legs out of bed, and thought: 'Now for it.' She would find the bird flown and a thousand-franc note pinned to the coverlet, and if I have time I'll leave a farewell poem with it. His head was heavy but had ceased to ache. He passed his hands over his face, and dropped them with disgust: they smelt of Negress. On the glass shelf above the wash-basin there was a cake of pink soap beside a spray, and an indiarubber sponge. He picked up the sponge, but an uprush of nausea came into his mouth, and he searched in his suitcase for his own washing-glove and soap. He washed himself from head to foot, splashing the water all over the floor, but that didn't matter. He combed his hair, took a clean shirt out of the suitcase, and put it on. The martyr's shirt. He was grim but composed. There was a clothes-brush on the chest of drawers, and he carefully brushed his jacket. 'But where can I have put my trousers?' he said to himself. He looked under the bed, and even between the sheets: no trousers: he said to himself, 'I must have been very drunk.' He opened the glass door of the wardrobe, he was beginning to be uneasy, the trousers were not there. He stood for a moment in the middle of the room, in his shirt, scratching his head and looking round him, then a gust of anger came upon him, it was a perfectly ridiculous situation for a budding martyr to be marooned like this in his socks in a whore's bedroom, with his shirt tails flapping round his knees. At that moment he noticed on his right a cupboard set in the wall. He dashed towards it, but the key was not in the lock: he tried to open it with his nails, and then with a pair of scissors which he found on the table, but failed. He flung the scissors down, and stamped on the floor, muttering in a voice of fury: 'The little bitch! She has locked up my trousers to stop me going out.'

'On this matter, I can only say one thing: two men are now confronted: Monsieur Beneš and myself!'

The whole crowd began to yell. Anna looked uneasily at Milan. He had gone up to the radio, and was eyeing it with his hands in his pockets. His face had darkened, and there was something moving inside his cheek.

'Milan,' said Anna.

'We are two men of a different stamp. While Monsieur Beneš, during the great struggle of the nations, came and went about the world, keeping out of danger, I, as a faithful German soldier, did my duty. And today, here I am, face to face with him – I, the soldier of my people.'

They cheered again. Anna rose and laid a hand on Milan's

280

arm: his biceps were contracted, his whole body had stiffened into rigidity. 'He'll fall down,' she thought. 'Swine,' he stammered.

She gripped his arm, but he pushed her away.

'Beneš and I!' he stammered. 'Beneš and I! Just because you've got seventy-five million men behind you.'

He stepped forward: she thought: 'What is he going to do?' – and dashed towards him: but he had already spat on the radio twice.

The voice went on:

'I have only a brief statement to make: I am grateful to Mr Chamberlain for all his efforts. I have assured him that the German people want nothing else but peace: but I also made clear to him that the limits of our patience are now set. I furthermore assured him, and I repeat it here, that – once this problem is settled – there is no other territorial problem for Germany in Europe. I also assured him that, from the moment when Czechoslovakia settled these problems, that is when the Czechs shall have come to terms with their other minorities, not by oppressive measures, but on a pacific basis, I shall have no further concern with the Czech State. On that point I give him my pledged word. We do not want any Czechs among us. But at the same time, I declare now before the German people, that in so far as the problem of the Sudetens is concerned, my patience is at an end. I made Monsieur Beneš an offer which is nothing more than the realization of the assurances he has himself already made. The decision is now in his hand: peace or war. Either he will accept these proposals, and now give the Germans their freedom; or we shall go and take it ourselves.'

Herrera raised his head exultantly. 'Well, I'm damned!' he said. 'Did you hear that? It's war.'

'Yes,' said Gomez. 'Beneš is tough: he won't give way: it's war.'

'Well,' said Tilquin, 'I wish it may be so!'

'What's this?' asked Chamberlain.

'The final message,' said Woodehouse.

Chamberlain took the papers and began to read. Woodehouse eyed his face uneasily. After a few moments the Prime Minister looked up, and smiled amiably.

'Well,' he said, 'there's nothing new here.'

Woodehouse looked at him with surprise. 'Chancellor Hitler has expressed himself with a good deal of violence,' he observed.

'That doesn't mean anything,' said Chamberlain. 'He had to.'

'Today I march at the head of my people as their first soldier: and behind me, as the world should know, marches a nation, and a nation which is quite different from what it was in 1918. In this hour, the entire German people are with me. They feel my will to be their will, just as I regard their future and their destiny as the motivating power behind my action. We must strengthen this joint will – the will of those great days, when I, an unknown private soldier, set forth to conquer an Empire, never doubting of success nor final victory. Around me is arrayed a band of brave men and women, who then marched with me. And now, my German people, I ask this of you all: March behind me, men and women of Germany. At this hour we must have but one will. A will must be stronger than any difficulty or any danger: and if it is so, it will master all difficulties and dangers. We are resolved. It is now for Monsieur Beneš to decide.'

Boris turned towards the others and said: 'It's all over.'

They did not react at once: they went on smoking with an air of concentration. After a few moments the landlord said: 'Well – so we're going to smash him?'

'I don't think!'

The landlord leaned over the bottles, and turned the knob: for a moment Boris felt uncomfortable: it was as though a void had been created. Night and a faint breeze came in through the open door.

'What did he say?' said the Marseillais.

'Well, at the end he said: all my people are behind me, I am ready for war. It is for Monsieur Beneš to choose.'

'My God!' said the Marseillais, 'So it's war?'

Boris shrugged his shoulders.

'Well,' said the Marseillais, 'it's six months since I've seen my wife and my two daughters, and I shall have to go back to Marseilles just to say good night, and wave a hand, and then off to barracks.'

'I very likely shan't even have the time to see my mother,'

said Chomis. 'I come from the north,' he said, by way of explanation.

'Well, well,' said the Marseillais, wagging his head.

They fell silent. Charlier knocked out his pipe against his heel. The landlord said: 'What about another? As it's to be war, I'll stand this round.'

'Right – the same again, thanks.'

The air from out-of-doors was cool and dark, they could hear the distant band from the Casino: possibly Lola was singing.

'I've been to Czechoslovakia,' said the man from the north. 'And I'm glad I have: it's a good thing to know what one is fighting for.'

'Did you stay there long?' asked Boris.

'Six months. On a timber deal. I got on well with the Czechs. They're workers.'

'As to that,' said the landlord. 'The Germans are workers too.'

'Yes, but they get across everybody. The Czechs are quiet folk.'

'Good health,' said Charlier.

'Good health.'

They clinked glasses, and the Marseillais said: 'It's getting chilly.'

Mathieu awoke with a start. 'Where are we?' he asked, rubbing his eyes.

'Marseilles, Gare Saint Charles: all change.'

'Right,' said Mathieu.

He took his weatherproof off the peg, and his suitcase from the luggage-rack. He felt adrift. 'Hitler must have finished his speech,' he thought with relief.

'I saw the boys go off in '14,' said the man from the north. 'I was ten years old. It was quite different then.'

'They wanted to go?'

'I should think they did – they were all yelling and singing and waving!'

'I expect they didn't realize what it meant,' said the Marseillais.

'I dare say not.'

'Well, we do,' said Boris.

A silence followed. The man from the north was looking straight in front of him. He said: 'I saw the Fritzes at close quarters. Our place was occupied for four years. They pretty well stripped us bare. The village was destroyed, for weeks and weeks we used to hide in the quarries. So you can understand that when I think it's all going to start again . . .' He added: 'That doesn't mean that I won't do my duty like the rest.'

'My trouble is,' said the landlord smiling: 'that I've a horror of death. Ever since I was a small boy. However, I've got over it a bit lately by saying to myself: The rotten thing is death: and whether you die of influenza or an exploding shell . . .'

Boris smiled a beatific smile: he liked these fellows, and he thought: 'I prefer men to women.' One good thing about war was that it was solely a male concern. For three years – five years, he would see only men. 'And I'll transfer my leave to fathers of families.'

'What counts,' said Chomis, 'is to be able to tell yourself that you have lived. I'm thirty-six, and I haven't always had a gay time. There have been ups and downs. But I have lived. They can cut me into little pieces, but they can't deprive me of that.' He turned to Boris. 'For a lad like you it must be even harder.'

'Oh,' said Boris briskly: 'I wonder how long people have been telling me that there's going to be a war.' He flushed, and added: 'It must be worse for married men.'

'Yes,' said the Marseillais, with a sigh. 'My wife has plenty of courage, and besides she has a profession: she's a hairdresser. I worry about my little girls: but it's better to have been a father, isn't it? Anyway, men who go to the war don't inevitably get killed.'

'Of course they don't,' said Boris.

The band was silent. A couple came into the bar. The woman was red-haired, and wore a long, green, low-cut frock. They sat down at a back table.

'None the less,' said Charlier, 'war is just too silly. I don't know anything sillier.'

'Nor do I,' said the landlord.

'Nor I,' said Chomis.

284

'Well,' said the Marseillais, 'what do I owe you? There's one round on me.'

'And one on me,' said Boris.

They paid. Chomis and the Marseillais went out arm-in-arm. Charlier hesitated a moment, turned on his heel and sat down, taking his glass of brandy with him. Boris was still standing at the counter, thinking to himself: 'They're good fellows': and was glad. There would be others like them in the trenches, thousands of them, just as good fellows as these. And Boris would live with them, he would not leave them day or night: and he would have plenty to do. He was in luck compared with the poor young men of his own age who had been run over in the street, or had died of cholera, he had to admit that he had been lucky. He had not been taken unawares: this was not one of those wars that wreck a man's life without warning, like a street accident: this war had proclaimed its advent six or seven years ahead, people had had time to see it coming. Personally Boris had never doubted that it would break out in the end: he had awaited it like a Crown Prince who knows from childhood that he is born to reign. They had begotten him for the purpose of this war, they had educated him for it, they had sent him to the Lycée, to the Sorbonne, they had trained his mind accordingly: the idea began that he should become a professor, but that story had always seemed to him extremely thin: he now knew that they had meant him to become an officer in the Reserve, and no expense had been spared to ensure that he should become a fine, fresh, healthy casualty. 'The ludicrous thing is,' he thought, 'that I wasn't born in France, I'm merely a naturalized Frenchman.' But after all, that was not a point of much importance: if he had remained in Russia, or if his parents had fled to Berlin or Budapest, it would have been just the same: it isn't a question of nationality, it's a question of age: young Germans, Hungarians, Englishmen, and Greeks, had been dedicated to the same war, the same destiny. In Russia, there had first been the generation of the Revolution, then that of the Five Year Plan, and now, that of the world conflict: to every man his portion. Ultimately a man is born for war or peace, just as a man is born a worker or a bourgeois, there's nothing to be done about it, everybody hasn't the luck to be born a citizen of Switzerland. 'A fellow who would have the right to complain,' he thought, 'is Mathieu: now there is a man definitely born for peace: he has always been convinced that he would die of old age, and has already acquired his little habits: at his age a man does not change. Whereas, as far as I'm concerned, it's my war. The war made me, and I shall make the war: we are inseparable: I can't even imagine what I should be like if it hadn't broken out.' He thought of his life, and it no longer seemed to him too short. Lives are neither short nor long. It was a life, that's all: war at the end of it. He felt as though he had been suddenly invested with a new dignity, because he had a function in Society, and also because he was going to die a violent death, and his modesty was hurt. It was surely time to go and fetch Lola. He smiled at the *patron* and hurried out.

The sky was cloudy: here and there some stars were visible: the wind was blowing in from the sea. For a moment, Boris's mind was clouded, then he thought: 'My war', and was surprised because he wasn't used to thinking about the same things for any length of time. 'How frightened I shall be!' he said to himself. 'My God, I shall get the wind up properly!' And he burst into shocked but rather complacent laughter at the notion of such fear. But he stopped laughing after a step or two, under the access of a sudden anxiety: after all, he must not be *too* afraid. He would not make old bones, certainly, but that was not a reason for spoiling his life, and allowing himself too much latitude. He had been pledged from birth, but he hadn't been robbed of any luck, his war was a *vocation* rather than a destiny. Obviously he could have wished for a different one: that of a great philosopher, for instance, or of a Don Juan, or a great financier. But one does not choose one's vocation: one succeeds or fails in it, that's all: and the unpleasant aspect of his own was that he wasn't allowed a second try. There were lives that resembled the *Baccalauréat* examination: the candidate sent in several papers, and if he failed in physics, he could make up in Natural Science, or Philosophy. But his own life rather suggested the Certificate of General Philosophy, in which a candidate is judged on one test alone: which was a terrible ordeal. However, it was in those conditions that he must succeed, not in any others – and it wouldn't be an easy job. He must behave decently, of course, but that wasn't enough. He must acclimatize himself to the war, find his due place in it, and try to take full advantage of all his experiences. He must bear in mind that, from a certain point of view, all have their value: an attack in the Argonne is as good as a trip in a gondola, the dishwater drunk in the trenches in the early morning is as good as the coffee in Spanish railway stations at dawn. And then there are other fellows, life in the open air, parcels, and above all the spectacle of war: a bombardment must be a good show, anyway. If I am afraid, I rob myself of life, I remain a tadpole. I won't be afraid, he said to himself.

The lights of the Casino brought him out of his dream, from the open windows came snatches of music, a black car drew up silently at the entrance. Another year to go, he thought with vexation.

It was past midnight, the Sportspalast was dark and deserted, full of piled chairs and cigar-ends, M. Chamberlain was talking on the wireless, Mathieu strolled along the quays of the Vieux-Port, thinking: 'It's a disease, simply a disease: it has come upon me by chance, it does not concern me, it must be faced like gout or toothache.' M. Chamberlain said: 'I hope the Chancellor will not reject this proposal, which is made in the same spirit of friendship with which I was greeted in Germany, and which, if accepted, will satisfy the German desire to unite the Sudetens with the Reich, without bloodshed in any part of Europe.'

He waved a hand to indicate that he had finished, and moved away from the microphone. Zézette, who could not get to sleep, was standing at the window, looking at the stars above the roofs, Germain Chabot was taking off his trousers in the lavatory. Boris was waiting for Lola in the hall of the Casino: everywhere, on every wave-length, unheard or nearly so, a dark flower struggling into blossom: *If the moon turns green*, played by the jazz orchestra at the Hôtel Astoria, and relayed by Daventry.

Tuesday, 27 September

TEN-THIRTY. 'Monsieur Delarue!' said the concierge. 'This is a surprise! I didn't expect you for a week.'

Mathieu smiled at her. He would have preferred to slip through unobserved: but he had to ask for his keys.

'You, at least, are not called up'

'Me?' said Mathieu 'No.'

'So much the better,' she said. 'It will come soon enough. Oh dear! Just think of all that has happened since you went away. Do you think there's going to be a war?'

'I don't know, Madame Garinet,' said Mathieu. And he added briskly: 'Any letters?'

'I forwarded them all on to you,' said Mme Garinet. 'Only yesterday I sent on a circular to Juan-les-Pins: you should have let me know you were coming back – but here's something that came this morning.'

She handed him a long grey envelope: Mathieu recognized Daniel's handwriting. He took the letter and put it into his pocket unopened.

'Do you want the keys?' said the concierge. 'What a pity you couldn't let me know: I would have had time to clean up the flat a bit. As it is . . . the shutters aren't even open.'

'That doesn't matter,' said Mathieu, taking the keys. 'Good night, Madame Garinet.'

The house was still deserted. From outside, Mathieu had noticed that the shutters were closed. The stair-carpet had been taken up for the summer. He walked slowly past the first-floor flat. Once there had been some noisy children there, and Mathieu had often tossed about at night, deafened by the yells of the last-born. Now the rooms were dark and desolate behind their closed shutters. Holidays. But he thought, in his inmost self: war. This was war – blank, bewildered holidays, curtailed for some, prolonged for others. The second floor was occupied by someone's girl-friend: her scent often percolated under the door on to the landing. She was no doubt at Biarritz, in a huge hotel prostrated by the heat and the stagnation of business. He reached the third floor and turned the key in the lock. Below him and above him, stones and night and silence. He made his way into the darkness, and put down his bag and weatherproof in the darkness: the hall smelt musty. He remained motionless, his arms at his sides, enveloped in shadow, then brusquely turned the switch and walked into all the rooms in his flat, one after the other, leaving the doors open: he turned on the lights in the sitting-room, the kitchen, the bathroom and lavatory, and in his bedroom, one by one, and a current of continuous light circulated from room to room. He stopped beside his bed.

Someone had slept there. The bedclothes were in a huddle, the pillowcase was soiled and crumpled, and there were bread-crumbs on the sheets. Someone – myself. 'It was I,' he thought, 'who slept there. Me, on 15 July, for the last time.' But he eyed the bed with disgust: that bygone sleep of his had grown cold within the sheets, indeed it was now someone else's sleep. I shan't stay here.

He turned into his study: his disgust remained. A dirty glass on the mantelpiece: on the table, near the bronze crab, a broken cigarette, with strands of dried tobacco hanging out of it. When did I break that cigarette? He squeezed it and felt the crackle of dead tobacco leaves. Books. A volume of Arbelet, another of Martineau, Lamiel, *Lucien Leuwen*, the *Memoirs of an Egoist*. Someone had undertaken an article on Stendhal. The books remained, and the intention, now petrified, had become an object. May '38: it was not yet ridiculous to write about Stendhal. An object: like the grey covers of the books, like the dust that had gathered on their backs. An opaque and passive object, an impenetrable presence. My undertaking. My undertaking to drink, now visible as a dim deposit in the transparent glass – to smoke, to write. Here was the green leather arm-chair in which the man sat in the evening. It was evening now: Mathieu looked at the arm-chair and sat down on the edge of a straight one. '*Your arm-chairs are corrupting*,' a voice had said, in this very place: Your arm-chairs are corrupting. On the divan a fair-haired girl had angrily shaken her curls. At that time the man had barely seen the curls, barely heard the voices: he saw, he heard, his future through them. And now the man had gone, carrying off his old, mendacious future: the presences had grown cold, they remained like a film of grease on the surface of the furniture, and voices hovered at the level of the eyes: they had floated up to the ceiling, dropped down again, and were now hovering in the room. Mathieu felt like an intruder, he went to the window, and swung the shutters back. A faint daylight lingered in the sky, a radiance that came from nowhere: he drew a deep breath.

Daniel's letter. He reached out a hand to take it, then dropped his hand on to the window-bar. Daniel had left down that street one evening in June, he had passed beneath that street lamp: the man had stood by the window, and watched him go. It was to that man that Daniel had written. Mathieu didn't want to read his letter. He turned abruptly, and surveyed his room with a sort of arid satisfaction. They were all there, immured and dead, Marcelle, Ivich, Brunet, Boris, Daniel. Thither they had come, there they had been entrapped, and there they would remain. Ivich's explosions of anger, Brunet's remonstrances – Mathieu *remembered* them already as an event, like the death of Louis XVI, and in the same dispassionate way. They belonged to the world's past, not to his: he no longer had a past.

He closed the shutters, walked across the room, paused, and, on reflection, left the table lamp alight. Tomorrow morning I'll come back for my suitcases. He shut the outer door upon them all, and went downstairs. He felt devoid of weight or content. Up above and behind him, the lights would shine all night like tapers on his dead life.

'What are you thinking about?' asked Lola.

'Nothing,' said Boris.

They were sitting on the beach. Lola was not singing that evening, there was a gala at the Casino. A couple had just passed them, followed by a soldier. Boris pondered.

'Do be nice to me,' said Lola, in a pleading voice: 'tell me what you're thinking about.'

Boris shrugged his shoulders. 'I was thinking about that soldier.'

'Really?' said Lola. 'And what was in your mind?'

'What does one think about a soldier?'

'Boris,' groaned Lola, 'what's the matter with you? You've

been so nice to me lately and so affectionate. And now you're just as bad as ever. You have hardly spoken to me all day.'

Boris did not answer, he was thinking of the soldier: and what he thought was: 'He's lucky: I've got another year to go.' A year: he would go back to Paris, he would walk down the Boulevard Montparnasse and the Boulevard Saint-Michel, both of which he knew by heart, he would go to the Dôme, to the Coupole, and he would sleep every night at Lola's place. If I could see Mathieu, I could just endure it all, but Mathieu will be in the army. And my Diploma, he suddenly reflected. For added to all this, there would be an untimely jest known as the Higher Diploma. His father would certainly insist on his taking the examination, and Boris would be obliged to submit a thesis on Imagination, according to Renouvier, or Habit, according to Maine de Biron. Why do they keep up this farce? he thought irritably. They had bred him for war, as indeed was their right, but now they meant to compel him to pass his Diploma, as though he had a whole life of peace before him. A sorry prospect: for a whole year he would sit in libraries, pretend to read the complete works of Maine de Biron in the Tisserand edition, pretend to take notes, pretend to prepare for his examination, and all the while he would be thinking about the veritable ordeal that awaited him, wondering whether he would be afraid, or whether he would be able to hold out. 'If it wasn't for her,' he thought, throwing a malevolent look at Lola, 'I would join up at once, and pay them out properly.'

'Boris!' cried Lola in affright. 'You mustn't look at me like that! Don't you love me any more?'

'On the contrary,' said Boris through clenched teeth, 'you don't know how much I love you. You haven't the faintest notion.'

Ivich had lit her bedside lamp, and lay outstretched on her bed, naked. She had left the door open, and could see out into the passage: there was a circle of light on the ceiling, and all the rest of the room was blue. A faint haze hovered above the table, the room smelt of lemon, tea, and cigarettes.

She heard a rustle in the passage, and an enormous shape silently passed her door.

'Hi!' she exclaimed.

Her father turned, and eyed her with disapproval.

'Ivich, I have spoken to you about this more than once: you must either shut the door or put some clothes on.'

He had flushed slightly, and spoke with an almost melodious intonation. 'I'm thinking of the maid.'

'The maid has gone to bed,' said Ivich composedly. And she added: 'I was watching out for you. You pass so quietly, I was afraid of missing you. Turn round.'

M. Serguine turned round, she got up and put on her dressing-gown. Her father was standing stiffly in the doorway, with his back towards her. She eyed his neck, his stalwart shoulders, and began to laugh noiselessly.

'You can look now.'

He was now facing her. He sniffed two or three times and said: 'You smoke too much.'

'It's because I'm so nervy,' she said.

He did not reply. The lamp lit up his large, rough-hewn face. Ivich rather admired him in the way she might admire a mountain or the Niagara Falls. After a pause he said: 'I'm going to bed.'

'No,' pleaded Ivich. 'No, papa: I would like to listen to the radio.'

'What!' cried M. Serguine. 'At this hour?'

Ivich ignored his tone: she knew he left his room every evening about eleven o'clock on his way to his study to listen to the news on the sly. He was as elusive as an elf, despite his thirteen stone.

'You go alone,' he said, 'I have to get up early tomorrow.'

'But, papa!' pleaded Ivich. 'You know I can't work the radio.'

M. Serguine burst out laughing. 'Ha-ha-ha!' he exclaimed. 'You surely don't want to listen to the music?' he asked, resuming his solemn air. 'Remember your poor mother is asleep.'

'"Of course I don't, papa,' said Ivich furiously. 'I want to know how they're getting on with their war.'

'Come along then.'

She followed him barefooted to the office, and he leaned over the radio. His long, powerful hands manipulated the knobs so gently that Ivich was quite touched, and regretted their vanished intimacy. When she was fifteen, they had been inseparable, and Mme Serguine became jealous: when M. Serguine took Ivich to a restaurant, he sat her opposite him, and she ordered her own dinner: the waiters called her Madame which gave her much delight and he looked complacent, like a man who is dining with a pretty girl. They heard the closing bars of a military march, and then a German began to speak in rasping tones:

'Papa,' she said reproachfully, 'I don't know German.'

He eyed her quizzically. 'He did it on purpose,' she thought.

'The best news comes on at this time.'

Ivich listened attentively to see if she could catch the word *Krieg* of which she did know the meaning. The German stopped talking, and the orchestra launched into another march: Ivich was quite stunned, but M. Serguine listened to the end: he did not dislike military music.

'Well?' asked Ivich in an anguished voice.

'Things are going badly,' said M. Serguine. But he did not look much concerned.

'Ah,' she said hoarsely, 'the Czechs are still the trouble, I suppose?'

'Yes.'

'How I loathe them,' she said passionately. And she added after a pause: 'But if a country refused to go to war, it couldn't be forced to do so, could it?'

'Ivich,' said M. Serguine severely, 'you are a child.'

'Am I?' said Ivich. 'I dare say I am.'

She suspected that her father was as much mystified as she was.

'Is that all the news?'

M. Serguine hesitated.

'Papa!'

He is furious with me for having come. I've spoiled his little celebration. M. Serguine loved secrets, he had six padlocked suit-cases, and two bolted trunks, which he inspected sometimes when alone. Ivich eyed him with affection, he was so likeable that she very nearly told him what her trouble was.

'In a moment or two,' he said regretfully, 'we shall hear the French news.'

His pale eyes looked down at her, and she realized that he was no use to her at all. She merely said: 'What will happen if there is a war?'

'The French would be beaten.'

'Pfui! Would the Germans invade France?'

'Of course.'

'They would get to Laon?'

'I imagine so. I imagine they would make for Paris.'

'He doesn't know a thing about it,' thought Ivich. 'He's a comedian.' But her heart was throbbing wildly.

She was sorry she had asked the question. Since the Bolsheviks had burned his country houses, her father rather enjoyed catastrophes. He half-closed his eyes, and wagged his head.

'Ah!' he said: 'Aha!'

Eleven-thirty. A dead street, immersed in shadow: at rare intervals an arc-lamp. A nondescript street, edged with tall, nameless mausoleums. All the shutters closed, not a single glint of light. It was once the rue Delambre. Mathieu had crossed the rue Cels, the rue Froidevaux, walked along the Avenue du Maine and even the rue de la Gaîté: they were all alike: still warm, already unrecognizable, already streets of war. Something had perished. Paris was no more than a vast street-cemetery.

Mathieu went into the Dôme because the Dôme happened to be there. A waiter hovered round with an ingratiating smile: a puny youth in spectacles, very deferential. He was a new waiter: the old one used to keep the customers waiting for an hour, then strolled up nonchalantly, and took the orders without even a smile.

'Where's Henri?'

'Henri?' said the boy.

'A tall dark fellow, with rather goggle-eyes.'

'Oh yes. He's been called up.'

'And Jean?'

'The fair one? He's been called up too. I'm taking his place.'

'Bring me a brandy,' said Mathieu.

The boy ran off. Mathieu blinked for a moment or two, and then considered the room with surprise. In July the Dôme had no precise confines, it overflowed through the windows and the revolving door into the street, and spread over the road, the passers-by were flooded in the milky haze that lit up the hands and left cheeks of the taximen on the rank in the centre of the Boulevard Montparnasse. One step more, and the haze reddened, the taximen's right profiles were red too: the Rotonde. But now the outer darkness surged against the windows, and the Dôme was reduced to its own essence: a collection of tables, benches, glasses, dry and unresponsive, denuded of that diffused glow which shadowed them by night. Gone were the German émigrés, the Hungarian pianist, the alcoholic old American lady. Gone were all those charming couples who held hands under the table and talked of love until the small hours of the morning, their eyes red with sleep. On his left a major was having supper with his wife. Opposite, sat a little Annamite tart dreaming over a café-crême, and at the next table a captain was eating a dish of sauerkraut. On the right, a lad in uniform had his arm round a woman's waist. Mathieu knew him by sight, he was a student at the Beaux-Arts, tall, pale, and diffident: but he looked quite truculent in uniform. The captain raised his head, and his look pierced through the wall: Mathieu followed it – what it envisaged was a railway station, flares, gleaming railway lines, men with ashen faces, and sleep-swollen eyes, sitting stiffly in the carriages with their hands on their knees. In July we sat together underneath the lights, our eyes fixed on each other, and none of our looks was lost. Now they are lost indeed, they speed towards Wissembourg, towards Montmédy: people are now divided by abysses, space, and darkness. The Dôme has been mobilized – transformed into a piece of basic equipment: a buffet. 'Ah well,' he thought with satisfaction, 'there's nothing I regard with any affection or regret, I leave nothing behind.'

The little Indo-Chinese smiled at him. She was a pretty little thing with tiny hands: two years ago Mathieu had decided to spend a night with her. This would be the moment. I should slide my lips over her chilly skin, and inhale a musty, insect smell; I should be just a naked entity beneath her professional fingers: I have in me certain antiquated notions that would die of such a contact. He would just return her smile.

'Waiter.'

The waiter ran up. 'Ten francs, please.'

Mathieu paid and departed. I already know her too well as it is. It was dark. The first night of war. No, not quite. There were still squares of light on the side of houses. In a month, or a fortnight, the first alarm would extinguish them: for the moment it was no more than a dress rehearsal. But Paris had in fact lost her pink cotton ceiling. For the first time Mathieu could see a dark vaporous pall of sky overhanging the city. The sky of Juan-les-Pins, Toulouse, Dijon, Amiens, the same for the country and the town, and for the whole of France. Mathieu stopped and gazed up at it. A quite ordinary and un-privileged sky. And myself a nondescript entity beneath that vast indifferent arc: that's war. A patch of light caught his eye, and he said to himself, listening to his own voice, 'Paris, Boulevard Raspail.' But all those lovely and familiar names had also been mobilized – all those delicious names, they looked as though they were printed on a staff map, or in a war communiqué. Nothing was left of the Boulevard Raspail. Roads they were, just roads, speeding south to north, west to east: just numbered roads: paved for a mile or two here and there, set between side-walks and houses, and named rue, avenue, and boulevard. But they were still segments of the same road. Mathieu, facing towards the Belgian frontier, was walk-ing along a section of the Route Departmentale which de-bouched from Route Nationale, No. 14. He turned into the long, straight highway that formed a continuation of the Ouest Railway, once the rue de Rennes. A flame enveloped him, a street-lamp flashed out of the shadows and vanished: a taxi passed, speeding towards the railway stations on the right bank, followed by a black car, filled with officers, then silence fell once more. Along that road, under that indifferent sky, the houses had been reduced to their crudest function: they were now just blocks of buildings. Dormitory-refectories for those about to be mobilized, and for the families of those already mobilized. Their ultimate purpose could already be surmised: they would become 'strategic points', and, in the end, targets. And that would be the end of Paris: the city was indeed already dead. A new world was coming into being: the austere and practical world of functional objects.

A ray of light gleamed through the curtains of the Café des Deux Magots. Mathieu sat down on the terrace. Behind him the last-to-leave customers were whispering in the darkness. The night was chilly.

'A beer please,' said Mathieu.

'It's nearly midnight,' said the waiter. 'We aren't serving any more drinks outside.'

'Just one beer.'

'All right – but you must hurry.'

Behind his back a woman burst into a laugh – the first he had heard since his return; and it quite shocked him. Not that he felt at all depressed, but he did not want to laugh. In the sky a storm cloud parted and two stars appeared. 'It's the war,' thought Mathieu.

'Would you pay now, please? Then I needn't bother you again.'

Mathieu paid, the waiter went back into the café. A pair of shadows rose, glided between the tables, and departed. Mathieu was left alone on the terrace. He looked up and saw, on the other side of the square, a fine new church, white against the black sky. A village church. Yesterday a very Parisian edifice had stood in its place: the church of Saint-Germain-des-Prés, an historic monument, Mathieu had met Ivich outside the porch. Tomorrow, perhaps, in front of the Deux Magots only a ruined edifice would remain; a hundred guns would fire from it and fire again. But today . . . today Ivich was at Laon, Paris was dead, peace had just been buried, war had not yet been declared. The church was just a large white shape standing under a white integument of night. A village church. A new and handsome church which served no purpose. A light wind rose: a car passed without lights, then a cyclist, then two lorries that shook the ground. The stone image quivered faintly, then the wind dropped, silence fell, and once more it stood, white, purposeless, in-human, and in it stood, amid all those vertical implements beside the highway to the east, the impassive, naked destiny of rock. It was eternal, a tiny black speck in the sky could blow it to powder, and yet it was eternal. A man alone, forgotten, devoured by darkness, confronted that fragile eternity. He shivered and thought: 'I too am eternal.'

It had all happened without any shock. There had once been a kindly, rather diffident man, who was fond of Paris and enjoyed walking in its streets. The man was dead. As dead as Waldeck-Rousseau, or Thureau-Dangin: he had become engulfed in the world's past, together with the peace, his life had been put away in the archives of the Third Republic: his daily budget would provide material for statistics of the middle-class subsistence level subsequent to 1918, his letters would serve as documents for the history of the bourgeoisie between the two wars, his anxieties and his hesitations, his feelings of shame and remorse, would be of the highest value for the study of French social life after the fall of the Second Empire. This man had shaped a future to his measure, a decorous, arid, uncomplaining future, overburdened with human contacts and schemes. An historic and mortal little future: the war had thundered down upon it and crushed it to powder. And yet, up to that minute, there was still something that could call itself Mathieu, something to which he clung with all his strength. Something, indeed, beyond analysis. Perhaps some ancient habit, perhaps a way of choosing his thoughts in his own likeness, of choosing *himself* from day to day in the like-ness of his thoughts, of choosing his food and clothes, the trees and the houses that he looked at. He relaxed his grip and let it go: all this happened deep in his inmost self, in a region where words possess no meaning. He let go, and nothing remained but a look. A new and passionless look, a mere transparency. 'I have lost my soul,' he thought with satisfaction. A woman crossed that transparency. She clat-tered along in a hurry, glided into that motionless look, a harrassed mortal denizen of time, devoured by a thousand little schemes, she lifted a hand and smoothed back a stray lock of hair. It was like her once: a hive of schemes. Her life is *my* life: beneath that look, under the indifferent sky, all lives are equivalent. The darkness swallowed her up, as she pattered into the rue Bonaparte; human lives melted into the shadows, clacking heels were silent.

My look. He looked at the quenched whiteness of the belfry. Everything is dead. My look and those stones: eternal, rock-like, like that white church. In my former future, men and women would be looking out for me on 20 June 1940, on 16 September 1942, and 8 February 1944, and would be glad to see me. At present my look and nothing else awaits me, as far as the eye can reach, just as those stones await themselves, stones wait for stones, tomorrow, next day, and for ever. A look and a delight as vast as ocean: a great day, indeed. He laid his hands on his knees, he must keep calm: may I not tomorrow revert to what I was yesterday? But he was not afraid. The church may collapse, I may tumble into a shell-hole, or drop back into my life: nothing can rob me of this eternal moment. There had been, and forever would be, that cold glare upon those stones under the black sky: the absolute, forever: the absolute, without cause or sense or purpose, without past or future save a gratuitous, fortuitous, splendid permanence. 'I am free,' he said suddenly. And his joy shrivelled into horror.

Irène was bored. Nothing happened, except that the orchestra was playing *Music, Maestro, please*, and Marc was looking at her with seal-like eyes. Nothing, indeed, ever happened, or if, by chance, it did, it passed unnoticed. She was watching a Scandinavian girl, a tall blonde who had been dancing for over an hour without even sitting down between the dances, and she thought dispassionately: 'She's very well dressed': Marc was also well dressed, everyone was well dressed except Irène, who felt shabby in her garnet-red frock, not that she cared, I know I have no taste in dress, besides I can't afford any new ones, but she went about so much among rich people, she must try not to look conspicuous: there were already half a dozen men with their eyes on her: and a cheap and rather flashy dress encouraged them to regard her as an easy prey. Marc was at his ease, because he was rich: he liked to take her among rich people, because it put her in a position of inferiority, and so he believed, more inclined to let him have his way.

'Why won't you?' he asked.

Irène started. 'Why won't I what ... ? Ah, yes ...' She smiled, and did not reply.

'What are you thinking about?'

'Only that my glass is empty. I'd like another Sherry Cobbler.'

Marc ordered another Sherry Cobbler. It was rather amusing to make him pay, because he wrote down his day-to-day expenses in a notebook. This evening he would write: 'Went out with Irène, one gin-fizz, two Sherry Cobblers: a hundred and seventy-five francs.' She noticed that he was stroking her arm with the tip of his forefinger – he had no doubt been doing so for some minutes, but she hadn't noticed it.

'Do tell me, Irène. Why?'

'Oh,' she yawned. 'I just don't know.'

'There you are, then: if you really don't know . . .'

'Not at all: it's just the other way round: when I sleep with someone, I want to know why I'm doing so. Either because he has nice eyes, or for something he said, or because he's good-looking.'

'I am good-looking,' said Marc in a low tone.

Irène laughed, and he blushed.

'Look here,' he said sharply. 'You understand what I mean.'

'Of course I do,' she said.

He grasped her wrist. 'Irène – Oh God, what is there I can do?'

He leaned over her with a sort of peevish, pleading look, his emotion made him gasp for breath. 'How bored I am,' she thought.

'Nothing: there's nothing you can do.'

'Ha!' he exploded.

He let her go, and flung his head back, exposing his teeth. She looked at herself in the mirror, and saw a dowdy girl with fine eyes; she thought: 'Well, I never! What a fuss about *that*!' She felt ashamed for him, and for herself, everything was so stale and boring: she couldn't even understand why she refused to sleep with him: I'm making a lot of trouble: much better say: 'All right, I don't mind.' Half an hour in a hotel bedroom, a little dirty business between two sheets, after which we'll come back here to finish the evening, and you'll leave me alone. But apparently she still attached too much importance to her wretched body: she knew she would not yield.

'I think you're a very odd girl,' he said.

He rolled his fine eyes at her, looking quite distraught, he'll go for me, that's what they always do, and then ask me to forgive him.

'You do make a fuss,' he went on ironically. 'If I hadn't known you for four years I should have thought you were virtue personified.'

She looked at him with sudden interest and began to reflect. When she reflected, she felt much less bored.

'You're right,' she said: 'It's very odd: I'm an easy sort of girl, and that's a fact, and yet I would rather be cut in pieces than sleep with you. Now try to explain that!' She considered him dispassionately and concluded: 'I can't even say that you really disgust me.'

'Not so loud!' he said, and added venomously: 'That little voice of yours does carry such a long way.'

They were silent. People danced, the band played *Caravane*: Marc twirled his glass over the tablecloth, and the ice in it clinked.

'The fact is,' he said suddenly, 'I've let you see too clearly that I wanted you.'

He had laid his hands flat on the table, and began to smooth out the cloth: he was trying to recover his human dignity. It didn't matter, he would lose it again in five minutes. But she smiled at him, glad of a chance to analyse herself.

'Well,' she said, 'there's something in that, no doubt.'

Marc appeared to her through a haze. A quiet little haze of astonishment rose from her heart to her eyes. It was a feeling she enjoyed, asking herself all the illimitable questions to which there is no answer.

'When a man is too keen on me,' she explained, 'I get shocked. Look here, Marc, I feel ridiculous: Hitler will very likely have attacked us by tomorrow, and you sit there fussing because I won't sleep with you. You must be a poor sort of creature to work yourself up over a girl like me.'

'That's my business,' he said in an angry voice.

'It's my business too: I hate to be overrated.'

A silence followed. What animals we are, to set so much store upon an instinct. She looked at him out of the corner of her eye: ah – he'll soon subside. His features drooped, the crisis had still to come: once, at Melody's, he had burst into tears. He opened his mouth, and she said to him briskly:

'Be quiet, Marc, please: I know you're going to say something silly or unpleasant.'

He did not hear what she said: he wagged his head with an ominous air on his face.

'Irène,' he said softly, 'I'm going away.'

'Away? Where?'

'Don't be stupid. You understood.'

'Well, then?'

'I did think you might feel it a bit.'

She did not reply: she eyed him fixedly. Then he went on, with averted eyes: 'In '14 lots of women gave themselves to men who loved them, just because they were going away.'

She said nothing: Marc's hands began to quiver.

'Irène, it means so little to you, but for me it's so important, particularly at this moment. . . .'

'Nothing doing,' said Irène.

He turned upon her savagely: 'After all, damn it – it's for you I'm going to fight.'

'Swine!' said Irène.

He subsided at once: his eyes reddened.

'I can't bear the idea of being killed without having slept with you.'

Irène got up: 'Come and dance,' she said.

He got up obediently and they danced. He held her close, and swung her round the room; suddenly she caught her breath.

'What's the matter?' he asked.

'Nothing.'

She had just recognized Philippe, sedately seated beside a Creole, rather handsome but not young. 'So that's what he was up to when they were searching for him all over the place.' He was looking rather pale, with dark circles round his eyes. She manoeuvred Marc into the centre of the throng: it was essential that Philippe should not recognize her. The band stopped, and they went back to their table. Marc sank back on to his seat. Irène was about to sit down, when she noticed a man bowing to the Negress.

'Sit down,' said Marc. 'I don't like to see you standing.'

'Just a moment,' she said impatiently.

The Negress got up lazily, and the man put his arms round her. Philippe eyed them for a moment with a stricken air, and Irène felt her heart contract: then suddenly he got up and slipped out.

'Excuse me a minute,' said Irène.

'Where are you going?'

'To the lavatory. There – are you satisfied?'

'You'll pretend to go, and then clear out.'

She pointed to her bag on the table. 'I've left my bag.'

Marc grunted: she crossed the dancing-floor, pushing through the dancers.

'That girl's crazy,' said a woman. Marc had got up too: she heard him cry: 'Irène!'

But she was already outside: he would need five minutes to pay for the drinks. The street was dark: 'How silly I am,' she thought: 'I've lost him.' But when her eyes had grown used to the half-light, she saw him hurrying in the direction of the Trinité, keeping close to the wall. She started to run: 'It's a pity about my bag: I shall lose my powder-box, a hundred francs, and the two letters from Maxime.' She had ceased to feel bored. They thus covered a hundred yards or so, both running, then Philippe stopped so abruptly, that Irène nearly bumped into him. She stepped aside, passed him, went up to a door, and rang the bell twice. The door opened just as Philippe passed behind her. She paused for a second, then slammed the door violently, as though she had just entered the building. Philippe was now walking at a normal pace, it was easy enough to keep on his track. From time to time the shadows swallowed him, then under the luminous drizzle of a street lamp he emerged out of the darkness. 'This is very amusing,' she thought. She adored tracking someone: she could walk for hours behind people whom she did not even know.

The boulevards were still crowded and it was easier to see, owing to the lights in the cafés and the shop-windows. Philippe stopped again, but this time Irène was not taken by surprise: she slipped behind him, and stood in a dark corner, waiting. 'Perhaps he's meeting somebody.' He turned, his face was livid: suddenly he began to speak, and she thought he had recognized her: and yet she was sure he could not see her. He stepped backwards, and muttered something: he was looking frantic. 'He's gone crazy,' she thought.

Two women passed, one young and one old, wearing rather old-fashioned hats. He went up to them, his face was that of an exhibitionist.

'Down with the war,' he said.

The women walked on faster: apparently they had not understood. Two officers came up: Philippe let them pass. Then came a scented prostitute whose perfume struck Irène full in the face. Philippe eyed her wildly: she was already smiling at him, and said in a strangled voice:

'Down with the war, down with Daladier! We want peace!'

'Silly fool!' said the woman.

She passed. Philippe shook his head, looked to right and left with a furious air, and then plunged suddenly into the darkness of the rue Richelieu. Irène laughed so loud that she nearly gave herself away.

'Wait two minutes.'

He turned the knob, and a jazz tune leapt forth – four notes from a saxophone, like a shooting-star.

'Leave it on,' said Ivich. 'It's lovely.'

M. Serguine turned the knob once more and the wail of the saxophone was replaced by a long, rasping crackle: he eyed Ivich severely: 'I deplore your taste for savage music.'

He despised Negroes. He had retained some vivid memories of his student life at Munich, and a cult of Wagner.

A voice shook the instrument: a characteristic French voice, calm and suave, translating the tortuosities of the speech into decent phraseology – it was the penetrating and persuasive voice of an elder brother. She smiled at her father, and said casually, to recapture a little of their old intimacy: 'I hate French voices.'

M. Serguine emitted a faint chuckle and he raised a hand enjoining silence.

'Today,' said the voice, 'the British Premier's representative was again received by the Chancellor of the Reich, who intimated that if he had not received a satisfactory reply from Prague by two o'clock tomorrow on the subject of the promised evacuation of the Sudeten districts, he would reserve the right to take the necessary measures.

'It is thought that Chancellor Hitler was referring to general mobilization, the order for which was expected on Monday, in connexion with the Chancellor's speech, and which was no doubt only delayed in consideration of the letter from the British Prime Minister.'

The voice was silent. Ivich, whose throat was quite parched, looked up at her father. He had absorbed the announcement with an air of fatuous complacency.

'What exactly does mobilization mean?' she asked in an indifferent tone.

'It means war.'

'Not necessarily?'

'Of course it does!'

'We shan't fight,' she said violently. 'We can't fight over the Czechs!'

M. Serguine smiled amiably: 'When mobilization takes place . . .'

'But as we *don't want* war.'

'If we didn't want war, we shouldn't have mobilized.'

She eyed him with bewilderment. 'Have we mobilized too?'

'No,' he said, with a blush, 'I was referring to the Germans.'

'Oh! I was talking about the French,' said Ivich dryly.

The voice continued quiet and benign: 'In foreign circles in Berlin, it is generally thought . . .'

'Ss'sh!' said M. Serguine.

He sat down again, his face turned towards the radio. 'I'm an orphan,' thought Ivich. She tiptoed out of the room, crossed the passage and shut herself into her bedroom. Her teeth were chattering: they will go through Laon, they will burn down Paris – the rue de Seine, the rue de la Gaîté, the rue des Rosiers, the Bal de la Montagne-Sainte-Geneviève: if Paris burns, I'll kill myself. 'Oh,' she thought, sinking on to her bed, 'and what about the Musée Grevin?' She had never been there, Mathieu had promised to take her in October, and they would bomb it out of existence. That very night, perhaps. Her heart contracted, her arms and hands turned cold: what is there to prevent them? Perhaps at this very hour Paris is in ashes, and the fact has been concealed to prevent a panic. Unless it was forbidden by international agreements. How was she to know? 'There must,' she thought angrily, 'be people who do know: I don't understand a thing about it, I've been kept in the dark, I've been set to learn Latin and no one has told me any-thing, and now look where we are! But I have the right to live,' she thought distractedly: 'I was brought into the world that I might live, I have the right to live.' She felt so deeply wronged that she collapsed on to her pillow, and burst into sobs. 'It's too unfair,' she murmured: 'at the best, it will last six years, even ten years, all the women will be dressed as nurses, and when it's over I shall be old.' But no tears came, there was an icicle in her heart. She sat up abruptly: '*Who – who* wants war?' Taking people as individuals they were not bellicose, they thought solely of food, making money, and begetting children. Even the Germans. And yet here was war, Hitler had mobilized. 'All the same, he couldn't decide it on his own,' she thought. And a phrase passed through her mind, where had she read it? – in a newspaper, surely, unless she had heard it at lunch from one of her father's customers: '*What is behind him*?' she repeated it in an undertone, looking gloomily at the toes of her slippers: 'What is behind him?' and she faintly hoped that it would all be cleared up. She passed in review the names of all those sinister powers which control the world – Freemasonry, the Jesuits, the Two Hundred Families, the armament manufacturers, the Gold Lords, the Wall of Silver, the American Trusts, International Communism, Ku-Klux-Klan: all of them more or less backing him, and very likely yet another secret and formidable association, whose very name was unknown. 'But what can they want?' she asked herself, as two tears of rage coursed down her cheeks. She tried for a moment to guess their reasons, but there was a void within her, and a circlet of metal revolved inside her skull. 'If only I knew where Czechoslovakia was!' She had pinned a large blue and gold water-colour to the wall: a map of Europe, which she had amused herself by colouring last winter, copying from an atlas but slightly readjusting the contours: she had put rivers everywhere, indented such coastlines as seemed to her unduly flat, and she had carefully avoided inscribing any names on the map: names looked learned and pretentious: no frontiers either: she detested dots. She went up to it: Czechoslovakia lay somewhere in the central mass of territory. There – for instance; or was that Russia? And where was Germany? She looked at a large smooth yellow shape, edged with blue, thought: 'What an enormous country': and felt bewildered. She turned, slipped out of her wrap, and eyed her naked image in the looking-glass, which usually had a soothing effect on her nerves. But what she saw was a foetus-like figure, a skin slightly crinkled by the shivers, and tip-tilted nipples – a horrid, hospital body, made for mutilation, they'll probably rape all the women, I dare say they'll cut off one of my legs. Yes, if they came into her room, and found her stark naked in her bed, they would say we'll give you five minutes to dress, then they would turn their backs as though she were Marie Antoinette, but they would hear everything, the soft thud of her feet as she got out of bed, and the rustle of fabrics against her skin. She picked up her pants and stockings and put them on quickly – disaster must be confronted standing up and dressed. When she had slipped on her skirt and blouse, she felt rather more secure. But as she put on her shoes, a bass voice in the passage began to croon in German: *Ich hatte einen Kamerade* . . .

Ivich dashed to the door and opened it: she found herself face to face with her father, who looked both grave and cheerful.

'What's that you're singing?' she said angrily. 'How dare you sing such a song?'

He looked at her with a quizzical smile: 'Wait,' he said, 'wait a bit, my little frog: we shall see our holy Russia once again.'

She went back into her room and slammed the door. 'I don't care a curse for Holy Russia, I don't want Paris to be destroyed, and if they dare to do such a thing, I bet the French aeroplanes will drop bombs on Munich.'

The sound of footsteps died away down the passage, and silence fell once more. Ivich was standing stiffly erect in the centre of the room, averting her eyes from the reflection in the mirror. Suddenly she heard three blasts on a whistle – calls from the street, and shivered from head to feet. Outside in the street: everything happened outside: her room was a prison. Human lives were decided everywhere, north and east and south, everywhere in that poisoned night, pitted with flashes, echoing with whispers and secret meetings, everywhere except here where she remained immured, and where, indeed, nothing whatever happened. Her hands and legs began to tremble, she picked up her bag, slid a comb through her hair, opened the door noiselessly and slipped outside.

Outside. Everything is outside: the trees on the quay, the two houses by the bridge that lend a pink flush to the darkness, the petrified prance of Henri IV's steed above my head; solid objects, all of them. Inside – nothing, not even a puff of smoke, there is no *inside*, there is nothing. Myself: nothing. I am free, he said to himself, and his mouth was dry.

Half-way across the Pont-Neuf he stopped and began to laugh: liberty – I sought it far away: it was so near that I can't touch it, it is, in fact, myself. I am my own freedom. He had hoped that one day he would be filled with joy, transfixed by a lightning-flash. But there was neither lightning-flash nor joy: only a sense of desolation, a void blurred by its own aspect, an anguish so transparent as to be utterly unseeable. He reached out his hands and slid them slowly over the stone parapet, it was wrinkled and furrowed, like a petrified sponge, and still warm from the afternoon sun. There it lay, vast and massive, enclosing in itself the crushed silence, the inspissated darkness, that constitute the interior of objects. There it lay: a plenitude. He longed to clutch to that stone, and melt into it, to fill himself with its density and repose. But there was no help in it: it was outside, and forever. There lay his hands on the white parapet: bronze hands, they seemed, as he looked at them. But, just because he could look at them, they were no longer his, they were the hands of another, they were outside, like the trees, like the reflections shimmering in the Seine; severed hands. He closed his eyes and they became his own again: there was nothing in contact with the stone save a faintly acid and familiar flavour, a whiff of formic acid. My hands: the inappreciable distance that reveals things to me, and sets me apart from them forever. I am nothing; I possess nothing. As inseparable from the world as light, and yet exiled, gliding like light over the surface of stones and water, but nothing can ever grasp me nor absorb me. Outside the world, outside the past, outside myself: freedom is exile, and I am condemned to be free.

He walked on a few steps, stopped again, sat down on the parapet, and watched the water flowing past. What shall I do with all this freedom? What shall I do with myself? His future lay marked out by definite tasks: the railway station, the Nancy train, the barracks, and the handling of weapons. Nothing was any longer his: war seamed the earth, but it was not *his* war. He was alone on this bridge, alone in the world, accountable to no man.

'I am free *for nothing*,' he reflected wearily. Not a sign in the sky, nor on the earth, the things of this world were too utterly immersed in the war that was theirs, they turned their manifold heads towards the east. Mathieu was moving swiftly over the surface of things, but they were unconscious of his presence. He was forgotten: by the bridge beneath his feet, by the roads that sped towards the frontier, by that city that rose slowly upwards to look at a fire on the horizon with which it had no concern. Forgotten, unknown, and utterly alone: a defaulter: all mobilized men had gone two days ago, he had no business now to be here. Shall I take the train? What did it matter? – go, or stay, or run away – acts of that kind would not call his freedom into play. And yet he must risk that freedom. He clutched the stone with both hands and leaned over the water. A plunge, and the water would engulf him, his freedom would be transmuted into water. Rest at last – and why not? This obscure suicide would *also* be an absolute, a law, a choice, and a morality, all of them complete. A unique, unmatchable act, a lightning-flash would light up the bridge and the Seine. He need only lean a little further over, and he would have made his choice for all eternity. He leaned over, but his hands still clutched the stone, and bore the whole weight of his body. Why not? He had no special reason for letting himself drop, nor any reason for not doing so. And the act was there, before him, on the black water, a presentiment of his future. All hawsers cut, nothing now could hold him back: here was his freedom, and how horrible it was! Deep down within him he felt his heart throbbing wildly: one gesture, the mere unclasping of his hands, and I *would have been* Mathieu. An effluence from the river bemused his senses: sky and bridge dissolved: nothing remained but himself and the water: it heaved up to him and rippled round his dangling legs. The water, where his future lay. At the moment *it is true*, I'm going to kill myself. Suddenly he *decided* not to do it. He decided: it shall merely be a trial. Then he was again upon his feet and walking on, gliding over the crust of a dead star. Next time, perhaps.

She ran down the main street, she heard two or three more whistle-calls, then nothing more, and now the street had become a prison too: nothing was happening there, the façades of the houses were blind and flat, all the shutters closed, the war was elsewhere. She leaned for an instant against a street-fountain, anxious and disappointed, but she did not know what she had hoped to see: lights, perhaps, open shops, people who would comment on events. There was nothing: in the great capitals, embassies and palaces were ablaze with light: she was immured in perpetual night. 'Everything always happens somewhere else,' she said, tapping her foot on the pavement. She heard a rustle, as of someone gliding close behind her. She held her breath and listened for a long while: but did not hear the noise again. She was cold, and her throat was dry with fear: she wondered whether she would not do better to go back. But she *could not* go back, her room revolted her: here at least she walked beneath everybody's sky, she kept in contact, through the sky, with Paris and Berlin. She heard a persistent scratching sound behind her, and this time she had the courage to turn round. It was a cat: she saw its eyeballs glisten as it crossed the street from right to left; a bad omen. She continued on her way, turned into the rue Thiers, and there stopped, quite out of breath. 'Aeroplanes!' A dull mutter – they must still be far away. She stood and listened: the sound did not come from the sky. Surely . . . 'Yes,' she thought with vexation: 'It's a snore.' It was Lescat, the notary, she recognized the brass plate over her head. He was snoring, the windows were open. She could not help laughing, and then suddenly her laugh turned harsh: they're all asleep. I'm alone in the street, surrounded by sleeping people, ignored by everyone.

All the world over they are asleep, or in their offices preparing for their war, not one of them has my name in his head. 'But I am here,' she thought, resentfully. 'I am here, I see, I feel, and I exist, no less than Hitler.'

After a moment she continued on her way, and came out on the terrace. Beneath her a bleak plain stretched away into the distance, dotted with points of light: but they brought her no solace, Ivich knew too well what they were – the lights of railway stations, level-crossings, piles of stones, shunted trucks on sidings. At the extremity of the plain lay Paris. She breathed again: if the city was in flames, there would be a glare on the horizon. The wind flapped her dress against her knees, but she did not move. 'Paris is there, still ablaze with light, for perhaps the last night of her existence. At that very moment people were walking up and down the Boulevard Saint-Michel, others sitting at the Dôme who no doubt knew her and were talking to each other. 'The last night – and I am here, in this dark water, and when I am free, I shall find nothing but a pile of ruins, and tents among the stones. O God,' she pleaded, 'let me see it just once more.' The station was there, immediately below her – that red patch at the bottom of the stairway: the night train left at twenty minutes past three. 'I've got a hundred francs in my bag,' she thought triumphantly.

She was already running down the stepped incline, Philippe was already running along the rue Montmartre – so I'm a coward, am I, just a dirty coward? Well, they shall see. He came out into a square, opposite the dark, gaping entrance of a clamorous alley-way that smelt of cabbage and raw meat. He stopped outside the iron gates of a Métro station, where a row of empty bins stood on the edge of the pavement: scraps of straw and muddy lettuce leaves were strewn about the roadway: on the right, shadows passed and repassed in the white light of a café. Ivich went up to the booking-office window:

'Third to Paris.'

'Return?' asked the clerk.

'Single,' she replied firmly.

Philippe cleared his throat, and yelled:

'Down with the war!'

Nothing happened: the shadows continued to move to and fro past the café. He cupped his hands over his mouth:

'Down with the war!'

His voice was a thunderous bellow. A few shadows stopped, and he saw some men approach him, mostly wearing caps. They strolled up to him, and eyed him quizzically.

'Down with the war!' he shouted at them.

They were now quite near: among them were two women, and a dark and rather graceful youth. Philippe liked the look of him and, without taking his eyes off him, shouted:

'Down with Daladier: down with Chamberlain: we want peace!'

They were all round him now, and he felt at ease, for the first time in forty-eight hours. They eyed him curiously, and said nothing. He wanted to explain to them that they were victims of capitalist imperialism, but he could not control his voice: 'Down with the war!' It was a sort of paean. A fist struck him on the ear, and he continued to shout; again on the mouth, again on the right eye; he fell on his knees, and stopped shouting. A woman – he could see her legs and flat-heeled shoes – struggled with his assailants, crying: 'You dirty swine. He's just a kid, you leave him alone!'

Mathieu heard a shrill voice crying, 'You dirty swine. He's just a kid, you leave him alone.' Someone was struggling in a throng of men in caps: a small woman, with uplifted arms, and rumpled hair. A dark youth with a scar under his ear, seized and shook her, and she cried: 'He's right, you're a pack of cowards, you ought to be at the Concorde, demonstrating against war: but you'd sooner knock a boy about, it's safer.'

A fat old prostitute opposite Mathieu surveyed the scene with glistening eyes:

'That's it – strip him!' she said.

Mathieu turned wearily away: this sort of thing must be happening at every street corner, on the eve of war and battle: just a picturesque interlude which concerned him not at all. Suddenly he decided that it did. He pushed the old whore aside, elbowed his way into the throng and clapped a hand on the shoulder of the dark-haired youth.

'Police,' he said. 'What's all this?'

The man eyed him with mistrust.

'It's the lad on the ground. He was shouting: "Down with the war."'

'And you beat him up, eh?' said Mathieu severely. 'Couldn't you find a constable?'

'There wasn't one,' said the prostitute.

'Hullo, Carmen.' said Mathieu. 'I don't want any of your lip.'

The dark youth looked uneasy. 'He isn't much hurt,' he said, licking his bruised knuckles. 'Someone clouted him on the head.'

'Who did?' asked Mathieu.

The man with the scar eyed his hands with a sigh. 'I did,' he said.

The others had stepped back: Mathieu turned to them. 'Do you want to be called as witnesses?'

They stepped a little farther back, and did not reply. The prostitute had vanished.

'Move on now,' said Mathieu, 'or I'll take your names. You stay,' he added, to the scarred youth.

'So,' said the latter, 'At a time like this, Frenchmen are to be jugged for knocking out a Boche who tries to make trouble?'

'Mind your own business. I'll get to the bottom of this.'

The onlookers had dispersed. Two or three stood in a café doorway still staring at the scene. Mathieu bent down over the boy: they'd made a mess of him. His mouth was bleeding, and his left eye was closed. With his right eye, he looked fixedly at Mathieu.

'I shouted,' he said proudly.

'That was a very silly thing to do,' said Mathieu. 'Can you get up?'

The boy staggered to his feet. He had fallen into the lettuce-leaves: one was sticking to the seat of his trousers, and there were strands of muddy straw all over his jacket. The small woman brushed him with the flat of her hand.

'Do you know him?' Mathieu asked her.

She hesitated: 'N-no.'

The boy laughed. 'Of course she knows me. It's Irène, Pitteaux's secretary.'

Irène looked darkly at Mathieu. 'You aren't going to take him to the station?'

'I've got to do my duty.'

The scarred man tugged at Mathieu's sleeve: he was looking rather abashed.

'I earn my living, Inspector, I'm a worker. If I go with you to the station, I shall lose my night.'

'Your papers, please.'

The man produced a Nansen passport, his name was Canaro.

Mathieu laughed. 'Born in Constantinople!' he said. 'So loyal to France that you attack the first person who abuses her.'

'France is my second fatherland,' said the man with dignity.

'You'll join the army, I hope?'

The man did not answer. Mathieu wrote his name and address in a notebook.

'Now get out,' he said. 'You'll be called as a witness. Come along, you two.'

The three of them turned into the rue Montmartre and walked a little way. Mathieu supported the boy who was very unsteady on his legs.

'You'll let him go, won't you?' said Irène.

Mathieu did not answer: they were still too near the Halles. They walked on, then, when they reached a street-lamp. Irène faced Mathieu, and eyed him venomously.

'Dirty cop!' she said.

Mathieu laughed: her hair had slipped down over her face, and she had to peer through her dishevelled locks.

'I'm not a cop,' he said.

'Is that so?'

She tried to shake her hair out of her eyes. In the end she gripped it angrily and flung it back, revealing a rather mask-like, wide-eyed face. She was quite pretty: she did not seem much surprised.

'Well, if that's so, you had them on properly,' she observed.

Mathieu did not reply. He was bored by the affair. He had a sudden impulse to walk down the rue Montorgeuil.

'Well,' he said, 'I'll put you both into a taxi.'

There were two or three on the rank in the middle of the street. Mathieu went up to one of them, dragging the boy behind him. Irène followed them. With her right hand she held her hair in place on top of her head.

'In you go.'

She blushed: 'I'd better tell you that I've lost my bag.'

Mathieu laid one hand between the lad's shoulder-blades, held the door open with the other, and pushed him into the cab.

'Feel in my jacket-pocket,' he said: 'the right one.'

After a moment or two Irène took her hand out of his pocket.

'Here's a hundred francs and some change.'

'Keep the hundred francs.'

A final push and the lad collapsed on to the seat. Irène got in after him.

'What is your address?' she asked.

'I no longer have one,' said Mathieu. 'Good-bye.'

'Hi!' cried Irène.

But he had already turned on his heel: he wanted to have another look at the rue Montorgeuil, and at once. He walked on for a minute or two and then a taxi drew up beside the pavement at his side.

The door opened, and a woman leaned out: it was Irène.

'Get in,' she said. 'Quick.'

Mathieu got into the taxi.

'Sit on the flap-seat.'

He did so. 'What's the matter?'

'The boy is crazy: he says he wants to get himself locked up: he keeps on trying to open the door and throw himself out: I'm not strong enough to hold him.'

The boy was lying huddled on the seat, his knees higher than his head.

'He wants to make a martyr of himself,' explained Irène.

'How old is he?'

'I don't know: about nineteen, I should think.'

Mathieu eyed the boy's long, thin legs: he was about the age of his oldest pupils.

'If he wants to get himself in quod,' he said, 'you haven't the right to stop him.'

'You're a queer fish,' said Irène indignantly. 'You don't know what may be coming to him.'

'Has he done someone in?'

'Of course not.'

'What's his trouble, then?'

'It's a long story,' she said gloomily. He noticed that she had coiled her hair on the top of her head: which gave her rather an oddly obstinate appearance, despite her graceful drooping mouth.

'It's his own affair, anyway,' said Mathieu. 'He's a free agent.'

'Free, indeed!' she said. 'I've just told you he's crazy.'

At the word free the boy opened his solitary eye and muttered something which Mathieu did not catch, and then, without a word of warning, flung himself at the handle of the door and tried to open it. A car, at that same moment, grazed past the standing taxi. Mathieu laid a hand on the boy's chest and pushed him back on to the cushions.

'If I wanted to get myself into prison,' he continued turning to Irène, 'I shouldn't like anyone to stop me.'

'Down with the war!' said the boy.

'Yes, yes,' said Mathieu. 'Quite.' He was still holding him down on the seat. He turned to Irène.

'He certainly does seem cracked.'

The driver slid the glass back: 'Where to?'

'15 avenue du Parc-Monsouris,' said Irène triumphantly.

The boy clawed at Mathieu's hand, then, when the taxi had started, he decided to keep quiet. They remained silent for a moment: the taxi sped through dark streets unknown to Mathieu. From time to time Irène's face emerged from the darkness and then plunged into it again.

'Are you from Brittany?'

'No. From Metz. Why do you ask?'

'Because of the way you do your hair.'

'Rather silly, isn't it? It's a friend who likes me to do it that way.'

She was silent for a moment, and then said: 'How is it you haven't got an address?'

'I'm moving.'

'Ah yes. . . . You're mobilized, I suppose?'

'Yes. So are most men.'

'You don't like war?'

'I don't know. I've never been in one.'

'Well, I'm against it,' said Irène.

'I noticed that.'

She leaned towards him with an anxious air. 'Tell me, have you lost somebody?'

'No,' said Mathieu. 'Do I look as if I had?'

'You look odd,' she said. 'Take care!'

The boy had reached out a stealthy hand, and was trying to open the door.

'Will you keep quiet?' said Mathieu, flinging him back into his corner. 'What a little squirt!' he said to Irène.

'He's the son of a general.'

'Is he? Well, I don't suppose he's proud of his father.'

The taxi had stopped. Irène got out, and the boy had to be extricated next. He clung to the elbow rests and kicked. Irène began to laugh: 'How tiresome he is: now he won't come out.'

Mathieu finally put an arm round him, and lifted him on to the pavement. 'Ouf!'

'Wait a second,' said Irène. 'The key was in my bag. I must get through the window.'

She walked up to a small two-storied house with one window half-open. Mathieu held the boy up with one hand: with the other he felt in his pocket and handed his loose change to the driver.

'Keep it all.'

'What's the matter with the chap?' said the driver genially.

'He's been knocked out,' said Mathieu.

The taxi restarted. Behind Mathieu a door opened, and Irène appeared in a rectangle of light.

'Come in,' she said.

Mathieu entered, pushing the now silent boy ahead of him. Irène shut the street door.

'On the left,' she said. 'The switch is on the right hand.'

Mathieu groped for the switch, and the light flashed on. He saw a dusty room, containing a box-bed, a water-jug, and a wash-basin on a dressing-table: a wheel-less bicycle was suspended from the ceiling.

'Is this your room?'

'No,' said Irène. 'It belongs to some friends.' He looked at her, and laughed: 'Your stockings!'

They were white with dust, and torn at the knees.

'It's from climbing through the window,' she explained nonchalantly.

The boy stood in the middle of the room, swaying precariously, and surveying his surroundings with his solitary eye. Mathieu pointed to him and said:

'What's to be done with him?'

'Take off his shoes, and make him lie down: I'll wash his face.'

The boy made no resistance: he appeared to be in a state of coma. Irène returned with a basin and some cotton-wool.

'There we are,' she said. 'Now, Philippe, behave yourself.'

She leant over him, and dabbed an eyebrow with a wad of cotton-wool. The boy began to mumble.

'Yes,' she said in a motherly voice. 'It smarts, but it will do you good.'

She put the basin on the dressing-table. Mathieu got up.
'Right,' he said. 'Now I'll be off.'

'No – please!' she said eagerly, adding in an undertone: 'If he tried to get away, I'm not strong enough to stop him.'

'But you don't expect me to stay on guard over him all night?'

'You aren't very helpful,' she said with vexation. And she added after a pause, in a more conciliatory tone: 'You might at least wait until he gets to sleep: it won't be long.'

The boy tossed about on the bed, muttering unintelligibly.

'How on earth can he have got himself into such a state?' asked Irène.

She was a plump girl with a sallow skin, a little too forthcoming, rather moist and faintly grubby: she looked as if she had just got out of bed. But her head was good: thin, rather drooping lips, large eyes, and small pink ears.

'There!' said Mathieu. 'He's asleep.'

'Do you think so?'

They both gave a start as the boy suddenly sat up, and said in a loud voice: 'Flossie! My trousers!'

'Damn the fellow,' said Mathieu.

Irène smiled: 'You're here till the morning.'

But it was a touch of delirium that gave way to sleep: Philippe fell back again, moaned two or three times, and almost immediately began to snore.

'Come along,' said Irène in a low tone.

He followed her into a large room with chairs upholstered in pink cretonne, and a guitar and a ukulele on the wall.

'This is my room. I'll leave the door open so that I can hear the boy.'

Mathieu observed a large unmade four-poster bed, a pouffe, a gramophone, and a pile of records on a Henri II table. On a rocking-chair lay a heap of worn stockings, feminine knickers, and vests. Irène followed his eyes: 'I furnished my room,' she said, 'from the junk market.'

'It's very nice,' said Mathieu.

'Do sit down.'

'Where?' asked Mathieu.

'Wait a minute.'

On the pouffe stood a boat in a bottle. She put it on the floor, and then cleared the underclothes on to the pouffe.

'There. I'll sit on the bed.'

Mathieu sat down, and rocked himself to and fro.

'The last time I sat in a rocking-chair was at Nîmes, in the hall of the Hôtel des Arènes. I was fifteen.'

Irène did not reply. Mathieu visualized the great dim hall with its glass door sparkling in the sun: that recollection still belonged to him, with others of the same kind, intimate and indistinct, that hovered all around him: I have not lost my childhood. The age of maturity, the age of reason, had collapsed, but his childhood remained, still quite warm: he had never been so close to it. Again he thought of the boy on the dunes at Archachou, who insisted on being free, and, confronted by that pigheaded little rascal, Mathieu ceased to feel ashamed. He got up.

'Are you going away?' said Irène.

'I'm going for a walk,' he said.

'Won't you stay a little longer?'

He hesitated: 'Frankly, I rather wanted to be alone.'

She laid a hand on his arm: 'Do stay with me, you won't notice I'm here.'

He looked at her: she talked rather oddly, in a flat and toneless voice: she barely opened her thin lips, and shook her head slightly as though to get words out.

'All right, I'll stay,' he said.

She did not look pleased. Indeed her face was very inexpressive. Mathieu walked across the room to the table, and picked up a few records. They were much worn, some of them cracked, and most of them without their covers. Jazz tunes, a potpourri of Maurice Chevalier, the *Concerto for Left Hand,* the Debussy quartet, the Toselli *Serenade,* and the *Internationale,* sung by a Russian choir.

'Are you a Communist?' he asked her.

'No,' she said. 'I have no political opinions. I think I should be a Communist if men weren't such swine.' And she added, after a moment of reflection, 'I'm a pacifist.'

'You're rather illogical, aren't you?' said Mathieu. 'If men are swine, you oughtn't to mind whether they die in battle, or otherwise.'

319

She shook her head with obstinate gravity: 'The point is,' she said, 'that as they are such swine, it is even more disgusting to use them to make war.'

A silence fell. Mathieu looked at a cobweb on the ceiling, and began to whistle softly.

'I can't offer you a drink,' said Irène. 'Unless you would like some fruit syrup. There's a little left in the bottle.'

'Hum!' said Mathieu.

'Yes, I rather thought you wouldn't. Ah – there's a cigar on the mantelpiece – would you care for it?'

'Thanks,' said Mathieu.

He got up and took the cigar, which was dry and rather dilapidated.

'Can I put it in my pipe?'

'Do what you like with it.'

He sat down again and crumbled the cigar between his fingers: he felt Irène's eyes upon him.

'Make yourself at home; if you don't feel inclined to talk – don't.'

'All right,' said Mathieu.

After a few moments she said: 'Wouldn't you like to go to sleep?'

'Thank you – no.'

He felt as though he would never want to go to sleep again.

'Where would you be, at this moment, if you hadn't met me?'

'In the rue Montorgueil.'

'What would you be doing there?'

'Walking down it.'

'It must seem odd to you to be here.'

'Not at all.'

'True,' she said in vague reproach. 'You aren't really here at all.'

He did not reply: she was right, he thought. These four walls, and that woman on the bed, were an unimportant accident, a transitory vision of the night. Wherever night was, there was Mathieu, from the frontiers in the north, to the Côte d'Azur: he was indeed absorbed into the night, and he looked at Irène with all the eyes of night: she was no more than a faint flicker in the darkness. A yell startled him out of his reflections.

'Poisonous little wretch! I'll go and see what's the matter.'

She tiptoed out of the room, and Mathieu lit his pipe. He no longer wanted to walk along the rue Montorgueil: the rue Montorgueil was there, passing through that room: all the roads of France passed through it, all its trees grew there. Four timber partitions from nowhere in particular had been set down to make it. Mathieu came from no matter where. Irène returned and sat down: she was no matter who. No, she didn't look like a Breton woman: she was much more like the little Annamite at the Dôme. She had the same saffron skin, blank face, and ineffectual charm.

'It's nothing,' she said. 'He's having a nightmare.'

Mathieu drew quietly at his pipe. 'That boy must have been through it.'

Irène shrugged her shoulders, and her face changed suddenly. 'Pah!' she said.

'You sound rather censorious, all of a sudden,' said Mathieu.

'Well, it annoys me to hear people pity a boy like that – what does a poor little rich boy know about trouble?'

'Still, that doesn't prevent him being unhappy.'

'You make me smile. My old man chucked me out when I was seventeen: I couldn't get on with him, of course. But I didn't go about saying I was unhappy.'

For a fleeting moment, Mathieu descried beneath that pampered face the hard and haunted visage of a suffering woman. Her voice flowed on, a slow, rich voice, with a sort of monotony in its indignation.

'People are unhappy,' she said, 'when they are cold, or ill, or hungry. The rest is all flummery.'

He laughed: she was puckering her nose, and opening her mouth wide so as to ger her words out. He scarcely listened: he *saw* her. A look. A vast look, an empty sky: she struggled in that look, like an insect in a shaft of light.

'No,' she said. 'I'm quite willing to take him in and look after him, and stop him from making a fool of himself: but I won't have him pitied. Because I know what trouble is! And when these bourgeois pretend they're unhappy . . .'

She eyed him intently, recovering her breath: 'But you are a bourgeois, of course, aren't you?'

'Yes,' said Mathieu. 'I am a bourgeois.'

She sees me. Swiftly he seemed to harden and shrink. Behind

those eyes there is a starless sky, and there is *also* a look. She sees me: as she sees the table and the ukulele. And for her, I am; a particle suspended in a look, a bourgeois. It is *true* that I am a bourgeois. And yet, he never managed to feel that he was. She was still looking at him.

'What is your job? No – let me guess. Doctor?'

'No.'

'Lawyer?'

'You aren't a crook, are you?'

'I'm a professor,' said Mathieu.

'That's odd,' she said, with a slightly disappointed air. But she added briskly: 'Not that it's of any importance.'

She looks at me. He got up and took her arm, a little below the elbow. The soft, warm flesh dimpled under his fingers.

'What are you up to?' she said.

'I wanted to touch you. With all due respect: because you were looking at me.'

She leaned against him, and the look was dimmed.

'I like you,' she said.

'And I like you.'

'Have you a wife?'

'I have no one.'

He sat down beside her on the bed. 'And you? Is there anyone in your life?'

'There are . . . a few.' And she added, with a rueful air: 'I'm not very particular.'

The look had vanished. What remained was a little Chinese doll, smelling slightly of mahogany.

'Indeed? And what then?' said Mathieu.

She did not reply. She put her head between her hands and looked gravely into space. 'Ah, the reflective type,' said Mathieu to himself.

'When a girl hasn't many clothes, she can't afford to be particular,' she said after a pause.

She turned uneasily to Mathieu: 'I don't make you nervous, do I?'

'No,' said Mathieu with regret. 'No, you couldn't do that.'

But she looked so forlorn that he took her in his arms.

322

The café was deserted.

'It's two o'clock in the morning, isn't it?' said Ivich to the waiter.

He wiped his eyes with the back of his hand and glanced at the clock. It indicated half past eight.

'Something like that,' he growled.

Ivich settled herself sedately into a corner, pulling her skirt up to her knees. I'll be an orphan girl going to join her aunt in a Paris suburb. She thought her eyes might be too bright, so she let her hair fall over her face. But her heart was brimming with almost joyful excitement: one hour to wait, a road to cross and she would jump into the train: I'll be at the Gare du Nord about six o'clock, I shall go to the Dôme first, I shall eat two oranges, and then go on to Renata, and borrow five hundred francs. She wanted to order a brandy, but an orphan doesn't drink alcohol.

'Will you bring me a lime tea?' she said timidly.

The waiter turned, he was horrid but she simply *had* to get on terms with him. When he brought the tea, she looked at him with soft and startled eyes.

'Thank you,' she sighed.

He stood confronting and sniffed perplexedly.

'Where are you off to like this?'

'To Paris,' she said. 'To stay with my aunt.'

'You aren't the daughter of Monsieur Serguine who owns the sawmill back there?'

The fool!

'Oh no,' she said. 'My father died in 1918. I'm a national orphan.'

He wagged his head several times and departed: the man was an oaf, a mere moujik. In Paris the café waiters have velvety eyes and believe what they are told. I'm going to see Paris again. The moment she got out of the Gare du Nord, she would be recognized: she was expected. The streets would be expecting her, the shop-windows, the trees in the Montparnasse cemetery, and . . . and people too. Certain people who would not have gone away – like Renata – or who would have come back. I shall rediscover myself; it was only there that she was Ivich, between the avenue du Maine and the Quais. And some-one will show me Czechoslovakia on a map. Ah, she thought passionately, let them bomb the city if they will, we shall die together, and my Boris will be left to regret us.

'Switch off the light.'

He obeyed, the room melted into the vast night of war; two looks were dissolved into the night: nothing was left but a glint of light at the edge of the half-open door, an elongated eye that seemed to see them. This annoyed Mathieu, who groped his way to the door.

'No,' said the voice at his back. 'Leave it open: I want to be able to hear if the boy calls out.'

He retraced his steps in silence, took off his shoes and his trousers. The right shoe dropped rather noisily on to the floor.

'Put your clothes on the arm-chair.'

He put down his trousers, jacket and shirt on the rocking-chair, which creaked as it swayed to and fro. He stood naked, his arms at his sides and his toes contracted, in the centre of the room. He wanted to laugh.

'Come along.'

He lay down on the bed beside a warm and naked body: she was lying on her back, motionless, her arms close to her sides. But when he kissed her, just below the neck, he could feel the throbbing of her heart, heavy mallet-blows that shook her from head to foot. He remained for a while motionless awed by that palpitating immobility: he had forgotten Irène's face: he stretched out a hand and slid his fingers over an expanse of sightless flesh. No matter who. People passed, not far away – Mathieu could hear their shoes creak: they were talking loudly and laughing together.

'Tell me, Marcel,' said a woman's voice. 'If you were Hitler, would you be able to sleep tonight?'

They laughed: their footsteps and their laughter receded, and Mathieu was alone.

'If I have to take any precautions,' said a sleepy voice, 'you'd better tell me at once.'

'No need to do that,' said Mathieu. 'I'm not that sort of fellow.'

She did not reply. He could hear her strong and regular breathing. A meadow – a meadow in the night: she breathed as a plant breathes, or a tree; he wondered whether she had not already gone to sleep. But an awkward, half-closed hand flickered over his hip and thigh, with what might pass for a caress. He turned gently over, and took her in his arms.

Boris dropped back on to his side, and pulled down the sheets. Lola had not moved: she remained outstretched on her back, her eyes closed. Boris curled himself up so as to avoid as far as possible the contact of the sheet against his perspiring body. Lola said, without opening her eyes: 'I'm beginning to believe you love me.'

He did not reply. That night he had loved all women in her person – the duchesses and all the rest. His hands, which an insurmountable modesty had previously confined to Lola's shoulders and breasts, had found their way everywhere: his lips too: and this time he frantically sought that half-oblivion into which he usually fell at the height of his enjoyment, and which so disgusted him: there were thoughts he wanted to escape. He felt clammy and unclean, his heart was throbbing violently: it was not an unpleasant sensation, and at that moment it was better not to think too much. Ivich always said to him, You think too much: and she was right. He suddenly noticed a trickle of moisture oozing from the corners of Lola's closed eyelids into two little pools, which gradually welled up each side of her nose. What could be the matter now? he wondered. He had gone through the last twenty-four hours with a sense of dry agony in the pit of his stomach, and was not in a melting mood.

'Give me my handkerchief,' said Lola. 'It's under the pillow.'

She wiped her eyes, opened them, and looked at him with a hard, suspicious air. 'What have I done now?' But, to his surprise, she said in a toneless voice: 'You'll be going away.'

'Where to? . . . Oh yes: but not at once: in a year's time.'

'What is a year?'

She looked at him intently: he reached a hand out from under the sheets and smoothed his hair down over his forehead:

'In a year the war may be over,' he said cautiously.

'Over? Don't you believe it: we know when a war begins, we never know when it is going to end.'

Her white arm leapt from underneath the sheets: she began to feel Boris's face as though she were blind. She passed a hand

325

over his temples and his cheeks, traced the contours of his ears, she caressed his nose with the tips of her fingers: he began to feel ridiculous.

'A year is a long while,' he said bitterly. 'Plenty of time to think about it.'

'That shows you're just a kid. If you knew how quickly a year passes – at my age.'

'Well, it seems to me a long while,' said Boris obstinately.

'So you want to fight?'

'It isn't that.'

He felt a little cooler, turned over on his back, stretched out his legs and came into contact with a piece of fabric at the end of the bed – his pyjama trousers. He went on, gazing up at the ceiling:

'In any case, since I've got to go to the war, I would sooner go at once, and not talk about it.'

'And what about me?' cried Lola. Then she added, catching at her breath: 'Don't you mind leaving me, you little wretch?'

'But I shall have to leave you anyhow.'

'Not yet awhile,' she said passionately. 'And I shan't survive it. Besides, I know you, you won't write for days together, you're so lazy, and I shall think you're dead. You don't know what it will be like.'

'You don't either,' said Boris. 'Wait till it happens, before you make such a fuss.'

A silence followed, then she said in a rasping voice that he knew only too well: 'Well, it shouldn't be very difficult to wangle you out of it. The old lady knows more people than you think.'

He swung himself on to his side, and eyed her with fury.

'Lola, if you do that . . .'

'Well?'

'I'll never speak to you again.'

She had composed herself; and she said to him with a quizzical smile. 'I thought you had a horror of war? You have often told me you were an anti-militarist.'

'I still am.'

'Well, then?'

'That's not the same thing.'

She had closed her eyes again, she was no longer agitated,

but her face had changed: the two familiar wrinkles of weariness and anguish had appeared at the corners of her lips. Boris made an effort:

'I am an anti-militarist because I can't stand officers,' he said in a soothing tone. 'I quite like the footslogger.'

'But you'll be an officer. They'll force you to become one.'

Boris did not reply: it was too complicated: he was himself confused. He detested officers, that was certainly a fact. But from another standpoint, since this was *his* war, and he had been dedicated to a brief military career, he *must* become a second-lieutenant. 'Oh dear,' he thought, 'if only I could be there now with my platoon, and not have to go through all this fuss.' And he said abruptly: 'I keep on wondering whether I shall be afraid.'

'Afraid?'

'Yes – it worries me.'

He thought she did not understand: it would have been better to confide in Mathieu, or even in Ivich. But since she was here . . .

'All this year we shall read in the newspapers how the French advanced through a storm of steel and fire, and so on – you know the sort of thing. And every time I shall ask myself whether I shall stand it. Or I shall ask the men on leave whether it was awful, and they will say it was: and I shall feel queer. It's going to be very jolly.'

She began to laugh and, in a mirthless imitation of his own words she cried: 'Wait till it happens before you make a fuss. And even if you were afraid, you little fool – who cares?'

It wasn't worth trying to make her understand. He yawned, and said: 'Shall we switch off the light? I'm tired.'

'If you like,' said Lola. 'Kiss me.'

He kissed her, and switched off the light. He hated her, and he thought to himself: 'She doesn't love me for myself, or she would have understood.' They were all the same, they pretended to be blind: they've transformed me into a fighting-cock, a bull for the arena, and now they won't face the facts, my father wants me to take my Diploma, and this creature wants to wangle me into a soft job because she once slept with a colonel. After a moment or two he felt the impact of a feverish, naked body against his back. 'I shall have to lie beside this

327

body for another year. She exploits me,' he thought; he
hardened his heart, and withdrew to his own side of the bed.

'What are you doing?' said Lola. 'You'll fall on to the
floor.'

'You make me so hot.'

She muttered something unintelligible, and drew away
from him. A year. Another year in which to wonder whether
I'm a coward, a year in which to be afraid of being afraid. He
heard Lola's regular breathing, she was asleep: and then her
body again flopped down on to him: it was not her fault,
there was a dip in the middle of the mattress, but Boris quivered
with rage and desperation: she'll be sprawling over me until
the morning. Men were the best companions – every man to
his own bed. Then a sudden dizziness came over him, he lay
wide-eyed and staring into the darkness, an icy shiver rippled
down his perspiring back: he had just remembered that he had
decided to join up next day.

The door opened and Mme Birnenschatz appeared in a
nightgown and a scarf wrapped round her head.

'Gustave,' she said loudly, to drown the noise of the wireless, 'do please come to bed.'

'Go to sleep,' said M. Birnenschatz. 'Don't you worry
about me.'

'But I can't sleep if you aren't in bed.'

'Nonsense!' he said with a jerk of irritation. 'As you see,
I'm waiting for an announcement.'

'What announcement?' she said. 'Why do you keep on
fiddling with that abominable radio? The neighbours will be
complaining soon. What are you waiting for?'

M. Birnenschatz turned to her and gripped her arm: 'I bet
it's a bluff,' he said. 'I bet there'll be an official denial during
the night.'

'What are you talking about?' she cried.

He signed to her to be quiet. A calm, deliberate voice had
begun to speak:

'A denial has been issued from authorized circles in Berlin
of all reports which have appeared abroad, either regarding
an ultimatum addressed to Czechoslovakia by Germany to
expire today at 2 p.m., or an alleged general mobilization said
to have been decreed immediately following that hour.'

'Listen,' said M. Birnenschatz. 'Listen.'

'It is considered that these reports are calculated to spread panic, and create an atmosphere favourable to war.'

'A denial has also been issued of an announcement stated to have been made by Minister Goebbels to a foreign newspaper regarding the ultimatum in question, adding that Dr Goebbels has not received any foreign journalist for some weeks past.'

M. Birnenschatz listened a little while longer, but the voice was silent. Then he waltzed Mme Birnenschatz round the room, exclaiming: 'I told you so, I told you so; it's a war climb-down, it's a pitiful climb-down. There'll be no war, Catherine, the Nazis have got it in the neck.'

Light. The four walls suddenly reared up between Mathieu and the light. He raised himself on his hands and looked at Irène's face: the nudity of that feminine body had risen into her face, the body had reabsorbed it, as nature reabsorbs forsaken gardens: Mathieu could no longer isolate it from those shapely shoulders, those small pointed breasts, it was now a flower of flesh, serene and dimly seen.

'I hope I wasn't very dull?' she asked.

'Dull?'

'Some men find me dull because I'm not very active. One got so bored with me that he departed in the early morning and never came back.'

'I wasn't bored,' said Mathieu.

She slid a finger over his neck. 'But you mustn't think I'm cold, you know.'

'I don't,' said Mathieu. 'And now stop talking.'

He took her face between his hands and leaned over her eyes: two glacier pools, transparent and infinitely deep. She looks at me. Behind that look, body and face had vanished. Deep in those eyes there is the night. The virgin night. She has admitted me into her eyes, and in that night I now exist: a naked man. I shall leave her in an hour or two and yet I shall remain in her for ever. In her, in this nameless night. He remembered that she did not even know his name. Suddenly, he felt so attracted by her that he wanted to tell her his name. But he refrained: words would lie: what drew him was, not so much the woman, as the room, the guitar on the wall, the boy asleep on the box-bed, the occasion, and events of the night.

She smiled: 'You're looking at me, but you don't see me.'

'Yes I do.'

She yawned. 'I should like to go to sleep for a bit.'

'Do,' said Mathieu. 'But set your alarm at six: I've got to look in at my flat before going to the station.'

'Are you off this morning?'

'This morning at eight o'clock.'

'Can I come to the station with you?'

'If you like.'

'Wait a moment,' she said. 'I must get out of bed to set the alarm, and put out the light. But don't look, I'm rather shy of my large behind, and my short legs.'

He averted his eyes, and heard her moving about the room, then she switched off the light. She said, as she got back into bed: 'I sometimes get up when I'm asleep and walk about the room. Just give me a clout on the head if I do.'

Wednesday, 28 September

Six o'clock in the morning.

She was very pleased with herself: she had not closed her eyes all night, but she did not feel in the least sleepy, though her eyes were smarting and twitching, her left eye itched, and shivers of weariness rippled up her back into her neck. She had travelled in a *horribly* deserted train, the last living creature she had seen was the station-master at Soissons, waving his red flag. Then, suddenly, in the hall of the Gare de l'Est, she came in sight of the crowd. A very uninviting crowd, largely consisting of old women and soldiers: but its countless eyes, the countless looks in them – besides, Ivich adored the perpetual heaving of a crowd, the jostling backs and elbows, the thrusting shoulders, and persistent undulations of the array of heads: it was so pleasant not to have to bear the burden of the war alone. She paused in one of the great outer gates, and stood in pious contemplation of the Boulevard de Strasbourg, feasting her eyes on it, and gradually visualizing her memories of the trees, the shuttered shops, the buses and the tramway lines, the cafés now just opening, and the smoky air of early morning. Even if they dropped their bombs in the next five minutes, or in thirty seconds, they couldn't take that away from me. She determined not to miss anything, not even the huge poster inscribed *Dubo – dubon – dubonnet*, on her left; then suddenly a wild impulse came upon her – she must get into the city before they came. She jostled past two Breton women carrying bird-cages, and planted her foot on a real Paris pavement. She felt as though she were entering a furnace – an uplifting, rather sinister sensation. 'Everything will be burnt – women, children, and old people, and I shall perish in the flames.' She was not afraid: anyway, I should have hated to grow old: but haste dried up her throat; there was not a minute to lose: so many scenes to be revisited, the Junk Market, the Catacombs, Ménilmontant, and other places that she did not yet know, such as the Musée Grévin: if *they* leave me a week, if *they* don't come before next Tuesday, I could see them all. 'Ah,' she thought passionately, 'a week of life, I'll pack a year's enjoyment into it, I'll die enjoying myself.' She hailed a taxi.

'12 rue Huyghens.'

'Right.'

'Go along the Boulevard Saint-Michel, the rue Auguste-Comte, the rue Vavin, the rue Delambre, and then by the rue de la Gaîté, and the avenue du Maine.'

'It's longer that way,' said the driver.

'Never mind.'

She got into the cab and shut the door. She had left Laon behind her for ever. She would never see it again: here we shall die. 'What a lovely day,' she thought. 'This afternoon we'll go to the rue des Rosiers and the Île Saint-Louis.'

'Quick!' cried Irène. 'Come here.'

Mathieu was in his shirt-sleeves, he was combing his hair in front of the mirror. He laid his comb on the table, put his jacket under his arm, and went into the other room.

'Well?'

Irène pointed sadly at the bed. 'He has bolted!'

'Well I'm damned,' said Mathieu.

He eyed the tumbled bed for a moment or two, scratched

his head, and then burst out laughing. Irène looked at him with a grave, astonished air, and then she caught the infection of his laughter.

'So that's that!' said Mathieu.

He slipped on his coat. Irène was still laughing.

'We'll meet at the Dôme at seven.'

'At seven,' she said.

He bent over her, and kissed her lightly.

Ivich ran upstairs and stopped at the third floor landing, quite out of breath. The door was ajar. She began to tremble. Perhaps it was the concierge. She went in: all the doors were open, all the lights on. In the hall she noticed a large suitcase: he must be there.

'Mathieu!'

No one answered. The kitchen was empty, but in the bedroom, the bed was unmade. 'He has spent the night here.' She went into the sitting-room and opened the windows and shutters. 'It's not such a bad place,' she thought, feeling a little touched. 'I was rather ungracious about it.' She would live there, she would write to him four times a week: no, five times. And then one fine day he would read in the newspapers that Paris had been bombed, and get no more letters. She pottered round the sitting-room, fingered the books and the crab paper-weight. A broken cigarette lay near a book by Martineau on Stendhal: she picked it up and put it in her bag among her mementoes. Then she sat down sedately on the divan. In a moment or two she heard footsteps on the stair, and her heart leapt. It was him. He stopped a moment in the hall, then he entered, carrying his suitcase. Ivich dropped her bag on to the floor.

'Ivich!'

He did not look astonished. He put down his suitcase, picked up the bag and gave it her.

'Have you been here long?'

She did not reply: she felt rather vexed with him because she had dropped her bag. He came and sat down beside her. She did not look at him: she looked at the carpet and the tips of her shoes.

'This is a bit of luck,' he said gaily. 'An hour later you would have missed me: I'm catching the eight o'clock train for Nancy.'

'What! You're going away so soon?'

She said no more, she felt rather put out and hated her own voice. They had so little time, she would have so liked to behave unaffectedly but could not manage it: when she had not seen people for a long while, she could not meet them again in an unaffected way. She had let herself sink into a sort of flaccid torpor not far removed from sulkiness. She kept her face averted from him, but let him see she was upset: indeed she felt more embarrassed than if she had been looking him in the face. Two hands reached out to the suitcase, opened it, took out an alarm clock and wound it up. Mathieu got up to put the clock on the table. Ivich raised her eyes slightly and saw him, a black figure, against the light. He sat down again, still silent, and Ivich regained a little courage. He looked at her: she knew that he was looking at her. No one, for three months, had looked at her in quite that way. She felt like a precious, fragile object: a small dumb idol: which was pleasant, vexing, and not too painful. Suddenly she caught the ticking of the alarm clock and realized that he would soon be going. 'I won't be fragile, I won't be an idol.' She forced herself to turn to him. The look on his face surprised her.

'Well, here you are, Ivich.'

He did not appear to be thinking about what he said. She smiled at him, none the less, but felt quite frozen. He did not return her smile: he said slowly: 'It's you. . . .'

He surveyed her with astonishment. . . . 'How did you get here?' he went on, in a more animated tone.

'By train.'

She set the palms of her hands together and squeezed them hard, to make the joints crack.

'What I meant was – do your parents know?'

'No.'

'You ran away?'

'More or less.'

'Yes,' he said. 'Yes. Well, this is fine: you will live here.' And he added with interest: 'Were you bored at Laon?'

She did not reply: the cool, assured voice dropped on to her neck like a knife-blade.

'Poor Ivich!'

She began to tug at her hair.

'Is Boris at Biarritz?' he continued.

'Yes.'

Boris had got gingerly out of bed, shivering as he slipped on his trousers and his jacket, flung a glance at Lola who was asleep with her mouth open, noiselessly opened the door and went out into the passage, carrying his shoes in his hand.

Ivich glanced at the alarm clock, the time was already twenty minutes past six. 'What time is it?' she asked plaintively.

'Twenty minutes past six,' he said. 'Wait: I'm going to put a few things into my haversack – that won't take me long: then I shall be quite free.'

He knelt down by the suitcase. She watched him listlessly. She was no longer conscious of her body, but the tick-tock of the clock got on her nerves. In a moment or two he got up: 'All ready now.'

He remained standing in front of her. She noticed that his trousers were a little worn at the knees.

'Listen, Ivich,' he said gently. 'We must talk seriously: the flat is at your disposal: the key is on the nail beside the door, you can live here until the end of the war. I have arranged about my salary: I have given a power of attorney to Jacques, he will draw it, and send it to you every month. There will be some small bills to pay from time to time: the rent, for instance, and the taxes, unless serving soldiers are exempted – and you might send me a small parcel now and again. What remains is yours: I think you will manage all right.'

She listened in amazement to that level, monotonous voice, the voice of a radio announcer. How could he be so tactless? She didn't wholly understand what he was saying, but she could clearly picture his expression, his half-smile, his heavy-lidded eyes, and his air of calm complacency. She looked at him, to help herself to hate him more effectively, and her hatred vanished. He didn't look at all like his voice. Was he in distress? No, he didn't seem unhappy. It was merely a face that she had never seen on him before.

'Are you listening to me, Ivich?' he asked with a smile.

'Certainly,' she said. She got up: 'Mathieu, I wish you would show me Czechoslovakia on a map.'

'I'm afraid I haven't got any maps,' he said. 'Though wait – I must have an old atlas.'

He took down from his shelves an album bound in boards, laid it on the table, turned over the pages and opened it at 'Central Europe'. It was coloured in the crudest yellows and violets. No blue: no sea nor ocean being shown. Ivich looked intently at the map, and could not discover any Czechoslovakia either.

'It dates from before '14,' said Mathieu.

'And before '14 Czechoslovakia didn't exist?'

'No.'

He picked up his fountain-pen, and traced an irregular shape in the centre of the map.

'It's more or less like that,' he said.

Ivich looked at that large drably coloured expanse of waterless earth, and the contour line of black ink, which looked very obtrusive and ugly on the printed sheet. Inside it she read the word 'Bohemia' and said: 'So that's Czechoslovakia. . . .' It all seemed so futile, and she began to sob.

'Ivich!' said Mathieu.

She suddenly found herself half-lying on the divan: Mathieu was holding her in his arms. At first she stiffened: I don't want his pity, I'm behaving like a fool, but in a moment she relaxed, there was no war, no Czechoslovakia, and no Mathieu: only the soft warm pressure round her shoulders.

'Did you get any sleep last night?' he asked.

'No,' she said between two sobs.

'My poor little Ivich! Wait a minute.'

He got up and went out: she heard him moving about in the next room. When he returned, he had recovered something of the naïve, placid air she liked: 'I've put clean sheets on the bed and made it, you can go to bed as soon as I have gone.'

She looked at him: 'But . . . aren't I coming to the station with you?'

'I thought you detested platform farewells.'

'Oh,' she said, with an appealing air: 'on such a special occasion . . .'

He shook his head. 'I would sooner go alone. Besides, you must get some sleep.'

'Very well,' she said. Then she thought: 'How silly of me,' and suddenly felt cold and isolated. She shook her head vigorously, wiped her eyes, and smiled. 'You're right, I'm nervy from being tired: I'll go and rest.'

He took her hand, and raised her to her feet. 'I must first take you round the establishment.'

In the bedroom he stopped before a cupboard. 'Here are six pairs of sheets, some pillow-cases and blankets. There's also an eiderdown somewhere, but I don't know where I've put it, the concierge could tell you.'

He had opened the cupboard, looked at the piles of white linen, and laughed sardonically.

'What's the matter?' asked Ivich politely.

'All this stuff belongs to me. How absurd it seems!'

He turned towards her. 'I'll show you the larder too. Come along.'

They went into the kitchen, and he pointed to a cupboard. 'There it is. You'll find oil, salt, and pepper, and a few pots of preserves.' He lifted the cylindrical tins one after the other to the level of his eyes, and turned them round under the light. 'That's salmon, that's sausage-meat, and those are three tins of pickled cabbage. You put them in a double saucepan. ...' He paused, and again broke into a rasping laugh. But he said no more, he looked vacantly at a tin of peas and replaced it in the cupboard.

'Take care of the gas, Ivich. You must lower the lever on the meter every evening before you go to bed.'

They were back in the sitting-room.

'By the way,' he said, 'I'll let the concierge know as I go out that I'm lending you the flat. She will send Mme Balaine to you tomorrow. She's my charlady, not at all a bad sort.'

'Balaine,' said Ivich. 'What a funny name.'

She laughed, and Mathieu smiled.

'Jacques won't be back before the beginning of October,' he said. 'I had better give you a little money to get on with until then.'

He had a thousand-franc note and two two-hundred-franc notes in his pocket-book. He took out the thousand-franc note and gave it to her.

'Thank you very much,' said Ivich.

She took it and held it in her hand.

'If anything goes wrong, ring up Jacques. I'll be writing to him to say he's to look after you.'

'Thanks,' said Ivich.

'You know his address?'

'Yes – yes, thank you.'

'Then good-bye.' He came up to her. 'Good-bye, my dear Ivich. I'll write to you as soon as I've got an address.'

He laid his hands on her shoulders and drew her towards him. 'My dear little Ivich.'

She raised her forehead submissively, he kissed it, pressed her hand, and went out. She heard the outer door slam: she smoothed out the thousand-franc note, and looked at the design: then she tore it into eight pieces, and scattered them on the floor.

A tawny-bearded Colonial veteran with one hand on a recruit's shoulder, and pointing with the other hand to the African coast. 'Join – rejoin – the Colonial Army.' The young recruit looked abysmally stupid. Well, that would be his fate: for six months Boris would look just like that. For three months perhaps: war years count double. 'They'll cut my hair,' he thought, clenching his teeth. 'The brutes!' He had never felt more venomously anti-militarist. He passed a sentry, standing motionless in his box. Boris eyed him darkly, his heart sank, and he swore a silent oath. But he had decided, he must do the deed: and he walked rather limply into the barracks. The sky was ablaze, a light breeze carried a fragrance into these distant suburbs. 'What a pity,' thought Boris. 'What a pity it's such a fine day.' A constable was pacing up and down outside the police station. Philippe looked at him: he felt utterly forlorn, and he was very cold: his cheek and upper lip were smarting. It would be an inglorious martyrdom. Inglorious and joyless: a prison cell, and then one morning a firing-squad in the Vincennes moat: no one would ever hear of it: he had been disowned by everyone.

'The Superintendent of Police?' he asked.

The constable looked at him: 'On the first floor.'

I shall be my own witness, I am accountable to no one but myself.

'The recruiting-office?'

The two guards exchanged a glance, and Boris felt his

337

cheeks blaze: 'I must be looking my best,' he thought.

'The building at the far end of the yard, first door on the left.'

Boris saluted nonchalantly with two fingers and walked firmly across the yard, and then thought rather ruefully that he must also be looking like a bloody fool, and was no doubt an object of derision. 'A chap who comes here on his own, without being called up, must seem just silly to them.' Philippe was standing up in the full light, confronting a short man with a ribbon in his buttonhole, and thinking of Raskolnikov.

'Are you the superintendent?'

'I'm his secretary,' said the other.

Philippe spoke with difficulty, owing to his swollen lip, but his voice was steady. He took a step forward:

'I am a deserter,' he said firmly, 'and I am in possession of false papers.'

The secretary looked at him. 'Sit down,' he said politely.

The taxi sped towards the Gare de l'Est.

'You're going to be late,' said Irène.

'No,' said Mathieu: 'I shall just do it.' He added by way of explanation: 'There was a girl at my place.'

'A girl?'

'She had come from Laon to see me.'

'Is she in love with you?'

'Certainly not.'

'Are you in love with her?'

'No: I am lending her my flat.'

'Is she a good girl?'

'No,' said Mathieu. 'She is not a good girl. But she isn't a bad girl either.'

They were silent. The taxi was crossing the Halles.

'There – there,' said Irène suddenly. 'It was there.'

'So it was.'

'And only yesterday. Good Lord! – it seems such a while ago.'

She swung round and peered out of the small window in the back of the cab.

'So that's over,' she said, sitting down again.

Mathieu did not answer. He was thinking of Nancy. He had never been there.

'You don't talk much,' said Irène. 'But I don't mind.'

'There was a time when I talked too much,' said Mathieu, with a curt laugh.

He turned towards her: 'What are you going to do today?'

'Nothing,' said Irène. 'I never do anything: my old man makes me an allowance.'

The taxi stopped. They got out and Mathieu paid.

'I don't like stations,' said Irène. 'There's something sinister about them.'

She suddenly slipped a hand under his arm. She walked close beside him, in silent intimacy: he felt as though he had known her for ten years.

'I must take my ticket.'

They made their way through the crowd. It was a civilian crowd, sluggish and silent, interspersed with a few soldiers.

'You know Nancy?'

'No,' said Mathieu.

'I do. Tell me where you're going.'

'To the Aviation Barracks at Essey-lès-Nancy.'

'Yes,' she said. 'I know where that is.'

There was a queue of men with haversacks at the ticket office.

'Would you like me to get you a paper while you wait?'

'No,' he said, gripping her arm. 'Stay with me.'

She smiled at him contentedly. They moved forward, step by step.

'Essey-lès-Nancy.'

He produced his army book, and the clerk gave him a ticket. He turned round to her: 'Come with me to the barrier: but I would rather you didn't come on to the platform.'

They walked on, and then stopped.

'Well, good-bye,' she said.

'Good-bye,' said Mathieu.

'Just one night.'

'One night: yes, but you will be my sole memory of Paris.'

He kissed her: and she said: 'Will you write to me?'

'I don't know,' said Mathieu.

He eyed her for a moment without speaking, and then moved away.

'Hi!' she cried to him.

He turned. She smiled, but her lips quivered.

'I don't even know your name.'

'Mathieu Delarue.'

'Come in.'

He was sitting up in bed, in pyjamas, his hair, as always, so immaculate that she found herself wondering whether he wore a hair-net at night. The room smelt of eau de Cologne. He looked at her with bewilderment, hurriedly took his spectacles from the bedside table and put them on his nose:

'Ivich!'

'Yes, it's me,' she said good-humouredly.

She sat on the edge of the bed and smiled at him. The train for Nancy was moving out of the Gare de l'Est: perhaps in Berlin, the bombers had already taken off. 'I want to enjoy myself! I want to enjoy myself!' She looked round her: it was a hotel room, repellently luxurious. The bomb will go through the roof, and the floor of the sixth storey: this is where I shall die.

'I never thought I'd see you again,' he said with dignity.

'Why? Because you behaved like a cad?'

'We had been drinking,' he said.

'I had been drinking because I had been ploughed in the P.C.B. But *you* hadn't been drinking: you wanted to take me to your room: you were waiting for a chance.'

He was utterly at a loss.

'And here I am,' she said. 'Well?'

He flushed scarlet. 'Ivich!'

She laughed in his face: 'You don't look very formidable.'

There was a long silence, then a hand fumbled round her waist. The bombers had crossed the frontier. She laughed until the tears came into her eyes: anyway I shan't die a virgin.

'Is this place free?'

The stout old gentleman grunted.

Mathieu put his haversack in the luggage-rack and sat down. The compartment was full: Mathieu peered at his travelling companions, but it was still too dark to see them. He remained motionless for an instant, then came a sudden jerk, and the train started: Mathieu was conscious of a thrill of joy: it was all over. Tomorrow – Nancy, war, fear, death perhaps, and freedom. We shall see, he said: we shall see. He felt in his pocket for his pipe, and came upon an envelope: Daniel's letter: His impulse was to replace it, but a sort of shame prevented him: after all, he must read it sometime. He filled his pipe, lit it, tore open the envelope, and took out seven sheets of paper covered with close, even handwriting, without any erasures. 'He must have made a rough copy. What an epistle!' he thought with vexation. The train was now fortunately out of the station, and he could see better. He read:

'My dear Mathieu,

'I can too well imagine your amazement, and I feel profoundly how inopportune this letter must be. Indeed, I don't quite know myself why I am writing it: I suppose one confidence, like one crime, leads to others. When I disclosed to you, last June, a certain picturesque aspect of my character, perhaps I unconsciously chose you to receive my intimate experiences. This would be regrettable, because if I had to get you to endorse all my activities, I could not fail to regard you with active hatred, which would be tiresome for me, and not to your advantage. You may picture me *laughing* as I write all this. For several days past I have been conscious of a certain leaden resilience – I apologize for such a conjunction of words – and *laughter* has been vouchsafed to me as a supplementary grace. But enough: it is not any ordinary event in my life that I want to describe to you, but an *extraordinary* adventure. It will not, I am sure, appear to me completely real until it also exists for other people. Not that I rely greatly on your faith, nor even, perhaps, on your good faith. The rationalism which for the last ten years has been your livelihood – if I ask you to forget it for a moment in order to follow me, I doubt whether you would do so. But possibly I have rightly chosen to communicate this extraordinary experience to the one friend least calculated to understand it: possibly I hoped, in so doing, to get something like a counter-proof. Not that I expect a reply from you: I should be sorry if you felt obliged to favour me with those exhortations to be sensible which – pray believe me – I have not failed to address to myself. I must indeed admit so much: it is when I think of good sense, sane reason, and the positive sciences, that the manna of laughter tends to descend upon me most of all. Moreover I fancy Marcelle would be annoyed if she found a letter from you among my mail. She would think she had come upon a clandestine correspondence, and perhaps, knowing you as she does, would imagine that you are placing yourself generously at my service, by way of guiding my first steps in matrimony. But here is why your silence may serve me as a counter-proof: if I can picture your "hideous smile", without being distressed by it, and conceive the tacit irony with which you will view my "case", without abandoning the exceptional procedure I have chosen, I shall have convinced myself that I have acted rightly. I would add, to avoid all misunderstanding, and in thanking the astute psychologist for his good offices, that this time it is the philosopher I am addressing, for the following narrative belongs to the metaphysical plane. You will no doubt pronounce this highly presumptuous, since I have read neither Hegel nor Schopenhauer; but don't take offence; I am certainly not capable of formulating the present operations of my mind in the abstract, I leave that process to you, as being your profession: I shall be content to live blindly through the experiences you and your more percipient colleagues are able to express in professional terms. In any case, I don't think you are so easily moved: this laughter and these agonies of mine, these flashing intuitions – it is only too probable that you will feel constrained to class them among psychological "states", and explain them by my character and habits, despite what I revealed to you in confidence. Never mind: what I said, I meant to say: you may therefore use all this as you think fit, though you may misread me utterly. Indeed it is with a sort of furtive pleasure that I now set out to give you all the information necessary for establishing the *truth*, knowing that you will use it to plunge deliberately into error.

'Now for the facts. But here laughter makes me drop my pen. I laugh till the tears come into my eyes. A subject on which I tremble to embark, which I have never *mentioned* to myself, from modesty as well as self-respect, I now propose to formulate in words, and these words I shall address to *you*, they will remain on these blue sheets of notepaper, and you may even amuse yourself by re-reading them in ten years' time. I feel somehow I am committing a sacrilege against myself: and that is the most inexcusable aspect of the matter: but I have *also* realized that I am giving you away too: so the said sacrilege is rather a joke – I should never wholly value what I most care for, if I had not, at least once, laughed at it. Well, I shall have made you laugh at my new faith. I shall carry within myself a humble certitude, so vast as to be utterly beyond you, and yet wholly in your hands: what crushes me will be there diminished to the measure of your unworthiness. And so, if you are amused by this letter, I forestalled you: I am laughing, Mathieu, laughing: God makes man, himself surpassing all men and derided by them all, hanging open-mouthed upon the Cross, livid, speechless, unsullied by the multitude – what can be more *laughable*! well, whatever you may do, the delicious tears of laughter will never trickle down your cheeks.

'Let us see what words can do. Will you understand me, for a start, if I tell you that I have never known what I *am*? My vices, my virtues, are under my nose, but I can't see them, nor stand far enough back to view myself as a whole. I seem to be a sort of flabby mass in which words are engulfed: no sooner do I name myself than what is named is merged in him who names, and one gets no further. I have often wanted to hate myself, and, as you know, had good reasons for doing so. But my attempted hatred of myself was absorbed into my insubstantiality, and was nothing but a recollection. I could not love myself either, I am sure, though I have never tried to. But I was eternally compelled to *be myself*. I was my own burden: but never burdensome enough, Mathieu. For one instant, on that June evening when I elected to confess to you, I thought I had encountered myself in your bewildered eyes. You *saw* me, in your eyes I was solid and predictable: my acts and moods were the actual consequences of a definite entity. And through me you knew that entity. I described it to you in my words, I revealed to you facts unknown to you, which had helped you to visualize it. And yet you saw it, I merely saw you seeing it. For one instant you were the heaven-sent mediator between me and myself, you perceived that compact and solid entity which I was and wanted to be, in a just as simple and ordinary way as I perceived you. For after all, I exist, I *am*, though I have no sense of being; and it is an exquisite torment to discover in oneself such utterly unfounded certainty, such unsubstantiated pride. I then understood that one could not reach oneself except through another's judgement, another's hatred. And also through another's love perhaps: but here there is no question of that. For this revelation I am not ungrateful to you. I do not know how you would describe our present relations. Not goodwill, nor wholly hatred. Put it that there is a corpse between us. My corpse.

'I was in this attitude of mind when I went to Sauveterre with Marcelle. Sometimes I wanted to see you again, sometimes I dreamed of murdering you. But one fine day I realized our relationship was reciprocal. Without me, you would be that same insubstantial entity that I am for myself. It is by my agency that you can at times get an occasional and doubtless rather exasperating glimpse of yourself – as you really are: a rather limited rationalist, superficially self-confident, but fundamentally without convictions, well disposed to everything within the compass of your reason, blind and disingenuous towards anything else: rational by self-interest, naturally sentimental, by no means sensual: in brief, a cautious, moderate intellectual, an excellent middle-class product. If it be true that I cannot get at myself without your agency, you need mine if you want to know yourself. Thus I saw us, mutually sustaining our two nonentities, and for the first time I laughed a deep and all-consuming laugh: then I sank back into a sort of dark indifference, the more so as my sacrifice in that same month of June, which I then envisaged as a painful expiation, had become *horribly* endurable. But here I must be silent: I can't talk about Marcelle without laughing, and from motives of decency which you will appreciate, we mustn't laugh at her together. Then the wildest, craziest *chance* befell me. God sees me, Mathieu: I feel it and I know it. Now all is said: how I wish I were with you and could draw an even stronger certitude, if that were possible, from the spectacle of your laughter as you read these words.

'But enough of this. We have laughed quite enough at each other: I resume my narrative. You must have experienced, in the Métro, in the foyer of a theatre, or in a train, the sudden and irksome sense that you were being looked at

344

from behind. You turn round, but the observer has buried his nose in a book: you can't discover who was looking at you. You turn round, but you are sure that the unknown eyes are again upon you, there's a faint tingling all over your back, like a sudden twitch of all your tissues. Well, that is what I felt for the first time, on 26 September, at three o'clock in the afternoon, in the hotel garden. No one was there, you understand, Mathieu, no one at all. But the look was there. Try to understand: I did not see it, as one sees a passing profile, a forehead, or a pair of eyes; for its essential character is to be *beyond perception*. But I became more compact and concentrated, I was both transparent and opaque, I existed in the *presence* of a look. Since then I have been continually under observation – even in my solitary room: sometimes, the consciousness of transfixion by the sword-blade, of that eye upon me while asleep, awoke me with a start. I have, in fact, almost entirely lost the capacity for sleep. Ah, Mathieu – what a discovery: *I was seen*, I struggled to know myself, I seemed to be slipping out of my extremities, I claimed your kindly intercession, and all that time I was seen, the inexorable look, an invisible steel blade was on me, And you too – sceptic and scoffer as you are – *you are seen*. But you don't know it. I can easily describe that look: it is nothing: it is a purely negative entity: imagine a pitch dark night. It's the night that looks at you: but it's a dazzling night: night in fullest splendour: the night behind the day. I am flooded with black light: it is all over my hands and eyes and heart, and I can't see it. Believe me, I first loathed this incessant violation of myself: as you know, I used to long to become invisible: to go, and leave no trace, on earth or in men's hearts. What anguish to discover that look as a universal medium from which I can't escape! But what a relief as well. I know at last that I am. I adapt for my own use, and to your disgust, your prophet's foolish wicked words – I think, therefore I am – which used to trouble me so sorely, for the more I thought the less I seemed to be; and I say – I am seen, therefore I am. I need no longer bear the responsibility of my turbid and disintegrating self: he who sees me causes me to be: I am as he sees me. I turn my eternal, shadowed face towards the night, I stand up like a challenge, and I say to God: Here am I. Here am I, as you see me, as I am. What can I do now? – you know me, and I do not know myself. What can I do except support myself? And thou, whose look eternally creates me – do thou support me. Mathieu – what joy! what torment! At last I am transmuted into myself. Hated, despized, sustained, a presence supports me to continue thus for ever. I am infinite and infinitely guilty. But I *am*, Mathieu, I am. Before God and before men, I *am*. *Ecce homo*.

'I called on the curé of Sauveterre: an astute peasant of some education, with the worn and mobile face of an old actor. I don't much care for him, but I was not at all sorry that my first contact with the Church should take place through such an agency. He received me in a study lined with books all of which he has certainly not read. I started by giving him a thousand francs for his poor, and I saw that he took me for a reformed criminal. I felt I was going to laugh, and I had to bear in mind my tragic situation in order to retain my gravity.

' "*Monsieur le curé*," I said, "I want to ask you this one question: does your religion teach that God sees us?"

' "Certainly," he answered with astonishment. "He reads our hearts."

' "But what does he see there?" I asked. "Does he see the froth and foam of daily thoughts, or does he penetrate to our eternal essence?"

'The sly old gentleman gave me the following answer, in which I recognized the mark of secular wisdom:

' "Monsieur, God sees everything."

' "I understood that . . ." '

'Stale trash,' said Mathieu to himself. The window was down, he crumpled up the letter, and threw it out.

'No,' said the superintendent. 'You speak. I don't like talking to these senior officers: they treat one like an orderly.'

'I fancy this fellow will be rather more polite,' said the secretary. 'After all, we are returning his son to him: besides he is in the wrong: he should have looked after him properly.'

'You'll see,' said the superintendent. 'He'll manage to make himself unpleasant. Especially in the present circumstances: on the eve of a war, a general isn't likely to admit he's in the wrong.'

The secretary picked up the receiver and dialled the number. The superintendent lit a cigarette: 'Be tactful, Miraut,' he said. 'Keep it on an official level, and don't say too much.'

'Hullo!' said the secretary. 'Hullo! General Lacaze?'

'Yes,' said a rasping voice. 'What do you want?'

'I am the superintendent's secretary at the rue Delambre.'

The voice seemed to display a little more interest. 'Yes; well?'

'A young man called at my office about eight o'clock this morning,' said the secretary, in a noncommittal, rather drawling tone. 'He said he was a deserter and in possession of false papers. We have in fact found on him a rough forgery of a Spanish passport. He refused to reveal his identity. But the Prefecture had sent us your stepson's description and photographs, so we recognized him at once.'

After a pause the secretary continued, with rather less assurance: 'Of course, general, no charge can be brought against him. He is not a deserter, not having been called to the colours: he has a false passport in his pocket, but that does not constitute an offence, since he has not had the opportunity to use it. We hold him at your disposal, and you can come and fetch him when you like.'

'Did you put him through any sort of third degree?' asked the dry voice.

The secretary started.

'What does he say?' asked the superintendent.

The secretary put his hand over the receiver: 'He wants to know if we've third-degreed him.'

The superintendent raised his hands in the air, while the secretary replied:

'No, general: of course not.'

'Pity,' said the general.

The secretary permitted himself a respectful laugh.

'What did he say?' asked the superintendent. But the secretary turned his back on him and leaned over the telephone.

'I'll come this evening or tomorrow. In the meantime keep him at the station: it will be a wholesome lesson for him.'

'Certainly, general.'

The general rang off.

'What did he say?' asked the superintendent.

'He wanted the boy put through a third degree.'

The superintendent stubbed his cigarette in the ash-tray.

'Did he indeed!' he said ironically.

Six-thirty. Sun on the sea – the sun went on setting, the wasps went on buzzing, and war came nearer: she flicked away a wasp with a vague gesture: behind her, Jacques kept on drinking his whisky in unending little sips: 'Life,' she thought, 'is interminable.' Every year for fifteen years, father, mother, brothers, uncles, and aunts, had assembled in this drawing-room on fine September afternoons, stiff and silent like an array of family portraits: she had waited for dinner every afternoon, at first beneath the table, then on a little chair, sewing and wondering what was the good of being alive. There they all lay, those vanished afternoons, in the russet gold of this unreal hour. Father was there, behind her, reading the *Temps*. What is the good of being alive? What indeed! A fly climbed laboriously up the window-pane, slipped down, and then started again: Odette watched it, she was on the verge of tears.

'Come and sit down,' said Jacques. 'Daladier is going to speak.'

She turned towards him: he had slept badly: he was sitting in the leather armchair, with the childish expression he assumed when he was afraid. She sat on the arm of his chair. All days are alike. All days. She looked out of the window and thought: 'He was right, the sea has changed.'

'What is he going to say?'

Jacques shrugged his shoulders: 'He is going to announce the declaration of war.'

She was conscious of a slight shock, but no more. Fifteen nights. For fifteen anguished nights, she had pleaded in the void: she would have sacrificed everything, house, health, ten years of life, to save the peace. And now, good God in heaven! – let war break out. Let something happen at last: let the dinner-bell ring, let a thunderbolt plunge into the sea, let a gloomy voice suddenly announce a German invasion of Czechoslovakia. A fly. A drowned fly at the bottom of a cup: she herself was drowning in that placid catastrophic afternoon: she looked at her husband's thin hair, and she no longer quite understood why it should be worth while saving men from death, and their homes from ruin. Jacques put his glass down on the sideboard, and said gloomily:

'This is the end.'

'The end of what?'

'Of everything. I don't even know what we ought to hope for – victory or defeat.'

'Oh!' she said feebly.

'If we are beaten, we shall be Germanized: but I can assure you that the Germans will know how to re-establish order. Communists, Jews, and Freemasons will be cleared out. If we win, we shall be bolshevized, it will be the triumph of the *Frente Crapular* – anarchy, perhaps, worse. ... Ah,' he continued, in a plaintive tone, 'this war should never, never, have been started.'

She hardly listened to what he said: 'He is frightened, angry, and alone, she thought.' She bent over him and stroked his hair. 'My poor little Jacques.'

'My dear little Boris.'

She smiled at him, and looked so nice that Boris felt quite conscience-stricken. I must tell her all the same.

'It's silly,' Lola went on. 'I'm fidgety, I must know what he's going to say – though, you know, it isn't quite the same as if you were going off at once.'

Boris contemplated his feet and began to whistle under his breath. It was better to pretend not to have heard, otherwise she would call him a hypocrite into the bargain. As the minutes passed, it became more difficult. She would look pathetic and frightened, and say: 'How could you do such a thing and not tell me?'

'I'm not going to be popular,' he said to himself.

'Give me a Martini,' said Lola. 'What will you have?'

'The same.'

He went on whistling. Perhaps after Daladier's statement, there might be an opportunity; she would learn that war had been declared, which would inevitably be something of a shock: then Boris would take the plunge and say: 'I've joined up,' without giving her time to get her breath. There were cases in which a jolt of that kind provoked unexpected reactions: laughter, for instance: what a joke if she burst out laughing. All the same, I should be rather annoyed, he said to himself dispassionately. All the guests in the hotel were assembled in the hall, even the two priests. They had settled into their arm-chairs, trying to look at ease because they felt themselves under observation, but they were really very agitated, and Boris caught more than one of them glancing sidelong at the clock. All right, all right! You've got another half-hour to wait. Boris was in a bad mood, he did not like Daladier, and it infuriated him to think that there were hundreds of thousands of married couples all over France, countless families and priests awaiting like manna from heaven the words of a fellow who had torpedoed the Popular Front. 'It makes him seem too important,' he thought. And turning towards the radio, he yawned ostentatiously.

He was hot and thirsty, and three of them were asleep: the two next to the corridor, and the little old man with clasped hands who looked as though he were praying: the four others had spread a handkerchief over their knees and were playing cards – four quite presentable young men, their jackets dangling from the luggage rack behind them and ruffling their hair as the train rocked. From time to time Mathieu looked out of the corner of his eye at the brown, rather mossy forearms of his neighbours, a short fair man, whose hands, tipped with broad black nails, deftly manipulated the cards. He was a compositor: the fellow next to him was a locksmith. Of the two others in the opposite seat, the one nearest Mathieu was a commercial traveller, and the other played the violin in a café at Bois-Colombes. The compartment smelt of humanity, tobacco and wine, sweat trickled down their faces, and moulded them into glistening masks: on the little old man's bristly chin, between the stiff white thatch on either cheek, the sweat looked oilier and more acrid – a facial excrement. Outside the window, under the glare of sunshine, the grey, flat countryside stretched away into the distance.

The compositor had no luck: he was losing; he bent over the game, arching his brows with an air of dogged surprise. 'Well, I'm blowed,' he said.

The commercial traveller picked up the cards briskly and shuffled them. The compositor watched as they slipped from one hand into the other. 'It's not my day,' he said grudgingly.

They played in silence. After a moment or two, the compositor took a trick.

'Good!' he said triumphantly. 'Perhaps that will turn my luck a bit, boys. I may get a move on now.'

But the traveller had already shown his hands: 'Too good for you, I'm afraid.'

The compositor pushed his cards away. 'I shan't play any more. I'm losing too much.'

'You're right,' said the locksmith. 'Besides the train does rock so.'

The commercial traveller folded his handkerchief and put it in his pocket. He was tall, big man with a pale complexion, a flabby, frog-like head, large jaws, and a narrow skull. The three others treated him with slight deference, because he had some education and was a sergeant. He addressed them with familiarity. He cast a malevolent glace at Mathieu, and got up rather unsteadily.

'I'm going to get a drink.'

'A good idea.'

The locksmith and the compositor produced bottles from their packs: the locksmith drank straight from the bottle, then handed it to the violinist.

'Like a drink?'

'Not just now.'

'You don't know what's good for you.'

They fell silent, overcome by the heat. The locksmith puffed out his cheeks and sighed gently, the traveller lit a High-life. Mathieu thought: 'They don't like me, they think me stuck-up.' And yet he felt drawn to them, even to the sleepers, and the commercial traveller: they yawned, they slept, they played cards, the rocking train rattled their empty heads, but they possessed a fate, like kings and like the dead. A crushing fate barely to be distinguished from heat and weariness and buzzing flies: the compartment, shut close like the hot room in a Turkish bath, barricaded by sun and by speed, was jolting them all towards the same adventure, a gleam of light edged the printer's ear: the lobe of it looked like a blood-red strawberry: 'It is with men like these that wars are fought,' thought Mathieu. Until then he had pictured war as a tangle of twisted steel, shattered timbers, iron and stone. Now blood

351

was quivering in the rays of sunshine, the compartment was flooded with a russet light: bloody war was a fate: it would be fought with the blood of these six men, with the blood stagnating in their ear-lobes, with the blue current of blood beneath their skin, with the blood of their lips. They would be split like wine-skins, all the excrement would gush out of them – the locksmith's intestines, which now and then emitted a waggish rumble, would be dragged through the dust, as tragically as those of a disembowelled horse in the arena.

'Well, I shall go and stretch my legs,' said the compositor, as though to himself. Mathieu watched him get up and go out into the corridor: that phrase was *historic*. A dead man had uttered it in an undertone, one summer day, when he had been alive. A dead man, or – what came to the same thing – a survivor. Dead men – dead men already. That's why I can't talk to them. He felt quite dizzy as he looked at them, he longed to have a part in their great and historic adventure, but it was not permitted. He sweltered in their heat, he would shed his blood in the selfsame roads, and yet he was not with them, he was just a pale, eternal halo: a man without a destiny.

The compositor, who was smoking in the corridor, swung round and said: 'Planes overhead.'

'Where?'

'There – there.'

'I . . . oh . . . you don't say!' said the locksmith.

'Are they French?' asked the violinist, looking upwards with expressive and bewildered eyes.

'They're too high up, I can't see.'

'Of course they're French,' said the locksmith. 'What else could they be? War hasn't been declared.'

The compositor leaned towards them, with both hands on the framework of the doorway.

'How do you know? You've been in this train for the last eleven hours. I suppose you think they'll wait till you arrive before declaring war?'

This was a new idea to the locksmith. 'You're right. I say, boys, we may have been at war since this morning'

They turned to the commercial traveller. 'What do you say? Do you think we're at war?'

The commercial traveller looked unruffled. He shrugged his

shoulders contemptuously. 'You think we'll fight for Czecho-slovakia? Have you ever looked at Czechoslovakia on a map? No? Well, I have. And more than once. The place is a bloody nuisance. And about the size of a pocket-handkerchief. There are two paltry million inhabitants who don't even speak the same language. Do you suppose that Hitler would bother to make a fuss about Czechoslovakia? And Daladier? In the first place Daladier isn't Daladier: he's the two hundred families behind him. And they'll tell Czechoslovakia to go to hell.'

He surveyed his audience, and concluded: 'The truth is that this has been with us here and in Germany since 1936. So what did Chamberlain, Hitler, Daladier & Co. do? They said to themselves: We'll settle those folk: and they entered into a little secret treaty. Hitler's great dodge when the workers get restive is to shove them into the forces. That shuts their mouths for good and all. Got a grouse, eh? Two hours' fatigue. Still got a grouse? Six hours' fatigue. After that the chaps are on their knees, all they think about is how they can get a lie-down. So the other ministers said to them-selves: we'll do the same; and that will put a stopper on war. We shan't fight about Czechoslovakia, any more than about the Grand Turk. But, mark you, we've been mobilized, we'll be in uniform for three or four years, and in the meantime they'll crush the proletariat at home.'

They eyed him rather doubtfully: they were not convinced, or possibly they had not understood. The locksmith said, in a vague way: 'Well, as we all know, the big chaps break the glasses, and the small chaps pay the damage.'

The violinist nodded approval, and they fell silent once more, the compositor turned and laid his forehead against the large windows in the corridor. 'Ah,' said Mathieu: 'so they're not very keen to fight.' He thought of the men of '14, their mouths agape, and their rifles garlanded with flowers. And afterwards? These fellows are right. They talk in proverbs but their words betray them, there's something in their heads that can't be expressed by words. Their fathers were respon-sible for a fantastic massacre, and for the last twenty years they have been told that war doesn't pay. Well, can they be expected to shout: 'To Berlin!' However, their words and thoughts were no more than furtive flickers on the margin of their destiny. We shall soon be saying – the soldiers of '38, as we used to say: the soldiers of the Year II, the poilus of '14. They will dig their holes like the others, neither better nor worse, and then lie in them, because that is what they must do. 'And what about *you*?' he thought abruptly. You, their uninvited witness, who are you? What will you do? And if you get back, what will you be like?

The man tapped on the window.

'They're still there.'

'Who?' said the violinist with a start.

'The planes. They're circling over the train.'

'Circling? Don't be silly!'

'Can't I see them!'

'Now, now!' said the locksmith. The little old man woke up: 'What's the matter?' he asked, cupping a hand behind his ear.

'Aeroplanes.'

'Oh, aeroplanes.' He smiled beatifically and went to sleep again.

'Come and look,' said the compositor. 'There must be thirty of them. I've never seen so many outside Villacoublay.' The locksmith and the traveller had got up. Mathieu followed them into the corridor. He saw about twenty small transparent insects, shrimps in the water of the sky. They seemed to exist intermittently: when the sun was not on them, they vanished.

'Suppose they're Fritzes?'

'God forbid, we should be for it! Just imagine what a target this train would make.'

There were some twenty men in the corridor, all staring upwards.

'I don't like the look of them,' said the traveller.

They all looked nervous. One man was drumming on the window, another beating time with his foot. The squadron banked steeply and disappeared over the train.

'Phew!' said a voice.

'Wait a bit!' said the compositor. 'Wait! They're still over the train.'

'There they are – there!'

A tall lad with a moustache was leaning backwards out of a window. The planes had reappeared, one of them leaving a white track behind it.

'They're Fredolins,' said the man with the moustache, standing up once more.

'Quite likely.'

Behind Mathieu, the violinist sat up abruptly: he shook the two sleepers.

'What's going on?' asked one of them thickly, half-opening his reddened eyes.

'War is declared,' said the violinist. 'There'll be a mess-up soon: Boche aeroplanes over the train.'

Lola grabbed Boris's wrist.

'Listen,' she said. 'Listen.'

Jacques had grown pale. 'Listen,' he said. 'He's going to speak.'

It was a slow voice, deep and monotonous, with a faintly nasal intonation.

'I had announced that this evening I would make a statement to the country on the international situation, but early this afternoon I received an invitation from the German Government, to meet Chancellor Hitler, Monsieur Mussolini, and Monsieur Chamberlain tomorrow at Munich. I have accepted this invitation.

'You will understand that on the eve of such important negotiations, it is my duty to postpone my promised statement. But before my departure, I wish to offer the people of France an expression of thanks for their courageous and dignified attitude.

'I want especially to thank those Frenchmen who have been called to serve their country, for the steadiness and firmness of which they have given this fresh proof.

'My task is hard. Since the beginning of these present difficulties, I have not ceased to labour with all my strength to safeguard peace and the vital interests of France. I shall continue in that effort tomorrow, with the conviction that I have the support of the entire nation.'

'Boris!' said Lola. 'Boris!'

He did not reply, and she went on. 'Wake up, darling – what's the matter. It's peace: there's going to be an international conference.'

She turned towards him, flushed and excited. He swore softly between his teeth.

Lola's joy collapsed: 'But what's the matter with you, darling: you've turned quite green.'

'I've joined up for three years,' said Boris.

The train rumbled on, the aeroplanes circled overhead.

'The driver's crazy,' exclaimed someone. 'Why doesn't he stop? If they start dropping bombs, we'll be blown to bits.'

The compositor was pale, but calm: he held his head back, watching for the planes.

'Better jump out,' he said between his teeth.

'I don't fancy jumping out at this speed,' said the traveller. He produced his handkerchief and mopped his brow: 'Much better pull the alarm signal.'

The locksmith and the compositor eyed each other. 'Well, get on with it,' said the compositor.

'Supposing they were French? What should we look like?'

Someone bumped into Mathieu from behind: a large man was dashing up the train shouting:

'We're slowing down! Everybody to the doors!'

The compositor turned to the commercial traveller: he was a man of slow and hesitant gestures, with a half smile that exposed his teeth.

'You see: the blighter's slowing down: they're Fritzes. So it's all bunkum, is it?' he said, mimicking the traveller. 'Well, you can see for yourself if it's bunkum.'

'I didn't say that,' said the other feebly. 'What I said was...'

The compositor turned his back on him, and made his way to the head of the train. From all the compartments men crowded into the corridor, preparing to jump into the fields. Someone touched Mathieu's arm, it was the little old man, looking up at him with a perplexed expression.

'What's the matter? What on earth is the matter?'

'Nothing,' said Mathieu irritably. 'Go to sleep again.'

He leaned out of the window. Two men had got out on to the footboard. One of them gave a shout and jumped, touched the ground, staggered sideways, plunged against a telegraph post, and toppled head-foremost down the embankment. The train had passed him. Mathieu turned his head and saw a diminutive figure get up, wave his arms, and run across the fields. The other hesitated, leaning outwards, and clinging with one hand to the brass cross-bar.

'Don't push, for God's sake,' said a strangled voice. 'We're suffocating.'

The train continued to slow down. There were heads at all the windows, and all along the footboards men were standing ready to jump. A station appeared round a curve, some three hundred yards away: Mathieu noticed a small town in the distance. Two more men jumped and dashed over a level crossing. The train was already pulling into the station. 'And these,' thought Mathieu, 'are our future heroes.'

A vast hum burst from the station, bright dresses glittered in the sunshine, tall girls in straw hats waved hands and handkerchiefs, children ran laughing and shouting up and down the platforms. The violinist pushed Mathieu out of the way, and leaned half out of the window. He cupped his hands over his mouth.

'Take cover!' he shouted to the crowd. 'Aeroplanes!'

The station staff looked at him in bewilderment, as they smiled and shouted. He raised an arm, and pointed a finger to the sky. The answer was a roar of cheers. Mathieu could not hear at first, then suddenly he understood.

'Peace! It's peace, boys!'

The entire train yelled: 'Aeroplanes. Aeroplanes!'

'Hurrah!' shouted the girls. 'Hurrah!'

Then they all looked upwards and, waved their handkerchiefs in greeting to the aeroplanes. The commercial gnawed his nails.

'I don't understand,' he muttered. 'I don't understand.'

The train creaked to a standstill. A railwayman climbed on to a bench, with his red flag under his arm, and shouted:

'Peace! Conference at Munich. Daladier leaves this evening.'

The train remained silent, motionless, uncomprehending. And then, suddenly, came the yell:

'Hurrah for Daladier! Hurrah for peace!'

The blue and pink cotton frocks were engulfed in a tide of brown and black jackets: the crowd began to flutter and rustle like trees in the wind, flashes of sunlight sparkled on the throng, caps and straw hats circled round and round – they were waltzing. Jacques waltzed Odette round the drawing-room, Mme Birnenschatz clasped Ella to her bosom and moaned:

'How happy I am, Ella darling.'

357

Beneath the window a young lad, flushed and laughing like a maniac, leapt at a peasant girl and kissed her on both cheeks. She laughed too, her hair ruffled and her straw hat awry, and cried: 'Hurrah!' as he went on kissing her. Jacques kissed Odette on the ear, he was filled with happiness.

'Peace! And of course they won't stop at the Sudeten question. The Pact of Four. That's how they should have begun.'

The servant peered through the door.

'May I serve dinner, madame?'

'Do,' said Jacques. 'Do. And then go down to the cellar and bring up a bottle of champagne and a bottle of Chambertin.'

A tall old man in spectacles had climbed on a bench, in one hand he raised a bottle of red wine, and in the other a glass.

'A glass of wine, boys; a glass of wine to drink to peace.'

'Here you are,' yelled the locksmith. 'Hurrah for peace!'

'Aha, *Monsieur l'abbé*, I'm going to hug you!'

The curé recoiled, but the old woman seized him and hugged him, Gressier plunged the ladle into the tureen: 'Ah, children, it's the end of a nightmare.' Zézette opened the door: 'So it's true, Madame Isidore?' – 'Yes, my dear, it's true, I've heard it everywhere, and on the radio. Your Momo will be back soon, didn't I tell you the good God wouldn't stand for that sort of thing?' – He danced around shouting: Hitler's got it in the neck, but what does that matter now the war is off? – oh no, I had some inside information, at two o'clock I bought back everything, it's a two hundred thousand deal, listen, my friend, this is an altogether ex-cep-tional occasion, for the first time in history a war that seemed inevitable has been averted by the act of four Heads of State, their decision goes far beyond the present crisis: war is no longer possible, Munich is the first declaration of peace. O God, how I did pray – O God, I said, take my heart and take my life, and, O God, you heard my prayer, you are great and wise and merciful, the *abbé* drew back and said: But I have always told you, madame, God is wonderful. Blast the Czechs, let them get out of their own mess. Zézette was walking down the street, Zézette was singing, all the birds in my heart, the people in the street were smiling, and winked a greeting to each other as they passed. They knew, she knew, they knew that she knew, the same thought

358

was in everybody's mind, everybody was glad, let us all behave like everybody else: what a lovely evening, that woman
passing by – I can see into her heart, and that nice old man
sees into mine, all friends together now, she burst into tears,
everyone was kind and happy and like everyone else, Momo,
wherever he was, must surely be glad, she cried and cried,
everyone looked at her, and that gave her a warm feeling in
the chest and back, indeed the more people looked the more
she cried, she felt proudly unashamed, like a mother suckling
her child.

'I say,' said Jacques. 'You're drinking hard, aren't you!'

Odette was laughing to herself. 'I suppose they'll demo-
bilize the reservists soon?' she said.

'In about a fortnight, or a month,' said Jacques.

She laughed again, and took a gulp of wine. Then, suddenly,
her cheeks flushed.

'What's the matter,' asked Jacques. 'Your face is quite red.'

'It's nothing,' she said. 'I've drunk a little too much,
that's all.'

I wouldn't have kissed him if I had known he would come
back so soon.

'Get in! Get in!'

The train started slowly. The men ran up and down,
shouting and laughing, or hung in clusters on the footboards.
The locksmith's perspiring face appeared at the window,
which he was clutching with both hands.

'For God's sake pull me in, or I shall let go,' he said.

Mathieu heaved him up, he got one leg through the
window, and jumped down into the corridor.

'Phew!' said he, mopping his brow. 'I thought I was going
to leave my two legs behind.'

Then the violinist appeared.

'Well, here we all are.'

'What about a little game?'

'Sure.'

They went back into the compartment: Mathieu eyed them
through the window. They began with a hearty draught of
wine, then the commercial traveller produced his handkerchief,
which they spread over their knees.

'Your deal.'

The locksmith farted. 'That was a good one,' he said, pointing upwards to an imaginary explosion overhead.

'You old toad!' said the compositor delightedly.

'Why are they here?' thought Mathieu. 'And why am I here anyway?' Their destiny had vanished, time had resumed its haphazard, aimless course: the train, from mere habit, rumbled on: the road drifting along beside the train now led nowhere, it was merely a strip of tarred earth. The aeroplanes had vanished: the war had vanished. A pale sky in which peace was gently awakening as evening fell, a torpid countryside, men playing cards or sleeping, a broken bottle in the corridor, cigarette-ends in a pool of wine, a stench of urine – an aftermath now meaningless. 'The day after a party,' thought Mathieu, feeling sad at heart.

Douce, Maud, and Ruby were walking up the Canebière. Douce was very excited: she had always had a liking for politics.

'There seems to have been a misunderstanding,' she explained. 'Hitler believed that Chamberlain and Daladier wanted to make trouble, while, at the same time, Chamberlain and Daladier thought he meant to attack. So Mussolini came along and convinced them they were mistaken: now it's fixed up, and tomorrow all four of them will be having lunch together.'

'What a spread that will be!' sighed Ruby.

The Canebière looked very festive, the people sauntered along, some even laughing to themselves. Maud felt depressed. Of course she was happy it was all so neatly settled, but she was mainly glad for other people's sake. In any case she would have to spend another night in the smelly, squalid Hôtel Genièvre, and then, railway stations, trains, Paris, hard times, cheap restaurants and stomach-aches: the Munich interview, whatever came of it, would make no difference to all that. She felt utterly alone. As she passed the Café Riche, she gave a start.

'What is it?' asked Ruby.

'Pierre,' replied Maud. 'Don't look. He's at the third table on the left. There – he has seen us.'

He rose, resplendent in a linen suit, and with his manliest and most opulent air. 'Ah well,' she thought, 'it doesn't matter now'; she tried, as he came towards her, to recall his livid face in the ship's cabin, and the reek of vomit. But the sea-wind had blown away both smell and face. He hailed her with apparent self-assurance. She wanted to pass on without a word, but she found herself walking rather unsteadily up to him all the same. He said with a smile: 'Are we to part like this, without even a drink together?'

She looked him in the eyes, and said to herself – This man is a coward. But that fact was not *visible*. The man she saw had bold, ironic lips, taut cheeks, and a prominent Adam's apple.

'Come along,' he murmured. 'That's all ancient history.'

She thought of her hotel bedroom, with its smell of ammonia, and said: 'You must ask Douce and Ruby too.'

He went up to them and smiled. Ruby liked him because he looked so distinguished. And so, three flowers sat down at a table outside the Café Riche. The place was a bed of flowers: flowers, sunlit murmurous faces, flags and fountains and sunshine. She looked at the ground and drew a deep breath: the sunlight blazed into her eyes, no one should pass judgement on a seasick man. Peace had come for her, too.

'Why don't they like me?' He was alone in the bleak room, leaning forward with his elbows on his knees, resting his heavy head on his hands. On the bench beside him lay a plate of sandwiches and a bowl of coffee which a constable had brought him at midday: but he couldn't eat, this was the end. They would try to force him into the army, he would refuse, and that would mean the firing-squad, or twenty years in gaol: his life was over. He considered it with a deep amazement: a failure from start to finish. His ideas, dull and glib, drifted to right and left; one alone remained constant, an unanswerable question: why don't they like me? In the next room he could hear loud bursts of laughter, the policemen were obviously in good spirits. A deep voice exclaimed: 'We must have a drink on this.'

No doubt some of these policemen liked each other; people in the streets and in houses smiled and helped each other, treated each other kindly and politely and some liked each other very much, Zézette and Maurice, for instance. Perhaps because they were older: they had had time to get acquainted.

A young man is like a traveller entering a half-full compartment during the night: the other passengers detest him, and manage to make him think that there is no more room. But my seat was reserved on the day I was born. Perhaps there's something wrong with me. Another roar of laughter from next door, and he caught the word 'Munich'. Streets, houses, trains, and the police station: a brimming world, a world of men; and a world that Philippe could not enter. He would live out his life in a cell like this, the burrow provided by humanity for its rejects. He saw a short, plump, laughing woman, with glossy arms – the hetaira: 'Well, she'll wear mourning for me,' he thought. The door opened, and the general entered. Philippe slid into the far corner, and cried:

'Leave me alone. I'll take my punishment, I don't need your protection.'

The general laughed. He walked across the room with his usual brisk, quick step, and confronted Philippe.

'Your punishment, indeed! Don't be a young fool!'

Philippe's elbow rose in spite of Philippe, and remained at the level of his cheek, ready to ward off a blow. But he lowered it, and said in a firm voice:

'I am a deserter.'

'Deserter! My poor boy: Hitler and Daladier are signing an agreement tomorrow, there won't be a war, and you were never a deserter.'

He eyed Philippe with offensive irony.

'A man needs will and perseverance, Philippe, even to do wrong. You're just a timid, half-baked schoolboy: all you have done is to worry your mother nearly out of her wits.'

Several policemen peered through the half-open door and grinned. Philippe leapt to his feet. But the general gripped him by the shoulder and forced him down again.

'You will listen to what I have to say. This last escapade proves that your education must be started all over again. Your mother agrees that she has been much too weak. From now on I shall take charge of you.'

He had approached Philippe, who raised his elbow and cried: 'If you touch me, I'll kill myself.'

'We shall see,' said the general.

He forced down the boy's elbow with his left hand, and with

the right he struck him twice. Philippe collapsed on to the bench, and burst into tears.

There was a cheerful commotion in the corridor, a woman was singing *Va petit mousse*. How he hated all these tiresome women. The nurse came in, carrying his dinner on a tray.

'I'm not hungry,' he said.

'But you must eat, Monsieur Charles, to keep up your strength. Here's some good news to give you an appetite: there won't be a war: Daladier and Chamberlain are to have an interview with Hitler.'

He looked at her dumbfounded: true, this Sudeten business of theirs was still going on.

She was rather flushed, and her eyes were shining.

'Well? Aren't you pleased?'

They've dragged me like a parcel away from the place I know, and nearly killed me in the process, and now they aren't even going to fight. But he wasn't angry: it all seemed so very far away.

'What do you expect me to do?' he said.

Night of 29–30 September

ONE-THIRTY.

Messrs Hubert Masaryk and Mastny, members of the Czechoslovak delegation, were waiting in Sir Horace Wilson's room at the hotel in the company of Mr Ashton-Gwatkin. Mastny was pale and perspiring, with dark circles underneath his eyes. Hubert Masaryk paced up and down. Mr Ashton-Gwatkin sat on the chair.

Ivich had slipped away to her own side of the bed, she wasn't touching *him*, but she could feel his warmth and hear his breathing: she couldn't sleep, and she knew he wasn't asleep either. Shivers like electric shocks travelled through her legs and thighs, she longed to turn over on her back, but if she moved she would touch him: so long as he thought her asleep, he would leave her alone.

Mastny turned to Ashton-Gwatkin and said: 'It's lasting a long time.'

Mr Ashton-Gwatkin made a vague gesture of apology. The blood rose into Masaryk's face.

'The accused await the verdict,' he said in a dull voice. Mr Ashton-Gwatkin did not seem to hear.

'Won't the night ever end?' thought Ivich. She suddenly felt soft flesh against her hip, he thought she was asleep, she mustn't move, otherwise he'll realize that I'm awake. Flesh slid across her back, rather feverish and flabby flesh – it was a leg. She bit hard on her lower lip.

Masaryk continued: 'To complete the resemblance, we were welcomed by the police.'

'What do you mean?' said Mr Ashton-Gwatkin, assuming a look of astonishment.

'We were driven to the Hôtel Regina in a police-car,' explained Mastny.

'Tut, tut!' said Mr Ashton-Gwatkin disapprovingly.

And now a hand; it moved lightly, almost casually down her side; fingers flickered over her stomach. 'It's *nothing*,' she thought: 'it's an insect. I'm asleep. I'm asleep. I'm dreaming. I shan't move.'

Masaryk took the map handed to him by Sir Horace Wilson. The territories to be occupied immediately by the German Army were marked in blue. He eyed it for a moment, then flung it angrily on to the table.

'I ... I don't understand,' he said, looking Mr Ashton-Gwatkin in the eyes. 'Are we still a sovereign state?'

Mr Ashton-Gwatkin shrugged his shoulders, apparently to indicate that he had no say in the affair: but Masaryk thought he was more moved than he cared to show.

'These negotiations with Hitler are very difficult,' he observed. 'You must take that into account.'

'Everything depended on whether the Great Powers would stand firm,' replied Masaryk vehemently.

The Englishman flushed: then he sat up straight and said gravely:

'If you don't accept this agreement, you must come to terms with Germany on your own.' He cleared his throat, and added in a milder tone: 'Perhaps the French will say so in more elaborate terms. But believe me, they share our views: if you refuse, they won't do any more for you.'

Masaryk laughed harshly, and nothing more was said.

A voice whispered: 'Are you asleep?'

She did not answer, but she felt a mouth against her ear, and then a whole body in contact with her own.

'Ivich,' he murmured. 'Ivich!'

She mustn't cry out, nor struggle. I'm not the kind of girl one rapes. She turned over on her back, and said:

'No, I'm not asleep. What is it?'

'I love you,' he said.

Oh for a bomb that would fall from fifteen thousand feet up, and kill them on the spot!

A door opened and Sir Horace Wilson appeared: he did not look at them, indeed, he was looking downwards. Since their arrival, he kept his eyes averted when he spoke to them. Suddenly becoming aware of this, he raised his head, and eyed them absently.

'Will you please come in now, gentlemen?'

The three men followed him down long, deserted corridors. A floor waiter was asleep on a chair: the hotel seemed dead.

He laid his burning chest against Ivich's breasts, and she heard a soft sucking sound as the sweat poured off them.

'Then get off, if you love me,' she said: 'I'm too hot.'

'In here,' said Sir Horace Wilson, receding into the background.

He did not move, one hand flung off the bedclothes, the other seized her shoulder, he was lying on top of her now, gripping her shoulders and arms with vehement, predatory hands, as he murmured in a childish, pleading voice:

'I love you, Ivich darling – how I love you.'

It was a small, low room, brightly lit. Messrs Chamberlain, Daladier, and Léger were standing behind a table scattered with papers. The ash-trays were full of cigarette-ends, but no one was then smoking. Chamberlain laid two hands on the table. He looked tired.

'Good morning, gentlemen,' he said with a gracious smile.

Masaryk and Mastny bowed without speaking. Ashton-Gwatkin stepped briskly away from them, as though he could no longer endure their company, and stood behind Mr Chamberlain and beside Sir Horace Wilson. The two Czechs were now confronted by five men on the other side of the table. Behind them there was the door, and the deserted corridors of the hotel. There followed an instant of oppressive silence. Masaryk looked at them all in turn, and then tried to catch Léger's eye. But Léger was putting some documents away in a portfolio.

'Will you sit down, gentlemen,' said Mr Chamberlain.

The French and the Czechs sat down, but Mr Chamberlain remained standing.

'Well,' said Mr Chamberlain. His eyes were red with lack of sleep. He looked hesitantly at his hands, then stiffened abruptly, and said:

'France and Great Britain have just signed an agreement on the German claims in regard to the Sudetens. Thanks to the goodwill displayed by all parties, this agreement may be considered as embodying a definite advance on the Godesberg memorandum.'

He coughed, and was silent. Masaryk sat stiffly on his chair, waiting. Mr Chamberlain seemed to want to continue, but changed his mind, and handed a document to Mastny:

'Here is the agreement: perhaps you would read it out.'

Mastny took the paper: someone was walking softly along the corridor. The footsteps died away, and a clock in the town struck two. Mastny began to read, with a nasal and rather monotonous intonation: he read slowly, as though he were pondering between each phrase, and the paper quivered in his hands:

'The four Powers: Germany, the United Kingdom, France, and Italy, taking account of the arrangement already established in principle for the cession to Germany of the territories of the Sudeten Germans, have agreed upon the dispositions and conditions regulating the said cession, and the measures thereby involved.

'1. The evacuation will begin on 1 October.

'2. The United Kingdom, France, and Italy have agreed that the evacuation of the territory in question shall be completed by 10 October, without destruction of any of the existing installations. The Czechoslovak Government will assume responsibility for effecting this evacuation, in such a way that no damage shall be done to the said installations.

'3. The conditions of this evacuation shall be determined in detail by an International Commission composed of representatives of Germany, the United Kingdom, France, Italy, and Czechoslovakia.

'4. The progressive occupation by Reich troops of those territories where there is a German majority shall begin on 1 October. The four zones indicated on the attached map shall be occupied by German troops in the following order:

'Zone 1 – 1 and 2 October.

'Zone 2 – 2 and 3 October.

'Zone 3 – 3, 4 and 5 October.

'Zone 4 – 6 and 7 October.

'The other territories in which Germans predominate shall be determined by the International Commission, and occupied by German troops between this date and 10 October.'

The monotonous voice rose up into the silence, in the centre of that somnolent town. It stumbled, stopped, then quavered on; millions of Germans, as far as eye could reach, lay asleep, as it described how a historic murder was to be committed.

The pleading whispering voice – Oh my dearest darling, how I love your breasts, I love the very smell of you, do you love me? – rose into the night, and the hands beneath that burning body were committing murder.

'I should like to ask one question,' said Masaryk. 'What are we to understand by "territory in which Germans predominate"?'

He spoke to Chamberlain: but Chamberlain looked at him in silence, with a slightly dazed expression. Obviously he had not been listening. Léger replied, addressing himself to Masaryk's back. Masaryk swung his chair round until he could see Léger in profile.

'The reference is,' said Léger, 'to majorities calculated in accordance with the proposals already accepted by you.'

Mastny produced a handkerchief and mopped his brow, and then went on:

'5. The International Commission mentioned in paragraph 3 will determine the territories in which the plebiscite shall be held.

'These territories shall be occupied by international contingents until the completion of the plebiscite.'

He paused and said: 'Will these contingents be actually international, or will only British troops be used?'

Mr Chamberlain yawned behind his hand, a tear trickled down his cheek. He withdrew his hand, and said:

'That question is not yet finally determined. The idea is that Belgian and Italian soldiers shall participate.'

'This Commission,' Mastny continued, 'will also fix the conditions under which the plebiscite shall be conducted, taking as a basis the organization of the plebiscite in the Saar. It will, moreover, fix a date for the opening of the plebiscite, being not later than the end of November.'

He stopped again and said to Chamberlain in a faintly ironic tone: 'Will the Czechoslovak member of the Commission have an equal right of vote with the other members?'

'Of course,' said Mr Chamberlain benevolently.

A sticky flow, like blood, tingled over Ivich's thighs and stomach and slipped into her blood, I won't be violated, then she yielded, shivers of ice and fire thrilled up into her chest, but her head remained serene and secure, and, in her head, she cried: 'I hate you!'

'6. The final frontiers will be settled by the International Commission. This Commission will also be competent to recommend to the four Powers: Germany, United Kingdom, France and Italy, in certain exceptional cases, limited modifications of the strictly ethnological determination of the zones transferable without plebiscite.'

'Are we,' asked Masaryk, 'to consider that article as a

clause guaranteeing the protection of our vital interests?'

He had turned to Daladier and was eyeing him insistently. But Daladier did not reply: he looked aged and dejected, and Masaryk noticed the butt of a dead cigarette in the corner of his mouth.

'We were promised such a clause,' said Masaryk with emphasis.

'In one sense,' said Léger, 'that article may be considered as embodying the clause to which you refer. But we must not be too ambitious at the start. The question of guarantees for your frontiers will be a matter for the International Commission.'

Masaryk laughed curtly, and folded his arms.

'Not even a guarantee,' he said, shaking his head.

'7.' Mastny read on. 'There will be a right of option for inclusion in, or exclusion from, the territories transferred.

'This option shall be exercised within a period of six months from the date of the present agreement.

'8. The Czechoslovak Government will release, within a period of four weeks from the conclusion of the present agreement, all the Sudeten Germans who so desire, from military formations or police forces to which they may belong.

'Within the same period, the Czechoslovak Government will release the Sudeten German prisoners at present serving sentences of imprisonment for political offences.

'Done at Munich, 29 September 1938.

'That's all,' he said.

He looked at the paper as though he had not finished it. Mr Chamberlain yawned, and began to drum on the table with his fingers.

'That's all,' repeated Mastny.

It was all over, the Czechoslovakia of 1918 had ceased to exist. Masaryk gazed at the white document which Mastny then laid on the table: then he turned to Daladier and Léger and eyed them fixedly. Daladier was sitting hunched in his chair, his chin on his chest. He took a cigarette out of his pocket, looked at it for an instant, and then replaced it in the packet. Léger was rather flushed and looked impatient.

'Do you expect,' said Masaryk to Daladier, 'a statement or a reply from my Government?'

Daladier did not reply. Léger bent his head and said rapidly:

'Monsieur Mussolini has to get back to Italy this evening: there is not much time.'

Masaryk was still looking at Daladier. He said: 'Not even a reply? Am I to understand that we are *obliged* to accept?'

Daladier waved a hand wearily, and Léger, from behind him, answered: 'What else can you do?'

She had turned her face to the wall and was crying silently, her shoulders quivered.

'Why are you crying?' he asked hesitantly.

'Because I hate you,' she replied.

Masaryk rose, Mastny also: and Mr Chamberlain indulged in a prodigious yawn.

Friday, 30 September

THE small soldier came up to Gros-Louis waving a newspaper.

'It's peace!'

Gros-Louis set down his bucket. 'What did you say, mate?'

'I said it's peace.'

Gros-Louis eyed him dubiously.

'Peace? – but there hasn't been a war.'

'They've signed a peace, old thing. You've only got to read the paper.'

He handed it to Gros-Louis, who pushed it away.

'I can't read.'

'Is that so?' said the lad sympathetically. 'Well, look at the picture.'

Gros-Louis reluctantly took the paper, went up to the stable window and looked at the picture. He recognized Daladier, Hitler, and Mussolini, all smiles: they seemed to be good friends.

'Well I never!' he said.

He frowned at the lad, then said with a sudden chuckle:

'So they've made it up, have they? And I didn't even know why they'd fallen out!'

The soldier burst out laughing, and Gros-Louis laughed too.

'So long, old thing,' said the soldier.

He departed. Gros-Louis went up to the black mare, and stroked her neck.

'There, there, my beauty,' he said.

He felt confused, and said to himself: 'Well, and what am I to do now, I should like to know?'

M. Birnenschatz hid behind his newspaper: a vertical thread of smoke rose above the outspread pages: Mme Birnenschatz fidgeted in her seat.

'I must see Rose about that vacuum cleaner.'

It was the third time that she had mentioned the vacuum cleaner, but she did not go. Ella gazed at her frigidly, she wanted to be alone with her father.

'Do you think they'll take it away again?' asked Mme Birnenschatz, turning to her daughter.

'You keep on asking me that. I don't know, mamma.'

Yesterday Mme Birnenschatz had wept for joy, clasping her nieces and her daughter to her bosom. Today the same joy rather baffled her: it was indeed a large amorphous joy, very like herself, which would soon be transmuted into prophecy, unless she found someone to share it with her.

She turned to her husband: 'Gustave,' she murmured.

M. Birnenschatz did not reply.

'You haven't got much to say to us today.'

'No!' said M. Birnenschatz.

However, he lowered his newspaper, and eyed her over his spectacles. He looked weary and old: Ella felt her heart contract: she would have liked to hug him, but it was better not to indulge in any demonstrations before Mme Birnenschatz, who was only too disposed to them.

'Well, I hope you're pleased, anyway,' said Mme Birnenschatz.

'Pleased about what?' he asked curtly.

'Oh come,' she said. already in a tone of lamentation: 'You told me over and over again that you didn't want war, that war would be a catastrophe, and that we ought to negotiate with the Germans, so I thought you would be pleased.'

M. Birnenschatz shrugged his shoulders, and went back to his newspaper. Mme Birnenschatz fixed a surprised, reproachful look on the rampart of newspaper: her lower lip was quivering. Then she sighed, rose with difficulty and made her way to the door.

'I no longer understand either my husband or my daughter,' she said as she went out.

Ella went up to her father and kissed him gently on the top of his head.

'What is it, papa?'

M. Birnenschatz laid down his spectacles and looked up at her: 'I have nothing to say. I was no longer of an age to take part in this war, was I? So the less said the better.'

He folded his newspaper with meticulous care: then he muttered: 'I was in favour of peace. . . .'

'Well?'

'Well?'

He tilted his head to the right and raised his right shoulder in an oddly childish movement.

'I feel ashamed,' he said darkly.

Gros-Louis emptied his bucket into the lats, carefully squeezed all the water out of the sponge, then put the sponge in the bucket and carried it back into the stable. He shut the stable door, crossed the yard, and entered the building. The barrack-room was deserted. 'They aren't in a hurry to go,' Gros-Louis said to himself: 'I suppose they're enjoying themselves.' He took his civilian trousers and jacket from underneath the bed. 'I'm not,' he said, beginning to undress. He didn't dare rejoice yet, and added: 'I've been mucking around here for a week.' He slipped on his trousers, and laid out his uniform. He didn't know whether his master would take him back. 'I wonder who is looking after his sheep just now?' He picked up his haversack and went out. There were four men outside the wash-house, who looked at him and grinned. Gros-Louis waved a hand at them, and crossed the yard. He hadn't a penny left, he would have to walk back. 'I can do a turn at the farms on my way, just to earn my food.' Suddenly, he saw the sky, pale-blue, above the heathland of the Canigou, the sheep's small jostling rumps, and realized that he was free.

'Hullo, you! Where are you off to?'

Gros-Louis turned: it was the corpulent little company-sergeant-major, Peltier.

'What's the meaning of this?' he said running across the yard.

He stopped two paces away from Gros-Louis, gasping and crimson with rage.

'Where are you going?' he repeated.

'I'm going away,' said Gros-Louis.

'Going away!' said the sergeant-major, folding his arms. 'Going away! ... And where are you going to?' he asked furiously.

'Home,' said Gros-Louis.

'Home!' said the sergeant-major. 'Home! I suppose you don't like the menu, or your bed's uncomfortable.' Then he added in a harsh and menacing tone: 'Kindly turn round and go back at once – at the double, please. I'll look after you, my son.'

'He doesn't know it's all over,' thought Gros-Louis. And he said: 'Peace has been signed, sergeant.'

The sergeant seemed not to believe his ears. 'Are you pretending to be crazy, or trying to pull my leg?'

Gros-Louis remained unruffled. He turned and continued on his way. But the fat sergeant pursued him, grabbed his sleeve, shoved his belly into him, and shouted:

'If you don't obey orders at once, you'll be court-martialled.'

Gros-Louis stopped, and scratched his head. He thought of Marseilles, and his head began to ache.

'I've been mucking around here for a week,' he said quietly.

The sergeant shook him by the tunic and yelled:

'What's that?'

'You've been mucking me around for a week,' roared Gros-Louis.

He took the sergeant by the shoulder, and hit him in the face. He had to slip an arm under the man's shoulder to hold him up, then he went on hitting him, until he was collared from behind, and someone seized his arms and twisted them. He released the sergeant-major, who dropped silently on to the ground, and tried to shake off his assailants, but he was tripped up and fell. Then they set about him, and as he swung his head from right to left to avoid the blows, he gasped:

'Let me go, boys, let me go – it's peace, I tell you!'

Gomez scraped the bottom of his pocket with his nails, and produced a few strands of tobacco mixed with dust and bits of thread. He put the mixture in his pipe, and lit it. The smoke had an acrid, suffocating flavour.

'Is the tobacco ration finished?' asked Garcin.

'Yesterday evening,' said Gomez. 'If I had known, I would have brought back more.'

Lopez came in with newspapers. Gomez eyed him, and then looked down at his pipe. He had understood. He saw the word Munich in large letters on the front page.

'Well?' asked Garcin.

Gun-fire could be heard in the distance.

'Well, we're bitched,' said Lopez.

Gomez clenched his teeth on the stem of his pipe. He listened to the guns, and thought of the quiet night at Juan-les-Pins, and the jazz band on the seashore: Mathieu would spend many more evenings of that kind.

'The bastard,' he muttered.

Mathieu paused for an instant in the doorway of the canteen, then he went out into the yard and shut the door. He was still in his civilian clothes; there had not been another tunic in the store. The soldiers were walking up and down in little groups, looking bewildered and uneasy. Two young men approached him, and both yawned.

'Well, you look pretty cheerful,' said Mathieu.

The younger of the two shut his mouth, and said with an air of excuse:

'It's all a bloody mess.'

'Hullo,' said someone behind Mathieu.

It was a certain Georges, his neighbour in the dormitory, a man of moonlike, melancholy countenance. He smiled.

'Well,' said Mathieu. 'How're things?'

'Not so bad,' said the other. 'Not so bad.'

'I'm sorry for you,' said Mathieu. 'You oughtn't to be here, you ought to be on the job.'

'So I should,' said the other. He shrugged his shoulders: 'But I don't much care.'

374

'No,' said Mathieu.

'I'm glad, because I shall see my little girl again,' he said. 'Otherwise . . . I shall go back to the office, I don't get on with my wife . . . we shall read the papers, and worry about Dantzig: just like last year.' He yawned and said: 'Life's the same everywhere, isn't it?'

'It is.'

They smiled feebly. There was nothing more to say.

'See you soon,' said Georges.

'See you soon.'

Beyond the gates, someone was playing the accordion. Beyond the gates lay Nancy, Paris, fourteen lectures a week, Ivich, Boris, Irène, perhaps. Life was the same everywhere, it was always the same. He steered slowly towards the gates.

'Look out!'

Some soldiers waved him out of the way: they had marked a line on the ground, and were nonchalantly throwing coins. Mathieu paused: he watched a few coins roll across the line, then some more, and then some more. From time to time a coin spun like a top, quivered for an instant, and fell, partly covering another: the players stood up and shouted. Mathieu walked on. So many trains and lorries streaking across France, so much misery, so much money, such floods of tears, such vociferation on the wireless all over the world, threats and challenges in every language, councils in high places – and what was the end of it all? Men strolling round a barrack yard, or throwing coins in the dust. All these men had striven to get away dry-eyed, all of them had suddenly seen death face to face, and all, with varying degrees of self-command, had made up their minds to die. And here they were, dazed and baffled, embedded for one more moment in a life which they no longer knew how to use. A day of dupes, he thought. He grasped two bars of the gate and looked out: sunlight on the empty road. In the business quarters of every town, peace had reigned for the last two days. But barracks and fortifications were still encompassed by a faint, dissolving haze of war. The invisible accordion was playing *Madelon*: a warm breeze eddied the dust in the road. 'And my own life – what am I going to make of it?' Quite simple: in the rue Huyghens in Paris, a flat awaited him, two rooms, central heating, water, gas, electricity, green leather arm-chairs and a bronze crab on the table. He would go back home, unlock his front door, and go back to his desk at the Lycée Buffon. Nothing would have happened. Nothing at all. His life awaited him, the life he knew so well, he had left it in this sitting-room, and in his bedroom. He would slip into it again – quietly and without fuss; no one would allude to the Munich interview, in a month it would all be forgotten – nothing would remain but an almost imperceptible scar or fracture in the continuity of his life: the memory of a night when he thought he was off to the war.

'No,' he said, gripping the bars with all his might. 'It shan't happen like that!' He turned abruptly and smiled, as he looked at the windows glittering in the sunlight. He felt strong: he was conscious of a now familiar little stab of pain that had begun to give him confidence. A nobody from nowhere in particular. Possessing nothing, he now was nothing. The sad night hours of yesterday would not be lost: this upheaval would not be wholly futile. Let them sheathe their swords if they so pleased, let them have their war, or not, I don't care: I am not fooled. The accordion was mute. Mathieu resumed his walk round the yard. 'I'm free, and shall remain so,' he thought.

The aeroplane circled over Le Bourget, where the landing-ground seemed to be half-covered by a dark and undulating deposit. Léger leaned towards Daladier, pointed downwards, and shouted:

'What a crowd!'

Daladier looked in his turn: it was the first time he had spoken since their departure from Munich:

'They are going to mob me, I suppose.'

Léger did not protest. Daladier shrugged his shoulders: 'I appreciate their feelings.'

'Everything depends on the reception arrangements,' said Léger with a sigh.

He came into the room with the newspapers: Ivich sat drooping on the bed.

'It's all right, they signed last night.'

She raised her eyes, he looked pleased, but said no more, daunted by the expression in her eyes:

'Do you mean there won't be a war?' she asked.

'Yes.'

No war: no aeroplanes over Paris: no bomb-shattered ceilings: life must now be lived.

'No war,' she sobbed: 'no war – and you look pleased!'

Milan came up to Anna. He swayed a little, and his eyes were red. He touched her belly and said:

'Well, I know who's going to be unlucky.'

'What do you mean?'

'The baby.'

He limped up to the table, and poured himself out a glass of spirits, the fifth since the morning.

'Do you remember,' he said, 'that time you fell downstairs? I thought you would have a miscarriage.'

'Well?' she said curtly.

He turned towards her, glass in hand – almost as though he were drinking a toast.

'It would have been better if you had,' he said with a grin.

She looked at him: he raised the glass to his lips with a slightly shaky hand.

'Perhaps,' she said. 'Perhaps it would.'

The aeroplane had grounded. Daladier climbed heavily out of the cabin, and set his foot on the ladder: he was pale. A vast clamour greeted him, the crowd surged through the cordon of police, and swept the barriers away: Milan drank, and said with a laugh: 'To France! To England! To our glorious allies!' Then he flung the glass against the wall: they shouted: 'Hurrah for France! Hurrah for England! Hurrah for peace!' They were carrying flags and flowers. Daladier stood on the top step, and looked at them dumbfounded. Then he turned to Léger and said between his teeth:

'The blind fools!'

MORE ABOUT PENGUINS

Penguinews, which appears every month, contains details of all the new books issued by Penguins as they are published. From time to time it is supplemented by *Penguins in Print*, which is a complete list of all books published by Penguins which are in print. There are well over three thousand of these.)

A specimen copy of *Penguinews* will be sent to you free on request, and you can become a subscriber for the price of the postage. For a year's issues including the complete lists) please send 25p if you live in the United Kingdom, or 50p if you live elsewhere. Just write to Dept EP, Penguin Books Ltd, Harmondsworth, Middlesex, enclosing a cheque or postal order, and your name will be added to the mailing list.

Some other books published by Penguins **are** described on the following pages.

Note: *Penguinews* and *Penguins in Print* are not available in the U.S.A. or Canada

THE BLOOD OF OTHERS

Simone de Beauvoir —

Many of the ingredients of the philosophy associated with the name of Jean-Paul Sartre go into the making of this story, based on the agony of the French Resistance: the universal responsibility of each and every man, the damning cloud of guilt, the emptiness of life, the hovering death-wish.

Jean Blomart, patriot leader against the German forces of occupation, waits throughout an endless night for his wounded lover, Hélène, to die. He is bitterly assailed by guilt for her death, and the onset of despair. And the very technique of narration calls up a world that is shattered and disintegrating.

Also available

MEMOIRS OF A DUTIFUL DAUGHTER

THE PRIME OF LIFE

FORCE OF CIRCUMSTANCE
(The volumes in her famous autobiographical trilogy)

SHE CAME TO STAY

A VERY EASY DEATH

NOT FOR SALE IN THE U.S.A.

WORDS

Jean-Paul Sartre

'I loathe my childhood and all that remains of it.' After his father's early death Jean-Paul Sartre was brought up at his grandfather's home in a world even then eighty years out of date. In *Words* he recalls his illusion-ridden childhood – dominated by a false conception of life, ideas and literature – and considers its effect on his work. Essential background to the philosophy of one of today's profoundest thinkers, this self-analysis is also a brilliant study in child psychology and a witty, lucid story that will delight all those who have previously found Sartre over-complex.

The first volume of Sartre's trilogy 'Roads to Freedom'

THE AGE OF REASON

This novel by one of France's greatest post-war writers covers two days in the life of Mathieu Delarue, a teacher of philosophy, and in the lives of his acquaintances and friends. Mathieu is trying to raise money for the abortion of a woman with whom he has been living for seven years, and at the same time he is obsessed with a desire for personal freedom. Individual tragedies and happiness are etched against the Paris summer of 1938, with its night clubs, galleries, students, and café society.

But behind it all there is a threat, only half realized at the time, of the coming catastrophe of the Second World War.

'There is a wonderful feeling of suspense about the book' – Henry Read in the *Listener*

'Constantly delights with its brilliance' – *Spectator*

'A dynamic, deeply disturbing novel' – Elizabeth Bowen

NOT FOR SALE IN THE U.S.A.

The final volume, Iron in the Soul, *is described overleaf.*

IRON IN THE SOUL

Jean-Paul Sartre

This is the third part of Sartre's ambitious long novel, *Roads to Freedom*. The first two parts, *The Age of Reason* and *The Reprieve* (both available in Penguins), traced the thoughts and actions of a group of characters in 1938–9, the dreary time of Munich and the 'phoney war'.

In *Iron in the Soul* the same characters at last face reality, in the shape of defeat and occupation. Around a graphic narrative of the fall of France, Sartre weaves a tapestry of thoughts, feeling and incidents which portrays – as few books about war have done – the meaning of defeat. As in the earlier books, the school-master Mathieu is the most articulate character: able to reflect on the nature of freedom even as he fires his last rounds against the oncoming enemy.

'*Iron in the Soul* must be saluted as a profound, subtle, and terrifying piece of writing' – *The Times Literary Supplement*

'The only great historical novel of our time. The energy of his imagination is comparable to Zola's' – *Listener*

Also available

NAUSEA
ALTONA AND OTHER PLAYS
KEAN, NEKRASSOV, and
THE TROJAN WOMEN
(*Three Plays*)